MW01131361

MIST'S EDGE

A Novel of the Broken Lands

T.A. White

To Tess—my first fan and amazing little sister

PROLOGUE

B irdon Leaf hasn't responded to roll call in over seven months."

Hunched over his desk, the man squinted through a set of bifocals at a report on a disturbing trend that had been on the rise in the eastern part of the Highlands. He didn't bother looking up as he gave his reply. "That village tends to run its pathfinder a little thin. I wouldn't worry about it yet."

The younger pathfinder waited at the desk, her hands fidgeting at her sides.

The man looked up, his glasses giving the impression of a bird. This was helped along by the tuffs of hair sticking up all over his head. "Was there anything else?"

"It's just that Pathfinder Shea was assigned to that village, and her name wasn't attached to any of the reports coming out of there for several months prior to our sending out a roll call." She bit her lip and clasped her hands in front of her, one finger rubbing the inside of her wrist.

He frowned, and his gaze went distant as if he were having an internal conversation with himself. He sighed and sat back.

The younger pathfinder rushed to add, "It could be like you said. She could be out on assignment and just hasn't had the chance to respond."

The older pathfinder tapped his quill on the desk and studied the younger woman from under lowered brows. She was new. Not quite trained yet and prone to panicking over the least provocation.

"It's not like Shea to miss a roll call," he finally said. Especially given that debacle in the Badlands. Poor kid hadn't been entirely at fault but had suffered the cost all the same. The labels of troublemaker and bad luck had followed her until the guild banished her to the backwards of beyond.

If any other pathfinder had missed roll call like this, he would have already waved away his assistant's concern. Seven months or longer wasn't really that long to go without communication from some of these villages. When a single trip could take up to a year, a pathfinder had to be given some leeway in sending word back to the Keep.

Given it was Shea who'd missed roll call, a woman who never missed anything in her life, he could understand why his assistant was hovering over his desk while he tried to make heads or tails of this report. No one wanted to be responsible for losing track of Shea Halloran due to negligence.

His assistant bobbed up and down, almost quivering with excitement. "Shall I send one of our Eyes to investigate?"

He frowned, already regretting the amount of paperwork this would generate and the time he would have to waste coordinating resources. "I suppose."

His assistant leaned forward, saying in a hushed voice, "You know she will have to be told."

His frown became even more pronounced. A disgusted huff escaped him as he lumbered to his feet, his bones crackling as he moved, like he was some ancient machine of their ancestors that needed oiling. An apt description since he could feel every one of his years when the air held a crisp hint of the coming winter.

"I'll be the one to inform her. Speak with the quartermaster to begin arrangements." His face was grumpy and his voice crotchety as he moved toward the door.

"You're going alone?"

He gave her a gimlet glare. "Were you planning on volunteering?"

She shook her head, her eyes getting even wider despite all odds.

"I didn't think so. It's best not to ask stupid questions."

She rolled her lips between her teeth and stared at him in repentance.

"Have the arrangements finished by the time I get back."

"Of course, master."

He sighed. These young ones made him feel so old sometimes.

The heavy wooden door creaked open as he plodded into the hallway, making his way toward the tower, his old bones already protesting the coming exertion. He passed several pathfinders, each finding better things to do given the grumpy expression on his face.

As he approached the tower, a young man with eyes the palest blue descended, whistling a jaunty tune. The sound trailed off as he noticed the old man.

"Pathfinder Whelan, it is a rare occasion to see you outside of your cave," the younger man said, referencing Whelan's habit of isolating himself in his offices and seeing no others for long spans of time. "What brings you to the tower?"

"Pathfinder Reece, you are as nosy as you've ever been," Whelan said, feeling out of sorts at the coming climb and the thought of facing her.

Reece flashed a charming smile, his eyes alert as he studied Whelan. "It is a trait that has served me well in the past."

Whelan made his way up the steps, holding tight to the railing and cursing the coming climb. "I'm sure it will again in the coming weeks. I wouldn't go too far if I were you. I'm sure she will call for you shortly."

"Oh, why's that?" Reece asked.

"A pathfinder missed roll call—one that has a special tie to you."

Reece's head tilted and then understanding dawned. "Shea."

Whelan cackled. "That's the one. I've no doubt that they'll pull you into a special assignment before too long."

Leaving the other pathfinder behind, Whelan continued up the long steps. For the amount of trouble this was going to generate, that girl had better be involved in something dire or he'd have her head.

CHAPTER ONE

W e're agreed then. What says the Telroi?"

Shea tuned back into the conversation to find twelve sets of eyes on her. She blinked at them and looked around with unease as she fought the urge to shift. The Trateri favored pillows instead of chairs. It made sitting for long periods painful for those not used to it. Shea had chosen to kneel since she'd assumed this meeting wouldn't last long. Her mistake. It was an assumption she really should have known better than to make.

"Do you have an opinion on this?" Gala asked, giving Shea an expectant look—one shared by many at the table. It was unfortunate Shea didn't have an opinion one way or another. Mostly because she'd stopped paying attention fifteen minutes into the meeting when it became clear that she had little to contribute.

Gala was a middle-aged woman, plump and soft with curves. Her brown hair, threaded through with grey, had been bound back in a smooth bun that Shea couldn't hope to ever replicate, even before she had chopped off all her hair in an attempt to disguise herself as a boy. Though that subterfuge had been uncovered several months prior, Shea's hair was at that weird length where it was considered neither long nor short. It had been unruly at both lengths, but at the in-between stage it was a mess of curls that refused to be tamed.

Youngest at the table by a few decades, Shea's presence would normally not be required nor appreciated among the elders of the Trateri clans. Her status as the Telroi, beloved of Fallon Hawkvale, warlord of the Trateri and conqueror of the Lowlands, had afforded her certain responsibilities—uncomfortable and outside her normal skill set though they might be.

Daere, a woman several years older than Shea though still much younger than the rest, leaned forward from where she sat behind Shea. Since she wasn't a clan elder, she didn't have a seat at the table and was forced into the role of observer. In a low voice, one only meant for Shea's ears, she said, "They're discussing where to house the new clans that have joined us."

Shea gave a slight nod, her face creased in a thoughtful frown. Or at least she hoped it was thoughtful. This was the third such meeting she'd been forced to attend, and she felt no more comfortable than she had at the first one.

Unfortunately, she'd also been unable to convince Daere of the uselessness of her presence. Daere was Fallon's cousin on his father's side and had been assigned to be Shea's shadow. Well, technically she'd been assigned to mentor and guide Shea in her new role in Trateri society.

The woman saw Shea's lack of social graces as a personal affront and had set about trying to integrate Shea into their way of life. She'd started with these meetings, and Shea was already trying to think of several ways to avoid Daere for the foreseeable future. It was difficult, since the woman evidently had eyes in the back of her head.

Daere was a tall woman, even taller than Shea who towered over most Lowlanders. Since the Trateri people as a whole grew tall and muscular, this wasn't unusual. Her reddish-brown hair was tied back from her face, setting off her sharp features and giving her no-nonsense glare an extra push as she aimed it Shea's way, telling her without words to pay attention.

Shea turned back to the assembled elders. Though mostly women, there were a few men scattered into the mix. Shea heaved an internal sigh. She missed the days when she was a pathfinder and scout, one who wasn't expected to comment on anything but the possible obstacles on her chosen routes.

"You want my opinion," Shea stated, hoping someone would volunteer some information on the particulars of what had been discussed. A few stared at her with expectant expressions. Others verged closer to outright hostility at having to listen to a stranger, someone who wasn't even Trateri.

Gala eyed her with a vexed expression and pointed at a spot on the map. "As we've discussed, we'd like to add the additions to this side of the camp."

"I still say that's a mistake. The Ember clan and the Rain clan both have blood feuds with the Earth clan," Calvin said, his mouth turned down into a sour frown.

Shea looked at the map, grabbing one side and sliding it closer to her. She ignored the slight huff from the woman from the Lion clan—a woman whose name she had forgotten. Again.

Hm. Camp was a little cramped already. The Forest of the Giants lived up to its name. The giant soul trees that were the size of mini mountains made finding adequate space for Fallon's army difficult. With roots the size of houses poking up out of the ground, it was a challenge keeping the camp from breaking into several scattered settlements. It was too easy for any isolated sections to be attacked by beast or man.

It had forced the Trateri to adapt. They'd packed the smaller tents so tightly together that they were nearly on top of each other while the larger tents the Trateri were known for were left packed away. The tight quarters had left many feeling irate.

"That's right under the Airabel village," Shea observed. The village was built among the treetops of the giant soul trees—trees so tall and wide that it was said only giants could tend them. The Lowlanders who made this place their home rarely ventured to the ground, and then only if it was in a hunting party. They'd been more than happy to let the Trateri set up their encampment below.

"We're aware of that," Sharri, an elder from the Earth clan, said.

"Then you don't care if the Ember clan and the Rain clan wake up with human waste decorating their tents," Shea said with a neutral expression.

Twelve sets of eyes looked at each other before aiming Shea's way. She greeted them with a pleasant expression.

"What do you mean?" Gala asked.

Shea slid the map back to the center of the table and began to lean back before catching herself at the last minute, remembering just in time that she wasn't in a chair. Her thighs screamed in protest.

"The Airabel have no way to build latrine pits since their homes are built into the branches of the great soul trees."

Their expressions said they had never considered how the Airabel handled waste. Shea wasn't surprised. The Trateri had never seen a sky village built into the canopy of a tree so tall it was difficult seeing the crown of it when you were standing right next to it on the ground. They had probably never even thought of the logistics of life up there. Unlike Shea, who'd spent many visits living and learning about the Airabel during her time as a pathfinder. Then, she'd lived in one of the tree top homes, instead of camping out on the forest floor as the Trateri did.

Shea sighed. They still weren't getting it. "They use chamber pots that they empty over the side of the village every morning. Anything below gets a nice coating of whatever they ate the previous day."

It was why the land below the village was so lush. Flowers and other vegetation had taken advantage of the nutrient rich soil derived from generations of fertilizer.

"They can't go there," Calvin said, staring at the map. "We'd never hear the end of it."

"I say put them there," an elder whose name Shea hadn't bothered to learn said. "They deserve what they get for waiting so long to join us. They should have been here months ago, instead of waiting to see if the Hawkvale's plans would succeed."

There was a murmur of agreement around the table.

Shea didn't know the particulars of the situation or why the two clans were just joining the other five now. She did know that putting them there was a disaster in the making. If nothing else, it would lead to additional meetings such as this as the newcomers aired their grievances. Shea would like to avoid that.

"What about here?" Shea asked, pointing to a corner of the map.

Gala and the rest leaned closer, frowning thoughtfully at the spot Shea indicated.

"That's the horse pasture," Calvin said.

"That we don't use," Shea said. "There are too many dangerous plants that could kill the horses. The horse master said he planned to move them further afield where there was less danger."

"So, you're saying the horses are more important than Ember or Rain."

Shea fought down a sense of frustration. That wasn't what she'd said at all.

"Not at all. Merely that they have the tools to make this spot safe for their people whereas the horses do not."

One elder harrumphed. "I say the horses are more important than either of those clans."

"They could see it as an insult on our part," another cautioned.

Shea forced herself not to roll her eyes. Because putting them in a spot where shit would be dumped on them every morning was less of an insult.

She couldn't take her sitting position any longer and shifted, easing her weight off her legs. They prickled with an angry buzzing sensation as feeling rushed back into them.

Daere aimed a disapproving stare her way. She probably thought Shea was showing weakness she couldn't afford, but Shea shrugged off the other woman's disapproval. If they chose to see her inability to kneel in one position for an indeterminate length of time as weakness, they would learn the exact depths of her strength should they choose to test her.

She propped her chin on her hand and listened as the elders debated the merits of the two spots. Daere gave her another frown and tilted her head as if to invite Shea to insert her opinion. Shea gave her a blank expression and feigned confusion as if she didn't know exactly what Daere wanted. Shea wasn't a peacemaker. If Daere wanted this fixed, she'd have to do it herself.

Daere's lips tightened before she aimed a serene expression at the rest of the group. "How about we give them a choice?" Daere said, stepping into the blossoming argument. "Let them decide which of the two areas would fit their needs best."

Gala and Calvin listened with attentive expressions before sharing a look with the rest of the group. They both nodded as a chorus of agreement came from the other elders.

Shea kept her heartfelt thanks that the meeting was over inside. She placed her hands on the table to begin leveraging her way to her feet.

"On to the next issue," Calvin said.

Shea froze. No. They were done. How could there be more?

Her eyes swung to Daere's, who gave her a meaningful stare combined with the barest hint of a victorious smirk before turning her attention back to the conversation. Shea's shoulders drooped, and she settled back into place. Her chance to escape the tedium had disappeared.

*

Shea strode down the small path sandwiched between several tents as she tried to ignore the woman pacing by her side. Daere was the epitome of the perfect Trateri woman—graceful with just a hint of that ferocious fire that said she would eviscerate any who got in her way. Adorned in the abundance of jewelry preferred by those Trateri not of the warrior caste, Daere's clothes were complex and yet simple, speaking of the highest craftsmanship.

Next to her, Shea felt like a homely usurper, wearing the pants and blouse she normally wore when on the trail. She'd had a much different plan for the day before Daere forced her into that meeting using placid smiles and artful words.

"We have time for a quick break for the midday meal and then we'll need to meet with the blacksmiths and armorers," Daere said as she smiled and nodded when three women greeted her in passing.

Shea stopped and turned to Daere. "What are you talking about?"

Daere was too refined to huff, but Shea was beginning to learn her expressions. The other woman was frustrated with her.

"The blacksmiths and armorers," she said in a patient voice even as the pleasant expression on her face grew strained. "There is a dispute that you will need to mediate."

Shea tilted her head. "I know nothing of either discipline. How do you expect me to mediate when I don't know any of the particulars?"

This time Daere's sigh was long suffering. "You just need to listen and then offer your best opinion."

"But if I don't know what I'm talking about, how can my opinion matter?"

Daere's smile dropped from her face. "I will be there to guide you."

That's what Shea was afraid of.

Daere gave her another smile, this one a thin stretching of lips that in no way reached her eyes. "Now, I suggest we visit the cooks' tents to grab something to sustain us for the afternoon."

Daere turned to set off but didn't get far before a man called her over to look at a tool in his hand. Shea glanced at Trenton, the ever-present shadow that Fallon had assigned as her guard. Trenton's lean frame and pretty hazel eyes belied the lethal swordsman who had tried to hammer some of those same skills into Shea's stubborn head. He had a thin face and pointed chin. Right now, he seemed preoccupied with scanning their surroundings for potential threats.

Seeing both of her keepers distracted, Shea slipped away, quickly merging into a stream of people heading in the opposite direction. Daere had claimed her morning; she wasn't getting her afternoon too.

An hour later, Shea leaned back on one arm, her legs swinging over the edge of her perch. High above in a soul tree, Shea allowed herself to relax. Daere wouldn't think to look for her up here. The Trateri weren't big on heights, being from the grass plains to the southwest where trees weren't common, and trees of this height were nothing but a myth.

Shea bent forward, cocking her head as she peered down. It was just a guess, but a fall from this height would probably result in her death. Not a cheery thought, but Shea counted the risk as acceptable. Solitude in the Trateri camp came at a high price—one Shea was willing to pay for an afternoon free from unwanted responsibilities.

Her perch was a knob of growth the Airabel villagers had turned into a resting place for travelers journeying to the crown. Even as high as she'd climbed, she was still only a third of the way up, and Airabel was barely visible through the branches of the soul tree it called home. A hundred men standing shoulder to shoulder wouldn't be able to surround the trunk of the tree completely. In a world filled with many odd and wondrous beings, it and its brethren were totally unique.

Fallon had marched his army halfway across the Lowlands to this Forest of the Giants after Shea had told him the story of this place. He'd decided that he needed to see the truth of her words for himself. She still hadn't gotten quite used to the power she held, but that was what she got for claiming the love of the most powerful man in the Broken Lands. She needed to be careful with what words she shared in the future.

If she could take the man and leave the warlord she would, but that was as likely as the sky falling to the ground. He'd poured his heart into the Trateri people, united the clans, and forged them into a unit capable of not only surviving the dangers of the Broken Lands but thriving in them. Getting him to walk away would be impossible.

Shea leaned back and sighed. She was bored. Bored and stifled. Of all complaints, she hated that one the most. It made her sound like some ungrateful child who needed to be entertained.

She would have settled for any small excuse to scout. A resupply mission. Maybe even something to do with reconnaissance. She'd even accept ferrying a letter to one of the Trateri squads on the outer perimeter of camp.

She'd tried. She'd been denied. Oh, they were polite enough—she was the telroi after all—but they made it clear in only the ways a fellow soldier could that her presence was a hindrance rather than a help. It had taken only one debacle of a mission to bring that point home.

As the telroi of the Trateri warlord, her position in this society had changed from that of a highly respected scout to someone tied to the most powerful man in the Lowlands. She still wasn't sure what place a telroi held. Somewhere between a wife and a mistress from what she could tell.

She couldn't even take her complaints to Fallon. He'd snuck off into the night after their last conversation—fight really—about her place and had been gone for a month and a half visiting his strongholds throughout the Lowlands and doing who knew what.

Shea certainly didn't—because he'd left her behind.

There was a commotion below. She leaned over the edge of her perch and frowned at the sight of two Trateri men hacking at a series of vines hanging from one of the giant, upraised roots. The vines were a deep verdant green and the smallest tracery of pale violet ran along the edges.

They really shouldn't be doing that. The vegetation in this forest was unpredictable and deadly if handled wrong. Those could be normal vines or they could be sleeper vines, whose purpose was to hunt and capture prey before dragging it back to the carnivorous flower at the vines' heart. The flower's pollen would sedate the prey as it slowly digested the animal while it was still alive.

"Oy, down below," Shea shouted. "You shouldn't be doing that. It's dangerous."

The taller of the men looked up and frowned before saying something to his companion. They both went back to hacking.

Did they not hear her? It was possible. She was pretty high up.

She narrowed her eyes at them. Some of the clans tended not to recognize Shea yet. She wasn't as well-known as Fallon and hadn't been with him that long. She thought it more likely they had ignored her.

She debated leaving them to their fate. The old Shea wouldn't have hesitated. She would have said their death was on their own heads if they chose to ignore her. Actions had consequences. New Shea was willing to give them a bit of reasonable doubt. These were her people if Fallon had his way. She needed to do her best by them even when it was a gigantic pain in the ass.

She grabbed the rope ladder she'd pulled up after her and tossed it over the edge, sending the secondary rope, which was anchored nearby, after it. Gripping the second rope with both hands, she hooked one leg around the thick rope and slid down.

Moments later she reached the forest floor. She released the rope and flexed her hands. They were a bit sore, but she hadn't gone so fast as to rip skin off, which was a relief. Injuries to the hands, even small ones like rope burn, hurt like hell and made even simple tasks difficult.

She turned to the men. They had given her descent a sideways glance but hadn't paused in their task.

Shea gave them a polite smile. "As I was trying to tell you earlier, what you're doing is dangerous. It would be better to get one of the Airabel villagers to spot you. They have a lot more experience with the flora and fauna in this forest and will know if you're messing with something that should be left alone."

The men shared a look before continuing with their hacking. Shea took a deep breath then released it slowly. That answered that. They'd definitely been ignoring her earlier. Should she continue to warn them or leave them to it?

She ran a hand through her hair, leaving the half-tamed mess disheveled and sticking up in odd directions.

She studied the plant. It was possible it was harmless. If so, confronting them was pointless and could lead to trouble later. On the other hand, if she let them continue and they managed to disturb a sleeper vine, they might die. Then there would be all these questions and accusations about how she'd failed them.

It was so much easier when she kept her own council and didn't care about getting along with the people she served.

"Are you really going to ignore me right now?" Shea asked. She pulled a face at her own stupid question. Of course they were.

She could try ordering them to listen, but she had a feeling that would make her feel even more stupid and ineffectual.

"Hey," she shouted.

"What?" one of the men finally snapped.

"Did you not hear me? You're hacking away at something that could kill you. Stop until someone can verify this is safe."

"We got mothers. We don't need the warlord's bed warmer telling us how to do our job."

Shea's eyebrows rose. She wanted to say the sentiment shocked her, but it didn't. She was only surprised that it had taken so long for someone to say something. It was a fact of life that people were going to assume what they wanted to.

Had she been someone different, those words might have hurt. Made her question her self-worth and position. The thing was, she'd earned her stripes through blood, sweat and tears. Her friends knew she wasn't just some pretty face to warm the warlord's bed. They knew what she was capable of. These men's words said more about their little minds than it did her.

Though, she did wonder why they weren't afraid to say such things to her. Most Trateri treated her like fragile glass, fearing word of their disrespect would get back to the warlord. He was not a man you wanted to make angry. She made a note of their clothes and the crest announcing their clan allegiance that decorated their backs. She'd have to investigate which it belonged to. She didn't think it belonged to any of the ones she knew. Perhaps one of the newcomers?

Shea disregarded the first two things she wanted to say. There were entirely too many curse words and threats in them. After a moment, she disregarded the third response. It was still a little bloodthirsty.

"I know you didn't show such blatant disrespect to someone who outranks you," a woman's voice barked from behind Shea.

The men snapped to attention in a way that was at complete odds with how they'd treated Shea.

Shea turned to find a shorter woman with dark brown hair pulled fiercely back from her face in several interwoven braids. Her amber eyes were flinty and fierce. There were three parallel scars across the line of her jaw. Her gaze flicked to Shea then back to the men.

"Who is your commander? Does he know the disrespect his men show their superiors?"

There was no answer.

"I'm sure Darius Lightheart or Fallon Hawkvale would be happy to personally discuss your lack—at length."

The men glared at the woman. Shea eyed her as well, surprised at the unexpected interference.

The woman looked familiar. Shea could have sworn she'd seen her before, but she couldn't have said where or when.

"I don't speak just for my own amusement," the woman said in an acerbic voice when the men failed to do more than glare. "Answer."

"Our commander is Patrick Cloud."

"Never heard of him," the woman said. To Shea, "You?"

Shea shook her head. "Not familiar to me either."

The other man looked impatient to have this over. "We're out of Dark Cloud under clan Rain. We were told to clear these vines out to make room for sleeping quarters and storage space."

The woman shot Shea a questioning look. Shea frowned and tilted her head in thought. Clan Rain. Wasn't that one of the new clans? The ones discussed at the interminable meeting this morning? She looked around the area. This wasn't either of the places they'd discussed hosting them.

It occurred to her that she should point that out. One look at the sullen faces before her convinced her to let someone else be the barer of bad news. She'd done all she planned on doing.

"We don't have time to humor a mother hen," the first man said. "We need this done by midafternoon so they can move some of the supplies in here before it rains again."

The second man looked at the trees above. "This place seems to have no shortage of rain."

A vine jerked. It was a small movement, easily missed. Shea's gaze sharpened. Was that her imagination or did it really move? The vine looked different than the ones the Trateri had been hacking at—some of which were strewn about the ground—the violet two shades darker and edged in white.

It flicked again and then rose. The rest of the vines shifted as if disturbed by a strong breeze. Only there was no breeze. Several of the dark purple vines, thicker and a deeper color than the rest, parted the curtain. They were silent as they snaked across the ground.

"Look out," Shea shouted.

She darted closer to the men, both of whom were just now realizing the danger they were in. A small vine closed around the tall Trateri's leg and jerked. He screamed as it dragged him toward the nest of vines.

His friend tried to help, hacking at the rest as they swarmed across the ground to him. Shea drew the short sword Trenton insisted she carry and rushed forward.

This was why she hated getting involved. Saving stupid people was a thankless task.

The woman darted past her, swinging a sword the length of Shea's arm. She cut one vine in half and then reversed her slash to take care of another.

Shea let the woman and the other man fight the vines while she concentrated on the one wrapped around the captive's leg.

She hacked at it, losing the proper form her sword instructors had tried to engrave in her body. All she cared about was getting the stupid vine to let go.

Her cuts fell in a flurry of strikes, a pale-yellow substance oozing out of the wounds. It quivered and then released the man's leg before slithering back behind the curtain of vines. The cloth the vine had touched was partially torn and bright red welts formed on the man's leg.

Shea grabbed his shoulder and heaved, half dragging him as he crab-walked backwards with her.

"Let's go. Get out of range of the vines!" Shea shouted at the other two.

She'd only taken two steps before a vine struck, wrapping around her leg and jerking. She hit the ground with a grunt, the sword falling from her grip. Her hands scrabbled at the dirt as the vine tried to drag her back toward the flower that was beginning to peek past the curtain of green.

A whistle cut through the air, ending in a thunk. The grip around her leg loosened and she scrambled forward.

"Move your ass," Trenton shouted as she gained her feet and raced away from the flower. She grabbed the man she'd saved and half dragged him across the forest floor to safety, as Trenton, the woman, and the second man worked to hold off the other vines.

Small feeler vines slithered across the ground after them but gave up the chase after a few feet.

Trenton's face was coldly furious as he looked back at Shea. His eyes held an accusation that she had no doubt would reach Caden and Fallon's ears when they returned from their trip. When she'd eluded Daere and Trenton, she'd known he wasn't going to be happy when he found her. It was just her luck that he caught up to her as she was being dragged to a grisly death. He'd no doubt have some choice words for her later.

"What the hell was that?" the second man asked in a shrill voice, interrupting Trenton's lecture before it could begin. His friend was seated on the ground, his hands hovering over the welts on his leg as he stared at the nest of vines that writhed and swarmed like a den of snakes.

Shea sighed and gave him a long-suffering look. "Had you bothered to listen, I would have told you that several of these types of vines are attached to a carnivorous plant, but hey, you seem to know what you're doing. Next time I'll leave you to it. I'm sure your families will be very proud when they're told their sons were eaten by a flower."

Both men stared at Shea in shock. They seemed almost as surprised at her response as they had been that a plant had tried to kill them.

The woman snorted. "You two louts should have listened to the stories. She's the scout who saved the Hawkvale's life from a spinner nest and from a village of crazy Lowlanders. When she tells you something, it's best to pay attention."

Several Trateri joined them then. There were exclamations of shock as they viewed the still writhing vines with something close to fear. It was one thing to be wary of the beasts that inhabited the Broken Lands, but a plant that could kill? The Trateri had no frame of reference for that.

"I'd leave the vines alone until you can get one of the villagers to help you safely clear the area," Shea said. Fire should do it, but she kept that part to herself. She didn't want to get drawn into this anymore than she was already.

Before they could ask her further questions, Shea walked away. The woman who'd interfered joined her, and Trenton trailed behind them, a grim and glowering shadow.

"Thank you for your help," Shea said after a beat. "I'm not sure it was needed, but it was appreciated regardless."

The woman's small grin flashed white teeth against a tan face. Her eyes crinkled with some private amusement.

"Don't mention it. I was in a nasty mood before I happened upon you. It gave me a chance to work through some of my aggression before I took it out on the men under my command."

Shea doubted that. The woman had seemed calm and collected when she dressed down those men. There hadn't been an ounce of unnecessary anger or aggression.

"You seem familiar," Shea said, saying what had been on her mind since the woman interceded.

The woman's grin became a full-fledged smile. "I should. We've met before."

Shea glanced over at her, startled. Had they? She took a closer look, trying to place the face. It was right there, but the memory wasn't coming.

"Let me see if this jogs your mind. Revenants and pickleberry juice."

The memory smacked her in the face. Shea's jaw dropped.

"You're the second command in Sawgrass. Perry's your commander, right?"

Shea remembered now, the woman had been in the company that had taken on a huge revenant pack on Shea's first mission as a Trateri scout. They'd have all died, despite every precaution taken and a hard battle fought, if Fallon hadn't joined the battle at the right moment.

"Yeah. My name's Fiona, in case you don't remember. You were just a Daisy then."

A Daisy was an untried scout, named for the yellow ribbon sewn into the collar and edges of the green jacket that all scouts owned. The jacket had been in a pack Shea had stolen on her way out of camp and was the reason why Eamon had assumed she was assigned to his scouting party.

Needless to say, she hadn't worn the yellow long. Only until the Trateri realized the extent of her skills and promoted her to a full scout.

"I'd forgotten the name, but I do remember the face," Shea admitted.

"Is that normal? How those men talked to you?" Fiona asked, tilting her head back at the Trateri they'd just saved.

Shea shot a glance over her shoulder. The Trateri massed around the vines. Most kept a careful distance, but some intrepid individuals poked at the vines with swords and jerked back when the vines tried to grab them.

"I've never had anybody be quite so blatant with their disrespect before." Shea's response was slow and careful. She wasn't one to talk about such matters, especially with strangers. Lately, she'd been trying to be a little bit more open, having experienced some of the friendships with the Trateri scouts she had worked with. It was a work in progress.

"In other words, there has been disrespect."

Trenton looked over with a frown. Shea ignored him and shrugged. Fiona could make of that what she would.

Fiona walked beside her in silence for a moment, her forehead wrinkled in thought. Shea was content to leave her to her internal musings, instead preoccupied with looking around the camp.

There wasn't enough room in the treetop village for the entire Trateri army, though the villagers had offered hospitality to Fallon and his top officials. They'd rejected it, giving the excuse that they needed to stay close to their men.

The truth was that they didn't trust the villagers, who had treated the Trateri horde as odd friends come to visit. The Trateri were used to at least a token resistance and were flummoxed at the lack of one upon their arrival.

Shea suspected that was because the villagers didn't see the Trateri as a true threat. While their military prowess would guarantee them victory on the ground, it would be difficult to fight a battle where the opponent had the advantage of the high ground. Quite literally in this case.

The moment the Trateri tried to ascend to the world above, the villagers could fade into the forest, using the numerous interlocking branches that created a network of paths. The Trateri would be hard pressed to follow.

Fallon and his generals knew all this, which was why they couldn't understand why the villagers had agreed to provide him with a tithe and a few of their hunters. Had in fact seemed overjoyed to do so.

Shea suspected it was because the villagers saw in the Trateri an opportunity. In many ways the tree people of the Forest of the Giants were advanced, more so than any in the Lowlands. They'd managed to build houses that defied gravity and logic. They did this because the dangers on the ground far outweighed those of the air.

There were two worlds in this forest, that of the below and that of the above. The forest floor had its beauty, but it was filled with numerous more dangerous plants and beasts than the canopies. Because of this danger, only the best hunters ventured to the forest floor. It led to their people being isolated with little trade with the rest of the Lowlands.

The Airabel saw the relationship with the Trateri as a way to become connected with the outside world again. Their population was small, and they were in danger of inbreeding. They hoped the exposure to the Trateri might lead to an influx of new blood.

Until the Trateri became a direct threat to the Airabel, they would act in good faith with Fallon. Since Shea was sort of responsible for their discovery, she hoped that continued to be the case. She'd like to avoid having their blood on her hands.

"I'm amazed these people could build that," Fiona said gesturing to the village suspended high above them.

Shea looked up. It was impressive. Breathtaking—the first, second, and third time you saw it. A feat that defied the imagination as it integrated seamlessly with the nature around it.

This place was one of Shea's favorite to visit. She respected them, and for her, that was rare. They worked with nature instead of against it, and it paid off.

"Are there more places like this?" Fiona asked.

"I'm not sure. I think there are a few other villages throughout the forest, but this is the only one I've ever visited."

"I was raised to see Lowlanders as weak, ineffectual people who wasted the abundance of riches their lands provided. For the most part, that view has held true."

Shea kept her own council. Fiona wasn't necessarily wrong. Shea had said something similar to Eamon and Fallon once. Still, it was more complicated than that, and Shea knew that you couldn't make sweeping assumptions with any accuracy.

"And now?" she asked. "How do you see them now?"

Fiona flashed a smile. "Still ineffectual and weak. Cowards for the most part." They walked several more steps. "But I'm beginning to realize that might not be true for all Lowlanders. That maybe there are a few exceptions."

Shea threw her a questioning look. That sounded like it was directed a little closer to home. Fiona looked back at her with an open expression.

"We Trateri are a hard race. We think we know a person's measure as soon as we meet them and can be slow to change our minds."

Shea looked away, wondering where Fiona was going with this.

Fiona continued after a beat. "Once our loyalty is given, though, it's forever. You've already started on that path. Don't let a few stupid people convince you to stray from it."

Ah, Shea saw now. Fiona was trying to comfort her, give her something to hold onto when things got rough. Shea was tempted to tell her it was unnecessary, that she'd been here before, and the things said then were much worse. She hadn't had friends like Eamon, Buck and Clark to stand up for her. She hadn't had the support of a warlord.

She didn't say any of that though, taking the advice in the vein it was meant. She gave Fiona a respectful nod.

"Don't worry, I'm a lot more stubborn than I look. It would take more than a few harsh words to run me off," she assured.

Fiona snorted. "Good. I'd expect nothing less from the Warlord's Telroi."

The two parted ways shortly after, Fiona heading to see if her commander had any need of her and Shea off to see the scout commander of the Western Wind Division. She wanted to see if she could twist the commander's arm into sending her out on a mission. He owed her a favor or two from all the times she'd saved his ass.

CHAPTER TWO

Shea stopped in front of a canvas tent with a dark blue banner that had a stylized image of a bird with wings spread on it. The tent dwarfed the last quarters she'd visited the commander in. He was certainly coming up in the world.

A man ducked out of the tent and blinked rapidly at the sight of her before freezing. By the looks of the stack of rolled parchment under one arm, he was a mapmaker.

Shea waited. As one of the cartographers, he would recognize her. She'd been instrumental in having one of their own executed for treason. To be fair, the man had passed out hideously inaccurate maps and tried to lure Fallon to his death. Somehow, she wasn't too torn up about his fate. For a scout, a map could mean the difference between life and death. Fuck with that and you get what you deserve.

The man gathered himself and offered a brusque nod and a low rumble of a greeting. Shea nodded back as he passed her.

Huh. That had been almost cordial. It made her want to chase the man down to ask him what was going on.

She had friends among the cartographers, but he wasn't one of them. The rest tended to see her as a mild threat at best and an ogre intent on their destruction at worst. It had led to some tense discussions when she ran into a supporter of the former head cartographer.

She stepped inside to find the commander of the West Wind Division surrounded by a mound of paper as he stared down at his desk with a perplexed frown. Trenton followed her moments later.

"Eamon, you look like that paper is going to jump up and bite you on the nose," Shea said with a grin.

It was a scene so at odds with the environment Shea normally associated him with. She was used to him as the scout master, the one fearlessly leading them into the great wilderness and possible death. The person who insisted they complete their mission even when sanity said they would be better served to give up and go home. Death by an avalanche of paper was not even in the realm of possibility for her old scout leader.

Eamon Walker lifted his head and aimed a grin her way. He was in his late thirties with brown eyes and a face chiseled with grooves. He liked to tell her that some of those grooves had her name on them. The sharp planes and valleys of his face made it easy for him to appear a stone-faced cynic. A fact he'd used to his benefit to intimidate idiotic commanders when he and Shea used to run missions together.

"Look who finally arrived. You were only supposed to be here several hours ago." Despite the harsh words, the smile in his voice let her know he didn't mean anything bad by it.

Shea gave him a careless shrug. "I got a little sidetracked."

He aimed a look her way that said she wasn't fooling anyone. "You mean you wanted to avoid her at all costs."

Shea's lips twitched at the corners.

"You know you can't do that forever."

Shea snorted. Who did he think he was talking to?

He grimaced and rephrased. "You know you shouldn't do that forever. Running isn't doing you any good, girl."

Maybe not, but it delayed the inevitable and it made her feel like she had a tiny bit of control. Something she desperately needed without the release valve that scouting provided. Before, when her emotions threatened to boil over, she could disappear into the wilderness. By the time she came home, whatever had been bothering her would have disappeared, given up, or resolved itself with no effort or emotional distress on her part.

Her safety valve was gone, and for the first time in a long time she was forced to directly confront how truly ineffective she was at dealing with other people. She hated feeling that way, which was why she'd taken to dodging things she didn't want to deal with.

"Well?" Eamon asked.

"Well, what?"

"What happened to cause your guard to glare at you in such a fashion and the warlord's cousin to corner me and interrogate me regarding your whereabouts?"

"Daere was here?" Shea glanced around as if the woman might spring out at any moment.

Eamon inclined his head. "Don't worry; she left a while ago."

Shea breathed a sigh of relief.

"You know whatever she's done, she's only trying to help."

"Unfortunately, it's not the kind of help I need," Shea said.

19

"Hmm."

Shea narrowed her eyes at Eamon. That sounded like the opposite of agreement. She folded her arms and leaned back in the pillow chair, this one had a back, thankfully. She chose to ignore his comment for now.

Eamon worked in silence as she sifted through her thoughts. She glanced briefly at Trenton, wishing he'd step outside. She was a private person and having someone watch every interaction made her want to hold back even more than she did normally.

"I'm not Trateri. Trying to shape me in their image isn't going to make everyone around me any more likely to accept me." There, that sounded neutral enough.

"I seem to remember you taking our venom. Your very survival says you're Trateri."

"That's not what I meant."

"What did you mean?"

There was quiet as Shea sorted through her thoughts, choosing and discarding words that didn't quite convey what she wanted to say. It was difficult to explain to someone who had never questioned who they were or their place in the world.

"I'm not sure I can explain."

"Try."

Her smile came involuntarily. "There are degrees of acceptance. You were born Trateri. You grew up learning every social cue, breathing in the culture and molding yourself to fit. Even if I had twenty years to do the same, I wouldn't fit here the way you do. For you, being Trateri is instinctual."

His face was thoughtful as he considered her words. "I see your point."

Shea released a breath. Eamon's opinion meant a lot to her. He and the other scouts on their team had managed to become a quasi-family during their months together. Extreme danger had a way of deepening relationships at a quick pace.

"Have you considered that Fallon and Daere aren't trying to mold you into a Trateri woman, but rather are trying to give you a set of tools that you'll need to navigate our society?"

Shea sat back and studied him. "What makes you say that?"

Eamon peered at her with a pensive expression. He had the look of a man who was weighing his words and trying to decide how much truth he wanted to share. He set his papers aside and sat back.

Shea braced herself. The last time he had shared truths, he'd pointed out how her lack of people skills made her inefficient at scouting. It had been something she had always known but not necessarily wanted to face.

"What future do you see for your life?"

Hm, not the tack she thought he was going to take.

"What do you mean?"

"What's your ultimate goal? Where do you see yourself years from now?"

She'd never really put much thought into the future, content with surviving the present.

"I've only ever seen myself as a scout."

It was mostly the truth. She'd once wanted to be a gatherer, a rare type of pathfinder responsible for gathering and safe guarding knowledge from the time before the cataclysm, an event so catastrophic that much of what had gone before had been lost, leading to the current state of the Broken Lands. The gatherers recorded the history of the world for future generations. That dream had died after a mission in the Badlands had destroyed any hope of achieving that future.

Eamon's expression said he knew she wasn't telling the entire truth but was willing to let it go for now.

"That would be a shame," he said instead. "There's so much more to you than someone who acts as a glorified guide to those much stupider than yourself."

"That's not all a scout does," Shea argued, outraged. "It takes hard work and extensive training."

Eamon held up a hand, forestalling any further protest. "You're right, but you're capable of so much more. I see that. I've seen it since that first mission. Fallon sees it too. You're wasted as a simple scout. I think you know that too. It's why you had so much trouble keeping your thoughts locked down tight when you're given an order."

He did have a point there, loath as Shea was to admit it. Seeing someone she led make stupid decisions and not being able to call them on it was akin to feeling like her skin was being stripped away one piece at a time.

"All I've known is this life. I don't know if I can do anything else."

"Evolve, adapt, learn. It's the only way to get through," Eamon said. "A Trateri scout typically only stays in the life for a short time before moving on to other endeavors. This lifestyle is too stressful on the body to stay at indefinitely."

He gave her a look that said 'come on'. She had to give him that point. It was similar for the pathfinders in her former guild. Once they got to a certain age, they started transitioning into other roles. They became trainers or rotated to one of the easier assignments, some took on roles in leadership and the governance of Wayfarer's Keep.

Eamon spread his hands to encompass the tent around him. "Look at me. I loved scouting just as much as you did. Now I'm the commander of the Western Wind division. Things change; learn to change with them or life will right stampede over you."

Shea studied Eamon and then she looked around the spacious tent. It was sparse compared to Fallon's tent, which was decorated with the spoils of war and items made from the best Trateri craftsmen. Eamon's quarters were considered sparse even by other commanders' spaces. That was probably because Eamon hadn't taken the time to outfit his tent with what his station now required. As a scout, he wouldn't have had much, and it would take time to accumulate furnishings and luxuries.

Still, Eamon seemed to be doing well. More surprisingly, he seemed to be enjoying the challenge of the position. Something Shea would have sworn was impossible before seeing him in action.

He was like her. Happiest on the trail doing what he loved.

"You still get to go out. Leave all this behind on occasion and enjoy what's waiting beyond the camp's perimeter," Shea pointed out, not willing to concede.

"Not as much as I would like."

"How do you do it?" Shea asked, curious. "How do you stay when you want to be in the thick of things?"

His forehead wrinkled as he considered her questions. "I'd be lying if I said I didn't miss it sometimes—the adventure, the surprises lurking in the shadows, but I've found happiness doing this. I suppose it's because there are challenges to be faced and overcome here. I might miss the trail sometimes, but not all the time. Not even most of the time."

Shea was quiet for a long moment. Eamon, used to her long silences, went back to his papers.

"You think I should give Daere a chance," Shea stated.

Eamon lifted his head. "I think you should see what she has to offer before you make any decisions. No running and no avoiding."

Hm.

That would take some effort. Shea didn't know if she was up to that or if she even wanted to try.

"What are you working on?" Shea asked, shifting the topic.

Eamon gave her a look that said he knew exactly what she was trying to do. That avoiding the conversation would work for now but it wouldn't work forever. He played along anyway.

"I'm studying a route for tomorrow. I wanted to make sure I familiarized myself with the map before we headed out."

"Oh?" Eamon was leaving camp? After just spending the last few minutes lecturing her on branching out? "Where are you heading?" She feigned mild interest when what she really wanted to ask was if she could come with him.

Eamon didn't look fooled. "Fallon's due back soon. I wanted to take a group out tomorrow and meet him a few days out so we can ride back with him."

Shea straightened in her seat. "And you didn't bother to tell me this sooner?"

He shrugged. "I'd planned to tell you this afternoon when you were supposed to be here, but someone decided to go jaunting about camp without a care in the world."

Shea's mouth snapped closed on her retort. She narrowed her eyes at him. He looked entirely too satisfied with himself.

"I'm going with you." The words were out of her mouth before she could stop them. She fought against a wince, knowing Eamon didn't like being ordered. It would have been better to phrase that as a question.

He lifted an eyebrow.

"Please." There, that was a little better.

His smile was slow in coming. "Fine." Trenton shifted in his corner. Eamon's eyes lingered on him. "But you're bringing your guards."

"Of course, I am," Shea agreed immediately. "The best there is."

"I don't mean me either. My men and I don't count."

"What? Come on. I know you're taking at least a dozen men. That should be more than enough."

"Nope." He leaned back and laced his hands behind his head. "I'm not the one who's going to explain to the Warlord why his Telroi is wandering around without the protection of his Anateri."

The Anateri were Fallon's personal guard, handpicked by him and trained by a sadistic old man. They were deadly and fiercely loyal to Fallon and by extension Shea. Most didn't make it through training, but for those that did, it brought honor to their families and clan.

Once upon a time, before her gender was discovered, Fallon had intended to have Shea join their ranks. She'd gotten a small taste of their training and could attest to its difficulties.

Trenton had been merciless trying to teach her the finer points of sword work. She rubbed one thigh in remembered pain.

"I don't suppose I could get you to change your mind?" Shea asked. She aimed a sour look Trenton's way, knowing that even if she did the nosy man regarding her with a placid expression would make it his business to ensure she didn't step foot out of camp without a full complement of guards.

Eamon knew it too and shook his head. He didn't even have the courtesy to look regretful.

She huffed at him. "I'll remember this."

"You do that. As long as the warlord remembers it too."

She made a rude gesture at him.

"Hello, hello," a voice called from the entrance of the tent. Seconds later a man popped his head through the door way. Seeing the two of them, he stepped in.

Blond, with a sly look in his eyes that said he got into more than his fair share of trouble, the man crossed the tent towards them. He had a broad forehead, an angled jaw, and moved with a dynamic energy.

"Look who it is. Our prodigal daughter come to visit the small folk."

"Buck." Shea greeted him with a smile as he clasped her on the shoulder. Buck's real name was Gerard, but only his superiors and boring people—his own words—called him that. "Where've you been?"

"Oh, you know, about. Old slave driver there had me and my team scouting the forest to the east."

Shea fought the wistfulness she felt at his words. She was happy for him. She was. It was a big deal to be given your own squad, and she knew how hard he'd worked for it. He deserved it, but she couldn't help feeling left behind.

"Find anything interesting?" she asked.

Buck took a seat on a pillow next to her before setting a pair of maps down on Eamon's desk.

"As a matter of fact, I did. A herd of giant elk nearly trampled my team. We would have been goners if we hadn't found a nice boulder to wait out the stampede on. Craziest thing I ever saw. They came out of nowhere, and I didn't see any predators driving them."

"Where was this?" Eamon asked.

Buck leaning forward and gestured to the map. "A few days east of this stream. We didn't see any sign of humans up that way, but with how thick this forest is and how good these people are at hiding, that's not saying much."

Shea leaned forward to look at the map. It was a strange story, but then strange things tended to happen in these lands. Until they had more information, it was considered peculiar but that was about it.

"I'll make a note of it in my reports." Eamon looked up at Buck. "There's been several sightings recently that are out of the ordinary. I'll have the men keep an eye out for similar occurrences."

Buck snorted. "Since when aren't there odd things about in this land?"

Eamon's expression said he half agreed.

Buck seemed willing to let that be the end of it. He leaned back and smiled at the two of them. "It's like old times. If we were on the trail, it would be exactly like them."

"We're heading out with a small group tomorrow if you'd like to join," Eamon volunteered.

Shea blinked, not expecting the invitation. Normally, Eamon kept things closer to the vest. It made her wonder if he missed their old team.

"What? Both of you?" Buck asked, looking between them.

Eamon and Shea nodded.

"I'm in. This'll be exactly like old times. Let's just hope Shea doesn't have to jump onto the backs of any shadow beetles."

"That was one time," Shea protested. "And it saved your worthless hides."

Buck snickered. "I'll never forget the sight of you free falling through the air. I was sure you were going to bounce off and get stepped on."

"That was a controlled fall. I knew what I was doing." That last part might have been a bit of an exaggeration. To this day, she wasn't sure how she survived that stunt. "Besides, Eamon is making us take the Anateri. They're not going to let me do anything even remotely dangerous."

Buck's face brightened. For a moment he looked like a child about to meet his heroes. "They're coming? Even better."

"Maybe for you," Shea muttered.

"How can you say that?" Buck asked. "They're the elite of our elite. I don't know anyone who has even come close to joining their ranks." He paused. "Well, except for you—before Fallon discovered you were a woman."

"Shea's just chafing at the fact that there's somebody who questions the more reckless decisions she makes before she has a chance to act on them." Eamon gave her a censorious look, having counseled her on similar topics when he was her squad leader.

She stuck her tongue out at him.

"You think they'll give me a few pointers?" Buck asked.

"I thought you were happy as a scout."

He shrugged. "I am, but if an invitation ever came to join their ranks, I wouldn't pass it up. Besides, I've never seen better swordsmen. Getting tips from them might prolong my life out there." He made a gesture meant to encompass the world outside.

Shea stood, preparing to take her leave. "You'd be better served spending your time studying the beast board. If it comes down to a fight against beasts, you're more likely to lose no matter how skilled you are with a blade. Better to study and learn so you avoid danger in the first place."

He blew a raspberry at her. "You're no fun. There's nothing to say I can't do both. Right, Eamon?"

One side of Eamon's mouth quirked up. "Don't get me involved in this."

Shea shook her head, chuckling, as she walked away.

"That means you'll do it, right? You'll put in a good word for me?" Buck yelled at her back.

She lifted a hand and waved. "You'll owe me one."

"Just put it on my tab."

CHAPTER THREE

Shea stepped out of the tent she shared with Fallon when he was home—a tent bigger than any house she'd lived in. It had to be to accommodate his guests on the occasions when he entertained. Shea had only been present for a few of those occasions, but she was glad to have the space.

She took two steps forward and stopped.

Daere waited for her, arms folded over her chest and an implacable expression on her face.

Shit. Trenton must have informed Fallon's cousin of Shea's planned activities for the day.

Shea hesitated before straightening her shoulders and meeting Daere head on. She was an adult and fully capable of letting Daere know that she was riding out to meet Fallon. The other woman could argue as much as she wanted, but it wouldn't change Shea's plans.

"Going somewhere?" Daere asked. Her expression left Shea no doubt that Daere already knew the answer to that.

"I'm joining Eamon when he rides out this morning to meet Fallon."

"Are you now?" Daere's eyebrow lifted.

"Yup. That's what I'm doing."

"And when were you going to inform me of this?"

Shea thought the answer to that question was fairly obvious. Instead of giving a response that would have guaranteed Daere's wrath, she said, "I'm informing you now."

Daere's jaw tightened, a vein throbbing in her neck. Shea waited.

"You are a stubborn, stubborn woman."

Shea nodded, acknowledging the claim. She was. There was no getting around it. She was also hardheaded and horrible with people. She fully acknowledged her failings.

"If I didn't know Fallon as well as I do, I would question his sanity in choosing you, of all people, as his telroi."

Shea narrowed her eyes but didn't respond. She wanted this over with and continuing to engage would just prolong it.

"Nothing to say?" Daere hands went to her hips. "It's like talking to a rock."

Shea let a brief smile cross her face. She'd been told that before.

"You know Fallon asked me to do this."

"That's the problem," Shea said. She didn't see a way out of this encounter; Daere just didn't seem in the mood to get fed up and stalk away. Shea would have to share. "He had no right to do that. I don't need someone to mold me into a Trateri woman."

"You think you can fit in without my help? Become the helpmeet he needs?"

Shea shook her head, frustrated. "Of course not. That would be impossible."

Surprise registered on Daere's face. "Then why have you been such a pain in my ass over the past few months?"

"There's nothing wrong with me. Nothing wrong with who I am. Fallon knew who I was when he made his offer."

"Is that what you think?" Daere didn't sound angry, just curious. "That he's trying to change you?"

Shea shrugged, uncomfortable with the questions. What else was she supposed to think? He'd banned her from joining the scouts and wouldn't let her go out with the regular army either. Eamon seemed to think that her path led to bigger things than just trail work, but she wasn't sure if she believed that. What she did know was that she was not equipped to be someone who supported Fallon from behind the scenes. She needed something that gave meaning to her life, something that made her feel like she had purpose.

Daere's sigh was resigned. "That's not it. I'm not here to try to mold you into what I am."

Shea arched an eyebrow at her. She could have fooled her.

Daere's nod was an acknowledgement of her unspoken point. "That might have been my intention, but not Fallon's. He believes that the more you know, the more power you will have to guide events in a direction you choose."

Movement in Shea's peripheral vision drew her attention. Shea glanced to the side, noticing Trenton and Wilhelm, the second Anateri Fallon had stuck her with. Wilhelm was striking in a way that had a good number of the women in camp making doe eyes at him every time he walked by.

Fallon's Anateri were another point of conflict between them. Shea had argued that their presence would be a giant pain in her ass. Fallon had countered with that stone-faced expression he got when he thought she was being unreasonable. She'd lost by the sheer fact that he'd left before she woke the next morning and the two men wouldn't take orders from her when those orders pertained to leaving her alone.

"Is everyone planning on coming with me?" Shea muttered.

"Despite what you might think, your station is not the same as when you were some faceless scout. You can no longer walk around the encampment unattended or venture out there without people to watch your back."

"I've never had a problem before now."

"Before, you were just one of many. Fallon has spent a lifetime accumulating enemies. You've helped uncover a few of them." Daere gave Shea a meaningful glance. Shea looked away. She still had trouble thinking about her involvement in those deaths. "That was just the beginning. There are many who would strike at him through you. If you care about him at all, you won't fight his men when they try to protect you."

Shea didn't have anything to say to that. Daere's words made her feel like a willful child putting herself in needless danger.

The men joined them. Trenton's gaze darted between the two women. He'd witnessed many of these scenes where Daere lectured Shea, and Shea steadfastly ignored it.

"Glad to see you two are ready," Wilhelm said in an affable voice.

Shea could never tell if he felt the tension or just failed to notice. Either way, he'd broken up several stare downs between Daere and her over the last few weeks.

Shea had met Wilhelm at the same time she'd met Fallon—when she saved both from execution by a mob of angry lowland villagers who were convinced the two of them were snooping around in preparation of stealing their horses. She hadn't known who Fallon and Wilhelm were then, just that the villagers had tried to kill two of her own men, and she wasn't going to let them have the satisfaction of killing anyone else.

Shea was grateful for his presence. Of the two Anateri, Trenton was more likely to egg Daere and Shea on, but then, he was a sadistic bastard. She had bruises from their latest training session that could attest to that.

"We'd better get going. I don't think Eamon will wait," Wilhelm said.

Trenton's mouth quirked in a half smile as he observed the two women. His eyes gleamed as he took in their tense postures.

Daere gave Shea a considering look, her amber eyes giving no hint to her internal thoughts. Shea stared back with a calm expression. It was the same one she used to give to her charges when she fully intended to ignore whatever they said and do things her own way.

"Let's get moving," Daere said, shocking Shea by giving in. "As Wilhelm said, the Western Wind Division's commander is likely to leave without us if we're late."

She turned and strode to where Shea just now noticed a pack similar to the one she was carrying lying on the ground. Daere shouldered it and walked off in the direction of the horse corrals near the Wind Division side of camp.

Shea blinked at Trenton and Wilhelm as they lost no time in following Daere. Trenton winked at her as he passed.

What had just happened? She'd expected a much bigger argument from at least two of them.

Not wanting to question her good fortune, Shea followed in their wake. If only getting her way was always that easy.

*

The horse shifted under her, its uneasiness reflecting Shea's own. She'd been antsy all morning, her skin feeling like a swarm of angry bees buzzed under it. It was a familiar feeling, but not one she'd ever thought to have this deep into the Lowlands.

Daere, as had become typical over the last three days, stuck close to Shea, riding just to her left. She was always within one or two horse lengths. Shea didn't know if it was because Daere worried she'd bolt or thought she could prevent Shea from doing something stupid if she stuck close.

The two Anateri were a little better, hanging back and giving Shea some semblance of space.

The rest of the party was spread out, Eamon and Buck somewhere in the front, and the rest of Eamon's men bringing up the rear.

Despite the height of the horses, they were like ants next to the soul trees and the rest of the forest. Everything here grew on a massive scale—mushrooms that reached up to Shea's shoulders, a flower that flourished in the shade of the trees and grew so high its leaves brushed the tops of their heads as the horses clopped their way past stalks as thick as Shea's waist.

"How is everything so big?" Daere asked, staring up at the flat leaves of the flower. "It's like it was built for giants."

Shea agreed. "The villagers like to say that the gods were once giants and that they created this garden full of wondrous and terrible life. They fed it with their blood to help it take root and grow, then tended it by watering it with their nectar. That even when the gods left this world, their creation remained and grew, flourishing through the years."

Daere looked over at Shea. "What do you believe?"

Shea tilted her head back, staring up into the canopy above. "That during the last years of the cataclysm, a great and terrible battle was fought near here. One that involved powerful magics that found root and affected everything nearby, causing

29

some type of rapid and atypical growth in the plants and animals. I doubt gods had anything to do with this place."

Daere didn't comment on Shea's observation, making a noncommittal sound in the back of her throat and going back to observing the forest around them.

Shea probably shouldn't have shared her thoughts. They were the sort of thing that she had been taught from a young age to keep secret from those who weren't part of the Pathfinder Guild. Most didn't want to hear or believe what she knew to be true.

Since Shea had decided to make the Trateri her people in truth, she decided it would be best to share what she knew in little drops. It was why she'd taken a chance in telling Daere a bit about the history of this place. History that her people had uncovered piece by piece as the villagers shared their oral history.

The feeling under Shea's skin surged, the angry buzzing turning into prickles just this side of pain, running along Shea's spine and arms and down the backs of her legs.

She hissed.

This was impossible. It couldn't be here.

She reigned her horse to a stop and slammed her eyes closed, ignoring Daere's exclamation and Trenton's questioning rumble. She listened, tuning out her companions as she strained to feel the world around her.

There. She was right.

Her eyes popped open, the fear in them silencing Daere's question.

She touched her heels to the horse's sides, sending it galloping for Eamon. Daere, Trenton and Wilhelm were right behind her.

"Rally your men," Shea shouted as soon as she got within hearing distance of him.

He didn't waste time asking questions, putting a small bullhorn to his lips and blowing on it in three short bursts.

Shea didn't wait for the rest of his men to assemble, swinging one leg over her saddle and digging through one of her saddle bags. She pulled out a coil of rope.

"Get off your horses," she ordered those that were close.

"What's going on?" a man asked.

"You want to live and see your family ever again, get off your horses and listen to what I say." Shea's voice brooked no argument—her eyes flinty.

Daere obeyed without question. Shea handed her a length of the rope and then did the same with Trenton and Wilhelm. Others followed suit, creating a chain of people holding rope when Eamon made it clear that Shea wasn't to be questioned.

The sense of urgency under Shea's skin grew, lending her movements a frantic speed. It was almost here. She was running out of time.

"What do we do with the horses?" Buck asked.

"Put as many of them on a string as you can, but don't lose sight of us. If you do, you're gone."

One of the men gave a small laugh as if he thought this was a joke or that Shea had finally cracked, showing signs of Lowland weakness after all.

Eamon and Buck didn't laugh, and they didn't act like this was a joke—their faces deadly serious as they gathered the closest horses and threaded their own rope through their reins.

White mist blew through the trees fifty yards in front of them, swarming across the ground in an unstoppable, unavoidable wall. Tentacles of it rolled in front of the main body, like they were horses pulling ahead of the herd.

"Leave the rest and get back on the line!" Shea shouted at Buck and Eamon.

Eamon yelled at Buck and another man, telling them to go as he tied off the line. Buck sprinted the short distance to Shea and the line of rope she'd made everybody grab. Eamon was seconds behind him, the mist looming behind, threatening to swallow him. The third man scrambled after.

"Hurry!" she screamed.

If the mist swallowed him, if he lost sight of them, his chances of finding them again were slim. Shea wasn't sure she'd be able to save him.

He reached her just as the mist engulfed them, bathing the world in a thick white that covered everything, including the man who'd been only a step or two behind Eamon. Holding her hand in front of her face, Shea was barely able to see the outline of her fingers.

"Richard," one of the men on the line called. No answer came. He was gone.

"Whatever you do, don't let go of the rope," Shea ordered.

"What is this?" Trenton asked, his voice seemed to echo from everywhere.

Shea could only see Daere, grasping the rope next to her. The rest of the men were just voices in the mist, the visibility almost zero.

"It's the mist," Shea said.

"So?" someone asked. "We have this in the Outlands. Never this thick but it won't hurt you."

"Not like this," Shea said. "I doubt you have anything like this in the Outlands. As far as I know this is something that only affects the Highlands and the Badlands. It's the first time I've seen it this far into the Lowlands."

"Where's Richard? Why isn't he answering?" the man who'd called for his friend asked.

Shea was quiet for a moment. "He's gone. If he's lucky, he'll find his way out."

"What is it?" Eamon asked, the mist making it nearly impossible to pinpoint where his voice was coming from.

"It's the bogeyman parents warn their children about. Be careful of mistfall, lest you never find your way home again. You get lost in this and chances are you won't come out. You'll wander lost and alone, searching for the way out—never to find it."

Even without being able to see them, Shea could sense the unease among the rest of the group.

"How is the rope supposed to save us?" someone asked. "We would have been better off trying to run and avoid it."

"You'd never have made it," Shea said. "It moves too fast, or otherwise I'd have tried just that."

She peered out at the foggy world, even knowing it would do little good. This was one of the thickest mists she'd ever encountered, not just turning the world odd and dreamy but wiping it completely clean.

"Can you get us out of here?" Eamon asked.

Shea was quiet for a moment. "Yes."

Relief filtered through the air.

"That's not our only problem, though."

Eamon understood without her needing to elaborate.

"Fallon."

"Yes."

There was a low curse.

Daere shifted next to Shea, her movements stirring the mist. Shea ignored her, needing to focus on the task at hand.

Eamon had given Shea a copy of the map, knowing she'd want to monitor their progress for herself. Also, it was a good way to check the accuracy of the maps. Neither one thought it was likely the cartographers would give them inaccurate maps—not after the last time, but it paid to not trust blindly and verify whenever they could.

By Shea's estimation, Fallon and his entourage wouldn't be too far from them. The mist could very well have swallowed them, and unlike Shea's group, they had no pathfinder trained to navigate its miasma.

No one spoke as Shea wrestled with deciding the best course of action. She knew she could lead them out. It might take a day or two, but it wasn't anything she hadn't done before.

"If you can navigate this, shouldn't you be able to find Fallon and get him and his men out?" Buck asked.

That was the crux of the problem. Leading people out was one thing. Finding them in the mist was another. Shea knew of no pathfinder who had walked into the mist blind and been able to accurately find the lost to lead them out.

"I don't know," she said.

"What does that mean?"

Shea wasn't sure who'd asked that.

"It means I don't know if that's even possible. No one I know of has attempted it. Once the mist takes you, that's it. If you're not anchored or with a pathfinder, you're just gone."

There was a long silence as they digested that.

Shea stared into the mist, angry and scared in a way she hadn't been in a very long time. She wasn't ready for this to be the end—for Fallon to disappear, not dead, but not alive either.

No, she wasn't ready at all.

"I have a theory about the mist. It's a risk though and could end with all of us dead."

There was the sound of something hitting another thing.

"Ouch."

"I knew she would have a plan. Didn't I tell you?" Buck asked.

"Like I said. It's a risk."

"We'll take it," Buck returned. "I'm sure it'll work."

"I'm not," someone muttered.

There was another thud and then a different person said, "Hey."

"Sorry," Buck apologized.

Shea was very much afraid that Buck's faith was misplaced this time. She wasn't lying when she said it was a risk, and the chances of success were small. If she were still a pathfinder, still answering to the guild, she would never have been allowed to even consider this option. There were too many things that could go wrong, costing her not just Fallon's life but the lives of everyone with her. It was a heavy burden to contemplate.

Her plan meant finding a large enough object, preferably living, to anchor this group to. Villages in the Highlands rarely went missing. The mist might pass them by but could do little to totally displace them, unlike those wandering the forest.

The soul trees might work. They were definitely big enough and were firmly rooted in this world. It was still a risk—something that had never been attempted before—but it wasn't as great a risk as leaving them standing in place awaiting her return. She could end up losing all of them, Eamon, Fallon and all the rest.

She kind of wanted to kick her own ass for even considering a plan so asinine. Then she thought of what her life would be like without Fallon in it, and she was willing to risk the world itself for the chance to see him again. It was a selfish desire. Dangerous and at odds with a pathfinder's duty.

"What's your plan?" Eamon said.

Last chance. She could follow her training, lead her charges to safety.

What had playing it safe got her before? Betrayal, punishment and heartache. No, she was Trateri now and life was a calculated risk. She could do this. She would do this.

"The soul trees. In the myths, it's said their roots and branches stretch between many worlds. I know they are rooted deeply in this world. If I can find one here in the mist, it should give you an anchor to our world. After you're anchored, I'll head out to find Fallon."

"Thought you said it had never been done before."

"It hasn't, but there's a first time for everything."

Shea didn't need to see Eamon's face to know the concern that would be on it.

"Fallon wouldn't want you to risk yourself on such a thin margin of success," Daere said in a soft voice.

"He's not here to stop me." Shea's voice was hard. "I decide what risks I take."

The mist stirred, giving a brief glimpse of the hazy silhouette of the figures clinging to a thin rope that was all that anchored them to her.

"Do it," Eamon said. "We've been in tough situations before. I have faith that you'll find a way. The Hawkvale is worth the risk. We owe it to him to try."

"My life for the Hawkvale," Wilhelm said, his words making it clear he found the potential risk in this plan acceptable.

"If we make it out alive, it may very well be our lives when he finds out we let her do this," Trenton said. He sighed. "Oh well, at least it means we'll be alive to face his wrath."

Shea took a deep breath and released it.

"What now?" Eamon asked.

"Everyone needs to be as quiet as possible," Shea said.

"Understood."

The others settled, only the faint sound of feet scuffing against the ground letting Shea know that she wasn't alone. The rope tugged gently in her hand as someone shifted.

Shea's breath rasped in her ears as she breathed deep and exhaled. She stared out at the whiteness, unseeing. Her eyesight worthless.

Humans have many senses beyond vision— hearing, touch, taste, smell. None of which were any more reliable here where the mist caused sound to echo, the warmth of the sun to be a faint memory, and the only smell that of damp earth and desperation. No, the normal senses would be all but useless, waiting to betray you at the soonest opportunity.

In the last test before an initiate was elevated to the rank of pathfinder, they were led deep into the wilds and abandoned in an area that was constantly ravaged by the mists. Their only hope was to find their way out on their own. Many lost their lives, some made it out but were mentally broken from their time spent in its grasp. Only those remaining gained the ability to navigate its treacherous heart.

The ability gained was hard to describe to the uninitiated. The closest Shea had ever come was likening it to a homing pigeon. There was some sense that enabled her to hone in on the direction that was home, whether that be the Highlands or the Lowlands. It was a tug in her heart that pulled her from the mist even when it was at its thickest and most dangerous.

She resisted that tug, trying instead to hone in on something closer. Something that could keep her friends safe until the mist relented.

She strained, sensing things in the mist that she hoped would continue to ignore the small existences of her and her friends. There were creatures here that made beasts look like tame puppies. She had no desire to run into them.

There. Her sense caught on something bright and warm. It felt big, an immense presence eclipsing the denizens of the mist by many factors. Her mind's eye sensed that it wasn't just of this world, its branches reached into many. Her curiosity sparked. If there had been time, she would have liked to study this effect. Perhaps explore those branches—see where they led.

"Follow," Shea ordered, moving forward. Her footsteps were sure and confident as she headed toward what she hoped was a soul tree.

The others made no protest as she led them through the whiteout. There was the faint nicker of the horses as someone tugged on the lead. Their hoof beats echoed in the air, seeming to come from everywhere.

Time passed, slow and fast at the same time. That was the way of the mist though. It was hard to judge how long you spent wandering. It could be hours or days as they made their way to the tree, a shining beacon in this colorless world. Shea had to push down the sense of urgency growing in her chest. If Fallon was caught in this too, time would have that weird distortion to it as well. She sensed that if too much time passed, her opportunity to find him would close.

At last, the great tree loomed in front of Shea— a dark figure that rose high above them. Shea tugged on the rope, sliding it through her hands until Daere's hands touched hers. Daere looked up at the tree with trepidation.

Shea caught her hands and placed them on the tree. "As long as one of you is touching this, you should be fine. Wait here until the mist dissipates or I come for you."

"How do you know this will work?" Daere asked.

"I don't. It's the only hope I've got, but it's better than nothing." Shea didn't mention she'd based this theory off two sentences of a tale that was so old that her people didn't even know when or where it had originated from. It was a story Shea's mom liked to tell her when she was younger—a cautionary tale about a man who'd been separated from his wife by the mist. Shea hoped their outcome was a little happier than that man's.

Whispers echoed through the mist. Voices barely heard, their words indistinguishable.

"What is that?" Buck asked, his voice hushed.

"Ignore it," Shea ordered.

Damn, it looked like something had found them after all. She'd hoped they wouldn't have to deal with them.

"I think I recognize that voice," a man she didn't know said.

"You don't. They're shadows taken from memories. Whatever you hear, whatever you see, it's not really there. They're temptations meant to make you stray from safety. Don't fall for it."

"Will they attack us?" Eamon asked.

"They shouldn't. The shades don't have form. They attack by imitating the voices and faces of loved ones, usually those lost in tragedy. As long as you stay with the soul tree, you should be safe."

She felt decidedly less confident now that she knew shades had found them. It made her hesitate, question what she planned to do.

Sensing she was waffling, Eamon said, "We'll be fine, Shea. I'll make sure we don't leave the safety of the tree. You concentrate on saving Fallon. That's your task, that's what's important."

Shea took a deep breath and released it. That was what she loved about the Trateri. They didn't take the easy path, even when death lurked on the harder road. They didn't leave their people behind just because it was dangerous. They were stubborn, hardheaded and courted a death wish more often than not. She fit in perfectly.

"I should go with you," Daere said.

"No, you'll only slow me down. I need to be able to move fast and without distraction if I'm going to do this."

What Shea didn't say is she didn't want the responsibility of another soul if this went wrong. She was as sure as she could be that they would be fine as long as they ignored the shades and kept in contact with the tree. Even with the shades present, what she was about to do was infinitely more dangerous.

"If it's possible, I'll bring him back." It was a promise Shea intended to keep.

Shea could sense that Daere was torn, not wanting to let Shea take this chance but also not wanting to be the one responsible for Fallon's death.

"Don't fail," she ordered.

Shea made a small sound of assent. She didn't intend to.

"And come back safe," Eamon added.

Shea took a deep breath. Her hand dropped, the rough texture of the rope sliding from her fingers. She took a step back and then another. A thick wave of mist blew between them, obscuring Eamon, Daere and the rest, muffling their voices until Shea was standing alone with only the sound of her own breathing to keep her company.

CHAPTER FOUR

S hea made her way through a landscape unrecognizable from the one she'd set out in that morning. Even with the hazy white around her, she could tell this place was not the Forest of the Giants. It was a desolate place, filled with a deep quiet that swallowed Shea's soft footsteps. Even if she screamed, that quiet would consume the sound, leaving not even the memory of it behind.

There was nothing holy or divine about this place. It was instead, oppressive and threatening with its inescapable never-ending sameness. If you got lost in this, you'd wander, never getting hungry or thirsty or tired. You'd just walk and walk. Forever. No purpose, no joy, no pain, no happiness, no sorrow. Just existence. Or so the stories said.

Shea couldn't think of a worse fate.

The rock under her feet and vaguely similar landscape was the same as previous trips into the mist. She'd never gone this deep though. Normally she was trying to escape, not venture further into it.

When she was a child on a trip with her father, the mist had descended unexpectedly. She'd gotten cut off from the group and since she hadn't been through the necessary training to develop a talent for finding her way through, she should have died. Instead, she'd discovered something odd. Something she'd never had the chance to verify because to do so was too dangerous.

On that long-ago day, she'd gone silent and still and listened, concentrating on her father until he was a dim beacon at the edge of her conscious. It was possible that had been the imagination of a scared child, lost and alone. She'd never experimented to find out for sure.

She suspected the connection had to be strong. It wasn't something you could do with an acquaintance or even a close friend. It had to be someone that you loved with all your heart. The connection had to run deep, with tentacles all through your soul that couldn't be severed even through death. That day, she'd been a terrified child intent on seeing her father again. It had been enough that she stumbled into his path against all odds.

Today, she hoped her feelings for Fallon would be strong enough to lead her to him.

Shea stopped walking, knowing she was deep enough in the mist. She concentrated, ignoring the tug that said she needed to go back. That way led out of the mist. She wasn't going anywhere until she found Fallon.

There. It was small, almost unnoticeable. She was half convinced it was her imagination, but there was something there. Some unexplainable feeling leading deeper into the haze.

It occurred to Shea it could be something else, a trap meant to lure her in. Her feet took her in that direction regardless. It was more than she had a moment ago. She'd come this far. Might as well see it through to the end.

She followed that feeling, a tiny spark under her skin. Wending her way deeper and deeper into the blanket of white that had descended on the world.

Sounds reached her, echoing from all directions. Voices that seemed familiar.

Shea stopped briefly. It could be shades trying to lure her deeper. She hadn't heard them since she left the others, but they could have found her again.

She decided to take a chance.

"Fallon! Fallon, are you there?"

There was a breathless moment as Shea waited, her ears straining as she stared unseeing into the white, her heart thumping with a painful hope.

"Shea! We're here."

Her breath gushed out of her, her exhale sounding almost like a sob. Thank all the gods both past and present.

She followed that strange sense, trusting it to lead her to him. It was several long interminable minutes as Fallon and his men kept shouting, trying to give her something to follow. Their voices echoed oddly in the mist, but at least she knew they were out there.

She cut through the mist, almost running as the sound of their voices got louder. She knew better than to run here, but hope lent urgency to her movements.

Between one moment and the next, the mist thinned and she could see him, his whiskey eyes an intense blaze in a face too masculine to ever be considered beautiful. His features were too rigidly defined, a forceful blade concealing the charismatic personality inside. A small scar along his strong jaw gave testament to the type of life he'd led up to now—one of violence and danger. Shea knew that the skin of his hands would be rough against hers, a perfect counterpoint to the gentleness he used when touching her.

The glare he was giving the mist would have been enough to make his men drop whatever they were doing so they could give him anything he desired. It was an expression that dared the world to thwart him. The kind that signaled that he would decimate any who stood in his way.

Normal people would have fled in terror having that glare leveled on them. Shea felt an immense sense of relief at its sight. She would suffer a thousand glares just for the knowledge that he was still part of this world.

Her steps didn't pause for a second as she ran to him. He opened his arms and grabbed her close, his hug a tight vise around her, threatening to crack her ribs. It was a welcome feeling, and she hugged him back with as much of her strength as she could muster.

They held each other for a long moment, his face buried in her hair and hers in the crook of his neck. She let herself luxuriate in the safety of his arms, the warmth and certainty that this man would fight the world itself for her. Even if that feeling was an illusion. There was no safety in the mist. Only loss and hopelessness.

His strength made her feel strong, made her doubts and uncertainty fall away. With him, it felt like this crazy plan of hers had an actual shot.

She drew back and looked up at him, his face holding a tenderness that only ever came out around her.

"How did you get here? How did you find us?" Fallon asked, his warlord mask not quite in place yet. There was relief in his eyes at the sight of her. Relief and happiness. Shea felt an answering warmth in her own expression.

"Eamon brought a company to meet you on the trail. I tagged along."

He frowned. "Alone?"

She gave him a look that said 'don't start with me.' "No, Daere and the Anateri guards you assigned insisted on coming with us."

His eyes went to the white haze behind her. Finding no evidence of the guards, they returned to her, his thoughts evident in their whiskey depths.

She raised one eyebrow. Really? That was what he wanted to focus on in this situation. Giving her grief about leaving her guards behind?

A small smile tugged at the side of his mouth, a faint expression that would have been lost on any who hadn't spent much time with him. Shea had heard others describe Fallon as hard to read, a stone-faced warrior that gave no indication of his thoughts before he struck. He wasn't that way to the people who knew him.

"We can discuss your lack of protection later, when we're safe," he conceded.

She gave a small snort. Yeah, they were going to talk about it, but she didn't think he was going to like what she had to say.

A wider smile touched his face as he read her expression. He seemed to find her anger by turns amusing and frustrating. For now, humor won out. She doubted that emotion would last.

"I'm glad you're here." His hands gave a light squeeze to her arms before dropping away.

"How are you here?" a gruff voice asked from behind Fallon.

Shea peered over Fallon's shoulder at a slightly older man, who eyed her with a healthy dose of suspicion. He was blond, which was rare for the Trateri who tended to have dark hair and brown eyes. His face was striking, refined by age and stamped with authority. The set of his lips said he wasn't terribly impressed by her either.

Shea could tell he was someone important, though she had no idea who. She was still learning the hierarchy in the Trateri ranks and was often at a loss as to a person's status. She usually found out once she'd already put her foot in it.

Although Fallon had united the clans, the idea of one structure of power was a new one that was still taking hold. As a result, the Trateri followed a military power structure, but they also needed to follow the power structure in their clan as well. It made things complicated and gave Shea a headache even on the best of days.

She didn't have the patience for it today.

"I had to leave Eamon and his men behind so I could move quick enough to find you," Shea explained to Fallon. "I left them by a soul tree. Its roots are heavily anchored to the Broken Lands, so they should be fine as long as they don't stray from its shelter."

"What does that mean?" the other man asked.

Fallon's eyes were considering as he looked at the mist swirling behind him. He was smart enough to know this was not a natural phenomenon, for which Shea was grateful. It meant she'd have little trouble of convincing him of what needed to be done.

"It means that you're in the mist," Shea finally told the other man. "Finding your way out is not going to be easy. Most who get lost here are never seen again."

"Superstition." The man's dismissive voice rubbed Shea the wrong way, reminding her of other missions, others whose assumptions and ignorance put people in danger.

Before Shea could make a cutting remark, Fallon stepped in. "Braden, enough. You know as well as I do that something is wrong. We've been wandering for days in land that is unfamiliar when it shouldn't be."

"Days?" That was worse than Shea had feared. It meant escaping had just become significantly more difficult.

"As best as I could figure." Fallon's deep voice was a steadying influence.

"At least three, maybe four. Time is difficult to gauge when you can't tell whether its day or night," Braden said.

"How many men do you still have?" Shea asked.

"We started with a hundred and are down to seventy," Fallon said. "We're lucky we had stopped for the night when it descended, or we would have lost many more. As it is, I barely gathered the men in time."

More of them had survived than she had expected. She had anticipated only being able to locate Fallon. The rest were a bonus.

"I think I can get us out of here," Shea said. "But it's going to require you to trust me."

Fallon pushed a lock of hair behind Shea's ear. "Always."

She gave him a smile, one that lit up her face. "Do you have rope or some way to stay connected with each other?"

"Yes, it's how we kept them from getting lost over the past few days. We tried to just walk close to one another that first day, but more than one ended up getting separated from the group. After that, I had them tie themselves to each other with rope so we wouldn't lose any more men."

That quick thinking had probably saved them. Shea wasn't sure she would have been able to locate Fallon if he'd been any deeper. The men with him would have delayed their descent further into the lands the mist shrouded. She was just grateful she'd found them in time.

"How long before your men can be ready to move?" Shea asked.

Fallon turned his head and barked a command. The sound of movement came from around them.

"We're ready to go now."

She noticed the rope tied around his waist for the first time. He shifted slightly when it pulled at him as the men arranged themselves.

She couldn't help the smile that took over her face. She did love efficiency.

"All right then, I'll take lead."

"Wait, we're really trusting her to lead us out of here?" Braden asked. "We stopped so we could get our bearing. How do we know she can find her way out when none of us could?"

The mist began moving again, veiling Braden and Fallon from Shea's eyes. She reached out and grabbed Fallon's arm before he could disappear entirely.

"I trust her with my life. If anybody can do this, she can."

Shea's hand slid down Fallon's arm until she gripped his fingers.

The tug in her chest toward home was faint here, almost nonexistent. For a moment she feared she'd lost it—that she had ventured so deep into the mist after Fallon that there was no way out.

Then she caught it.

She stepped forward, Fallon's hand clasped securely in hers. One by one, his men followed as they progressed slowly through the mist. Much slower than the pace Shea had set on her journey in. It was a necessary precaution with such a long chain of people.

Fallon was a silent presence at her side, as if he sensed that she needed quiet. That her connection was tenuous at best and she needed her focus. Though she couldn't see him nor he her, she could almost feel his eyes boring into her back. It was a comforting sensation as they crept through the haze.

*

So focused on that tug leading her out of the mist, Shea almost didn't notice when the haze thinned. Such an imperceptible change at first, that it was easy to miss. Only the slight flex in Fallon's hand around hers warned her.

She looked back, noticing she could see his form and face almost without hindrance for the first time in hours. Her eyes drifted to those beyond his shoulder. Three others, including Braden, were visible as well.

Good. This meant they were close to being out of this infernal haze.

A renewed sense of hope lent speed to her footsteps. The forest, the same one she'd been in before the mist, towered above them. A silent testament to their success.

It didn't take long before Shea began to hear the sounds of the forest around them. It was only then that she realized how oppressive the silence in the mist had been. A forest is never quiet. There is always some sort of sound, whether that be the sound of branches rustling in the wind, birds calling to each other, or the hum of insects.

Now that she could hear that song again, she felt that tight spot in her chest loosen. Not all the way, but it wasn't wound as tight as before. She doubted it would totally relax until she'd confirmed Eamon and his group had made it out as well.

Still, she hung onto Fallon's hand until the mist had disappeared, not even leaving a faint memory of its presence.

"We should be safe now. You can tell your men to untie the rope."

Fallon's serious eyes studied her and then the air around them. Coming to the same conclusion she had, that the mist was no longer a danger, he nodded and turned to give the order. "You can untie but stay close. I want everyone to be within a few feet of each other in case this becomes a problem again."

Shea didn't take offense to his hesitation. She would have done the same in his situation. The mist was unlikely to make another appearance, but stranger things had happened.

She stepped away and peered over her shoulder, only dimly aware of his men's movements as they shrugged out of the rope they'd tied to themselves. She stared at the path behind them, questions swimming in her mind.

"What are you thinking?" Fallon asked, coming to stand beside her.

Shea was quiet for a long moment as she composed her thoughts. Used to the way she tended to hesitate before speaking, Fallon waited.

"I'm thinking that this shouldn't have happened."

His eyes shifted to her. "How so?"

"It's been so long since the mist appeared this far into the Lowlands that even my people only have second and third hand accounts of it ever happening. Those accounts come from records hundreds of years old. I don't think anyone living near here has ever experienced it."

"You're worried that Airabel is going to suffer losses." He made a guess, but it was a good one. He'd become used to the way her mind worked since their relationship had deepened.

She made a 'hmm' sound. Yes, part of her regretted the inevitable deaths that would occur simply because the Lowlanders didn't know how to survive the mist.

But a bigger part of her questioned why this was happening at all. First, she'd run afoul of the frostlings, a being not seen since the last cataclysm, that had killed several while putting the rest of the expedition to sleep. Now this, an event that hadn't been seen in these parts for several generations. Something was wrong in the Broken Lands. Something dark and dangerous.

It could be that this was some freak occurrence. That the mist, the frostlings, and others of its ilk wouldn't be a concern in the future. A sinking feeling in the pit of Shea's stomach said that would be a false assumption. She had a feeling all of these events were symptoms of a bigger problem. She just didn't know what.

"Fallon, the men are eager to keep moving. Being this close to the mist's edge makes them antsy. I can't say that I blame them," Braden said from behind them.

Shea turned. Braden's gaze was fastened entirely on Fallon, never once straying to Shea.

"We'll be underway in a few minutes. Prepare them for movement," Fallon said.

Braden gave a nod of acknowledgement. He turned and walked away without once glancing at Shea.

"Who is he?" Shea asked.

"He's the general of my forces in the south. I thought it would be good to have him accompany me back to the main camp. He had some interesting insights that I wanted him to share with some of my other top officials."

If he was in the south, Shea had to wonder if he'd been in charge of one of the city states and the surrounding territory.

"He doesn't seem to like me," she observed in a neutral voice.

Fallon didn't bother trying to convince her otherwise. She knew he'd seen what she had and wouldn't waste time denying the obvious.

"He doesn't like change. He's a good man and a better general. He'll see your good points soon enough."

Shea cut a glance to Fallon, letting him know she wasn't holding out much hope.

He chuckled. "I have faith in you both."

She snorted and walked away. "Fat lot of good that's going to do me in the meantime."

He followed her. "As if you really care what anybody else thinks."

Shea had to give him that. At the end of the day she didn't really care what the general thought of her. It would be nice if he was cordial, but it wasn't a requirement.

Fallon's men were preparing the horses. There weren't enough for everyone to ride, since they hadn't been able to tie all of the horses onto leads before the mist separated them. They'd only saved about a quarter of them.

Shea knew that had to hurt. Being a migratory people, the Trateri tended to form strong bonds with the horses they owned. For them, a horse thief was treated to an even harsher penalty than a murderer. It had taken getting used to when Shea first joined them; her people relied mostly on their own two feet for transport since the Highlands were often too mountainous to take horses in many places.

After some discussion, it was decided that several of the Trateri would take the horses and ride ahead and report in. They'd come back with mounts for the rest of the group.

Shea planned to stay with the group who were walking. She had no desire to rush back to camp. The walk would do her good and give her a way to work through some of her restlessness. She didn't know how she was going to explain that to Fallon though.

Under normal circumstances she'd just inform him of what she planned to do then do it regardless of his objections. With the general and his men here, none of whom were familiar with her, she didn't want to start something that might have consequences for herself and Fallon later.

He caught the reins someone tossed him and gestured for her to mount. She sighed. She should have broached this subject with him while they were talking earlier. Now she had to make a stand in front of these people while making it look like she hadn't challenged his authority.

She stepped up to him, placing one hand on the horse's neck. "I need to stay here."

Fallon was quiet as he studied her with an implacable impression, the mask she associated with the warlord falling into place.

"You need, or you want?"

"Both." Lying wouldn't help her cause and he knew her well enough by now to understand her tells.

"Explain." She could tell by the set cant of his mouth that he wasn't happy with her choice. She was surprised he hadn't already tried to order her on the horse. He was the warlord, more comfortable with orders than listening.

45

She petted the mane of the horse trying to find the right words for what she needed.

"I left Eamon and Buck behind so I could find you." She didn't look up at him as she made that statement. "They knew there was no other choice if I was going to reach you in time, but I can't leave without at least trying to find them."

"How do you plan to do that?"

She shrugged. To tell the truth, she hadn't gotten that far. She just knew she wasn't ready to go back to camp and looking for Eamon and Buck was as good an excuse as any. More so because it was true.

It felt wrong to leave them behind without at least trying to look for them, even if she had little hope of finding them.

"You're not going back into the mist." The words were an order, an implacable will behind them, letting her know that he wasn't going to even consider that option.

Her eyes rose to his in surprise. He didn't look expressionless now, his face filled with anger and a stubbornness that would outlast even hers. The part that caught her and made her unable to respond in a manner she normally would have was the glimpse of fear behind it all. A fear that reached out and struck her in the chest, leaving her with an inescapable feeling of doom.

"I didn't plan to," she said honestly. If they were in the mist, there wasn't anything she could do for them. She was close with Eamon and Buck, but they didn't have the depth of connection that she had with Fallon. There would be no following that connection to them.

His shoulders loosened and relaxed, as if a great weight had been removed from them. Her hand covered his. She knew he had a problem with the idea of her in danger. It was the biggest source of disagreement in their relationship and one they had made no headway in solving, since neither of them were willing to bend or compromise. A small part of Shea feared what would happen if they didn't find a middle ground.

"If that's not the case, why stay behind? You've already said that we came out of the mist in a different part of the forest. They could have as well."

That was true. It didn't stop her from worrying though. It was a feeling that would stick with her until she had proof they'd survived and made it out of the mist. She went back to petting the horse.

He waited a moment before asking, "Were they able to keep hold of their horses?"

She nodded. Yes, Eamon had gotten the last one on the lead before the mist descended.

"If they came out of it, they would head straight to camp knowing that they would have difficulty finding us out here."

46

He didn't say anything else, just leaving it at that.

Shea felt an irrational sense of annoyance. He was so certain that she would come to the conclusion he wanted. The worst part was that he was right. If she was truly worried about Eamon, Buck and the others, the best thing she could do would be to head to camp. She knew Eamon. If he'd managed to come out, he would have ordered his people home so they could warn others and put together a large search party if Fallon and Shea failed to make it back.

"Fine," she gritted out.

Fallon's lips moved just the slightest bit, enough to let Shea know he was fighting a smile at her expense. She reached over, pinching his side in retaliation. His hand covered hers and pressed it into his side, the thumb caressing the inside of her wrist. Tingles shot down her arm.

"Ride with me?"

She stepped closer and laid her head on his bicep. "I still want to walk back."

"Of course you do, but I haven't seen you in several months."

She lifted her head and glared at him.

"You don't fight fair."

Amusement was alive in his eyes as he released her hand.

"Of course not. I am a warlord after all."

Shea's sigh was heavy and loud. "You're not going to win every battle."

He swung onto the horse before reaching down to help Shea swing up in front of him. He whispered into her ear in a husky voice, "Is that a challenge?"

She fought against a smile, losing the battle as he kicked the horse to set it into motion. Those with horses followed him as he took the lead. The rest would make their way at a slower pace until mounts could be sent back to them.

CHAPTER FIVE

They rode into camp with little fanfare, moving at a fast pace past the outer perimeter and onto the lanes formed by the military lines the Trateri had arranged the tents by. The path was a little more jagged given the obstacles of the soul trees, but they were as straight as possible. Fallon didn't stop until he was in front of his tent, a structure easily twice the size of anything near it.

It had its own personal bathing area, a luxury only available in the highest ranks. The rest of the army used one of the communal bathing tents that were set up at each camp.

Two Anateri guarded the entrance, snapping sharp salutes when Fallon reined to a halt in front of them. Fallon dismounted, helping Shea down, as the rest of his men rode into the open space in front of his tent. One of the Anateri took his reins and led the horse away.

Shea followed Fallon toward his tent.

"Send for Darius and Henry," he ordered the other Anateri.

The general and a few of his men dismounted, handing their reins off to others in their party before heading for Fallon's tent. Shea had really hoped the general would elect to stay behind with those walking, but she wasn't that lucky.

"Braden, send several of your men to obtain mounts for the ones we left behind."

Braden gestured and one of his men nodded and left the tent.

Darius came in at a run. His eyes immediately went to Fallon, relief the emotion most present in them. He had the look of a man with the weight of an entire world on him, totally at odds with the easy-going nature he normally presented. He was a tall man with high cheekbones and a broad nose. His light blue eyes were startling against skin several shades darker than most Lowlanders. He was a close friend to Fallon, and one of his most trusted, having grown up beside him. Fallon often left Darius in charge when he had duties elsewhere.

He was also the man responsible for capturing her all those months ago at the village of Goodwin of Ria. Darius had arrived to collect the tithe the villagers owed—

wheat and several of their strongest men. Unbeknownst to anyone at the time, the villagers had made a deal with the elders from the village Shea served, convincing them to betray their own people and send a select few from Birdon Leaf who could stand as tithe in the villagers' place. Darius, having recognized her from when she'd saved Fallon, had known how important she would end up being to his warlord.

Fallon and Darius clasped hands, pulling each other into a back-thumping hug.

"We were getting worried," Darius said, after he'd stepped back. "You've been missing for weeks."

Shea stepped forward. "Have Eamon and his men made it back?"

Darius looked at Shea and nodded. "Yes, they arrived about a week after you left, telling strange stories about a mist capable of whisking people off. We thought they'd gone crazy at first until we lost three patrols under similar circumstances."

Shea let out a deep breath. That was one weight off her back.

"They're not stories," Braden said, his eyes serious as he poured himself a cup of ale from the carafe on the table.

Darius looked over at him. "Braden, I see he finally convinced you to come back. Thought you'd never leave the Outlands again."

"He can be persuasive when he has a mind for it," Braden said, with a wry smile aimed in Fallon's direction.

Fallon raised one eyebrow. "I didn't have to twist your arm too hard to get you here."

Braden chuckled. "If I'd known how interesting things were in the Lowlands I would have come much sooner. Who knew there was such danger given its people are so weak?"

Darius clapped him on the shoulder. "Whatever the reason, I'm glad Fallon could lure you from the Outlands. Your leadership will be appreciated given recent events."

Shea shifted in her seat, wondering if they'd notice if she left. Knowing Eamon and the rest had made it home safely had lifted that sick feeling from her stomach but had also left her exhausted. It had been a long day—one that evidently spanned weeks.

The time jump was a concern. She didn't think she'd ever lost that much time in the mist before. She would have to think on this. It made her wish that she still had access to the Wayfarer's Keep, the stronghold of the pathfinder's guild and where all pathfinders were trained. More specifically, she wished she had access to the library at the Keep. It might have some information that could help her understand what was happening.

She blinked, and her head nodded forward as exhaustion caught up to her. Using her abilities in the mist always took it out of her. This time was no different.

The voices of Fallon and his men were faint as she struggled to keep her eyes open. She didn't want to show weakness in front of the general. Not when he'd already made it clear what he thought of her.

Fallon, noticing the tiredness tugging at Shea, straightened and turned to his men. Darius was in the middle of briefing him about what had happened when Eamon had returned with no Shea and no Fallon. It had evidently caused quite an uproar. With several patrols missing, Darius had made the decision to recall anybody in the outlying areas until they could get a handle on what was happening. It was a decision Fallon agreed with.

"Braden has sent men to recover those we left behind," Fallon told Darius. "I want my top advisors here tomorrow morning so we can discuss this new obstacle."

Darius caught sight of Shea slumped over the table and nodded, understanding why Fallon had called the meeting short.

"Understood."

Braden opened his mouth to object, but at a sharp look from Darius, closed it and gave a gruff nod.

Fallon waited until the two men had departed before he made his way over to where Shea was tilting in her seat. He caught her and then picked her up and carried her to the partitioned area that hid their bed chamber.

She woke as soon as he swung her into his arms. Her eyes blinking up at his, her face sleep-softened and without the normal shields she hid behind.

"Fallon."

"I'm here, Shea."

"I was so scared that I wouldn't be able to find you."

His arms tightened around her. It was a fear he reciprocated. They'd been in there longer than Shea had even guessed. Long enough that he had nearly given up hope. It was a feeling he was not accustomed to, having spent his entire life raging against the odds and coming out victorious in the end.

"I know. Me too."

He set her on the bed and began to disrobe, pulling his shirt off as she watched him with shadowed eyes. As he unveiled a body defined by rigorous training and a lifetime spent at war, Shea took a deep breath. The smile that curved his mouth was pure sin. He recognized that sound, it was one he never got tired of.

He pulled her hips to the edge of the bed and grasped the bottom of the shirt she wore, slowly drawing it up to reveal soft skin stretched tight over lithe muscles. When he pulled the shirt over her head, she stared up at him with a yearning that matched his own.

He'd missed her more than he ever thought possible. This last month had been hard. Every day had been a battle to accomplish what needed to be done instead of saddling his horse and taking the shortest path back to her. If his men ever guessed how difficult he found it to be parted from her, they would write stories of how the great warlord had been ensnared by a beautiful pathfinder from the Highlands.

He ran the tips of his fingers over one smooth shoulder, relishing in the shiver that shook her. She tilted her head back, her eyes steady on his, demanding a kiss. One they both knew wouldn't end with just that. As soon as they started they would catch fire, consumed by a raging inferno of desire that would burn until two people became one, just to start all over again.

It was always like this. He kept thinking it would eventually abate. That this need inside him would fade, leaving him able to think and reason again. So far it only seemed to grow.

He leaned forward taking her lips in a hard kiss, one that was met with an equal ferocity of her own. She gave as good as she got. Always. It was one of the things he loved best about her. Even before he knew who she was. She'd never bow just because of his position.

He tumbled her into their bed, wedging one leg between hers and pressing it hard against the apex of her thighs. She broke away from the kiss, panting as her hands roamed over his back with just the hint of her nails skating against his skin.

Fallon buried his head in the crook of her neck. She writhed under him, the rough sensation of his unshaven cheek against her sensitive skin driving her crazy. His chuckle was gruff and raspy. He pressed a kiss against her shoulder, one hand going to unlace her trousers. He barely touched her as he ran his fingers delicately over the skin revealed beneath.

She panted and arched up. He parted her folds, dipping into them before withdrawing. He stood, helping her yank off her trousers before doing the same with his own. Both of them bare to each other, he paused to look down at her, burning this memory into his mind, her hair spread across his bed and desire in her eyes.

Sometimes it scared him—the depth of feeling he had for this woman. He didn't know what he would do if he ever lost her. If the world thought him a monster now, it had better pray that she outlived him.

He crawled onto the bed taking a place between Shea's legs as he pressed his full body against hers, claiming her lips again for a deep kiss that held a fraction of his feelings. Breaking apart, he pressed a kiss to the side of her mouth, then her chin, her nose and both eyes. The feel of her lips tilting up in a smile softened that hard feeling in his stomach, the one that burned with conquest. She was his greatest challenge, a wild and untamed wind that defied every attempt to master it. He looked forward to the attempt despite the knowledge of his likely failure.

He kissed his way down her body, stopping to pay tribute to both breasts. He pulled one nipple deep into his mouth, biting down lightly as she made a sound in the back of her throat.

Fallon's fingers circled the folds between her legs, brushing against her clit before sinking inside her. Her stomach stiffened and then loosened. He thrust his fingers in once and then again before withdrawing them to circle that small bud of nerves.

He kissed his way further down her body, pausing when she jerked or shivered to investigate all of her sensitive spots. It was a game he enjoyed, seeing how far he could tease her before she lost patience with him. He blew against her wet curls and smiled as she twisted and turned in his hold.

A glance up her body revealed her bare breasts and a blue-eyed glare that told him she was about at that point where she would try to take matters into her own hands. His eyes were filled with a dark challenge as he pressed a kiss to either side of the spot she most wanted his mouth.

Shea panted as Fallon took his sweet time exploring her body. Need quaked through her as he pressed another kiss against a spot below her belly button before nibbling at the skin beneath. The look in his eyes was intimate, almost more than she could bear, and full of knowledge of the torture he was inflicting on her.

Shea's eyes flared and she grabbed a handful of hair, tightening her grip until it was just this side of painful. Firm, but not so tight that it would hurt him.

His chuckle was full of naughty things. He knew exactly what he was doing to her. He enjoyed it.

She arched as he speared two fingers into her. A mewl escaped her as he pressed an open-mouthed kiss against her, his tongue stabbing at that bundle of nerves before he began to suck. She moaned, her legs tightening around his head, as desire spiraled inside her. Each wave pushing her closer and closer to the edge, drawing her nerves tighter and tighter. He flicked his fingers up, finding a spot inside that threw her over that edge.

She came with a long moan. The feeling almost too much, as she both wanted to press closer and move away, trying to escape as it threatened to burn her alive.

Finally, when he had wrung every drop of sensation, he rose above her, need and desperation on his face. He pulled her legs up and pressed her knees to her chest before fisting himself in one hand, pumping once then twice. Fallon guided himself inside her, filling her up until she was almost too full.

His gaze was too intimate like this. It made Shea feel like he saw inside her in a way nobody had before. Like he could reach out and touch her inner most self.

He began moving in her, each thrust sending need spiking through her. Her head fell back as it threatened to send her crashing back into the deeps. He grabbed her chin, pulling it down and meeting her eyes with his own. His hand was a searing brand against her skin. It slid down until it lightly circled her neck before coming to rest on her chest. He tweaked one of her nipples and added a twist to his thrust, reaching a new spot inside her.

She jerked, one hand pressing against his chest, her nails digging in just slightly.

He grunted as his thrusts picked up pace. He reached, down circling her clit.

"I'm close. Get there." Fallon's voice was rough with desire.

Breathy sounds escaped Shea as sensation quickened and the wave rolled back, bigger than before. Her skin pulled tight, as if the faintest brush of air against it would send her catapulting out of this world.

He thrust deep one last time with a long groan. The wave crested and she gave a strangled shriek as she slid down that deep tunnel of feeling with him.

Spent, he collapsed on top of her, his weight a welcome feeling as they came down from the high. Both panted with the intensity of the experience.

Shea brushed her fingers up and down Fallon's back in a relaxing caress as she stared up at the ceiling of the tent.

He slipped out of her though he didn't move from his position, just shifting slightly so his weight didn't crush her. He turned his head to look at her from where he had buried it in the pillow. "What are you thinking?"

She threaded her fingers through his hair, letting the strands slide against her skin. "That as good as you are at that, it doesn't mean you're off the hook for sneaking out of camp when you left."

His grin was slow in coming as she turned to face him. "I wouldn't expect anything less from you."

"I'm serious. Once I've had a chance to sleep and recover from this escapade, we're going to have a talk."

He pressed a kiss against her nose. "Later."

She made a small sound of assent. Yes. Later. When they weren't in the postcoital glow. She wanted clothes and plenty of space between them when they had that talk so he couldn't distract her.

He pushed up, holding his weight above her with just his arms. She looked down his body and smirked. He did look nice like that, all firm and hard—the ridges and planes of his chest and abs on display.

Noticing her glance, he tweaked a nipple as he shifted to the side. She slapped his hand away even as she giggled, a sound she only seemed to make around him when he brought out her playful side.

He drew her into his arms, wrapping her tight. With anyone else she would have felt constricted, but with him she'd never felt so safe or cherished. This was what she'd missed when he'd been gone. The weight of him, the warmth of his body in their bed and the wordless comfort a simple embrace could offer.

Fallon pressed a kiss to the top of her head as he drew meaningless designs on her back. She shivered, the sensation threatening to spark another conflagration, before she settled again.

"I have missed you," he said.

She shifted against him. She was glad to hear that, even if that was entirely his fault.

"I've missed you too."

"Have you been up to anything interesting while I've been gone?"

She frowned against his shoulder before tilting her head back and attempting to pierce him with her best glare. It was missing a huge component since she was currently pressed naked against him, but she tried anyway.

"No, actually, I haven't because you assigned a woman to me with all the sticking power of a burr. She's been relentless in trying to train me to be the perfect Trateri woman."

Fallon stared down at her with a rare expression for him—surprise. It helped allay the worst of Shea's ire. Until right then, she hadn't fully believed Daere when she said that Fallon hadn't planned to change her into a Trateri woman.

"What are you talking about?"

"She's spent the last few months trying to drill me in the etiquette and behavior befitting the Telroi of the Trateri Warlord. She's lucky I didn't feed her to any sleeper vines."

"Sleeper vines?" he asked in a curious voice.

Ah, that's right he probably hadn't been acquainted with them before he headed out.

"They're a carnivorous plant that camouflages itself among regular vines. When its prey comes near, it snatches the prey and drops it into its flower where it can digest and break the meat down into nutrients for the rest of the plant."

He moved his head to look down at her in disbelief. She hid a smile in his chest. "Really? You're not making that up, are you?"

"It's all true. I swear. I had to save two of your men from one when they wouldn't listen to reason."

He settled back. "Next time just let the plant have them. It'll save me from having to weed the idiots from my ranks."

Shea made a sound of agreement. Sleep had latched its tentacles around her and was fast dragging her down. Her eyes closed as she relaxed into Fallon, the feel of his hands rubbing her back lulling her further into sleep.

"Wait, where were your guards?"

Exhaustion stole the filter from her mouth. "You didn't actually think I would listen to that order, did you?"

His chest tensed under her. She opened one eye to peer up at a set of whiskey colored eyes glaring down at her. She closed the eye and snuggled back into him. She was too tired for this conversation.

"Maybe not you, but them, definitely."

She patted his stomach. "It's cute how you think they could stop me."

There was an angry huff above her head. This time she didn't open her eyes, letting sleep pull her under. A kiss pressed against her ear and then Fallon pulled the covers up over her shoulder.

"You know that's not why I left Daere with you?"

"What is?" her question was a drowsy murmur.

"I never wanted you to act as a normal Trateri woman. She's there to provide guidance when you need it—to ease your path when possible."

"Hmm," was her only response.

"Sleep, Shea. We can discuss this when you've rested." A short time later she thought she heard him whisper, "What am I going to do with you?"

She had no answer for him as she lost the battle against her exhaustion and fell into sleep's embrace.

CHAPTER SIX

Voices woke her, the partition doing little to shield her from the sound. Shea blinked sleepily at the empty pillow beside her. She stretched, sending one arm questing through the covers, already knowing she would find no warm body next to hers. The sheets still held a hint of his heat, meaning he hadn't been gone long.

Shea sat up, the sheets pooling in her lap. Her hair was a tangle of curls around her face. She ran one hand through them, pulling them back.

She squinted at the partition as she tried to figure out what she should do. Her mind had that cottony feeling that she got when she just woke up after not getting enough sleep and her mind didn't feel like it was processing things fully yet.

It took everything in her to gaze dumbly at the other side of the room and not just collapse back onto the bed and go back to sleep. She was tempted, her body telling her it hadn't quite had enough rest after the demands she'd put it under.

Her bladder, on the other hand, was saying that sleep would have to wait. She knew from experience that getting up now would mean returning to sleep once she'd taken care of business would be near impossible, especially with the briefing currently taking place in the next room.

That left her sitting on the bed in the semi-dark as she debated each option, torn between trying to sleep a little longer and giving into the inevitable and staying awake. In the end, her bladder decided for her.

She grumbled as she grabbed Fallon's shirt from the carpeted ground by the bed. She tugged it over her head as she made her way by feel to the chamber pot located in a room attached to the bed chamber.

Her bladder appeased, Shea went to her trunk and pulled out a clean set of clothes. She'd long given up the battle of doing her own laundry, Fallon's personal attendants making it clear in a non-vocal fashion that that was their job and they wouldn't allow her to have it any other way. It had taken two weeks of them holding her clothes hostage except for a single set laid out each morning before she bowed to the inevitable and let them wash them every night. As long as they put them back in the trunk when they were done, Shea had decided to let them have their way.

Once dressed, she hesitated. She didn't really want to deal with whatever was happening on the other side of the partition. Unfortunately, there was only one way out of their living space and it was through there. Shea had broached the idea of two entrances and was told no. It would be too difficult to secure both.

Unfortunately, that left her with the decision of whether it was worth interrupting or just waiting until everyone went away. It was a decision she wrestled with on a regular basis.

For her, some of it stemmed from the awkwardness of what to do when on the other side of the partition. Did she join Fallon and his advisors? Listen even as she felt more and more like an outsider? Or did she continue on to her affairs and hope her disinterest in their conversation didn't offend?

Leading the Trateri was Fallon's calling. Shea had no desire to lead anybody. Hell, she hadn't even liked leading the groups she took into the wild country. It made the decision to stay or go during these little gatherings a particularly loathsome one. Which was why she was dithering in her bedroom, in what Fallon insisted was her home, while she had never felt like more of an outsider. A feeling that she hated.

No, she was done with this. She'd do what she felt was best, and if they didn't like it, they could kiss her ass.

Shea batted the curtain aside and stepped through, her jaw set as she took in the scene at a glance. Fallon sat at the head of a long table, Darius to one side and Braden to his other. Eamon sat at the table as did Buck and Trenton. Some of the clan heads were in attendance, and there were a few other faces she didn't recognize.

Daere looked at her with a questioning expression, one eyebrow rising as if in challenge.

Shea ignored her, not wanting to let the other woman distract her from her goal—escaping the tent without having to interact with anyone there.

Fallon gestured to her, "Shea, join us."

For a moment, Shea debated the merits of refusing. She discarded that idea, tempting though it was. With Eamon, Buck and the others from the mission that ended with the mist present, Shea knew they wanted to tap into her knowledge to understand what they were facing.

Shea heaved an internal sigh and walked over to them. There was a brief reshuffling as room was made on Fallon's left. Braden was forced to slide down so Shea could have his spot. She would have been just as happy on the end, but knew from one of the lessons with Daere that the position was considered one of honor, given to his most trusted advisors, or in this case, the Telroi. The only position above it was the spot to his right. As Fallon's second in command, it was a position that Darius would always be entitled to.

Shea had no idea how she'd remembered all of that, given how much effort she made to ignore anything Daere had said.

Braden avoided looking at Shea as she took a seat. Fallon distracted her, as he poured her a cup of ale and fixed her a plate of food. The first time this had happened, Shea had nearly had a fit, assuming it meant that he was trying to control her. Another of Daere's lessons had explained the logic behind his actions.

For the Trateri, fixing a plate for someone, especially a prospective mate, fulfilled two purposes. The first being to show that the fixer was able to provide their mate with a comfortable life full of food and plenty. The second was to show the esteem with which they held the other person. Preparing a plate was normally one of the attendant's jobs. By preparing a plate for Shea, Fallon was saying without words what hold she had over him. Had Shea been present from the beginning, Fallon would have made sure her plate was prepared first.

Shea picked up a piece of flat bread and dipped it into a sauce before taking a bite. The flavors burst on her tongue—the bread warm with a savory and salty taste, the cool bite of the sauce tantalized and teased the senses. Shea knew from experience that it would be easy to mindlessly eat the bread and sauce until she was stuffed.

Knowing she needed to replenish vital nutrients and energy after her adventures, she forked up some of the meat next. It was seasoned to perfection, just enough to complement one of the wild birds they'd trapped but not to overwhelm the natural flavor of the meat.

Fallon waited until she stopped to take a sip of the ale before addressing her. "Eamon was about to share what happened after you left them to search for us."

Shea took another sip and then sat back, turning her attention to Eamon.

He gave her a respectful nod, addressing both her and Fallon with his next words. "Your plan worked. The soul tree kept us anchored to this world. After the mist swallowed you, the shades, as you called them, spent several hours trying to tempt us away from its safety."

"There was something else in the mist?" Braden sat forward in interest, his blue eyes pinning Eamon in place.

Eamon looked at Shea before turning to address Braden. "Yes. Shea called them shades. They spoke with the voice of our loved ones who had gone before. Even with Shea's warning, we nearly lost two of our number."

"Are you sure it wasn't something your imagination dreamed up? Maybe something influenced by the superstitions of others?" Braden carefully didn't look in Shea's direction as he said that last bit. She got the message though. He didn't really believe. Even after his own experience, he doubted.

She didn't waste any of her breath trying to convince him otherwise. To do so would be pointless, and she loathed wasting her time on useless endeavors.

"I heard Daniel's voice," Daere said without looking in their direction. "As clear as on the day he died. Do you think I too imagined it, Braden?"

Braden stared at Daere, who didn't acknowledge his attention. He had an expression on his face, sadness with a hint of longing in it. There was history there. The kind that ended in tears and heartbreak.

A different person would have been tempted to poke and prod until they knew all the details. Shea made a mental note to avoid any mention of the name Daniel and to keep away when the other two were near each other. She didn't want to get sucked into whatever was going on between them.

"I heard him as well," Trenton said into the tense quiet. "I also heard my mother. It was harder to resist their words than it should have been."

"The shades know your innermost fears, those thoughts and dark urges that we like to pretend don't exist," Shea said, setting her ale down. "Their voices can be mesmerizing and are difficult to resist even for seasoned pathfinders."

"You said there were other things hidden there," Eamon said.

All eyes found Shea as she gazed unseeing at the table. She came back to herself when Fallon spoke, "Have any others gone in and been able to come back?"

Darius shook his head. "None that we know of so far, but we haven't re-established communication with a small group that was supposed to head south last week. I'm still waiting to hear back from my scouts."

"What are the chances that we would have come out of that without your help?" Fallon asked Shea.

She frowned in thought. "It's doubtful you or your men would have made it out. Quite frankly, it's a miracle I found you. Everything I've ever been taught says you and your men should be lost. Eamon's team is a little more difficult to gauge. They weren't as deep in as you. One or two of them might have wandered back out by sheer luck. Unlikely, but still possible."

Shea stiffened as she realized what she'd just admitted. Fallon's expression was a cold tundra as his hands clenched around the goblet he'd been holding. After a long, tense moment where the rest of the people at the table found places to turn their eyes, Fallon took a deep breath and released it very slowly.

"How do we make it so that their chances are higher?" Fallon asked, his tone measured, with a false sense of calm.

Shea rubbed her thumb against the smooth wood of the table. She didn't want to answer that, knowing before she spoke that he wouldn't like her reply.

"It's not possible."

Braden made a derisive sound that Shea ignored.

"There's a reason pathfinders play such a significant role in the Highlands. If there was a way to cut them out and learn the mist's secrets, the villagers there would have done so by now," Shea said.

"You know these secrets though," Braden said, his eyes hard.

Shea turned to face him, her expression outwardly calm while inwardly she took exception to his tone. It made her want to take her fork and stick it in his neck.

"Some, but not what enables us to travel the mist."

"That is convenient." There was a pause before the word convenient as Braden made it clear what he thought of her excuse.

"Now see here," Buck started, his voice angry. Eamon touched him on the shoulder and gave a minute shake of his head. Eamon's face was hard as he turned back to the table.

Their reactions weren't unexpected. It was something that might have happened when they worked together, someone casting aspersions on her abilities, and Buck or Eamon coming to her defense. What was unexpected was the sour look on Trenton and Wilhelm's faces, their expressions darkening at the implication behind the general's words.

It was a surprise, given Shea had been half convinced the two merely tolerated her for Fallon's sake.

Their anger helped spark her own. She was tired of the superior attitude and veiled disrespect Braden had treated her to since she'd appeared. She didn't know what problem he had with her. Quite frankly she didn't care. She was done with it.

She pinned him with her gaze and did something she rarely contemplated with people who annoyed her. She explained why things were the way they were. "The last part of our training is very ceremonial. Much like your cleansing ceremony to be adopted into the Trateri, if I had to guess. I can give you parts, but that won't help you, since the critical component, the thing that makes us able to walk through it without getting lost, is my people's most closely guarded secret. They only reveal it to those responsible for the last part of our training. I couldn't give it up even if I wanted to."

Braden held her eyes with his own. Whatever thoughts he had were hidden behind an impenetrable mask. He reminded her faintly of Fallon before she'd learned how to read him.

"That is unfortunate," Braden said. "Without the Telroi's abilities, it will be difficult to protect our forces from this new danger."

He'd backed down. Shea had half thought he would continue to push. She took another sip of her ale and listened as the conversation moved away.

"We're looking at a fifty percent attrition rate if we continue to lose our men to this. If reports are to be believed, this mist can appear and disappear in seconds with no rhyme or reason," Darius said, looking around the room.

"And we can't keep our men in camp for long. Our supply chains would collapse," Henry of the Horse clan said. He was the oldest person in the room, his hair white but his eyes clear and sharp. Shea had heard rumors that he had founded the Stray Wind Troop, a group widely known throughout the Trateri as being spies.

"We could go into the Highlands. Find these so-called pathfinders and force them to show us how to tame the mist," Braden suggested.

Shea tensed. She'd dropped her guard too soon. She should have foreseen this. Of course, they would want to go into the Highlands, which at the moment had the largest population of people with a skill now in high demand. The general was like a dog with a bone.

"The thought had occurred to me," Fallon said.

Shea spun toward him, words of protest springing to her lips. His expression was shadowed and unclear, not giving her any hint of what path to take. She took a deep breath and let it loose. She couldn't say what she was thinking. Not here with so many people listening in.

Politics didn't come easy to her, but one thing that she did understand was the need to present a united front to their enemies. As far as she was concerned, anyone not Fallon had the potential to be an enemy. She would keep her knee-jerk objection to herself until she could confront him later.

Her decision turned out to be the right one when Fallon continued. "But it would be impossible. First, getting up the Bearan Fault cliffs would be a nightmare and would necessitate splitting our force in a manner that would leave us an easy target for our enemies. Second, we would be going into a territory that has even more problems with the mist than this one."

"Your Telroi can guide us," Braden said.

"She is only one person. She might be able to take a handful but not my entire army. We would need every person to breach the pathfinder's stronghold if stories are to be believed."

Not to mention his Telroi absolutely refused to do such a thing. She wouldn't take them to the heart of her people, not where weapons of unimaginable power waited. Fallon knew that. He'd given her the maps himself, so she could destroy any evidence of the routes her people took into the Highlands. She was the only one in the Lowlands with that knowledge, and she'd take it to her grave before she saw it compromised.

She might not agree with her people's stance on many things, but on protecting what the ancients had left behind, she would do all in her power to ensure those weapons remained hidden. Even if that meant leaving Fallon. Even if that meant her death.

Shea took a sip of her ale, keeping her face expressionless as they continued the discussion. He might believe she still knew how to get home, but she saw no reason to confirm it for him. What he didn't know couldn't be used against them.

She loved Fallon but his thirst for conquest sometimes scared her. What was he capable of in this mindless pursuit of uniting the Broken Lands? What was he willing to sacrifice? She still didn't know the answer to that. It meant she kept her council on many things that might threaten the life she was building with him.

"This doesn't leave us with a lot of options," Braden said, dissatisfied. "If we can't find a way to meet this challenge, we will lose much of what we've built here."

Yes, they would. Everybody's faces were grim as they considered the prospect.

"It is possible that this whole thing is a temporary situation," Shea said into the quiet.

Fallon shifted to his attention to her. "How so?"

"Even in the Highlands, the mist waxes and wanes, coming in cycles. It is not an ever-present threat. In the Lowlands, the threat of the mist has faded until it is little more than a myth of the times after the cataclysm. It is possible that this is a fluke, one that will not remain."

"Or it could be the first sign that the worst is yet to come," Fallon said.

She nodded. That could very well be the case. They were in uncharted territory. Shea really knew nothing for sure.

"Are you able to teach some techniques for dealing with it?" Eamon asked. "Things like tethering to the soul tree? It might not be much, but it could be the difference between losing everyone and just losing some. You might not be able to teach us how to navigate it, but you might be able to show us how to survive it."

Shea thought about his words. It was a long shot, but it was better to try than give up out of hand. "I will think on what might help. It would be wise to talk to the villagers above. They might have something worthwhile to contribute."

"I thought you said the mist hasn't reached down here in hundreds of years," Darius said.

"It hasn't, but I noticed something strange about the trees when we were in the mist. I don't think it's a coincidence that their ancestors chose this area to settle. There might be some nugget of information in their oral stories that could help us now."

"Trenton and Wilhelm will help you." Fallon's words were an order thinly veiled as a request. Shea had no doubt he intended them to also guard her from danger—something she had little need of up there. The villagers had never been hostile, accepting her into their midst and treating her with a respect Shea was not used to.

"In the meantime, I'm giving the order to keep all patrols in camp unless its mission critical," Fallon told the rest. "Until we know how to deal with this, I don't want to risk losing men on nonessential tasks. All expeditions are to be cleared by myself, Darius or Braden."

There was a murmured assent from those at the table. It wasn't a long-term solution but it would do for now.

By some unspoken command, Eamon and his men stood, giving Fallon and Shea respectful nods before departing. They were followed by several others, people Shea guessed were in similar positions as Eamon. Trenton and Wilhelm stood and followed them.

The group was whittled down, leaving behind only the clan heads, Braden, Darius, and Daere.

Shea glanced around, not knowing if she should remain. Whatever they planned to talk about was probably important, and she doubted she would play any part in it. She set her glass down and began to stand. Fallon's hand on her wrist forestalled her, asking without words for her to remain.

She kept her sigh internal and settled back down. She was still not sure how she felt being included in these discussions. On one hand, she was flattered that Fallon respected her enough to have her be part of the decision making at the highest level. On the other, she hated the responsibility such a position gave her.

"As many of you know, I have spent the last few months journeying through much of the conquered southern Lowlands and inspecting our strongholds there."

It was why he'd been gone for the last few months. He'd wanted to see how his commanders were handling the larger city states and see the state of things for himself. It's why he had left Shea behind, despite her objections.

"What you don't know is that I also visited the Outlands and our people there." This was the first time Shea was hearing of it.

Judging by the surprise on many of the faces around them, this was news to the Trateri as well. Darius was the only one who didn't look taken off guard.

"One of my purposes was to convince Braden to lend his help to the efforts here. The other was to assess the situation there. Braden will share more." Fallon gave Braden a nod to begin.

Braden leaned forward and looked around the table with a grave face, his eyes pausing on Shea before moving on. Shea got the sense he would have been happier if she hadn't been present but had decided not to make an issue of it with Fallon sitting next to her.

"Things have gotten worse in the Outlands," he said. "There is a plague affecting the plants and animals. It started small but has taken hold of nearly half of the land. There is a rot at the root of the long grass. Insects and animals that feed off it have begun to sicken and die. Those that survive show madness. We lost an entire herd before we figured out the cause."

There was murmur of unease in the room as those around the table wore similar looks of dismay or grief. The loss of a herd was a hard blow. The bloodlines bred into that herd would be difficult for the Trateri to replace and the effects of their deaths would be felt for several generations.

"We've burned what we could before the dry season made burning too dangerous, but I fear it is only a matter of time before this rot infects the rest of our lands."

"Has the Sun clan been able to study it? They must have some way to treat this rot," Ben said.

Braden shook his head. "I've had Chirron's people working day and night to figure out a treatment, but they've had no luck. They are now hesitant to approach, as the rot started affecting those that worked with it. Chirron lost three of his people to madness after they handled the diseased plants. I'm not sure they will be able to figure out a solution before we reach a point from which there is no return."

The rest of the group sat back, the normally antagonistic banter that presided over one of these meetings absent for once.

"What is to be done?" Henry asked Fallon.

"I've given orders that the remaining herds are to be moved to the border with the Lowlands. There is less grazing room for them there, but that also means the blight is unlikely to reach them anytime soon."

"And our people?" Ben asked.

Braden looked at Fallon for permission to continue. Fallon inclined his head. "We've left half of the Sun Clan healers behind, so they might continue their work in finding a cure. The rest of our clans will follow the herds."

"You want to bring them all to the Lowlands?" someone Shea didn't recognize asked. "If we abandon those lands, the Azelii and the Keric will claim them for their own. We'll have lost our ancestral home."

"They'll claim nothing but a wasteland," Fallon said, his voice hard. "This is our only option if we want to survive. The resources in our lands already cannot support our current population. Those lands may be where our father and his father and his father before him were given a sky burial, but our oldest stories say it is not where our ancestors lay. It is simply the land we ended up in when we were driven from our homes during the cataclysm. Our ancestors will understand if we abandon them to ensure our survival as a people."

Fallon met each person's eyes with an implacable expression. The one that Shea had dubbed his warlord expression because it said that there would be no arguing with him, no challenging his wishes. He'd made a decree and he expected it to be followed.

The men and women at the table looked like they didn't have the energy to oppose him. The news Braden had brought seemed to drain them.

Daere stared into the distance, her thoughts far away. Henry seemed resigned, as if he had been expecting this but had hoped for better. Darius's expression was thoughtful and grim. Shea could almost see thoughts and plans being considered and discarded when they failed to meet his expectations. Darius was a strategist—the best besides Fallon. It looked like he was already factoring the news into his calculations.

Shea studied Fallon, his face like stone and his thoughts hidden behind a stern expression. She'd known that their home in the Outlands held limited resources for their people, but she had not realized the situation was quite so dire. It sounded like he was preparing to migrate all of the Trateri from their territory in the Outlands, instead of trying to extend their reach to the Lowlands.

This would change things, but Shea had yet to figure out how.

"That will be all. I have given you much to think on. I suggest you take the next few days to consider what I've said here. We have dark days ahead, ones where we will have to make hard decisions that might mean sacrificing to survive. I expect every one of you to be prepared if the worst comes to pass." Fallon dismissed the group.

He gave Shea a significant look, telling her without words to remain where she was as the others departed. When they were finally on their own, he turned to her, studying her face with a considering expression.

"Most of my army does not know how far things have deteriorated in our homelands. I'd like to keep it that way for now. Knowing could cause dissension and would distract them from where they need to be focused."

Shea frowned at him. She'd assumed as much, otherwise he wouldn't have dismissed Eamon and the other commanders before having Braden make his announcement.

Seeing the confusion on her face, he gave her a half smile, a small twist of the lips that managed to convey his ruefulness. "I know you understand, but I needed to make sure you didn't reveal this to your friends just yet."

"Of course." She understood, perhaps better than most, how important information was and what effect it could have on people. After all, controlling the flow of information and knowledge was how the pathfinders began.

He reached out and tugged on a strand of hair that had fallen out of the small braid she'd attempted. "Would you spend the afternoon with me?"

There was a hint of vulnerability to his face that took Shea off guard. The word, "Yes," was out of her mouth before she could stop it, even though she'd thought to follow up with the Airabel on the problem of the mist.

His half-smile widened, lighting up his entire face. An answering warmth filled Shea. She frowned, nonplussed that someone else's emotions could have such an impact on her own. She wasn't sure she liked it.

"I was planning to head to the treetop to get started on research, but I can take you around the village up there instead." She gave him small smile of her own. "There's something I've been meaning to show you."

"Oh, and what's stopped you before?"

She gave him a reproachful look. "Who is the one who decided to sneak out while I was asleep?"

He grinned repentantly. "You were sleeping so soundly; I couldn't bring myself to bother you."

Her glare said she was not amused. His statement reminded her of the argument they were going to have soon. The one she had put to the side in favor of the twin issues of the mist and the blight on his homelands distracting them.

"We will be talking about that," Shea informed him. "And soon."

He inclined his head. "I would expect no less."

She huffed at him and stood. The moment wasn't right, her issue seeming inconsequential in comparison to the other dangers they faced. She'd wait a little longer, maybe after she'd shown him some of the village.

She turned to the door saying with a backwards glance, "Are you coming?"

He rolled to his feet, his stride that of a lethal predator as he stalked behind her. "An army couldn't keep me away."

She snorted and shook her head. Such a way with words.

CHAPTER SEVEN

It took over an hour to reach Airabel, a tree-top village made up of an interconnected maze of pathways built by rope bridges and ladders. These shortcuts from thick branch to thick branch allowed the inhabitants to travel throughout the village without having to backtrack to the trunk of the tree. The trunk was the center around which life revolved; the village sprouting around it like a wheel, the branches being the spokes on which life flowed.

The villagers had risen to meet the challenges of life suspended hundreds of feet in the air by carving their homes directly into the tree. Some were nestled into the great trunk at the village's heart. As the village population had grown along with the tree, they'd carved the base of their dwellings into the wood of the thick branches that reached out from the tree's heart. They'd coaxed smaller branches to grow from the thicker limbs until they interwove, weaving them together to create the walls and roofs. Surprisingly, this process didn't kill the branch or harm the tree.

Shea had asked how they were able to create living houses that grew and changed even as its inhabitants did but was told that it was a secret only the architects of their people knew. Though her curiosity had nearly consumed her, she had left them their secrets. The wonder she felt when she viewed these living houses was enough. She didn't need to know how they were created to know they were special.

Around the base of the trunk, larger dwellings had been carved out to create meeting places for the entire village to gather. These buildings were much older than the ones further down the branches. As a result, the roofs towered high above the floor, the wood smooth and patterned with age.

The first time Shea had stood in one of those great chambers, she'd been left with an almost spiritual feeling—the space seeming almost holy with the lifeblood of the tree flowing all around it.

Today, Shea didn't intend to show Fallon the trunk, as he'd seen it when he and his people had first come to a halt under the branches of the soul tree. No, there was something else she wanted him to see. Something that she had only discovered recently during one of the many times she had slipped away from Daere and the Anateri guards.

But first, she needed to locate one of the storytellers. They were her best bet in finding out some of the history behind why Airabel's first inhabitants had chosen to settle here in the branches of the soul tree.

She led Fallon across one rope bridge after another, using the rope ladders to ascend or descend in a circuitous path that took them to the opposite side of the tree. They stopped in front of a red wooden door that sheltered a small hut. Though they were a fair distance from the trunk of the tree, the little house looked old and well cared for. The small branches to the sides and front of the building had little flowers sprouting from them, resulting in the house looking colorful and cheerful.

Shea raised her hand and knocked. She waited until the door creaked open and one pale-colored eye peered out through the crack.

"Good afternoon, Teller Laura. I was hoping I could have a moment of your time."

The eye's gaze shifted from Shea to Fallon and then disappeared into the darkness. The door yawned open.

Shea turned to Fallon. "I'll just be a moment."

Shea didn't wait for a response, stepping in after the old woman as she shuffled to her back door. The little house had a small deck that the teller had set a rocking chair and a small desk on. It was a nice space, one that would allow the older woman to sit and enjoy the quiet and peace of the tree and its splendor without every passerby being able to see her.

"You've come about the mist," Laura said as she lowered herself into her chair and picked up the yarn and knitting needles she had stashed in a basket at her side. She rocked back and forth as she worked the needles, the small scrap of knitting growing with each movement.

"I have. Is there anything in your stories about it?"

Laura's smile was crooked as she looked up at Shea before turning her attention to Fallon who had followed Shea inside. "And who's this?"

Fallon stepped forward, impressing Shea as he kept his nod polite and his voice respectful. "Fallon Hawkvale, Warlord of the Trateri."

"Conqueror of the Lowlands. Would-be ruler of the Broken Lands," Laura finished for him. "I've heard about you. Whoever tells your story in the end will be remembered for a long time."

Fallon's lips tilted into a grin. "Perhaps, lady, you will do me the honor."

Laura snorted. "I doubt I'll be around long enough for that. The years come quick when you get to my age."

"You'll probably outlive us all, Laura," Shea said. "You look much the same as the day I first came here."

Laura's knitting paused. "How long's that been?"

Shea thought about it. "Ten, maybe twelve years?"

Laura went back to rocking. "The days just float on by when you get to my age. Time was, such an event as the mist appearing would have sent me into a tizzy of worrying."

"So, your people do have record of it," Shea said.

Laura nodded. "We do, as I expect most villages that kept up with their past do. As your own people do."

"Do your stories mention anything about the soul trees?"

Laura's knitting paused, and her faded blue eyes swung to fix Shea with a long stare. "They might. What's it to you?"

"I'd like to hear them. When we were lost, I thought I noticed something about the trees."

Laura looked into the distance, her gaze faraway. She was silent for a long time— long enough for Fallon to step closer to Shea and place his hand on her back as he leaned down to say in a low voice, "Are you sure this woman is the right person to ask about this?"

"She's one of the oldest in the village. She's also a respected teller, someone who keeps the Airabel's oral history and speaks it to her people at gatherings and when asked. If anybody knows anything, it will be her."

Fallon gave her a look that said he had serious doubts that Laura was in the right mind to share anything of note.

"She's also in possession of perfectly good hearing," Laura said acerbically, fixing Fallon with a gimlet stare.

Amusement tinged Fallon's eyes as he gave her a courteous bow of contrition.

Laura harrumphed. "You asked about the trees. I may know something."

Shea leaned forward in interest.

Laura's eyes shifted to Shea. "Did you feel it when you were there? The connections?"

Shea nodded. She had.

Laura put her knitting in her lap and looked out at the tree before her. "Our history says these trees exist in many worlds. That their branches lead to different places, ones not ravaged by magic or mist, ones where beasts do not exist and the world was never broken."

Fallon made a small movement at Shea's side. She looked up to catch a fleeting grimace before he schooled his face to impassivity.

Laura's smile was sly as she looked at Fallon. "You don't believe. That's alright. I didn't either for a long time and then I followed one of these branches to a place so utterly unlike this one that I fled in terror. That day, I learned that every story that was passed on to me, even the ones we no longer tell as anything but myth, was true. You see, these trees don't just protect us from the mist. In a way, they call it to us. They're one and the same. Two halves of a whole. With the mist will come other things, some wondrous, many terrifying." Laura picked up her knitting and began rocking again. "You have your work cut out for you, future conqueror. Pick your teller wisely."

*

Shea and Fallon were quiet as they walked along one of the thick branches, its bark covered by a mossy plant except in the middle where hundreds of feet had worn a path through many years. Each digested the teller's words and predictions. One thing she now knew was that the tree would protect those touching it from being lost in the mist, but it sounded like it could be dangerous in its own way too.

Shea and Fallon climbed one of the ladders hanging from the branches above, then made their way across one of the many rope bridges as they traveled further and further from the village's heart.

The air was cool against Shea's face, while patches of sunlight warmed her as she passed under them. She took a deep breath then released it. She let go of some of the worry eating at her. They were away from all of the responsibilities and duties that came with the Trateri. She was determined to enjoy the next few hours.

The sun was setting the world aflame with a golden glow as it sunk behind the horizon when they finally reached the spot Shea had picked. The golden tint picked up the deep auburn in Fallon's hair, a color that was only obvious at times like these.

Fallon stopped beside Shea, taking in the scenery around them. Shea had chosen a spot where the branches of the soul tree and the trees surrounding it had interwoven so closely that it blocked out any but the briefest glimpses of the world below. On one side of the branch floor was a deep groove where water had pooled, creating a series of mini pools. From a branch above, a small stream of water trickled down, creating a small waterfall shot through with the hues of sunset. Moss covered everything as it drenched the small scene in lush, verdant greens. A small purple flower that Shea had learned only grew in spring lent a pop of color to the world.

"How did you find this?" Fallon asked, his face expression alight with wonder.

Shea's shoulder jerked in a half shrug. She didn't think he would enjoy learning she left her guards behind as she wandered outside of the safety of the camp and village.

The censorious glance he leveled on her said he guessed how but didn't feel like arguing with her before he turned his gaze back to the small oasis.

"This is beyond anything that I've seen before," he said, as his eyes took in their surroundings.

Shea gave him a small, pleased smile. She thought he might like it, since he was used to the rocky plains of his homeland and the forested mountains of the Lowlands. Nothing like this. Even with all her travels, this place stood out—a place that most of the world didn't even know existed, for the simple fact that so few people look up.

"You haven't seen anything yet." She shrugged out of the pack and set it on the branch at her feet. "I brought food for dinner and a change of clothes for both of us. We can stay the night up here if you'd like."

The gaze he shot her said she'd surprised him.

"Or we can go back. I know you're busy with everything; I just thought it might be nice to take a night to ourselves before things get even crazier."

They hadn't had one in a while—if ever. There always just seemed to be something in the way, whether that was one of the clan heads demanding his help with an internal clan issue, or him needing to visit with his soldiers, or having to make battle plans because one of the villages decided to rebel. Shea just wanted a little time to themselves.

"No. No, I'd like this." Fallon's gaze was warm on her and Shea gave him a happy smile.

"Good. Race you to the pool." She pulled her shirt over her head and tossed it before taking off at a run for the cool water.

There was a long silence before Fallon gave a war cry and pounded after her, the wood under Shea's feet vibrating slightly as he gained on her. She hadn't made it even halfway there before he swooped her into his arms and tossed her over his shoulder as she shrieked with laughter. She wriggled madly until he slapped her on the ass. She yelped before wriggling even harder than before, laughing the entire time.

He walked to the edge of the pool and then stopped. Shea used her hands to lever herself partially upright.

"Don't you dare. These shoes take forever to dry, and I don't want to climb down with soggy boots," Shea told him.

His shoulders heaved in a sigh. One huge arm wrapped around her upper thighs to pin them against his chest. The other got busy unlacing her boots before tugging them off in a feat of strength and dexterity that impressed Shea, despite how hard she thrashed as she fought to escape.

He repeated the act with her pants and underwear until she was hanging over his shoulder, her ass bare to any passing breeze. One large hand came up to cup a cheek before squeezing it. He slapped it again, and this time it stung without the protection of a thin layer of cloth. She yelped and then whacked his ass in retaliation.

His shoulders bounced as a deep chuckle rumbled in his chest.

Shea's eyes closed and she slumped over his shoulder. Crap.

"Yeah, you didn't think that through, did you?"

"Fallon," was the only word she got out before she was sailing through the air. She took a deep breath before the water rose up around her, covering her head. She bumped against the smooth wood on the bottom. Her feet under her, she pushed, exploding up.

She slicked her hair back and blinked away water to glare at Fallon. That was her intention anyway. Fallon had disappeared.

"Fallon?" She waded a step toward where he'd just been, noticing belatedly the pile of clothes in his place.

A hand grabbed her ankle and then yanked. She went under with a shriek.

They surfaced at the same time. She splashed him in the face which triggered retaliation as he wrapped her in a bear hug and sank under again. She came up laughing, his hard chest pressed against her back and his arms wrapped around her front.

"Do you give up?"

Shea tilted her head so she could look at his face. "How did you even get undressed and into the water so fast?"

He gave her a smug smile. "I was very motivated."

She snorted and tried to splash him again. He dunked her twice more.

"Give up yet?" he said in her ear, sending shivers racing down her spine.

"Yes, yes I give up."

His arms loosened, and she took two steps forward, a smile pulling at her face. She gave him a sly backwards gaze before sending a wave of water his way, feeling victorious when it hit him square in the face.

"Victory is mine," she crowed before diving into the water and scissor-kicking for the opposite size of the grotto.

The muffled sound of splashing water reached her as he arrowed toward her. She evaded his grasp, slipping from his hand with a move that would have impressed a fish. They played this game for several more minutes until he cornered her at one end of the pool, her hands pinned behind her back and his face close to hers.

"What was that you were saying?" he murmured, a dark wicked look in his eyes.

"I don't know what you're talking about." Shea tried to keep a straight face but feared the mirth showed through despite her best efforts.

His smile was that of a conqueror, arrogant and dark, and just a little bit cruel. "If you were anybody else, such actions would have resulted in a swift and painful punishment."

She lifted one eyebrow. "Oh?"

He nodded solemnly. He leaned forward pressing a kiss to the side of her neck, following it up with a sharp nip. Shea bit down on her moan, warmth spreading through her core, but she wasn't ready to give up the game just yet.

"Well, you should know by now, Warlord. This pathfinder rarely does what she's supposed to."

Shea twisted her wrists, sliding out of his grip. At the same time, she kicked his leg out from under him in a move Trenton had spent considerable time teaching her over the last few months. Done properly, it could seriously injure someone. Ideally, it would send her opponent crashing to the ground. Fallon staggered but didn't fall. It was enough that Shea was able to slip past him.

She aimed a smile at him as she treaded water at the deeper end of the pool.

The look he gave her was half fascination, half determination, and all possession. It sent a thrill of adrenaline through Shea. She took off, avoiding his grab. The two of them romped for another hour, each giving as much as they got.

It was a rare opportunity to play, something Fallon told her he'd never had the chance to do as a child. So much of his life was spent protecting his mother or in training that he'd never been able to be a child. While she'd had plenty of opportunity to play games when she was younger, it was a forgotten art until she met Fallon. As an adult, she had to be serious and restrained when living in the villages, not wanting to give them any reason to see fault with her. She'd never realized how much of a strain it had put on her until she'd experienced the light-heartedness playing with Fallon could bring. He was the only person to bring out that part of her, and she took pleasure in these small moments, rare though they were.

Fallon lunged forward, catching her before she could slip away, his momentum carrying them to the side of the pool. A seriousness had entered his face. Shea stood still as he lowered his head ever so slowly to hers, giving her a dozen chances to turn away if that was what she wanted.

She lost patience with the slow tease, bridging that last little distance and pressing her lips against his. For a long moment, his lips remained hard, then they softened and suddenly he was kissing her like he intended to consume her. Like the world might end if he didn't get inside her. His hands gripped her ass, lifting her and crushing her against him. She helped him by wrapping her legs around his waist.

There were none of the teasing touches of earlier. No delaying the inevitable culmination. It was like someone had lit a match and they were going up in flames.

He was inside her between one breath and another, thrusting up into her and pressing frantic kisses against her throat and breasts. She threw her head back and moaned, feeling her womb pull tight, and those feelings spiral deep inside.

He reached down, rubbing the bundle of nerves just above where they were joined, building the tension in Shea. She was hurtled into climax before she could even think to guard against it. He followed moments later, his groan echoing through the trees.

Finished, he pressed her closer as he rested his forehead against hers. Shea was still breathing hard as she wrapped her arms around his neck and held on as he moved to the side of the pool and lifted her up to set her on it.

They were quiet as they dried off, each keeping their thoughts to themselves. They shared little touches with each other, a caress against the shoulder, a fleeting touch to the back, a press of lips against the chin, telling each other without words the depth of their feelings.

They dried off and dressed in the change of clothes Shea brought. She pulled out the food, mostly trail rations—nothing fancy—except for two pieces of fruit she saved for their dessert.

By now the sun had set and even its memory had faded from the sky, leaving only night in its wake. This high in the canopy there were gaps for the sky to be seen, and what a sight it was. This far from the camp and village meant there was no light pollution to obscure the heavens on this nearly cloudless night. It made for the perfect opportunity to lay next to each other and stare up, as the stars woke one by one, until they were a stream of light twinkling across the heavens, sometimes so thickly that they looked like a river of sparkling dust.

It wouldn't be long now until the main event—the reason Shea had wanted Fallon to see this. It was only visible for a limited time beginning a few hours after the sun set. Not every night, but often enough that Shea had risked the trip.

"This is beautiful, Shea. I can see why you brought me here."

Shea turned her head to find Fallon staring at her. She gave him a smile, only visible because of the moon and stars. Something over his shoulder caught her eyes. She tapped him and pointed. "Look."

The purple flowers that had been folded tight in daylight began to unfurl, looking nearly silver in the pale light. Out of each flower a light rose, slowly at first, then with ever-increasing speed until the little treetop grove was aglitter with moving, flickering lights. It turned the grove into a fantastical oasis as the tiny lights became nearly as numerous as the stars above.

"It's like the stars have come down for us to touch," Fallon said in a soft voice, reaching out one hand to touch a light that had drifted close.

"This is the only place I've ever seen these," Shea confided. "It seems to be a phenomenon unique to this area. This is a small showing. I'm told that deeper in the forest, the lights are so plentiful that it's brighter than the sun at midday."

"What are they?"

"Bugs, as near as I can figure it. The locals call them fairy lights. They're nocturnal and reside in the flowers during the day, using its cover as protection against predators. At night, when the flowers open, they wake up and come out."

Fallon caught one, gently cupping his hands around it. He held his hand out between them and unfurled his fist in a slow movement. In his palm, no bigger than

Shea's thumbnail was a miniature figure, almost humanlike with a head and arms and legs but no features, and wings that closed and opened in a lightning fast movement. As they watched, its wings flickered, creating the glow they'd been watching.

"How does it create light?" Fallon's face was intent as he tilted the fairy light in his hands, this way and that as if he could find the mechanism it used just by observation.

Shea shook her head, the movement visible by the fairy light. "The villagers don't know, and my people haven't spent enough time in this area to study it. There's a story the villagers tell about a race of people so tiny that they are almost invisible to the eye unless you look very closely. That the race was once so plentiful throughout these lands until the cataclysm, which forced them to retreat into obscurity to avoid annihilation. The fairy lights only come out at night when they feel safe, chancing the light only when predators or enemies aren't close."

Fallon looked up for a moment, the fairy light's wings opening and closing, its light turning off and on with each movement.

"Watch." Shea lifted her hands and clapped once, the sound a crack in the night. The lights closest to them winked off, including the one in Fallon's hands.

"It reacts to danger."

"Yes, which means the light can be controlled. Its reaction to threat is to hide, using the natural camouflage of the night as protection."

When Shea made no other movements, the fairy lights gradually drifted closer again in a slow meandering movement. Fallon slowly lowered his cupped hand when it became clear that the light he'd held was no longer there.

"The villagers harvest the fairy lights' waste to create artwork and ceremonial dress. For the summer solstice, they always have a celebration that they call the Joy of Light. It looks like a dance of the sun. I've never seen anything like it," Shea said.

Fallon's hand covered hers on the blanket. "I would like to see that someday."

Shea leaned her head against his shoulder as they watched the fairy lights move in swooping patterns over the pond, its water reflecting their light.

"When we have children, I'd like to bring them here," Fallon said, his statement startling in the quiet.

Shea lifted her head. "We're to have children, are we?"

"Of course. I must have someone to pass what I've created to—someone to take up the legacy and make something better, something stronger out of it. I'll sit them down here and tell them the story of how we met, how you exploded onto that platform like a goddess of old, like the stories my grandmother told me when I was a child."

"What if I don't want children?"

His shoulder shifted as he peered down at her. "Do you want children?"

Shea rubbed her chin against his shoulder and sighed. "Truthfully, I've never thought about it. I've been so focused on making a place for myself—and then when the Trateri caught me, on surviving—that the thought never crossed my mind."

"I think you would make a good mother, teaching our children how to read the trails and track beasts."

"Like my mother taught me."

"Not your father?" Fallon voice curious. "You so rarely talk about them."

Shea was quiet a long moment. Her first instinct was to clam up, to ignore the question and make it clear there were some things she didn't want to discuss. It's what she would have done not so long ago.

"My father did teach me some, but he was gone so often. He's a pathfinder; my mother is too, but her duties required her presence at the Keep more often."

"Was that difficult?"

She'd never thought of it in terms of difficulty or not. It simply was the way things were. "No, our family was happy. My father brought me trinkets from his trips, and my mother was the firm hand of discipline, teaching me the skills she thought I'd need when I took my place as a pathfinder. Turned out it was a good thing as it gave me an advantage over other initiates when I began my formal training."

"You speak as if they're dead."

She sighed. "They're very much alive, though they probably wish I'd done them the service of dying in the course my duties."

"That sounds harsh." There was no judgment in his voice. He was simply making an observation.

Her laugh was rough and ugly, hurting her throat as it left. "To them I'm a disappointment. Long before I was captured by the Trateri, I knew I hadn't lived up to their expectations. Now, I doubt they would want me to darken their doorstep. I'm the round peg among a world of square ones. I never quite fit, and once that cost the lives of other pathfinders, they made it clear I wasn't welcome."

Some of the peaceful feeling she'd had after viewing the night sky and seeing the fairy lights threatened to dissipate. She wasn't ready for that, wanting to hold on to the good while she still could.

"And you, what was your childhood like?" she asked, wanting off the subject of her past.

Fallon laid back, pulling her down so her cheek rested on his chest and his arms wrapped around her. It made her feel safe and comforted.

"You know some of it," he told her, staring up at the stars. "My father was a great man, grandson of the man who first united the clans. When I was a child, I would watch him fight. He was fierce; no man could beat him in a fair fight. He was able to take on five men, and they couldn't even land a single blow."

Shea was quiet, knowing that his father had not had a happy ending. She rested a hand on his chest, her fingers rubbing lightly along his pectoral muscle in a soothing caress.

Fallon continued without prompting. "He couldn't be defeated in a fair fight so when it looked like he might succeed in reuniting the clans, his uncle resorted to trickery to stop him. My father's allies used deceit and false promises to lure him from his stronghold. They attacked him with over thirty men, and even then lost two thirds to his blade, before several archers were able to put ten arrows in his body."

Shea's fingers stilled, and she closed her eyes at the pain in his voice. Her family might have its problems, but her childhood was nearly idyllic. Or as idyllic as a childhood in the Highlands could be. It was only because of her own mistakes that the divisions in their family took hold.

"My mother was forced to flee and take shelter with Henry's clan. He was one of the few who did not take part in the betrayal."

That must have been when she met Cale's father. Shea didn't bring his name up, knowing Fallon still regretted the necessity of executing his half-brother.

"Henry's the one who helped me track the men who killed my father. He helped finish the training my father started. When he deemed me ready, he put a blade in my hand, gave me a horse and told me to avenge my father."

Shea lifted her head and looked up at his shadowed face. "And did you?"

His face shifted down until he was staring at her. There was a dark pleasure in his voice as he said, "Every last one. Traderi across our plains heard what I'd done and began to gather. From there, I hunted down the clans that had betrayed my father and destroyed them—wiped their names from our history and made sure they could never recover."

Fallon fell silent after that, and Shea was content to let him. She pressed her hand flat against his chest and smoothed it across the hard ridges of his body.

"Is that why you're so stubborn when it comes to me being a scout?" Her question was soft. She almost lost her courage at the slight tension in his body, but forced herself to stay the course. If they had any chance of lasting, they needed to be able to communicate—even about the hard things. Shea knew deep in her bones, she couldn't go on as she had over the last few months. It would slowly destroy anything they attempted to build.

"Is that why you brought me up here?" he asked, his voice a quiet rumble against her ear.

Yes. And no. She knew they needed time to themselves, but she'd be lying if she said she didn't have an ulterior motive. How to put that into words, though?

She hesitated too long, and he took her silence as answer enough.

The moment shifted. He withdrew from her without ever moving a muscle. It was almost a physical feeling.

77

"No, that came later." The answer came after a long moment, one where she thought he was going to ignore her question.

She lifted her head and looked up at him, holding her breath. He'd shared some things, but only in passing. She knew most of his family was dead, but not how, or why it affected the present.

He fell silent again. Shea didn't push even though she wanted to. She had a feeling that the wrong words right now would cause him to close down and shut her out again.

"My mother was a lot like you," he said. "She was strong and brave and not diplomatic in the least."

She pinched him in retaliation for that last statement.

"She was a Lowlander?"

He made a 'hm' sound of agreement. "My father used to say that he was struck dumb the first time he saw her. She was standing in the door of her family home with an arrow aimed directly at his heart."

His father sounded like he had an odd sense of the mating dance. She could imagine being struck dumb at the sight of someone pointing a weapon in your direction, but not then wanting them as your telroi.

"She sounds like my kind of woman."

"She would have approved of you. She wouldn't have let you know that, but she would have." His hand cupped the back of her head, his fingers smoothing through her hair. "You know that my people have the custom of kidnapping our telrois from other clans or Lowland villages. She's one of the few that came willingly. She gave up her family and life because she saw something in him that called to her. When he died, something broke inside her. She was not the same for a very long time. Some days I don't think she ever got back to the person she was."

Grief will do that. It was like a many-headed beast; every time you chopped off one, two more heads sprung up to bite you in the ass. Left unattended, it could reach deep inside, ripping out the vital parts that made up a person.

"She met Cale's father in that time. Everyone knew the two of them were not a good match. He was ambitious but lacked the discipline to make his ambitions a reality. He latched onto her because she was the former wife of the Hawkvale and thought she would bring him the acclaim and recognition he craved."

Shea leaned against Fallon harder, letting him take more of her weight—wishing that she could prevent the ugliness that was coming.

"When that didn't happen, he changed, taking his frustration out on her. And me sometimes. Back then, I was small. He would taunt me about my inability to protect her. He did that until I was finally big enough and well-trained enough to put a stop to it. I took my mother and Cale and we left him. Henry helped with that too." His voice was hoarse by then. Shea's eyes smarted though all this happened years before she met Fallon. "I thought it was over then. My mother gradually became the woman I remembered. In the end I was wrong, that man was simply biding his time. Waiting until I was off getting our revenge before striking. He snuck into our tent one day and killed her and two others. He tried to kill Cale too, but Henry managed to get there in time to save him."

Fallon fell silent after that. Shea rubbed her chin against his shoulder, trying to give him wordless comfort. It was a poor offering, given what he'd shared.

"I understand your desire to cling to this notion that you can keep me safe," Shea finally said. She lifted her head to look up at him in the poor light. "It is a noble feeling, but you must understand that it is not possible to wrap me in swaddling to protect me from what's out there. Just look at what happened earlier with the mist. There are no guarantees in the Broken Lands."

"You cannot argue that the danger you are in increases every time you go outside the camp."

"That is true, but your enemies are more likely to do me in, than anything out there. You know this or else you wouldn't have put as many guards as you could spare on me."

She could tell by the loaded silence he didn't want to concede that point. Seeing a chink, she pushed on, "Fallon, you can't make me into something I'm not. I'll never be a pretty trinket on your arm or a ball of fluff sitting by your side. I deserve more; I am more."

The shadow of his head dipped in the dark and Shea got the sense his intense eyes were focused on her.

"What is it that you like about being a pathfinder?"

Shea drummed her fingers against his chest. She'd never really thought about it before. It was just the world she was raised in—the world she was born into.

He didn't wait for her answer. "Because from where I sit, you don't appear to like it."

Shea reared back. How could he say that? Yes, she might not be able to quantify what she liked about it, why it drew her, but that didn't make it less the case.

"How can you say that? I'm a damn fine pathfinder."

"Are you now?"

Shea opened her mouth to say yes, then shut it.

Sensing he'd scored a point, Fallon pushed his agenda, "You forget, my love, I talked with Eamon and your men before we ever began. I spoke with every one of my units that you led or worked with. I know what makes you tick, and you were one of the worst soldiers or scouts in my army."

Shea opened her mouth to protest; a warm palm covered her lips before she could.

"Not in skill. There you were better than any man in the clans. But there is more to being a scout, and I'd wager a pathfinder, than skill. From what I heard from both Eamon and others, you flirted with the edge of insubordination more than once. That if you hadn't been so damned talented, they would have had you strung up and whipped as punishment."

Damn Eamon and his big mouth. She knew exactly what incident had been at the forefront of his mind when he'd told Fallon that.

Her sigh was angry. There was little argument she could present. What Fallon said was true.

"I loathe stupidity," Shea finally muttered.

Fallon's chest moved under her as he chuckled. "I am well aware, as is anybody you worked with during your time as a scout." He settled under her. "I'm not just doing this because I want you safe. It's a big part, but not the only part. You're too good and too smart to be a follower, and at the end of the day that's all a scout is. They follow orders about where to go and sometimes how to get there. You're meant for more. I don't want a pretty trinket; I want a strong and powerful partner capable of ruling by my side."

"Shouldn't this be my decision?"

"No, not in this. I am the Warlord, and if I say you won't be a scout, you won't be a scout."

She sat up. This, this was what drove her crazy. They were having a reasonable conversation and now he was back to being an autocratic ass.

"I hate when you pull that card."

His arms came up to yank her back down. "I know. Why do you think I do it?"

She pushed against him, his strength no longer as amusing as it was earlier. "That's not how this works. You don't get to say something and then have it your way."

His sigh was heavy and frustrated. He rolled over, pinning her wriggling body under his. "We haven't seen each other in months. Do you really want to fight? Whatever our thoughts, this issue will not be solved tonight."

He pressed a few kisses along her jaw and one on her nose.

"Fine. For now. We'll pick this up at a later time."

He pressed another kiss against her neck and collar bone. She shivered.

"And in the meantime, can you at least try to find something meaningful that takes advantage of your unique skills here?"

Her silence was stony.

"Shea?" He kissed lower, using his chin to drag her shirt down until he was kissing the tops of her breasts.

She wriggled again, testing his grip but getting nowhere. "Fine, I'll look, but I make no promises."

She felt rather than saw his smile against her skin. "That's all I ask."
He resumed kissing her, sliding until he nuzzled the valley between her breasts.
"Really, again?"
A hand sliding under her shirt was her only response.

CHAPTER EIGHT

Warlord."

The hushed whisper woke Shea from where she'd nestled into Fallon, her body seeking his warmth in the cold of the night. Her back was pressed against his side and her head was pillowed on his bicep while both hands clasped his wrist.

Shea came to the realization that she was naked, never having put her clothes on after the last time she and Fallon coupled. She lay unmoving, playing possum and praying that the interloper would go away without noticing her.

"What is it, Caden?"

"There is a situation in camp that requires your attention."

There was a heavy sigh that held a hint of a growl. "Understood. We'll be ready in a few minutes."

"Yes, Warlord."

Shea didn't even hear the man leave, his stealthy movements would have made any assassin proud.

Fallon moved beside her, briefly spooning her from behind. He kissed her hair and then said into her ear, "I know you're awake."

Shea grunted, not quite past the mortification of being naked in front of Caden, a man she was pretty sure only tolerated her presence under duress.

"Dress, it's time to face the world again."

Shea sighed and rolled over to face him. Over Fallon's shoulder she saw Caden and two other men with their backs to them.

"How did they find us?" Shea wasn't sure how she felt about being awoken to three of Fallon's Anateri keeping watch.

"They've been with us the whole time."

Shea froze, her eyes meeting his as her shocked expression gave way to a glare. "Last night?"

He nodded, his expression guarded.

"So, while we were in the water? After?"

His nod would have been called cautious on another man—a word not often applied to Fallon, a man who liked to use brute force and evidently had about as much sensitivity as a rock.

She rolled away from him, snatching the underwear that was lying beside them. She had to walk a few more steps for the breast band and pants. She donned each item with angry motions, mortification and outrage making her nudity a concern of the past.

Shea hunted for her shirt, turning in a circle to find it. With each passing moment that she couldn't, her anger grew.

"Shea."

She turned in a sharp motion to see Fallon dressed and holding her shirt out to her. She looked at it for a split second, wanting more than anything to throw it in his face—a face she had spent considerable time kissing last night where every man in his command could watch and comment—but not being able to, because his men were standing right there and she was wearing nothing but a thin scrap of cloth across her breasts and a pair of pants.

She grabbed it from him and yanked it over her head—her blue eyes spitting chips of ice at him as they appeared above the collar.

She turned and stalked off, her strides eating up the distance. Fallon finished dressing and was a silent presence at her back as they made their way along the soul tree's thick branch. Caden took point while the other two positioned themselves at Fallon and Shea's back.

"Why are you so upset?" Fallon asked.

Shea's lip lifted on one side in a semi-snarl. She wished she was some great beast with the ability to breathe fire. It would perfectly punctuate what a stupid question that was.

"Not now."

"Shea."

Shea ignored him, continuing without sparing him a glance. She didn't know what made her more upset, the fact that Fallon's guards had been shadowing them the entire time when she thought they'd successfully left them behind, the fact that they'd probably overheard them last night when Shea had made no attempt to muffle her cries—something she at least tried to do in camp where the walls were canvas-thin. Or perhaps it was the fact that Fallon didn't even know why that would upset her.

He took hold of her arm in a firm grip, drawing her up short. "Shea, don't ignore me. Answer my question—why are you upset?"

83

She twisted her arm out of his grip in a move leftover from her training as a pathfinder. "I do not wish to discuss this now." Her eyes went to the guards at their back.

His gaze followed hers. Understanding dawned on his face.

He got it. Good. Took him long enough. Shea spun and continued on, not looking at anyone as her strides ate up the ground. She made no attempt to move quietly, rather liking the heavy thunk of her feet hitting wood. It made a nice accompaniment to her anger.

She'd always been a private person, or as private as you could be when half your life was spent on the trail with other people. There wasn't a lot of physical privacy to be had out in the wilds, but she managed for the most part. The thought that the Anateri had heard Fallon and Shea in the middle of sex, or even worse, that they had heard any of the conversation afterward was enough to send Shea's blood boiling.

The worst part was she should have known better. Fallon hadn't hidden the presence the Anateri had in his life. They went everywhere he did, but while in camp their presence wasn't quite as apparent. They were rarely in Fallon and Shea's quarters, and when they were out and about, they could easily be lumped in with the rest of the Trateri.

So yes, she was pissed at herself just as much as she was pissed at Fallon. It didn't help that the conversation last night hadn't had the outcome that she wanted, matters left unresolved. Again.

They were quiet on the journey through the twisting pathways of the treetop roads, Fallon content to let Shea have her way in this. The trip took a lot less time coming back than it had going, the two of them less willing to get distracted by the sights. They moved with purpose, and before long, the village came into view.

One of the elders waited on the branch leading into the village. He looked nearly as old as the tree behind him, his hair thin and pulled back in a dozen different braids. His face was wrinkled and gnarled like a tree, his skin almost the color of bark. His clothes were a bright splash of color, like the only flower in a meadow. He held a walking stick that he leaned on for balance.

"I see you showed your man our oasis," the elder said to Shea, his eyes sharp and knowledgeable in that old face.

"Yes, I thought he would appreciate it at nighttime."

"And what did you think of our little friends' home?"

Fallon was respectful of the older man, but not so much that it wasn't clear who was in charge. "I've never seen the like in all my travels. I will take the sight of your oasis at night to my grave."

The elder gave a gap-toothed smile full of innuendo—something hard to do when he was missing more than one tooth. "That place has a reputation among our village. A lot of babies have been born nine months after their parents have taken a dip in that water and spent the night under the fairy lights. A child conceived there is said to be touched by the gods."

Shea's cheeks caught flame as the Anateri suddenly found anywhere else to look. Fallon's eyes swung to hers, amusement in them. She hadn't known that. The elder hadn't bothered explaining that when he told her about the place last week. Why couldn't he have explained that little myth? And why did he choose now to reveal it?

"Is that right?" Fallon's arm slid around Shea's shoulders and he tugged her into his side. "We would welcome such an occurrence."

Shea's gaze shot up, a warning in her eyes. They were in no way ready for a child. They hadn't even finished settling their differences, too much was up in the air to even consider such a big step.

His face was thoughtful and considering as if the idea was not an unwelcome one. Shea's eyes widened and she shook her head at him. Nope. Not happening. Not any time soon. Besides them as a couple not being ready, she doubted she was. Not for the responsibility that such a tiny existence presented.

Fallon had brought it up in passing before, and Shea had been content to let it go with minimal protest, thinking that it was some theoretical future child. If the look on Fallon's face was anything to judge by, it was not quite so theoretical to him.

She made a note to bring up later the fact that she took an herbal supplement that made pregnancy very unlikely. It was a common herb in both the Highlands and Lowlands. All female pathfinders were taught how to recognize and prepare the herb to prevent pregnancy. Fallon might want children, but unless she stopped taking the herb, it wasn't happening.

"Elder Eckbert is the one who requested we summon you, Fallon," Caden said in a respectful tone of voice.

Fallon nodded and looked at the elder with a questioning look. "Is that right? What is it that you wish to speak with me about?"

Eckbert cackled. "It is, though if I'd known where you two were I would have delayed a few more hours."

Shea shifted again, silently cursing the fact that she'd ever wanted to take Fallon to that oasis. If she'd known everybody in the Forest of the Giants was going to comment and speculate on her and Fallon's whereabouts, she would have never given them anything to talk about.

"We're here now. You might as well speak of your concern."

"Very well." Eckbert narrowed his eyes on Fallon. "My people tell me you're taking fifty of our men."

Shea stiffened at Fallon's side, instantly on guard. The Trateri took honor very seriously. If you did anything to impinge on that honor, they reacted with decisive force, usually in the form of violence. While they had an odd respect for those who fought and lost in battle, they had only loathing for those who signed and then broke

85

a treaty. The consequences of such an action often resulted in complete destruction of the village. Any survivors would be enslaved and divvied out among the clans.

Eckbert's village had already agreed to the treaty. If they tried to go back on their word, Shea feared what might happen to them.

"That is the number that was agreed upon when you signed the treaty. Are you saying that you're unable to meet these terms?" Fallon's voice was calm, not giving any hint to his thoughts.

Shea looked up at him in concern, noting the suddenly alertness on his face, like that of a wolf that had just scented prey. His body was tense where it touched hers. She liked these people and didn't want to see them end, not when it was her stories that had led the Trateri to them.

His hold tightened on her and his eyes dropped to hers in warning. Her mouth thinned, but she kept her council. For now.

Eckbert waved his hand. "Bah, of course we can. That's not the problem. I want to know why you're not taking more of our hunters. I can easily give you double that."

The response was met with a long silence. Fallon blinked at Eckbert in a rare moment of surprise. Caden and the other Anateri studied the other man with undisguised curiosity.

"This is an unusual request," Fallon's response was slow in coming. "I'm afraid you have me at a loss."

Eckbert gave a grunt, sounding more like a crotchety old man. "Yes, I imagine so when you're dealing with the land dwellers. You'd be hard-pressed to find an honest one among them. For the most part, we avoid them since we've had trouble with them in the past. Greedy lot, but none of them want to work for what they have."

Fallon studied Eckbert, his expression calculating. Shea could almost hear the thoughts turning over in his head. "What is your reasoning behind offering me more men?"

"You take more men; they get to see the world. Maybe when they come home they bring wives." The elder's face turned crafty. "Maybe even Trateri wives."

One of Fallon's men choked, his laugh disguised as a cough.

Fallon nodded. Only someone who knew him well would be able to tell that the response amused him.

"I'm sure we can accommodate you. I will speak to my generals to find places for the extra men."

The elder threw his arms out wide, the cane hanging down uselessly, "Aiie, that is outstanding." He shuffled forward, his balance slightly wobbly without the cane. Fallon's guards stiffened as the elder got close to Fallon and Shea, his hands lightly patting both of their faces.

"And you must come for dinner tomorrow night. We will throw a feast to celebrate. There will be much entertainment."

He released Fallon and gestured forward several of his people, all women that Shea could tell. They giggled as they advanced, swarming toward Fallon and Shea.

Caden stepped forward, trying to use his body to usher the elder and the others back. "The Warlord is a busy man." He was only half-successful. He managed to keep Fallon out of reach, but the women transferred their attention to Caden, who quickly found several pairs of hands patting his cheeks—and other portions of his anatomy.

"We'll be there," Shea volunteered, finding herself inordinately amused by how uncomfortable the attention was making Caden, a man who usually possessed confidence and a raw power that warned others of his danger. She looked up at Fallon pointedly. "Won't we?"

Humor danced behind his eyes, before he broke her gaze and looked back at Eckbert and the women tittering every time one of them touched Caden. "We wouldn't miss it."

"Aiie, brilliant." Eckbert clapped his hands and started shuffling back towards Fallon. Caden grabbed him and tried to steer him away.

"That's enough. He gets it. You can't just grab onto the Warlord whenever you want. There's a protocol to these things." Caden's voice was irritated as he tried to keep from getting entangled in Eckbert and the other women's affections again.

Shea bit back a laugh, finding the sight of the normally austere commander flustered too funny to resist.

Fallon leaned down, saying into her ear, "I think we best get going before Caden feels his only recourse is to draw his sword."

Shea snickered and took the lead, skirting the women and Caden as Fallon chuckled and followed.

"Fallon, where are you going?" Caden asked, the faintest trace of outrage in his voice.

"You seem to have this well in hand," Fallon called back.

"Fallon! Damn it, Fallon?" Caden tried to keep the women at arms distance with little success. There were just too many of them. Together they were bolder than they would have been if there had been just one or two. "Curse it, I'm not a damn toy. Let me go."

By now Fallon and the other two guards were laughing outright at Caden's struggles as the rest of them continued past.

"We should run. He's going to be angry when he finally gets free." Fallon grabbed Shea's hand and took off. She followed, her unrestrained giggles making it difficult to keep up. Her humor in the situation lasted almost the entire trip down the tree.

*

Caden's molesting by the village women and the clear unease of the Anateri as they began their descent down the tree—something only possible through the use of ropes and flimsy ladders—lifted Shea's mood. Seeing hardened warriors pale-faced and wide-eyed when it came time to step out into nothing with only the promise of a sturdy rope in your hands to keep you from falling went a long way to restoring some of her dignity.

As soon as they set foot in camp again, Fallon withdrew, projecting the fierce warlord again. She hadn't realized how relaxed he'd become in her presence until now. Shea knew it was inevitable. He'd been easy-going and comfortable on the trip down, but as they got closer she could tell he was mentally drawing on the mantle of his station. It was enough that he'd been willing to have their brief interlude.

They hadn't even reached their tent when the new general approached, his eyes flicking to Shea and then away in dismissal.

"Fallon, I've been looking for you all morning."

Fallon stopped, turning his attention to his general. Shea continued on. She had no interest in getting caught in their conversation. She had many things to think on. Though their climb down had been pleasant, it did nothing to solve any of the many problems they faced. She needed to reassess—figure out how she felt about things. Listening to the general, a man who clearly had no respect for her, would not make that an easy task.

"Shea, a minute, if you please," Fallon said to her back.

Shea turned and looked at him, her eyebrow raising in question. He had a pleased expression on his face, like a smug feline. Her eyes narrowed on him. She didn't like when he got that expression on his face. It usually meant he was going to convince her to do something she definitely didn't want to do.

"Braden had a few questions about the beast board instituted by the Horse clan. He'd like to see if it's feasible to implement such a board throughout the rest of the army."

Braden's face was neutral as he looked from Fallon to Shea, but Shea got the feeling that he was impatient over having Fallon's focus split—that he'd have preferred if Fallon hadn't called her back. It was a feeling Shea reciprocated.

"Yes, I had heard mention that some of the other clans might be interested in replicating what Clark and Charles created."

"Why don't you show him the board and discuss how it's helped reduce casualties for the Wind Division?" Fallon's face made it clear that wasn't really a question.

Shea fixed him with an expression that warned him just how much she disliked this idea. She'd like nothing more than to not spend any extra time in the general's company. He'd already made his distaste of her clear. She was perfectly happy to steer clear of him for as long as it took for him to head out to his next assignment.

"I'm sure your Telroi has much better things to do than accompany me to the Wind Division's tents," Braden protested. "I'd hoped to speak to the creators and get more information on their methods. I've no doubt she would find such matters tedious and time-consuming."

Shea restrained her snort, seeing no reason to stop him as his objection helped serve her own purposes, even if he had just cast her as some dimwit unable to pay attention. This, after she had rescued his ass from the mist.

"There you have it. I'm sure the general will be able to get on without me." Shea gave them both a wide smile, prepared to excuse herself.

"Not so fast." Fallon's words had Shea heaving an internal sigh. She tried to tell him with her eyes to leave it, that she had better things to do even if she didn't know what those things were. "Shea would be the perfect companion since she helped create it and would know more about it and its beasts than any other."

Shea didn't know about that. The board's keeper would know more about the process and the way it was being used.

Fallon's smile held just a slight edge of wickedness to it. "Furthermore, since she will be responsible for helping you implement a similar board within your own command and other divisions, it makes sense to have her accompany you today."

Shea blinked and gave Fallon an appalled look. Since when? She didn't remember any discussion regarding this before.

Braden's face was guarded as he looked between Fallon's implacable expression, the one that said he wasn't going to be persuaded from his course, and Shea's slightly horrified one. He proved he was not without brains when he nodded. "It would be my honor to have the Telroi accompany me."

Shea gave him a smile that was little more than a baring of teeth as she grabbed Fallon's thick bicep and gave him a tug.

"I would like a word with the Warlord before we go."

Braden's expression didn't change a bit as she led a willing Fallon away, Caden and the other two guards watching with similar non-expressions on their face. No doubt each had their own thoughts on the sight of Fallon's Telroi leading him off. Shea decided to ignore that as unimportant for the moment.

"What are you doing?" she asked Fallon, her voice tight. She didn't like being blindsided, and she definitely didn't like being volunteered for something she had no desire to do.

"You said you were bored and wanted a challenge."

No, she hadn't. She didn't remember ever saying anything of the sort.

"That's not what I meant. You entirely missed the point of our conversation."

"Did I? I don't think so."

"Never once did I say anything about being bored," she hissed at him.

"Maybe not in so many words. I read between the lines."

He read—

Shea took a deep breath and released it. Her glare would have sent lesser men scrambling for cover. Fallon's lips only twitched, and he got a look on his face that said he thought her anger was adorable. It made Shea want to start punching things, preferably that face, just to show him how adorable her anger actually was.

"Fallon, you know that's not what I meant."

The humor fell from his face, leaving a solemn and serious expression behind. "Maybe not, but I don't think I'm that far off-base. Not to mention, you're the best person for this job. You wanted meaning; this is it. You can make a sizable difference in my warriors' ability to survive this land. You, more than any other in my army, know what they're up against. They can use every tool in their arsenal."

Shea's shoulders fell and she rubbed her forehead as she looked away.

"You're one person and while your skills are undeniable, you are limited by the fact you are only one person. I need you to teach others what you know. It's the best way that I can protect my people."

He was right. She hated to admit it, but he was.

"Fine." Shea's response felt like it was dragged out of her by wild horses. She gave him a sideways glance, noticing the mirth that was threatening to reappear. Her fist shot out, nailing him in the stomach. His breath whooshed out of him.

Braden, a few steps away, looked horrified at her action. Caden lifted an eyebrow but otherwise remained unmoved.

Shea stepped beside Fallon, who leveled a glare on her as he rubbed the place she'd hit. She gave him a negligent shrug that held not even an ounce of remorse. "You wouldn't want your men to see the Warlord smile, now would you?"

"Well played," he murmured. Now it was Shea's turn to bite back a smile. He leaned down, saying in a voice meant for only her ears, "I'll have my revenge later tonight."

She arched an eyebrow as she stepped around him before saying over her shoulder, "We'll see."

CHAPTER NINE

Well, I assume you'd like to visit the board now," Shea said to Braden as she walked up to him.

His eyes went above her head to where Fallon lingered behind her. "Yes, if the Warlord can spare you."

"I'm sure he'll manage without me." Shea's voice held an acerbic edge.

"Trenton and Wilhelm will be here shortly; they will accompany you," Caden said before they could walk away.

"I'm sure my presence will be enough protection in camp," Braden responded.

"The Warlord has made it clear that his Telroi is to have guards at all times, even while in camp."

Shea grimaced. She'd forgotten about that, having made it her business over the past few months to slip away from her guards whenever possible. Good thing Fallon hadn't been around to hear about that. She could only hope Trenton and Wilhelm kept silent. What Fallon didn't know wouldn't cause Shea problems.

By the significant glance Caden shot her way, she had a feeling either Trenton or Wilhelm—she was willing to bet Trenton, since he rejoiced at getting her in trouble—had spilled the beans.

"How unusual. She should be trained so she's not so defenseless," Braden said.

Shea gave him a look, but kept her own council. He seemed determined to twist everything. Why not let him?

"You are wrong," Daere said, striding up to them. "The Warlord holds Shea and her skills in the highest esteem. He simply wishes to ensure she is protected from every eventuality, including being overwhelmed by surprise or greater numbers."

Braden gave Daere a reserved nod, the gesture almost a half bow. Shea looked between the two with unease. The tension between them was already thick enough to cut.

Trenton and Wilhelm joined the group moments later, coming from the same direction as Daere. For once, Shea was happy to see them.

"Now that we're all here, shall we go?" she asked Braden.

His answer was a sharp nod before he turned and stalked off, his strides long and purposeful. Being a Trateri, he'd probably grown up in one of these camps, so he understood the chaotic organization better than Shea did. The first few times the camp had moved, it had taken her a few days to relearn where everything was. After that, she began to find the pattern in its set-up and got lost less and less frequently.

Braden walked with his hands clasped behind his back, Shea an uncomfortable presence by his side. Away from Fallon, he did not seem inclined to talk. Since Shea had never been one for idle chatter, it meant they traveled in silence.

Shea glanced behind them to see Daere looking lost in thought, content with keeping her own council. It was a trick Shea wished she had known months ago. Wilhelm and Trenton were behind her, their faces carefully blank—the perfect expression for a guard. None of them looked like they would be willing to help Shea out.

She looked at Braden's profile before glancing forward again. Was this one of those times that she was expected to say something? Enforce that horrible social behavior called small talk? What would she even talk about? The weather?

No. Better to be quiet. You couldn't put your foot in your mouth if you never said anything to begin with. Besides, who was she trying to impress? Braden? He'd already made it clear he didn't think much of her skills.

They passed several minutes in silence as they maneuvered through the bustling pathways of the tent city to the eastern side of camp where the Wind Division and Clark's beast board was located.

Normally, when there was space and not giant trees interfering with the camp's layout, Fallon and his closest advisors' tents were located at the center. They were the hub around which everything else revolved. From there, the camp was split into sections, like little pieces of a pie. The higher-ups in the different division and clans were located closer to the center ring. The further out, the less rank and status you were likely to have. On the outermost edge was where the training fields and horse corrals were located.

The beast board was near that outer edge so scouts could drop off their latest intelligence and pick up any new pieces of information on their way out of camp.

The Wind Division was mostly made up of Horse clan. They had some of the best scouts in Shea's opinion, in no small part because of the changes Eamon had implemented when Fallon promoted him. He'd made a policy requiring returning scouts to visit the board before being released from duty.

They were nearing the edge when a familiar face ducked out of a tent, an engaging grin already forming. Clark was young. About seventeen or eighteen and just growing out of his baby face. His wide brown eyes were entirely too trusting for a scout, but Shea knew he had a core of unexpected strength. He was an orphan and had adopted many of the scouts as his family, including Shea. The feeling was mutual, as she saw him almost as the little brother she'd never had.

He'd been the first to take her little journal and turn it into this amazing, life-saving thing. It had realized a childhood dream of Shea's from when she had wanted to be a gatherer, one of those pathfinders specifically dispatched to study the world and bring their observations home.

Clark fulfilled her dream in a different way than she'd imagined, but it had done more good for her little slice of the world than her former dream would have. If she'd ever achieved her original goal, her knowledge would have been hoarded and kept in the Wayfarer's Keep, where it would sit in a library, unlikely to ever be read or shared.

"Shea, where've you been?"

Shea's steps stuttered. Had she made a promise to visit him and forgotten about it in the excitement of Fallon's return?

"I would have thought since we're friends your first stop would have been here to share what you knew. Instead, I had to learn about this mist thing from the throwaways that were brought in with Fallon."

There was so much to address in that statement that Shea looked around in confusion for a long moment.

"First, what throwaways? And since when were you on speaking terms with any of the Lowlanders?"

"Throwaway" was a term the Trateri had coined to describe Lowlanders taken in tithe because their people had thrown them away to ensure their own safety for a while longer. Unless a scout was on a mission that dovetailed with collecting a tithe, they didn't have much to do with the throwaways, since scouts were considered too tactically sensitive to train their enemy in this position.

Clark got a shame-faced expression, as if it had just dawned on him that she might take umbrage with that term, having been a throwaway herself at one point. "I thought you knew. Some of the men Fallon brought back were former soldiers from the city states in the south."

Shea hadn't noticed any prisoners among the men escorting Fallon, but then the mist had been a bit distracting when she finally found them. Later, once they were out, Fallon had gathered the advance team and they'd ridden out. The throwaways must have been among those he left behind to follow at a slower pace.

"Still doesn't explain how you got to talking with them," Shea said, not wanting to dwell on a practice that made her uncomfortable.

Clark shrugged. "Some of the newcomers are being given to the Wind Division. Eamon wanted to debrief them in case they knew anything of value. I just happened to tag along."

"And who is this?" Braden asked, finally interrupting the conversation. His solemn eyes were intense as they studied Clark.

Clark looked around at the people accompanying Shea, for the first time realizing she might not have been here to see him. His eyes goggled in recognition at the sight of Braden.

Clark's mouth snapped shut and he sprung to attention, drawing himself up to his greatest height. Thankfully, he managed not to salute, though Shea could tell it was a struggle for him. "Clark of the Southern Plains, scout of the Dawn's Riders, Wind Division."

"You're an orphan then."

Shea's mouth dropped open and her head spun as she aimed a glare Braden's way. How did he even guess that from what Clark offered? And what kind of person said that on a first meeting?

"Orphans are named for the closest landmark. On occasion the clan is kind and lets them claim the clan's name as their own," Daere said softly at Shea's side.

Clark's face was stiff and guarded as he gave a wary nod.

"You are the one responsible for this board I hear so much about?"

His nod this time was less hesitant.

"Show me."

*

The beast class had assembled in a small clearing right next to the horses' paddock. Wooden seats made of stumps and logs had been set up facing in one direction. Charles, a slight man in loose clothing, stood in front of the gathered warriors talking animatedly.

Shea was surprised to see how many had gathered. Instead of the small group she had imagined, every seat was taken, and still others leaned against trees or stood in the back. Those with seats took notes as Charles gestured to a board that had been set up next to him. Several men nodded at what he was sharing, their expressions focused and intent.

Clark said, "I'll ask some of the men to move so you can sit."

"No, we'll watch from back here," Braden said.

Shea agreed. They'd learn more if they remained unnoticed.

"How long has this been going on?" Shea asked in a quiet voice.

"A few weeks now." Clark's voice was hushed. "They take turns standing up and speaking. We've even started noticing scouts from other divisions attending."

"Bet that causes problems," Trenton said.

Shea cocked her head, not understanding why it would.

Seeing the question on her face, he supplied, "The divisions are largely manned by the different clans."

She still didn't get it.

"Every clan hates every other clan," Wilhelm explained. "It's about the only thing you can always count on. Just because Fallon has united them in name doesn't mean that there aren't still blood feuds between them."

"There's a lot of history, spanning generations. It'll take time to truly unite them," Daere said.

Shea knew that. Eamon and the others had told her at some point, but she didn't know if she had fully realized what that meant. To most of the Lowlands, the Trateri were all painted with the same brush.

"It would help matters if the bloodlines mixed," Braden observed, not taking his eyes off the front. "If the Hawkvale had ties of blood to some of the other clans, they would be much less likely to fight him on some of his policies."

Shea sucked in a breath, the comment unexpected. She blinked rapidly, grateful that he wasn't looking at her so she could compose her expression. The shock. It had never occurred to her to think Fallon's position would be more stable if he had taken a proper Trateri woman as his telroi—and it should have.

She took another breath and let it go slowly.

Before she could think of a response, Daere stepped into the awkward silence. "Such a move could also result in further instability, as one clan is elevated above the rest."

"He could just have children with a woman from every clan. Of course, you'd face the same problem when it came time for one of those children to take up the mantle of leadership." The response was out of Shea's mouth before she could stop it.

The only acknowledgement from Braden of her sarcasm was a slight turn of his head toward her. Daere smothered a smile and lowered her eyes to the ground.

Shea fought to keep still, not wanting Braden to know how such talk of Fallon and other women had disturbed her.

Trenton stepped into the silence. "Until then, there are flare-ups when they come into contact with one another."

"As the Telroi you should understand this," Braden chided. "You cannot lead if you do not know how to control your people."

Shea stiffened next to him, taking issue with the rebuke in his tone. Daere quickly looked away, having said something similar a time or two. Shea narrowed her eyes at the two of them. For two people who barely talked to one another, they sure thought alike.

Shea gave Braden the same response she gave Daere. "I have no intention of leading. Fallon is the warlord; he's the leader."

Braden arched an eyebrow at her. "That is a surprisingly naïve outlook from someone I had assumed was smarter than this."

Shea gave him a stony-faced expression, not letting him know how those words smarted.

Braden kept speaking, his voice crisp and matter of fact. "Whether you have the intention or not doesn't matter. The fact that you stand at his side means people are going to look to you for leadership in times of crisis. How will you guide them if you don't even understand the most basic facet of their existence? To say nothing of those who covet your influence over the Warlord, and see you as a means to manipulate him by simply bending your ear to their agenda. A wise woman would learn all she can, so she can determine the snake in the grass before she is bitten."

Daere shifted beside Shea, drawing her attention. The other woman's face was impassive, offering Shea no insight to her thoughts. Shea looked between the two of them. Yup, basically the same speech. She wondered if Daere had coached Braden on what to say, or if he had come up with that little talk all on his own.

"I've heard something similar before," Shea finally said.

Braden looked briefly at Daere, who had still not given him her attention and was intently focused on the class. "It is sound advice."

Shea shrugged one shoulder. "Probably."

A man in the back raised his hand. He was dressed a little differently than the rest, his leathers a little rougher, and the crest on his back not one Shea was familiar with. A few of the others gave him a sideways glance that made it clear they weren't quite happy with this stranger in their midst. Shea assumed he was one of those not from the Wind Division that Clark had spoken about earlier.

Charles stopped speaking and looked at him expectantly. "Yes, you had a question?"

"What about this mist that seems to be popping up everywhere all of a sudden? You haven't given us any information on that."

Charles looked momentarily nonplussed, glancing around the class as if they might have the answer. When everyone looked at him expectantly, he said in a hesitant voice, "The mist is a new threat that we don't have a lot of information on yet. Does anybody here have any observations?"

There was a long pause as the rest of the men and a few women glanced around. None stood to offer their opinion. A few shook their heads and sat back.

Another stranger, this one also with a patch Shea didn't recognize, asked, "Isn't that what we're here for? So you can tell us how to survive this thing?" His voice was impatient, with the barest edge of derision in it.

The feeling of the crowd shifted, the undercurrents ugly and rife with anger as the scouts and soldiers from the Wind Division glared at the man.

Charles looked around with unease, sensing the worsening mood. Everyone was on edge. It was a situation that could explode into violence as the people present turned their skills to something they could control—beating each other senseless.

He made a placating motion with his hands. "We're all a little uneasy about what this mist is and what it can do. The purpose behind these classes is to bring our heads together so we can figure out sound strategies to overcome the obstacles we face on a daily basis."

"This is ridiculous. I bet you have no idea how to handle this. I can't believe my war band insisted I attend."

A man in the front stood up. He was big, easily taller than most of the men here. He looked like he had been cut from stone with a blunt chisel, his features rough and half formed. "How 'bout you keep your mouth shut if you've nothing helpful to add?"

If a man who looked like that—with a body built for violence and a face that looked like it belonged on a berserker—spoke to her like that, Shea thought she might do whatever he asked, especially when his question had a tone that made it clear what the consequences would be if you didn't listen.

Charles looked overwhelmed and out of his element as he tried to intervene. "Let's not let our emotions get the best of us. We're all just looking for answers."

"Stay out of it, cripple," the stranger snapped.

The other man's face darkened, and he looked like he was going to leap across the crowd to wrap his hands around the stranger's neck.

"You shouldn't run," Shea said, her voice ringing through the air. The statement was strange enough and out of context enough that both men paused to glance her way.

"Shea." Charles looked unhappy as he glanced from her to the other man.

Many of those gathered recognized her, having been on missions with her, or having heard her story. She was a bit notorious with the Wind Division scouts. Clark and Buck liked to brag on her, trying to convince any who listened that they knew her first and taught her everything she knew. A lie, for the most part.

"The first thing to know about the mist is that you shouldn't run from it. One— you'll never be fast enough, and two—it knows when someone acts like prey. Running will just attract it."

The stranger guffawed, a sound of stunned disbelief. "What's this? Superstition is what you're teaching these people? Who is this anyways?"

He took in her appearance, his lip curling in a sneer. Guess he didn't recognize her. She sighed. She'd thought she was past having to deal with idiots. Looked like she was wrong. She was beginning to think there was one in every group. Perhaps it was simply her burden to bear.

"Someone who knows considerably more about the mist than you, obviously."

Clark snorted back a laugh at her dry tone. He always got an odd joy when she put others down with the sharp edge of her tongue.

"I seriously doubt some throwaway knows anything of worth."

There was a rumble of anger at the last statement. Clark puffed up and looked like he was going to leap to her defense. Shea shook her head at him and he settled back.

Assured that Clark wasn't going make things worse or get himself hurt, Shea took the time to study the other man. His face was set in a belligerent expression, but she couldn't tell if that was a cover for fear or whether he'd come here specifically to start something. Knowing the Trateri, it could be either.

She gave him the benefit of the doubt and attributed some of his hostility to fear of the unknown and the rest to having to turn to his enemy for answers. Fear was difficult to gauge. Everyone reacted to it differently. Some took it in stride, using it as an opportunity to rise to the challenge and meet it head on. Shea had seen people pull together when faced with what seemed to be insurmountable odds and overcome them. Others, when faced with fear of the unknown, became their most base selves, committing atrocities previously at odds with their core beliefs. These were the people who would sacrifice everything—including pieces of themselves and others—to survive just one more day or even an hour longer. Their fear was a wind that fanned the flame of destruction, both in themselves and what they once loved.

Perhaps it was the cynic in her or just that she was unlucky, but Shea had considerably more experience with the second reaction, having seen it time and again.

How to address this? The easy answer would be to reveal she was the Telroi of the Hawkvale. She was actually surprised that the men with her or Daere hadn't already disclosed that little secret. She was grateful for their restraint. If she was to make a place here, to lead as Braden had said, she needed to make her own way, build respect on her own. The respect Fallon had built would only extend so far.

Shea gave an internal sigh. It seemed no matter how far she'd come, or what she did, she always came back to having to prove herself, to demonstrating she wasn't just some throwaway with air in her head or an insignificant woman wanting a seat at the men's table.

"The first time I walked into the mist, I was six. My mother thought early exposure would help me overcome it when it was time."

There was a murmur among those gathered at Shea's words. Daere's gaze jumped to Shea's face. Braden looked thoughtful at the revelation.

"The second time I was twelve and during my apprenticeship as a pathfinder. I've walked through the mist and come out the other side more times than I have fingers on my hands." Shea let that sink into their minds, noting that the stranger seemed watchful now, as if he was weighing her words and looking for loopholes.

"Treat the mist as you would a beast. It is mysterious, and dangerous, and beautiful. It will make you lose your way if it can, never to walk this world again. Be vigilant. Be brave."

"If we can't run, what should we do?" the question came from the mountain of a man in front, the one who had threatened the stranger.

Shea was quiet as she thought. She'd been truthful with Fallon when she said it was impossible for her to teach them how to walk in the mist. That would offer little comfort to these men who risked their lives every time they set foot outside the camp's perimeter. She needed to give them something to hold onto, no matter how small. Something that would offer some protection, even if it wasn't much.

"Carry rope on you at all times. Your biggest challenge in the mist is getting lost. It's easy to get separated. If you can, gather your people and have them hold onto the rope. It'll at least give you a chance."

As Shea spoke, she saw that several of those present began to write—their faces as attentive and intense as they had been when they listened to Charles. It made Shea uneasy to know they were giving her words such weight. She hoped she didn't fail them by offering useless advice.

"There are many things that are still unknown about the mist even in the Highlands where it is a constant threat." She rubbed her hands together as she thought. "This may just be observation and hypothesis. Not everything is proven. What I can tell you is that the mist has limitations. Most of the time it seems to avoid large populations of life, leaving it alone or barely skirting along the edges. Its effects are greatly mitigated where there are large settlements. You have more of a chance of coming back to this world in a group than you do by yourself."

She chose to leave out the fact that after the cataclysm, when the mist was at its worst, it could carry off entire cities teeming with people. That's how the Badlands formed. Once settled by thousands of people, they were now a desolate wasteland where only the insane, foolhardy, and desperate visited.

"Some of Eamon's men said you had them tie themselves to one of these trees," Fiona said from the front, her eyes piercing and intent.

Shea hadn't noticed her among the crowd. She nodded. "I did. The soul trees are deeply rooted in this world and their size acts as an anchor. My suggestion would be to find one and stay with it until the mist abates."

The stranger snorted, a sound filled with skepticism. "This is all you have? If you walked out of the mist when you were six and twelve, it doesn't sound too dangerous. Why should we believe you?"

Shea shrugged, the gesture careless. "Believe what you like. It's your life to live as you choose. Its loss makes no difference to me. I think, though, you know on some level that the mist is dangerous. Why else would you be here? Why else would any of you be here?"

"Easy words for a throwaway to say. You're not the one who is going to be out there. For all we know everything you just said will get us killed."

Shea gave him a long look filled with disdain. Guess she should have expected that as his next volley.

Before she could reply, Daere's voice was a whip through the air. "Watch how you speak to the Hawkvale's Telroi."

Her words had an immediate effect on those who didn't already know. The strangers and a few of Wind Division studied her with new eyes, assessing, cataloging, and trying to decide what about this throwaway had so drawn their warlord. Shea fought not to react, though she'd always loathed being the center of attention in matters not related to pathfinding.

She knew what they'd see, a woman with unruly hair just brushing her shoulders. One who was of average height and average looks. Sometimes she questioned what he saw in her too. She wasn't politically powerful, and since she'd burned the maps that showed the secret paths to the Highlands—she didn't have leverage with him that way. She'd be the first to admit she had a bit of a temper, and she wasn't the nicest of individuals on occasion.

Daere's words seemed to work, acting like a blast of cold water. However, Shea was pretty sure by the way the stranger was eyeing her that she hadn't managed to sway him much. She gave a mental shrug. He'd believe her, or he wouldn't. She'd tried. She'd even taken Eamon's advice and tried to explain rather than just tell. What he did with that information was now on him. She just hoped he didn't get others killed through his own hardheadedness.

A few of the others seemed to take her words to heart, dutifully inscribing them in the notebooks she knew Clark had passed out to any scout who would take them. At least someone would get something from this. It would have to be enough.

The crowd gradually dispersed. Charles walked over to them as the others left, some in groups as they compared notes, and others trickling off alone.

"Thanks, Shea. I don't know what I would have done without you here," he said, his gait stiff as he limped over to them. It was enough to ensure he was unable to become a soldier or join any other combat positions. He was smart, though. Smarter than most. His intellect should have guaranteed him a spot in the upper echelons, but his leg kept him back.

"Does that happen often?" Braden asked. If he thought less of Charles because of his physical ailment, he didn't show it.

"The scouts and soldiers from Wind Division don't usually challenge me like that. We're having more problems when some from other divisions join in a class. Most are respectful, but a few feel the need to throw their weight around. Soldiers from Ember and Lion seem to be the worst."

"Which clan and division was that man from?" Shea asked.

"Rain clan, Tempest division."

Hm. That was good to know. She thought the patches on the men from the sleeper vine incident were similar to that of the stranger's.

"That does not surprise me," Trenton said. "Rain took a lot of the exiles from Snake Clan when Fallon disbanded it. Their clan leader was good friends with Indra. They seem to hate everyone who is not them. It doesn't matter what clan or division you're in."

"You've got an interesting concept here," Braden told Charles. "It could use a little work and fine tuning, but the idea is sound."

Charles blinked at the general as if just realizing who he was. His mouth dropped open as surprise dawned on his face. "You're General Braden Thorisdon. You're responsible for the victory against the Oorumicon."

"I did fight in that battle, but there were many who fought alongside me." Braden's words were humble, sparking Shea's curiosity.

Who were the Oorumicon? Were they another enemy of the Trateri that she didn't know about? Had they been conquered and assimilated into Fallon's clans? There was so much to learn about the Trateri, their culture and history. It seemed never-ending.

"This is such an honor," Charles said. "I have listened to the stories and songs about you and have followed your path up the ranks."

Before Braden could respond, a woman with blond hair pulled back in a single braid and wearing a determined expression approached. She was trailed by a tall thin man with a long face and a pained expression. He was Trateri; Shea was willing to bet the woman wasn't.

"Eva, don't," the man warned in a soft voice.

His words caused the other woman to hesitate before she shrugged them off and lifted her chin. Her eyes fastened on Shea's. "I'm told you can help us."

Trenton turned and looked at the woman, edging her away from Shea with a subtle movement. "And who might you be?" he asked with a flirtatious grin.

Eva stopped short, eyeing Trenton for a moment before dismissing him and looking past him to Shea. "We're having problems in the pasture. We've lost three horses in the past week and two others were injured. We need help from somebody who knows this place."

"You should direct your complaints to your clan," Braden said.

The woman's face turned frustrated, her petite features belying the force of personality behind her eyes. "We have. They've neglected to do anything meaningful, and meanwhile we stand to lose even more." Her eyes turned to Charles, an accusation in them. "This is the second time I've come here for help and have been turned away."

Charles blustered, "The beast class isn't here to help a throwaway do their job. We have important business that takes priority."

Eva snorted. "You would think you people would care for your horses a little better, instead of just leaving them to be picked off one by one."

"Eva," the other man cautioned again, his eyes flicking from Braden to Trenton to Wilhelm.

Eva's mouth tightened, and her chin lifted, stubbornness written on every line of her body.

"Do you know what's attacking the herd?" Shea asked.

Eva's eyes turned to Shea, a cautious hope in them. Shea didn't know how this woman came to be among the Trateri, but it was clear she felt passionate about her horses.

"I found tracks. They look like bandisox, but they're about four times bigger and a lot meaner."

Bandisox were a rat-like animal that had bands of black circular rings around its body and white feet. It had a rodent-like face and a tail. They were normally not a threat. While carnivorous, they were too small to bring down a human and were mostly scavengers.

"You should take this to Mountain division," Charles complained. "The herd belongs to them."

Eva made a sound of frustration, one that sounded very like a growl. "I've already told you I did. They haven't been able to help. Aren't you all part of the same people?"

"While I sympathize with your plight, we are unable to help," Braden said, his tone a clear dismissal.

Eva's face fell before she rallied enough to hide her thoughts.

"I'll help," Shea said. "Can you show me where your herd is?"

Hope lit in Eva's eyes, and she gave a sharp nod, before shooting the rest of the group a grim look.

Charles looked offended. "The Telroi is too important to waste her time on such insignificant matters."

"I think I should be the judge in how my time is spent." Shea kept her voice gentle to soften the rebuke.

Charles felt the sting of it, nonetheless. His face flushed and his mouth tightened in a frown.

"If you don't mind the company, I'd be interested in seeing this as well," Fiona said. She and two other men stood off to Shea's left, watching them with curious eyes. "My men and I have a lot of energy to spend since we've been cooped up in camp for the last few weeks."

Eva studied Fiona and her men before nodding. "We'll take any help we can get at this point."

Eva's friend looked no less worried than he had before Eva had confronted Shea, but he did squeeze her shoulder in support. "If you'll follow us, we can show you where we keep the herd and the tracks we found."

Shea gestured for them to lead the way.

*

Eva was right; these did look like bandisox tracks, only they were bigger than any Shea had ever seen. Nearly as big as her head, they were also set almost an entire arm length apart. That meant the stride was pretty long. Shea was guessing from these that the beast was as tall as her waist and probably her weight as well.

Fiona crouched a few feet away and pressed her hand down into the track. "Piss and bollocks. This thing is huge."

"Looks like more than one of them," one of Fiona's men said from where he crouched.

"The smaller bandisox tend to scavenge in packs," Shea said, standing and walking along the tracks. "I wouldn't be surprised if these are the same."

While big compared to their smaller cousins, the bandisox in this forest would still be small when compared to many other predators. Horses, dangerous in their own right, and perfectly capable of killing their predators, were probably less aggressive than some of the other animals here. They would be easy prey if enough bandisox attacked en masse.

"What are you looking for?" Trenton asked as he shadowed Shea. She'd followed the tracks to a tree.

"A nest. There are too few tracks for this to be a colony. My guess is a few broke with their original colony when resources became plentiful and that they're setting up their own nest close to a food source."

Eva followed, listening with an attentive expression. "Are you saying there are going to be more of them?"

"Probably sooner than you think," Shea warned. "It's good that you brought this to our attention when you did. A colony can grow to several hundred strong. At that point, they wouldn't have only attacked the horses. You would have been prey as well."

Eva looked apprehensive at that news, her eyes going to the forest around them as her body tensed.

Seeing the alarm in her face, Shea gave her a reassuring smile. "Your warning came in time. I think this is a small nest so far. We shouldn't have a problem uprooting it."

Fiona and her men trailed Shea and Trenton as they swept through the forest. The horses were allowed to roam in the meadow that had popped up due to a gap in the canopy above. The wildflowers and long grass made it perfect for grazing, and the open space made it easy for Eva and her friend to care for them.

One of the horses, a white gray mare with a black mane and tail, and gray spots on her lower legs trotted up to Eva. She butted the woman playfully and then tossed her head. Eva patted her absently, her eyes on the meadow around them.

"She's a beauty," Fiona said, her eyes on the horse.

"Last herd master wanted to put her down because he thought she was too aggressive," Eva said stroking the mare's nose. To the mare, she crooned, "You just thought the man was an idiot, didn't you sweetheart?"

One of Fiona's men stepped close, his hand going up to touch the horse's neck. The mare squealed and wheeled, her lips pulling back as she tried to nip the man. Eva grabbed the horse's head and pulled before the mare could trample the other man.

"Hey, just ignore the fool," Eva told the mare, her voice soft and gentle. "Just because someone's rude doesn't mean we have to go get all bent out of shape."

Shea chuckled. She liked the herd mistress.

"How long have you been with this herd?" Shea asked.

Eva continued patting the mare even as she threw a glance at Shea. "Not long. A few months at most."

"We don't normally accept women as tribute," Braden said, thoughtful eyes on Eva.

Eva's smile was humorless. "I wasn't tribute."

"Someone claimed you as a telroi?" Trenton asked.

She shook her head. "My village cast me out. One of the warbands found me and offered to take me with them. I didn't see much of a choice."

"Brave," Fiona said, a bit of respect on her face. "Not many women would be so accepting."

Eva's smile was gentle as she looked up at the mare. "Their horses made the risk worth it."

The mare let out a loud snort as its ears laid back and its tail swished aggressively. It lifted its head and pawed the ground.

Eva stepped back, her gaze going to the forest around them as the mare alerted them to the danger. The others with them immediately went on alert, weapons coming out as they eyed their surroundings.

The forest was quiet—the trees looming like silent watchers.

The mare lifted half up and then came back to the ground, stomping as she released a scream of challenge.

Charles took several unsteady steps back, fear showing on his face. Clark had already drawn the bow and arrow he'd brought.

A large form, about the size of a dog, appeared in the grass not far from them. Its yellow eyes focused on Shea and her group. It was a bandisox, smaller than the tracks had indicated, but bigger than any she'd seen before.

The mare used her shoulder to herd Eva away from the bandisox.

"Don't shoot." Shea's voice was eerily calm.

"Kill it," Charles said, his voice tight.

"No, not yet. Look in the trees above it," Shea said.

Above them, massed on the branches like crows, were a swarm of bandisox. The grass rustled on both sides of their group.

"I was wrong. The colony is much bigger than I thought." Shea's voice was grim. It had probably grown in the weeks that it had taken for Eva to get someone to listen to her.

Two bandisox, ones that dwarfed those in the trees, slunk closer. A high-pitched chittering escaped them as they broke off to circle Shea and the others. The mare whirled as one of the bandisox came close, rising onto her hind legs and trying to stomp the rodent under her hooves. The bandisox darted out of the way, letting out a high screech of its own. Another sought to take advantage of the mare's distraction, sailing across the grass to attack the hindquarters.

Eva let out a war cry and hit it with a rock she grabbed from the ground. There was a pained grunt as the bandisox landed before turning on Eva. It didn't make it far before the mare gave a rear kick, sending it sailing back into the grass.

This seemed to be a signal for the rest. They surged forward.

The Trateri next to Shea let out bloodcurdling cries as they met the surge with naked blades and a fearsome ferocity. The next few minutes were a tangle of images as the Trateri fought off the bandisox, the mare at their side.

Shea wielded her blade against several as they converged on her. She suffered several bites as she stabbed and swung. One landed on her shoulder, its small teeth sinking into her back, before Trenton knocked it off her.

A mad light flared in his eyes before he turned to attack the next bandisox with a battle cry.

It wasn't long before they had killed all those that attacked them. Shea panted as she watched her surroundings, bandisox dead all around them.

"I think that's the last," Fiona said, coming to stand beside Shea. She clapped Shea on the shoulder. "Glad we tagged along with you. This was fun. We should do it again sometime."

Shea eyed the other woman with an expression close to disbelief. Fun. Right. Their definitions differed wildly.

"Your throwaway did a pretty good job herself," Fiona said, gesturing with her chin to where Eva stood, exhausted, the mare dropping her chin onto Eva's shoulder. "Better than some of us, anyway."

Fiona eyed Charles with a hint of distaste as the other man limped back towards them. He'd tried to abandon them when the bandisox attacked, leaving them to fend for themselves. Unfortunately, the bandisox had surrounded him so he hadn't gotten far.

"He's not a warrior," Shea said in his defense.

"Neither is the Lowlander," Trenton said in a soft voice at her side.

"Not everybody is made for battle," Shea returned.

The quiet that answered her made the others' stance on Charles clear. He'd lost respect by trying to run. Shea didn't fault him for his actions. Everyone's response to danger was different. The Trateri didn't see it that way, and there was a definite difference in how the others treated him, with the exception of Clark, who greeted the other man with relief.

Shea turned away and began walking into the forest.

"Where are you going?" Braden asked.

"There's a nest somewhere around here. We need to take care of it, or else Eva will have the same problem in a week or two."

Fiona and her men pulled themselves up. Fiona stepped forward. "My men and I will help. We're not bad trackers."

Shea gave them a nod of appreciation.

Eva patted the mare on the neck before joining them. "I will help as well since I'm the reason you're here."

Trenton and Wilhelm didn't offer their services. They didn't need to. Where Shea went, they did as well. Yet Shea couldn't help noticing the respect on both of their faces when they looked at Eva.

"Clark, take Charles and head back. This could take a while, and I'm sure you both have other duties," Shea said.

Charles' face darkened. "We can help. You don't have to protect us."

"Yes, you can," Shea agreed. "You can write up the description and a few points from this experience, and then make sure it gets into the hands of the rest of the herd masters. They need to know what to watch out for so they can protect their herds."

Shea wasn't lying. The task was an important one. Even if it hadn't been, she would have found some way to send Charles back. He wasn't suited for this work. Nothing wrong with that, but it didn't change facts.

The look on Charles' face said he doubted her reasoning but a glance at Braden told her he didn't want to argue in front of the general.

Clark covered for his friend. "Of course, Shea. We'll make sure that it's done."

106

The two set off towards camp.

"That was kind of you," Braden observed.

"Not particularly. I needed it done."

He made a hmm sound that was neither agreement nor disagreement.

Shea took the lead, trusting the others to follow. It was going to be a long afternoon.

CHAPTER TEN

S hea waited as Trenton and Wilhelm conducted their checks of Fallon's tent—though she didn't see much point to it, given the guards stationed at all times at the entrance. She was tired, and the scratches and bites she'd received from the bandisox stung. She just wanted to get inside, bathe, and rest for a little bit before dinner.

Trenton gave her a nod, indicating it was safe. She pushed past him, grateful the outer chamber was empty.

Passing through the partition that separated the private quarters from the public ones, she headed for the mound of furs piled on their bed. A bath would take time to draw up. In the meantime, the bed called to her. A short platform covered by a thick mattress, it was the heaviest piece of furniture in the room. It was elegant in its simplicity, not approaching the ornateness or heaviness of a bed found in a Lowland or Highland home. The mattress managed to be soft and firm at the same time, a welcoming cloud of comfort that Shea was loath to leave more often than not. Before Fallon, she would have said that a soft place to sleep was an unimportant luxury. A few nights in his bed had changed her mind.

After sleeping on the hard ground last night and then running around the forest chasing bandisox, she was sore—something she would never have noticed before her time with Fallon and his bed. She'd become weak. Dependent on its stupid softness.

She studied the mattress with half a mind to demand its absence, or at least consider sleeping on the ground more often. She'd never do it, too addicted to the way it cradled bones long abused by the work she demanded of them, but it was a thought.

She turned and sat, falling sideways onto the pillow. Another comfort that she wouldn't have said was important before now.

The pillow made an odd crinkling sound. She frowned. It had never done that before. She sat back up and stared down at it, noticing the edge of paper sticking out from under it. A note. It must have shifted when Shea had head-planted onto the pillow.

She picked it up, curious. Fallon hadn't struck her as the type to leave messages. She felt a thrill of excitement. Perhaps she had just discovered a previously unknown side of him.

The discovery felt like a gift, much like the feeling after visiting a place where she knew few had ever walked before. Excited, awed, and just a little bit humbled— she felt an odd mishmash of feelings that put a tight feeling in her throat. She'd never felt such things for a person before. It was something to think about.

With eager hands, she unfolded the note, careful not to accidently tear the paper in her excitement.

She smoothed it flat. Her excitement turned to confusion as she read the words. The letter fell to her side as she stared unseeing at the canvas walls, the words burned into her mind.

Come home.
Bring your friends.

A short message but a powerful one.

Shea didn't have time to process, to decide on a course of action before Fallon was pushing through the partition. Shea wasn't able to mask her unease before Fallon took note of her. He stopped at the sight of her, his big body going on alert as he examined the small space for potential threats.

"What is it?" Fallon asked, his eyes sharp and assessing as he noticed the slightly lost expression on Shea's face.

Shea stared back at him blankly. What did she say? Should she say anything?

Fallon's eyes dropped to the note in Shea's hands, correctly concluding that the piece of paper was what had so unsettled her. "What is that?"

Fallon advanced on Shea, taking a seat beside her, his presence a coiled, wild thing. The potential for violence was in every line of his body. Not against Shea. She'd never once felt threatened by him, not even when she had considered him, if not the enemy, then a potential hostile force. This violence was directed at whatever had threatened her, and against it, he would have no mercy.

She stared at him, noting how his gaze went to the note in her hand. He didn't reach for it, allowing her to decide.

She loved him for that. He could be such a dominant force, dictatorial, hard-headed, but when it counted—at least with her—he was patient. He recognized some things could not be forced. Even if you were a warlord used to getting your way.

How would things change once she revealed the note? Because they would.

There was no point hiding it. Nor would it have been right to do so, even if her first instinct was to pretend the note never existed. There was this dread in her, as if the note would signal a change so profound it would affect everything that had come before.

"I came in because I needed a moment to myself," Shea said. The note had thrown her off balance. It took a minute to find her words. "I'm not used to so many people all the time. It can be difficult."

Fallon's eyes had an intense focus as he scanned her face. "This is why you've been ducking your guards."

The statement surprised a laugh out of Shea. "I see Caden had a little chat with you."

His touch on her shoulder was gentle, there and gone in one moment to the next. "Of course, he did. He knew I'd want to know."

Of course, he had. Shea had known she wouldn't have much chance of convincing Caden otherwise. The loyalty of Fallon's Anateri would always be to him first and foremost.

"I hadn't realized that you were slipping away to escape the press of humanity though."

"Would it have made a difference?"

His expression was slightly lost as he looked at her—like he wanted to say something but didn't know how. There was an edge in his eyes, a heightened awareness.

"You know how I feel about your safety." She looked away. Yes, she did. That was the problem. His sigh was heavy. "Perhaps we can find a compromise."

It wasn't a capitulation, but it was a start.

"I came in here because I wanted a moment." She gave him the letter. "I found this. At first I thought it was from you."

She didn't say anything else, letting him read the words and draw his own conclusions.

Fallon read the note, his forehead furrowing. He read it once, twice, then a third time. His confusion transformed to understanding, and then into an incandescent rage—his expression filling with wrath, forming a visage terrifying enough that Shea could understand why villages surrendered immediately when he rode up to their front gates. His face was the stuff of nightmares, reminding people that there were monsters in the world. He was so darkly intimidating that Shea knew if he ever aimed such an expression her way that she'd surrender too. That, or run really far away to a place he could never find her.

"You're not going," he roared. He was on his feet and out of the room in the next moment.

Shea stared after him, surprised at the vehemence of his response. Concern in her eyes, Daere pushed aside the partition that had been partially ripped down and now sported a fist sized hole in the screen.

"What happened? Daere asked.

"A note was left for me."

"What was in the note?"

"It was from my people. They asked me to come home."

Daere gave a long whistle, the sound surprising from a woman Shea had always thought of as reserved and proper. "That would do it."

Fallon burst out of his tent, roaring for Caden and Darius—the note, the wretched, loathsome note, clutched in his hand. The familiar need to tear and rend ate at him. With no enemy in sight, he forced the feelings down. When he was younger, he didn't have such control, and with no outlet for his emotions, they would build up until he savaged any warrior in striking distance. Henry had helped him find ways to channel that bottomless anger, turning it into fuel for battle, and later conquest.

He could control it now, but this note and all it stood for tested that.

"Darius, Caden."

He would wipe this interloper from the face of this world—this person who had dared invade his home, who had threatened to take his Telroi. No. This would not stand. He would end this insignificant maggot in such an unpleasant way that Shea's people would never chance sending another person to steal her from him again. There would be cautionary tales told about this individual after Fallon got done tearing him apart with his bare hands.

Caden and several of Fallon's Anateri approached at a run, their hands on their swords as they scanned the area for threats.

"Fallon, what is it?" Caden's expression was cautious. He was the only one to look at Fallon, the rest of the Anateri were busy focusing on any incoming threats.

Their efficiency helped to calm some of the turbulent rage Fallon felt.

"This," his voice nearly a hiss, he thrust the note at Caden.

Caden took it as Fallon paced back and forth like a caged animal. The other guards were careful not to get too close, giving him the space to move as he needed. Wilhelm and Trenton waited by the entrance to Fallon's tent. They'd come to attention when he burst out of it, but hadn't moved from their guard positions.

The sight of them doing their job helped clear Fallon's mind further, enough that he was no longer thinking about doing bodily harm to the guards who had let this interloper slip through his security to leave that note on Shea's pillow.

What if she'd been there when this person invaded their space? What if he'd convinced Shea to follow him home? Fallon could feel that crouching rage begin to consume him again at the thought of losing her.

It took Caden seconds to read it. Like Fallon, he read it more than once. "I'm not sure I understand." His words were cautious as he looked up at Fallon.

"They want her back. She found it on her pillow in our tent—someone came into our home and left this on her pillow. They trespassed on our private space."

"Fallon." Darius approached at a quick pace. "I got word that you wanted me."

Witt, one of the Highlanders who had been part of the group caught with Shea, followed behind Darius. He looked curious and his face was filled with trepidation at facing an enraged warlord. The years had carved crow's feet into the corners of his eyes, and his mouth was bracketed with deep grooves. He was a serious man, one who weighed every word twice before it left his mouth.

Fallon had given him to Darius to keep an eye on when it was clear that the man had a bit of a soft spot for Shea. To Fallon's surprise, Darius had found him useful and used him to spot check his men. He was good at finding the flaws in their training and had a good head on his shoulders.

"Give him the note," Fallon ordered.

Caden complied, handing Darius the note.

"How did they get into our quarters, Caden?"

Caden's face was grim and his eyes filled with a burning anger that almost matched Fallon's own. He took any perceived failure as a personal deficiency. "I don't know, but I'm going to find out."

"You do that, and then you make sure this never happens again."

Caden gave a sharp nod and turned to one of the guards who'd followed him when Fallon had called. "Find me the two men who were on duty this afternoon. I want them in front of me in the next five minutes."

The other man nodded, his face equally grim. All of them knew that the lives of the two men who'd been on guard duty depended on what they had to say.

"Who is this from?" Darius asked. He turned the note over examining the other side before flipping it over to look at the handwriting on the front. Witt read over his shoulder, his eyebrows drawing to a deep V.

"It was left for Shea. Who do you think it's from?" Fallon didn't have the patience for stupid questions.

Darius nodded. "Whoever left it didn't use our paper. I don't recognize this blend."

"It's from the pathfinders," Witt said. "Their stationary always has a faint bluish tinge to it. This won't be the last note, I'd wager."

Fallon stilled as a thought occurred to him. "Shut down the camp; no one leaves. Whoever left this isn't one of us. They may still be here. Search every tent, every nook and cranny of this place until you find them."

Darius turned and strode off, snapping orders as he made Fallon's command a reality.

"You, stay. I want to know what else you know about the pathfinders," Fallon ordered before Witt could follow Darius.

The man nodded, his eyes solemn. "I'm not sure how much more I can share. I've told your people everything I could remember."

"Tell me again."

"If it'll help."

Fallon felt a little of his anger ease. Darius would do everything in his power to find this person or persons. Fallon wanted to be out there too, searching for this invader. It would give him no greater pleasure than to hunt him down and teach him the error of his ways.

For now, he had a few other things to take care of before he could join the hunt. He strode over to Trenton and Wilhelm, both of whom watched him come with an alert cautiousness that wasn't normally present.

"I want one of you with Shea at all times, even when she's here. She's not to leave your sight until this person is found."

The two men shared an uneasy look, both aware of how much trouble that would bring them with Fallon's Telroi.

Fallon acknowledged their hesitation, knowing it wasn't a reaction to his order. They were beginning to feel some loyalty to Shea. That was good. It was what he was hoping for, that they would feel the same need to protect her that they did him. He couldn't entrust this task to her friends from the scouts, knowing they didn't have the skills or desire needed to become an Anateri.

He made it easy on them. "Say the order came from me. She can take up her dissatisfaction with me later."

Trenton gave him a wry look. "I do not envy you that task. I've been caught on her bad side on more than one occasion and still have the bruises on my ego after she got through with me."

Fallon grunted. That was one of the things he liked about the woman. She always pushed back, never letting him have an inch if she could help it. She challenged him. It was something that had been missing from his life for a long time before her.

He turned to Witt. "With me."

Witt followed as they headed for a tent adjacent to Fallon's. It was where he conducted less friendly talks—the ones that might involve a more forceful display of his prowess. The tent was stripped of civilized trappings. It wasn't a place one lingered voluntarily.

There were no rugs on the ground to soften one's step. There was only one place to sit and that was on the ground. There was a table, but it contained devices only welcome in a nightmare—devices meant to compel someone to spill their innermost secrets.

Witt waited patiently by the entrance while Fallon prowled the small space. Patience wasn't always Fallon's strong suit, unless it was the patience needed for a hunt.

Fallon gave the other man credit, not once did Witt eye the space with fear. Instead he was a calm next to Fallon's storm.

"Start from the beginning," Fallon ordered. He folded his large arms and gave Witt a long stare, the kind of stare that drilled through a person's mask down to the soul beneath. It was meant to intimidate, to cause a man to squirm.

Witt stepped forward, his expression open as he held his hands wide as if to say he had nothing to hide. "As I've said before, Shea would be the best person for this. She was a pathfinder and knows more than me."

That wasn't an option. Not right now. Not in this situation. She was too close to this.

"Tell me what you can. I want to hear it again."

Witt was quiet for a long moment as he gathered his thoughts. His lips pulled down in a frown. "You know the pathfinders fulfill a vital role in the Highlands. They are the connective tissue that maintains what passes for civilization. Without them, the Highlands would be a collection of isolated villages that would probably fade and die given enough time. The pathfinders keep the communication and trade lines open. It's still isolated but nowhere what it would be without them."

Fallon's eyes were shadowed as he stared at Witt. He folded his muscular arms over his chest and adopted a wide-legged stance, as if he was bracing for whatever might come.

When he didn't interrupt, Witt continued, "They're also the only thing that passes for a government, though they're really only concerned about the tithes owed them, and that their pathfinders stay safe. Anger them and they'll cut your village off—excise it from the maps. Villages don't usually last long after that." Witt's face darkened and his gaze turned inward as if he was remembering something painful. He shook his head coming back to the present. "There are rumors that they have ways to call beasts down on those villages that displease them."

"What do you think?"

Witt frowned in thought. "I think it's too big a coincidence how quickly the excised villages fall into ruin. They do it rarely—only twice that I've heard of—but when they excise a village there are few survivors."

Ruthless—but Fallon didn't fault them for that. It was something he would do himself, though he wouldn't let the beasts do his dirty work. He'd ride into a village that threatened one of his own and kill the offenders face to face. It was more satisfying that way. It had the added benefit of making the rest fear you that much more. Fear, he'd found, was a powerful motivator for good behavior.

"Shea has mentioned there are different kinds of pathfinders."

Witt's nod was slow in coming. "It's not something they advertise. The pathfinders who serve the villages seem to be at the low end of their hierarchy. The smaller the village, the lower the status of the pathfinder. They send other pathfinders out into the remote corners of the Highlands and beyond."

"Their purpose?"

Witt shook his head. "I don't know. I only know about them because they hooked up with a caravan I'd joined when I was younger and trying to find a place for myself. They stayed with us for a month and then broke away to press further north."

"Perhaps they were heading to another village."

"There were no villages beyond our destination. I've never heard of a settlement where they were heading. Nothing up there but snow, mountains and beasts. As far as I could figure it, they were just looking around—exploring because they could."

Fallon grunted. That would fit with what he knew of Shea. She might have served as a village pathfinder, but he suspected that wasn't all she was. Her social skills were too poor and her mind too curious. He could see her exploring a remote stretch of land—so isolated that no one had ever visited it before—just to see what was there.

It was one of the things he loved about her, and one of the things he hated. That need to explore, the restlessness he could see in her eyes sometimes. It made him feel like he was trying to lay claim to air. There one moment and gone the next. He sometimes had nightmares of waking up and reaching for her, only to find her gone.

"They also have a type that they call a 'keeper,'" Witt said. "From what I understand from talking with other pathfinders, the keeper safeguards the knowledge they've gleaned through their service to the Highlands. I knew this guy from before, who said the pathfinders had a room in their keep that held all their knowledge from even before the cataclysm, great histories of a time lost to us. Art that has not been seen in nearly a millennium. Wonders that have long passed from this world."

Fallon found himself curious about these keepers. The ancients were said to have powerful weapons beyond anything that existed today. Such weapons might enable him to build an empire not seen since the cataclysm. The histories also interested him, having found that the mistakes of the past often formed the present. There was much that could be learned from their predecessors.

The Trateri had a strong oral tradition, passing stories of their great battles and strong leaders from one generation to the next. However, these stories tended to change after so many retellings until some clans had drastically different versions of the same story. Further, when a clan was wiped out, their stories and oral history died out with them. It left gaping holes in the history of his people.

"Have you ever met one of these keepers?" Fallon asked.

Witt shook his head. "They're usually kept close to their stronghold. I'd wager they realized how dangerous it would be for someone with that kind of knowledge to be wandering around the Highlands."

Fallon would expect as much. Someone armed with the knowledge these keepers were said to possess would have great power—dangerous power if it fell into the wrong hands.

These pathfinders and their hoard of knowledge reminded Fallon of a story the Trateri told as a cautionary tale to their young. In some versions the story featured an old man close to his deathbed, in others, it was a woman in her middle years. Both versions agreed that the person spent his or her life accruing material wealth—rugs of the softest material and finest weaving, tapestries from the best artisans among the Trateri people, and gold gilded furniture for them to rest their weary bones. Always gathering more and more. Every time their clan picked up and moved to the next hunting ground, to the summer camp or the winter camp, it would take longer and longer for this person to pack for the journey—until one day, they couldn't pack everything. Their clan offered to help for the small price of one item from the tent. Always this person refused, choosing to carry the burden of the possessions by themselves.

The story always ended with the old man and woman dying alone, far from their people as the terror of nature destroyed what they had spent their lifetime hoarding. In the end they lost everything and gained nothing.

These pathfinders and their knowledge of the world benefitted no one, including themselves, locked up in their stronghold where nothing could be shared.

"What about this mist?" Fallon asked. "Shea's mentioned that her fellow pathfinders possess a similar ability to navigate its depths."

Witt braced his hands on his hips and looked down, his face pensive. "I'm not sure how true that is."

Fallon's eyes sharpened, piercing in their intensity. "You're suggesting she lied."

Witt rubbed his neck with one hand, looking a shade uncomfortable. It reminded Fallon that Witt felt a depth of indebtedness that might affect how much he was willing to share. He didn't blame the man for the feeling. No, he respected him for it, even as he knew he'd have to compensate for it, or find another way to get the information out of him.

"Not so much lied, as downplayed her abilities," Witt finally said. "I've never heard of any pathfinder doing what she did when she went deeper to find you. It's not just heard of; it's damn near suicidal. I don't think any other pathfinder could have done that. They wouldn't have even tried."

Fallon felt his blood freeze in his veins at that statement. Shea had not shared with him just how dangerous her actions had been. The thought that he could have lost her did not sit well with him. It made some of that rage that had been banked surge forward.

Whatever expression was on his face was fierce enough that Witt stiffened, looking very like prey when faced with a bigger, much deadlier predator.

Fallon took a deep breath. He needed to maintain control. Losing his shit right then would help nothing and could cost him more than he was willing to afford. He had an invader to hunt and a woman to confront about her reckless actions.

"Even for a pathfinder, there are shades of abilities," Witt continued when Fallon didn't react further. The man was brave; Fallon would give him that. "Just like there are differences between great swordsmen. You pick your Anateri, your elite warriors, because they possess a level of ability, born with it or refined after endless hours of blood, sweat, and struggle. Shea lived and breathed that life. I don't know what happened to get her demoted to the back edge of beyond, but I know her skills are not easily replicated or replaced. I wouldn't count on other pathfinders showing the same level of ability when faced with the mist. Even they sometimes enter and don't come out the other side."

Fallon's face was grim as Witt finished his speech. He rubbed his chin in thought. A half-formed plan had been forming after Shea's display in ability—one that involved storming the Highlands to demand pathfinders for his army or finding a way to replicate their training in his own men. From what Witt had shared, that plan might not hold enough positive returns for such a risky undertaking.

That was to say nothing of the anger Shea would feel if he invaded her homeland. It was something he'd avoided until now, an action so at odds with his personality that some of his generals had questioned him. Among them was Braden, who upon hearing that Fallon had no immediate plans to invade the Highlands, had expressed extreme reserve about Fallon's relationship with Shea.

There were even whisperings of bewitchery and sorcery. As if Fallon was susceptible to such things. Those were ridiculous ideas designed to undermine Fallon and cast doubt upon Shea.

Fallon knew that he still had detractors among the Trateri. He could name three people off the top of his head who were actively plotting for his downfall so they could take over in his stead. It was one of the reasons he was so adamant that Shea have guards with her at all times. He knew she didn't realize the danger, being utterly uninterested in Trateri politics, or any politics he'd guess.

The advent of this mist would give them further fuel for their fire.

He'd rotated Braden back into the fold to consolidate his power base. With Darius and Braden at his side—his two most powerful generals, he had a chance at withstanding some of the storms that were gathering.

"Is there anything else you can share?" Fallon asked.

Witt shook his head. "Shea would be your best resource. She was one of them. If anyone would understand their reasoning behind the note, she would."

That was what Fallon feared.

CHAPTER ELEVEN

After Fallon left, Shea and Daere stared at each other for a long moment before the other woman excused herself.

Alone again, Shea laid down on the bed, her arms thrown over her head and feet on the ground as she stared unseeingly at the ceiling. It swayed gently in a stray breeze.

In every scenario she'd considered, each move she'd anticipated, she'd never expected the higher-ups to leave that note—to summon her home, for all intents and purposes. To bring her friends of all things. It was so outside the realm of possibilities that she was having a hard time believing it.

She sat up on her elbows. Maybe the note hadn't come from Wayfarer's Keep. Maybe it was a ruse. One aimed at impacting her relationship with Fallon. Or maybe the note writer had intended some other outcome Shea just couldn't anticipate right now.

One thing was for sure—Shea didn't trust that note and she had no intention of leading the Trateri on a suicide mission into the Highlands where the pathfinders and their guild held the advantage.

Shea spent over an hour staring up at the canvas ceiling, waiting for Fallon to come back. He never did, and she ended up falling into a fitful sleep.

It was late in the night when Fallon's warm weight slipped into bed beside her. His arms slid under her, shifting, and arranging her until she was sprawled on his chest. Her face automatically burrowed into his shoulder in a move that had become familiar over the months they'd been together.

Her fingers toyed with the bare skin of his chest, tugging lightly on his chest hair before soothing the sting. His hand settled over hers.

"Did you find the person responsible?" She held her breath, almost dreading the answer.

"No."

She exhaled.

It took a moment for her to realize how stiff his body was under hers, like a board instead of the warm heat she was accustomed to.

She lifted her head to look at him in the dark. He was glaring up at the canvas. "What is it?"

"We'll talk about it tomorrow." His voice was a whiplash of ice in the night.

She drew back a little to get a better look at him. His arms tightened around her in warning. She didn't appreciate him shutting her out nor did she appreciate the threat in his tone.

"Why not talk about it now?"

"Tomorrow, Shea."

Her jaw dropped at the autocratic command. He did not just say that. That wasn't how this worked. They were partners and partners shared things.

She pushed out of his arms and sat up, staring down at him. Her silence filled with angry words that she couldn't get out—her jaw locked tight. It was something that only happened when her temper started unfurling. She wasn't the best at speaking and sharing. When angry it was just that much worst.

After turning the words over in her head, she came to a decision. If he wanted to be an asshole warlord, he could damn well sleep alone. She rolled away from him in a sharp movement, getting out of bed.

His sigh was angry. "Where are you going?"

She didn't answer, grabbing a blanket from the end of the bed and her pillow. The partition had been partially repaired from his fit earlier, but it was still a little wobbly. She was careful as she pushed it aside, not wanting to deal with having their private space exposed to the communal side until the partition could be fixed.

"Shea."

"You wanted to discuss it tomorrow, Fallon. We'll discuss it tomorrow. Until then, have fun sleeping alone."

With those parting words she stalked into the other chamber and threw her pillow on the ground before settling down and pulling her blanket over her. She'd only been lying there for a few seconds before a pair of arms swooped down, picking her up, blanket and all.

Shea found herself against Fallon's chest being carried back to their bedroom.

"This is familiar," he murmured in her ear as he kicked the partition away, not being nearly as careful as she'd been.

"Yes, and not in a good way."

"We sleep together."

"Do we talk to each other too?" Her voice held an acerbic edge. She didn't enjoy when he dictated how things would be.

"Tomorrow, Shea."

"So, it doesn't matter what I want?"

He set her on the bed and climbed in after her, dragging the covers over them. He didn't answer. Shea took that as a no. Fine then, if that's how he wanted to play this.

She wiggled out of his arms and turned her back on him. Pressed up against the edge of the bed, she held herself as stiffly as possible, attempting to exude anger through every line of her body. She might not have a choice about sleeping elsewhere but that didn't mean she wasn't going to act like nothing was wrong.

His arm wrapped around her, and he attempted to slide her across the bed. She batted it off, before turning and pushing him away.

"No. Keep to your own side."

She turned back to the edge, curling up until she was as far away from him as possible.

"Shea."

"No, you wanted to talk tomorrow; we'll talk tomorrow."

This time it was his angry sigh that filled the air. The mattress moved as he turned onto his side to face away from her. The dark was filled with the things that went unsaid. Hurt feelings so thick that it felt like Shea would suffocate on them.

Despite it being her who had insisted on distance between them, Shea had never felt so alone. Her eyes stung as she stared at the shadowed canvas. It was a long time before she drifted back to sleep.

*

It was a slow progression to wakefulness for Shea. She woke to find herself curled into a ball with the undeniable feeling of being watched. Opening her eyes, she turned her head to find Fallon dressed and looking at her with an enigmatic gaze.

She closed her eyes and dropped her head back onto her pillow. For a brief moment, she was tempted to go back to sleep. It felt way too early for the confrontation she could feel brewing.

With a groan, she sat up and blinked at Fallon. A yawn cracked her face, the sleepless night leaving her slightly groggy.

She leaned back on one hand as she met Fallon's gaze. His emotions were locked down tight.

"It's morning," he said.

"That it is. You going to tell me what had you acting so dickish last night?"

He raised one eyebrow at her crude language. She raised an eyebrow right back at him, challenging him to say something about it.

Wise man that he was, he moved on. "Why didn't you tell me how dangerous it was for you to find me in the mist?"

Shea froze, all thoughts coming to a standstill. She stared at him, her eyes wide. Of all the things for him to ask her, he chose that. Why?

Her words were a long time coming. "You knew it was dangerous."

"Did I?" There went the eyebrow again. His body was tightly controlled as he tapped one finger against his leg. "I don't think I did."

She bent her knees and wrapped her arms around them. The urge to get up and walk out, to escape this coming confrontation was strong. It would be so easy.

He straightened, the movement that of a tightly coiled beast preparing to pounce. "Because the way I hear it, what you did pretty much amounted to a suicide mission."

Shea's hands tightened on her thighs, the knuckles turning white for a brief moment. Witt. It had to be. He was the only other person among the Trateri who would have had any inkling of just how big a risk Shea had taken.

"What was I supposed to do, Fallon? Just leave you there?"

"Yes, that's exactly what you should have done. For all you knew, we weren't in its grip."

She aimed a sharp look his way. "I knew. I could feel you slipping further and further away with every breath. Yes, it was dangerous, but it had to be done or you and your men would have never made it out."

"You promised to stay safe," he barked at her.

"I never did any such thing. This world is too dangerous to make such an asinine vow. I am a pathfinder; this is what I do."

"You're not. Not anymore." Thunder was in his face. "You left that life behind. It would be really nice if you acted like it for once, instead of rushing straight for the most dangerous, sure to get you killed, situation in a hundred miles. How am I supposed to trust you after this?"

A tight feeling took root in Shea's chest at those words. She looked away from him. "I'm well aware that path is closed to me. Thank you for pointing that out. That doesn't mean you can relegate me to the rear with the gear and expect me to sit pretty somewhere while you or others are in danger. That's not who I am, and you knew that before we started." She put every ounce of her frustration and resolve into her eyes as she met his thunderous glare. "You don't get to make this choice for me. You don't get to berate me and make me feel ashamed for having the skill and gumption to pull your ass out of the fire. If you can't accept this part of me Fallon, we won't last long."

There was a crack and then a crash as he kicked the chair he'd been sitting in. It flew back and clattered to the ground after it hit the tent wall with a loud thud.

There was movement in the other room and then Trenton came through the partition, sword in hand and his eyes scanning for a threat.

"Get out!" Fallon roared.

Trenton's gaze went to Shea as if to check that she was in no danger before he gave Fallon a short bow and backed out of the room.

"Do you feel better now?" Shea's voice was calm with a slightly sarcastic edge. She felt a tinge of pride that it showed none of her throat-gripping unease.

Fallon remained facing away from her. One hand went up to rub his face before going back to grip his neck. He stood like that for a long moment, his shoulders slightly bent and his head hanging down.

He looked so miserable that Shea almost softened. She stiffened her spine.

"Fallon, I don't take stupid risks for the hell of it. The risk to go deeper into the mist was a calculated one. Yes, it was more dangerous than I originally let on, but you can't expect me to sit back while you're in danger and do nothing. That's not who I am."

He still didn't turn. Shea sat there, the covers pooled in her lap and an ache in her chest.

"I don't know if I can do this," Fallon said without looking at her.

Every fiber of Shea went cold. A beast gripped her by the throat—one fueled by heartache, pain and desperation.

"What do you mean by that?" she asked, her voice eerily calm. A calm she in no way felt. There was a turbulence inside her that was just beginning to make itself felt. A turbulence that felt like it had the power to destroy her if she didn't hold perfectly still.

His sigh was long and held an emotion she had never thought Fallon capable of. Hopelessness. Dejection. Defeat.

"I don't know. I need to think."

He needed to think. Shea felt like he had just slapped her across the face. She was left blinking dumbly at him. He still hadn't turned to face her.

Well, wasn't that just ducky. He had to think. Fine. He could think. She'd give him all the time in the world to think.

"You do that, Fallon." She ripped the sheets off and crawled out of bed. The soft mattress made it difficult to convey the depth of her rage by its utter comfortableness and inability to give her motions any violence. She finally made it to the edge and swung her legs down. "You just remember—it wasn't me who started this relationship. I warned you before we ever began. You're the one who couldn't listen."

By this time, she'd found her pants and jerked them on in angry fits and starts, at one point almost falling before regaining her balance. She located her shirt and grabbed it, her movements sharp and angry. She pulled it over her head and got stuck, fighting with the material for a long moment, her arms sticking over her head as the material restricted her movements better than a rope ever could. A pair of large hands guided one arm into a sleeve and then the other arm into the other sleeve before grasping the bottom and giving one hard jerk. Shea's head popped out of the top. Her blue eyes spit sparks of fury as they met Fallon's whiskey colored ones.

It wasn't fair that his eyes were pools of warmth, trying to reach out and heat her insides. She stepped back and then moved around him, her hands smoothing the shirt into place. Not fair at all. Especially when they were fighting. Especially when he was threatening to end them.

Just like a man. When things get tough, take a break, run for the hills. He was a warlord, he was supposed to break obstacles with his pinky finger. Not give up when they reared their ugly little heads.

"Shea."

She didn't listen and stalked out of their chamber. Well, his chamber if he was serious about not being able to make their relationship work.

She stopped in the next chamber at the sudden realization that if they ever did end, what would happen to her? She assumed she wouldn't be able to keep this tent. It had been specifically built for the warlord, a man responsible for uniting the Trateri tribes. Not for his former telroi. Would she even be able to stay among the Trateri? Would they let her go back to being a scout, or would that door be closed to her now?

The righteous indignation she'd been using to shield herself from the hurt that was lurking deep inside drained out. She'd seen what happened to those unfortunates that had no place in either the clan or military caste. They lived on the fringes of Trateri society, relying on the kindness or lack of it from the clans. Their existence was meager and humble. Two things Shea had faced before, but not like this where you had to rely on the charity of others.

That wasn't the life for her. If Fallon and she were to end, it would mean she would have to leave, give up the life she'd been building here. Give up the friends who'd made her feel like she belonged for the first time in her life. She'd lose everything.

Fallon was a warm presence at her back as his hands came up to cup her shoulders. "You misunderstood. I'm not saying we're over."

She grunted, still reeling from her discovery, and shrugged him off. Her feet began to move again. Over her shoulder, she muttered, "I'll see you later. I think we both need a little space to decide how we feel."

She ducked out of the tent, noticing Trenton standing outside. "Just who I was looking for. Let's go train."

Surprise registered on his face before he looked over her shoulder. Understanding dawned. Shea knew without looking that Fallon had stepped out of their tent. His eyes were a heavy sensation on her back. She didn't look back, not wanting to see him.

"If that's what you want."

"It is." Her reply was terse. She started walking toward the special area that had been set up so the Anateri and Fallon could train whenever they wanted without having to waste time walking to the perimeter of the camp.

There was only the briefest hesitation that she knew involved Trenton conferring with Fallon through the non-verbal communication that all the Anateri seemed to share with their warlord. He caught up with her quickly as she stalked off.

"You don't typically lead the charge for training. Normally I have to drag you kicking and screaming." He didn't lie. Shea usually endeavored to do all in her power to avoid spending any time in the training ring with Trenton. The man was a sadist who took an inordinate amount of pleasure in leaving Shea black and blue after their sparing sessions. "Is this newfound enthusiasm because you've finally decided to get serious about weapons training, or are you just looking to blow off a little steam?"

A gemlike stare was his only response.

"Blowing off steam it is." He gave her the best half bow he could from his sideways walking position. "Happy to be of service."

Of that Shea had no doubt.

*

Trenton had been merciless in drilling her in defensive sword maneuvers, leaving a stinging rebuke anytime she failed to keep her guard up sufficiently. It left for an interesting number of bruises, several on her posterior, which seemed a favorite target of his when she over-extended her defense. Shea winced as she shifted position.

"Stop fidgeting," Daere said, without bothering to spare Shea a glance. "It makes you look uncomfortable."

Shea gave the other woman a sour glare. That's because she was uncomfortable.

Somehow Daere had convinced her to wear the Trateri version of formal clothes for this dinner, saying that they needed to present a united and impressive front to the villagers. Her hair had been half pulled back from her face in a nest of small, interwoven braids. The rest had been curled and left to spill down her neck. The girls had managed to leave Shea looking like she had way more hair than she had.

They'd brushed a shimmering brown-gold powder on her eyelids and tinted her eyelashes black. They then dusted a lighter version of that powder along her cheekbones and jawline. On her lips they'd left a stain so red that Shea looked like she'd painted them with blood. The effect was stunning, if the mirror they'd shoved her in front of was anything to go by.

Even her outfit hadn't been safe from their attention. They'd forced her into a sleeveless shirt of deepest blue, made of a silky fabric Shea had never felt before. She ran her fingers along the hem of the shirt, impressed by the feel of it against her skin. It felt cool and refreshing, despite the slumbering heat and humidity of the forest. It framed her breasts in a V while fitting well enough that she wasn't afraid she'd spill out during the climb up. A belt cinched her waist above an almost transparent loose skirt of the same color. The skirt had high slits on either side, almost up to her ass. Shea had refused to wear it when Daere first presented it, stating she had no plans on flashing everyone her personal bits just because Daere wanted to play dress-up. Daere had rolled her eyes and given her a pair of tight-fitting calf length pants the color of gold to wear under it. The outfit managed to be provocative and modest at the same time, striking a balance between Lowland sensibilities and the hedonism the Trateri embraced on occasion.

Around Shea's throat a torque of gold had been fitted. The two ends were that of a hawk's wings clasped around a sapphire stone—a symbol of the Hawkvale. The torque around her bicep had a hawk's head with sapphires for eyes.

Daere had a similar amount of gold around her throat and arms. She wore an outfit similar to Shea's, only her legs were bare of the pants Shea had insisted on. She looked regal and beautiful, and ever the Trateri.

It left a strange yearning in Shea. No matter how she tried, she just could never seem to fit in totally. It left her trying to own her strangeness. It was harder than it used to be, like a skin that was just a little too tight.

She fiddled with one of the bracelets clasped around her wrist, the weight an unaccustomed feeling.

"You look fine," Daere said. From the tone, Shea was betting Daere was trying not to roll her eyes.

Fallon, Braden and Darius came around the tree trunk, a low rumble the only warning of their approach. They, like the women, were dressed in Trateri finest. Their chests were bare and glistening, each wearing a sleeveless tunic. Gold torques similar to Shea's and Daere's were wrapped around their throats and biceps. Fitted leather pants completed the look.

Fallon's hair was pulled back on the sides in tiny braids. The top had been slicked into a half Mohawk. Black paint streaked along his temples to the corner of his eyelids, framing those whiskey-colored eyes and making them even more intense than they were normally.

Fallon stopped dead at the sight of Shea, his eyes sweeping down her, pausing at the gold around her throat and arms. A small grin tugged at the corners of his mouth, his eyes heating before they swung to Daere briefly then returned to rest on Shea.

"I appreciate that," he said.

Shea tilted her head, not quite understanding.

"I thought you might," Daere murmured.

Fallon closed the rest of the distance between him and Shea, reaching down and grasping her hand. He raised it, pressing a kiss to her knuckles, not taking his eyes off hers. Despite some of the anger and hurt still lurking in Shea, she felt a stirring of warmth, flutters of desire at the surprising gesture.

"The gold suits you," Fallon murmured, his eyes sweeping over her one last time in appreciation.

Shea blinked at him. That was such a strange compliment. Mentally she shrugged. Perhaps it was a Trateri thing. "You don't look so bad in it either."

There was a choked sound from Braden. Shea would have categorized it as a laugh, if it had come from any other person. She gave him a sideways glance, noting that his attention had already moved on. He was staring at Daere with an intense focus that Shea would have sworn was capable of scalding its recipient. Daere was made of stronger stuff though, determinedly ignoring his attention.

Shea waited, half expecting Braden to push the issue. Make a comment on how amazing Daere looked. He surprised her when he switched his attention back to Shea, noting her attention with a frown. She held his gaze for a long moment, determined not to be cowed or made uncomfortable for staring at what was probably a private moment for him. She felt like she'd spied on something she shouldn't have, even if he'd been making eyes in front of everybody.

A slight furrow formed between his brows before he turned away, making a point of not looking in Daere's direction again.

"Shall we ascend?" Fallon asked, holding his hand out to Shea.

Shea looked at it for a long moment, remembering the fight from the morning. She slipped her hand in his and offered him a small smile. "We shall."

Two of the Anateri had already started up the ladder to the first resting platform. They moved fast as Fallon steadied the rope ladder for Shea. His hand was a warm weight at her back as she stepped onto the first rung.

She met his eyes through the ladder. He leaned forward and pressed a small kiss against her lips before resting his forehead against hers.

In a quiet voice only meant for her ears, he said, "I'm sorry for this morning and last night."

Her eyes closed in relief. "I'm sorry too."

"Forgive me?"

She nodded. His hands tightened briefly around her waist before they slid away. "I'll be right behind you."

Shea gave him a playful grin. "We'll see."

She didn't wait for a response, scaling the ladder as fast as she could, leaving the rest behind. The rope swayed under her as Fallon stepped on and started climbing. She'd almost caught up to the Anateri above her when she had to slow down, not willing to crawl over them to get a further lead on Fallon. Not to mention, given how upset he'd been this morning, she didn't want to push him too hard this soon.

Fallon wasn't far behind her by the time they made the first platform. There, they took a brief rest, letting the rest of the group catch up. There were several strangers among them, four men that Shea recognized as Anateri and two others that she assumed were in the upper echelons of the clans. Witt was the last to join their group, his quiet calm suffusing his gaze as he glanced at Shea.

She took a deep breath and released it. She needed to talk to him about what he'd told Fallon, and why. The more pressing question was how he had known what he did. The pathfinders guarded any information about the mist and how to navigate it with a zealousness that bordered on mania.

The first of the strangers had hair that looked like someone had caught the sun and then poured its light into its strands. He was big, bigger than Fallon, and he walked with that perfect, self-aware balance that only warriors seemed to possess— the kind that said he was mindful of his surroundings and prepared to fend off an attack at any moment.

The other stranger was as dark as the first was fair. His skin looked nutbrown, and his hair had been tied entirely back from his face. His eyes were two pools of dark brown highlighted by streaks of amber. He was slight where the other man was muscled, and he moved with a dancer's grace. He looked at the others in the group with a friendly caution, not fully suspicious, but not at ease either.

Shea didn't engage with them, content to stay to her side of the platform and watch them from afar. The blond looked like he'd spent a little too much time training—she recognized him. He'd come out of several meetings that involved the clan heads. She was willing to bet he was one of those heads.

Trenton and Wilhelm moved to the next series of ladders and rope bridges and Shea followed close behind. There was a little chatter at this stage of the journey, but Shea knew it would soon drop off as the climb tested the group's physical endurance, forcing them to save their breath.

Shea and her guards would be in a better position later, as she'd made a habit of taking this trip whenever possible in the past few months, and they had been forced to tag along with her.

They'd just passed the third platform and were taking a breather on one of the rope bridges when Fallon came up to her.

"I can see why your climbing skills were so developed when we first met, if this was the kind of place you learned on."

Shea gave him a crooked grin. "This isn't where I learned to climb cliffs."

He arched one eyebrow, one side of his lips pulling up in a half grin. "Oh? A story you haven't told me then. I'd be interested to learn where you developed that particular skill set."

She gave him a wry look. "And if I tell you, will I wake to find the camp preparing to pick up and move?"

A smile cracked the stern mask he normally wore, lending warmth to his expression as a hint of playfulness peeked through.

"It's always a possibility."

She snorted and rolled her eyes. "Then perhaps I'll wait until a better time to tell you that story."

She looked away from him, still smiling. The dark-haired stranger watched them with a curious expression. His eyes drifted between Shea and Fallon with an almost perplexed look in them.

"Who are your friends?" Shea asked Fallon.

He glanced in the direction she was looking and then away, almost turning his back on the other two as he bent and said in a low voice. "The blond one's name is Van, clan leader of the Lion clan."

"And the other?"

"His name is Chirron. He's a friend of Braden. Technically, he does not hold any power in the clans."

"And in reality?"

"He's probably one of the most powerful men amongst the Trateri, with the exception of myself and possibly Darius."

Shea gave Fallon big eyes. How was that possible? Especially since he wasn't in the clan hierarchy.

"He's the leader of our healers. They denounce all ties to their clan once they take their vows. It's to prevent them from being biased and only offering their services to one clan. In reality, it gives them a voice in all clans."

And because they were healers, no one would want to risk angering them and having them refuse to assist their clan in times of need.

"Is he a friend or foe?" Shea asked.

Fallon looked over her head, his eyes distant. "I haven't figured that out yet."

"He sounds interesting, if you can't categorize him," Shea said, her eyes lighting up playfully.

His gaze came down to rest on her. He reached up and tugged on a loose curl, watching in fascination as it straightened and then sprung back when he let it go. She let him do that several times before she batted his hand away and gave him a warning look.

"It is not always easy to tell friend from foe. Chirron, especially, keeps his motives close. I can't tell if that's because he's planning something, or if it's a natural response from having to deal with the fractious clan elders."

Shea saw Wilhelm and Trenton begin to move again and knew their discussion was almost at an end.

"Probably a bit of both, I'd guess."

He made a sound of agreement.

She followed in Trenton and Wilhelm's wake, leaving the rest of the group to keep up. She was surprised at how well the two strangers were doing, less so with Darius and Braden who probably followed a similar training regime as Fallon and would have stamina for days.

They made the rest of the journey easily, Van and Chirron not falling back or voicing any complaints, even when their breathing turned slightly labored. It was one of the things Shea liked best about the Trateri. They rarely complained about things that couldn't be changed. It was a welcome departure from some of the charges she'd led while in the Highland.

CHAPTER TWELVE

Shea gave a full-bodied stretch once they'd stepped onto the last platform, hands above her head, back arched as she lengthened throughout her body. It felt sinfully good after the climb, her muscles stretching pleasantly to counterbalance the strain she'd put on them.

She felt Fallon at her back moments before his hand landed on her stomach. He leaned down, his breath tickling her ear. "What do you do to me?"

She tilted her head back to look at him questioning from upside down. "What do you mean?"

His gaze was searching and filled with dark things as he looked down at her. His eyes did strange things to her stomach as it dipped and flipped. She felt warm stirrings at the heat and intensity he was aiming her way. He sighed heavily, the erotic intensity in his gaze disappearing.

"Now's not the time," he murmured. He stepped around her, his hand sliding to her back and ushering her forward.

She blinked at him in confusion, not quite understanding what had just happened. That had come out of nowhere. It made her wish they were closer to their tent and bed, though she knew such a wish was selfish.

Eckbert stood at the head of his people as they waited for them on the other end of the rope bridge that marked the beginning of the village. They would have to cross that bridge one by one to greet the headman and those gathered.

Trenton and Wilhelm stayed at Shea's side while Fallon debated with his two advisors who should go first. Darius and Caden were in favor of anyone but Fallon being the first across the bridge, pointing out the need for caution since the Airabel, while allies, were still not to be trusted.

"I am not a child in need of protection," Fallon snapped. "I am perfectly capable of defending myself, having done it long before you formed the Anateri."

That last comment was aimed at Caden.

"No one is questioning your prowess with a weapon, Fallon. These people are unknown. Let one of us go first to test our footing before you come in," Darius said, frustration in his voice. "There's no need to take unnecessary risks."

"I've already met with the headman. If they'd wanted to kill us, they could have done so yesterday morning when there were fewer of us. Sending in a guard first makes us look weak—like we fear them when we don't. I cannot afford to look weak before them or anyone else."

Darius looked at Caden for confirmation on the first statement. Caden hesitated before giving a quick nod. A storm began gathering on Darius's face. "What were you doing up here with so few guards last night? Because I know damn well that Caden and the rest were down below getting some rest."

Fallon's jaw ticked as he met Darius's glare with a fierce one of his own. Shea stood very still not wanting to draw Darius's wrath. She hadn't taken into consideration Fallon's position or the potential danger to him when she'd dragged him up here last night.

Darius didn't need anyone to confirm who was at fault, his gaze swinging to take in the uncomfortable expression on her face. He swore and shook his head. "You're going to get him killed."

"Enough," Fallon snapped. "I've lasted this long without a problem. We were in little danger last night."

"That was before, Fallon," Darius snapped back, not cowed by Fallon's anger. "Before you went and united the clans and pissed off a lot of people. By the gods, Caden tells me you've had three assassination attempts in the last week."

Shea jolted forward. What was this? "What are you talking about?"

Darius's attention swung to Shea—for a brief moment he looked like a bull about to charge. "Maybe you should have considered that before you dragged him out of the protection of the camp."

"What are you talking about? What assassination attempts? I thought those were done."

"Enough, we're not talking about this anymore." Fallon's voice was a cold snap of winter.

"Fallon!" Shea protested.

"No, enough." He gave her a fierce warning glare, one strong enough to freeze the words on her tongue. His gaze moved slightly to the side. She snapped her mouth close. Van and Chirron watched the proceedings with a fascination that made her feel dirty, like she'd done something wrong.

She gave Fallon a nod, saying she understood. The warning look she gave him said that this would be one more thing they talked about later.

"Caden should go first," Shea blurted.

Caden and Darius looked at her in surprise.

"He's the captain of your Anateri. It makes sense that he would proceed you. They'll see it as an honor, not as an insult," she said in belated explanation.

Fallon didn't look happy as he watched her. Her eyes went everywhere but his as she waited for a rebuke or to have her suggestion overridden. If he pushed her suggestion aside, he'd be undercutting her in front of potential enemies and hinder any progress she'd made. The expression on his face said he knew it too and wasn't happy about it.

He jerked his chin down once in a nod that still managed to be an order.

Caden gave her a considering glance before he took off, tilting his head down in an almost bow before he strode across the rope bridge. It swayed under his feet.

Fallon waited beside her in a thunderous silence as they watched Caden greet the headman. It was only a few moments before he gave the signal for Fallon and the rest of them to approach.

Fallon went first. Then it was Shea's and her guards' turn. She took a deep breath before following Fallon's broad back. She looked past him to where Caden and the villagers waited, decked out in their best finery, much as the Trateri were. The generals followed her, then the clan heads, and Daere. Witt and the rest of the guards brought up the rear.

Eckbert stepped forward and gestured, several women breaking from the crowd to step forward with necklaces of brightly colored flowers.

"Welcome, friends. Welcome," Eckbert said giving them a wide grin.

Shea ducked her head and accepted the flower necklace with a smile, murmuring a thank-you to the young girl who'd placed it around her neck.

"What's this?" Chirron asked, picking up the braided flowers and examining them closely.

"It's tradition for the village to greet their guests with the mbel. It's a sign of their esteem."

"I wonder if these have any medicinal properties," he muttered, rubbing a petal between his thumb and forefinger.

Shea's mouth opened and then closed. "I don't know. You'd have to ask one of the villagers. They're familiar with the flora around here and could tell you more about its properties." She thought a moment then volunteered, "I do know that the bark of the soul tree when brewed at a high temperature can calm a cough."

She had personal experience with that treatment having had to sit through a few cups after she'd contracted a particularly nasty cough while visiting the area previously.

Chirron's eyes brightened as he looked at the tree trunk. "I wonder what temperature the water needs to be to achieve the best results, or if the treatment could be replicated in a paste."

Shea shrugged. "I couldn't tell you. I'm sure Eckbert will be more than happy to introduce you to their healer."

"I'd greatly appreciate that," Chirron said. The expression he bestowed on her was full of eager anticipation.

"Careful, Chirron. Your tendency to lose yourself in inconsequential things has begun to show again," Van said, clapping the other man on the shoulder.

Unlike the rest of them, he was not wearing one of the mbel. Shea looked back at the girl who had been the one to approach him. She was staring at the ground as several other women gathered around her and talked in hushed voices while shooting quick glances in Van's direction.

"A new method to treat a cough or fever is never inconsequential, Lion." The earlier anticipation in Chirron's gaze had disappeared, leaving him with a calm expression that bordered on serene patience.

"I'll be honest; I'm more interested in what kind of warriors they can contribute to our armies. You can treat as many coughs as you like; it'll never win us the war." Van's gaze was assessing as he took in those who had gathered to welcome them to Airabel. "Though from the sight of this lot, I'm willing to bet the pickings will be slim."

Chirron's eyes narrowed just slightly, but he didn't react in any other manner.

"I imagine a treatment for the fever one gets from an infected battle wound would be worth its weight in gold, if it had the ability to restore soldiers to the ranks, when otherwise they'd be consigned to the grave," Shea said before she could stop herself. Once the words were out, she was committed, and she met his gaze with an impassive one of her own.

Daere turned her body so she was half facing away, saying so only Shea could hear. "Well said. Now don't push him any further. You're not the one who will pay the price for his anger." Daere's eyes slid to the girl being led away by the other women.

Shea dipped her chin just slightly to show Daere she understood.

Van studied her, his face thoughtful as he pulled at one lip. "That is a fair point, but ultimately irrelevant. You have to win the battle before you have the luxury of treating your wounds. Only after you have been victorious, can the healers treat those unlucky or unskilled enough to be caught by their enemies' blade. Without the first, you cannot have the second."

Shea bit her tongue on the response she wanted to give him. His argument was flawed and shortsighted. Yes, winning the battle to then be able to treat your wounded was necessary, but how would you win the next battle or the battle after that if half your force was fighting off infection from non-mortal wounds. Eventually you'd run out of men with which to fight and you would lose.

Not to mention, luck had as much to do with surviving a battle as skill.

Chirron met her eyes from next to Van and shook his head once. Shea almost thought she'd imagined the movement because in the same motion he turned to speak to Braden who observed Shea and Van with a watchful expression on his face.

"General, have you been able to figure out the answer to the question I asked you earlier?"

The question came out of nowhere for more than Shea it seemed, because Braden blinked at the smaller man for a moment before responding, "I'm afraid I don't have a working theory for how the tree supports the weight of its trunk and branches without collapsing."

"It's largely hollow," a regal looking woman said, stepping up next to the headman. Ilyra had black hair threaded through with white that was pulled back from her face in an elegant knot. She wore the brightly colored garments of the other villagers. "Most of the soul trees are. I believe it allows them to grow to their immense height without being crushed under their own weight."

"Fascinating," Chirron said. He did look fascinated. "I would love to discover more about these amazing trees you call home."

She inclined her head. "I would be happy to share all I know over dinner." To Fallon and the rest, she said, "If you'll follow us, we will lead you to the feast."

"Lead on, lady. My Telroi tells me your feasts are the stuff of dreams," Fallon said.

Amusement dawned on her face. "High praise indeed from a pathfinder who has traveled most of the known world."

"It's only the truth, Ilyra," Shea said, stepping up to Fallon's side. "I've visited many villages and can honestly say that none of their people have quite the same touch as your cooks."

"Then it would be a travesty to keep you and your guests from our feast any longer. If you'd follow me."

Ilyra spun on her heel, her bare feet padding over the well-worn bark of a tree branch that could host three Trateri sleep tents set right beside one another. The path she chose followed the branch back to the trunk, the ground sloping down more and more the closer they got to the center of the tree.

She led the group to one of the village celebration spaces, a large chamber carved into the base of the trunk. The chamber had grown as the trunk aged and showed at a glance just how old Airabel was. The ceiling arched high above them in elegant whirls that followed the grain of wood. The villagers had carved sculptures into the knots, providing columns of intricate artwork as high as the eye could see.

"Your home is breathtaking," Daere said, her voice hushed with wonder.

Shea glanced at the woman beside her, realizing this was probably the first time she'd been in the trunk. Shea had been part of the negotiations when Fallon first made contact simply because she had a history with these people and wanted to make sure they didn't end up destroyed because of a simple miscommunication or an overinflated sense of pride.

"I've been many places but have never seen anything quite like it," Shea said, looking around while trying to see it through Daere's eyes. "Most humans attempt to force nature to flow around them. The Airabel have found a way to exist in harmony—coaxing it here and there into a certain form, but for the most part, existing parallel with it."

Daere touched one of the carvings just above their head. "They must have lived here for centuries."

"Longer, I'd imagine," Chirron said, coming to stand behind them with his hands clasped behind his back. "It's probably close to a thousand years or more. Though a lack of carvings in some of the spaces higher up speak to the idea that they may have abandoned this home for a length of time before resettling it."

"I would say you're correct," Shea said. "These trees grow painfully slow. It would have taken many years to create this space. My guess is that this is one of the oldest settlements in the Broken Lands. There are only a few to my knowledge that would rival it in terms of history."

"Oh?" Braden stopped near them. "I would be interested in hearing about these other ancient cities."

Shea gave him a tight smile. "Perhaps another time."

"I look forward to it."

She bet he did.

Fallon came up to her and touched the small of her back. "Are you enjoying baiting my generals?"

"Of course. They are so easy to bait."

His chuckle was warm against her ear. "He will find a time and place to interrogate you regarding those other cities. Of my generals, Braden takes the saying 'you can never have too much information' the most seriously."

"Not Darius?" The other general had always struck her as more of an information gatherer. The sort to keep one ear to the ground and an eye on everything around him.

Fallon's eyes were thoughtful. "He also subscribes to that theory but perhaps doesn't take it to such extremes as Braden. Darius excels at recognizing the best uses for a person's abilities and then leveraging them to their maximum capability. He's my strong right hand. Braden, on the other hand, is more like a spider sitting in the middle of his web and spinning intricate plots layered one on top of the other. I often think of him as my strategist."

Fallon would be the brain and the heart. The one person among all of them capable of inspiring the Trateri to follow him and the person with the big picture.

Shea looked at the two generals with a thoughtful frown. The two men were comfortable in each other's presence. The slightest smile was present on Braden's face, something Shea suspected was rare for him. Darius always looked like a man who thought the entire world was a game set up for his private amusement. He was the sort who didn't take things too seriously. With Braden, he looked more at ease, and the two shared a rapport similar to what she had with Eamon and Buck.

"Darius is the one who thought you might make a good Anateri if given enough time," Fallon volunteered.

Shea's head spun so she could give him gape at him. "That was a terrible idea."

"Was it?" Fallon raised an eyebrow. "I'd thought about making your alter ego Shane a general at one point before I knew who you were. Darius's idea was better. Many of my Anateri are picked not just for their skill with a blade but for other skills as well. Braden, for instance, was among my Anateri before he claimed the rank of general. Others have gone on to have high offices in my military."

"You never told me that."

He shrugged. "Once I found out who you were, it didn't matter. You could not be Anateri and my Telroi at the same time. We have rules against such things. A relationship of that sort would border on an abuse of power not to mention limit your effectiveness at your job."

"So, you decided for me?"

The corner of his lips quirked. "If you recall, you did not want to be Anateri in the first place."

Her mouth dropped. "How was I supposed to know what all that meant? All I knew was that you'd taken me from the scouts without even asking my permission."

"Every man or woman in my army serves at the needs of the army. Not the other way around."

Her lips firmed, and she narrowed her eyes at him. She couldn't argue with that, though she wanted to. Badly. It was the same with the pathfinders. You had some discretion, but at the end of the day it was the organization's needs as a whole that took precedent. It's the only way it could be. The sticking point was she'd only been an imposter at that point, a Trateri in name only and part of his army only as it suited her.

"And if I wanted to go back? To become an Anateri?"

There had been a time where she would have said it was impossible to read what Fallon was thinking. That time was gone. His eyebrows, the twitch of his mouth, these things were as plain as day when you knew what to look for. Right now, he was amused. It made Shea want to yank on his tail just to mess with him.

"You would have to give up your relationship with me." He gave her a look, one with slumberous eyes and a wicked tilt to his lips. "Is that what you want? To give me up?"

He was messing back. She considered him from beneath her eyelashes. Two could play this game.

"And if it is?"

"Then I would step aside."

"You would let me join the Anateri? You wouldn't try to stop me?"

"It would be your decision."

Shea narrowed her eyes on him. There was a catch in there—she could feel it.

The rest of the group moved towards the long tables set up in the middle of the chamber as their hosts began carrying large platters of food inside. Shea and Fallon didn't move, eyes locked on one another.

Try as she might, she couldn't find the catch. She finally broke his gaze to move towards the tables.

"Of course, I never said I wouldn't try to convince you otherwise."

A light touch trailed down the side of Shea's neck, setting off a wave of goosebumps that traveled down her spine. Her stride hitched, and she sucked in a breath at the demonstration of just how he would go about convincing her.

He stepped past her as he aimed a look filled with heat her way, one that reminded of her long nights tangled in sheets pressed skin to skin. She met his look with a smoldering one of her own. This time it was his turn to pause, his regarding her in that particular way—part wonderment and part unfiltered desire. It stole her breath as it always did.

"Lady, we have a surprise for you," Eckbert said as Shea stepped away from Fallon and the almost physical effect he asserted on her body.

"That wasn't necessary," Shea said. She figured it was another host gift, a common feature of these dinners.

"It was a surprise for us as well," Ilyra said. Her voice and face held a hint of caution, and she gave Fallon and his men a small glance before focusing back on Shea.

There was something in her tone. Something that put Shea's senses on alert.

"How about you show us what this surprise is?" Shea said, her eyes guarded now.

"It's not so much a what as a who," Eckbert confided. He seemed as reserved as Ilyra. It was a shift in the façade he'd presented earlier.

Yup, she was definitely not looking forward to whatever was coming.

Eckbert and Ilyra shared a glance. An entire conversation seemed to take space in the span of moments. With a huff, Ilyra gestured at one of the attendants who turned and walked off.

"What's this?" Fallon asked, as he looked at the two leaders as he would a possible threat.

"The villagers have a surprise for us," Shea said through gritted teeth.

"You don't sound pleased about this."

"Probably because I'm not." Her response was low, almost inaudible.

Fallon's gaze was thoughtful as he looked from Shea to their hosts. He made a gesture and the Anateri shifted, one moment seeming harmless and at ease, and the next second on their guard, watching their surroundings with suspicious eyes. There was a thread of tension that coursed through them and Fallon's generals. One that hadn't been there before. All from a simple gesture from their warlord.

There was a commotion at the entrance across from them as the villagers parted and two figures stepped inside. The first was the villager Ilyra had sent off.

Shea drew in a sharp breath at the sight of the second, a man only a shade taller than the villager. Shea knew even before getting a closer look that he would have eyes of the palest blue, the kind that Shea had only seen rarely in the very northern parts of the Highlands, where giant ice sheets marched back and forth across the land as the seasons changed.

"Reece." Her face was stricken.

It couldn't be. He was never assigned this far south, as he said the Lowlands were much too tame for the type of work he liked. No, they never would have sent him here.

His pale blue eyes flashed at her, and he gave her a mocking look, taking in the brooding warlord at her side. He cocked his head at her and shook his head.

"Warlord, Lady," Eckbert nodded to each of them respectfully. "May I present a traveler who came to us last night and requested an audience with your esteemed selves."

"And just who is this traveler?" Fallon asked, his voice a lazy whip. He was in warlord mode, his face a mask that said he could crush this entire tree without breaking a sweat.

"Pathfinder Reece, at your service." Even with the half bow, Reece managed to put a world of disdain and attitude into that statement.

"Pathfinder." Fallon's words were like a stone thrown into still water, bringing the focus of the entire gathering down on them.

The circle of Anateri tightened around the three of them. The two village elders had the sense to look uneasy at being between the Anateri and the stranger in their midst.

Reece rose from his mocking bow. "Indeed, much as your lovely companion there once was."

Fallon didn't take his eyes off the other man. Nonetheless, Shea knew what he was waiting for. "He's not lying. He is a pathfinder."

"What are you doing here, pathfinder?"

Reece cocked one eyebrow. "It seems you didn't respond to my note, so I was forced to take matters into my own hands."

The smile that broke across Fallon's face was the stuff of nightmares. It was victory and retribution all at once. Reece blanched, looking for a moment like he finally realized the extent of the predicament he was in.

"And are you the same person who left that note on our pillow?" Fallon's voice was silky. He didn't move but the space suddenly seemed a lot more cramped.

He didn't wait for the other man's assent, springing forward before anyone could react and grabbing Reece by the collar of his shirt. Fallon lifted him half off the ground and shook him. "I need to pay you in kind for that little stunt."

"Call off your brute, Shea." Reece glared at Fallon.

"He doesn't answer to me."

Reece sneered. "Then what good is he?"

"Oh, I don't know. I can think of a few things." Shea's voice was bored, as if what was taking place in front of her didn't affect her in the least. That was a lie. Her insides twisted and turned as if she'd swallowed a swarm of snakes.

"I never figured you for the type who was distracted by what was between your legs," Reece said. "He is handsome, I'll give you that, but you would have done better with someone a little less in touch with their inner barbarian. Someone more amenable to being led around by his nose."

The words stung, but Shea didn't let it show. Reece was the type to key onto what bothered you and then poke and poke until you snapped. Smart man that he was, he usually managed to escape the resulting blast. He'd done similar things to her growing up, while they were mentored under the same pathfinder.

Fallon bared his teeth and lifted Reece higher. The smaller man grimaced and tried to wiggle free. Fallon's grip didn't budge.

"I wouldn't antagonize him if I were you," Shea told Reece. "I'm not lying when I say he doesn't answer to me. He can and will snap your neck if it suits him."

He tossed him at Caden. "Take him into custody. No one is to interrogate him until I get there."

"Understood." Caden pulled Reece's arms behind him and slipped a tie around his wrists, binding him so he couldn't attack. Shea wanted to point out that Reece would need his arms for the descent to the encampment but kept quiet. They would figure that out themselves soon enough.

Fallon aimed a fierce frown at Eckbert and Ilyra. "Would either of you like to tell me why you provided shelter to one of my enemies?"

"Yes, I would be interested to know that as well," Van said, his voice gleeful. His look had the anticipation of a predator scenting blood. "I say we skip the explanations and you let me take care of this matter."

Ilyra blanched ever so slightly and Eckbert drew himself up as tall as his back stooped with age would allow him.

Fallon's lips tightened, and he seemed to be thinking it over.

"It's part of their culture," Shea blurted out. "The forest can be a cold and dark place. For that reason, they extend shelter and guest rights to any who visit. I've never heard of them turning a traveler away. If they'd wished to act against you, they never would have presented him at this dinner."

Shea faced Fallon and Van and kept her expression calm, even if it was the last thing she felt. There was a palpable tension on the air, one so thick that it seemed like the room could explode into violence at any moment. The Anateri, along with the generals, had dropped one hand to the blades at their waist. They eyed their surroundings with a hostility that increased by the minute.

Several of the villagers, hunters if Shea didn't missed her guess, had adopted similar positions. Out of the corner of her eye she saw movement. Men and women armed with bows and arrows took up position along the edge of the room. A few held spears and knives. They didn't raise them, but the threat was there.

Shea took a step, placing herself between the two sides. Fallon's eyes narrowed as he took notice of what she'd done. If either side attacked, she would be caught in the crossfire. Rage sparked to life behind his whiskey colored eyes, and his nostrils flared as he took a deep breath and released it. Just like that, all that anger was hidden, leaving her to deal with the impervious warlord.

She took a deep breath. She didn't know what she was doing. She just knew she couldn't stand by while the situation escalated.

"Ilyra, Eckbert, would you like to explain how Reece came to be a visitor here?"

Ilyra's eyes were careful. She knew the significance of what Shea had done. "He approached our heart late last night and requested guest rights."

"Your heart?" Fallon's question was a snap of sound

"It's what they call the village center that resides in the trunk of the tree," Shea told Fallon.

"You did not think it suspicious? His arrival so late at night?" Darius asked.

Eckbert shook his head. "We thought nothing of it. The pathfinders have long been visitors of this place and they often show up at odd times."

"And when he requested an audience with the Hawkvale?" Braden asked.

Eckbert shrugged. "We assumed he was seeking an alliance with your people much as we have. The Telroi was once a pathfinder. It is not outside the realm of possibility that the pathfinders would want to assure themselves of her health. It's our understanding that they take the continued well-being of their people very seriously no matter how far they stray."

Shea shifted uncomfortably. That was very true and might have been the case had she not fully aligned herself with the Trateri. Now, she doubted they would shed a tear if she was to meet with an unexpected ending.

"Yes, we had no idea you would have such an extreme reaction to the pathfinder's presence." Ilyra managed to sound both mildly reproachful and respectful at the same time.

Fallon studied them under veiled eyes, his expression not giving away any of his thoughts. Shea held her breath.

"Very well," he said at last. "Your explanation is reasonable. I believe you did not know of our feelings on this particular pathfinder and did not mean any harm in your actions."

Shea released a breath.

"That still does not negate the fact that a potential enemy got so close. Darius and several of my men will take up residence in your village to keep something of this nature from happening again."

"Is that really necessary?" Ilyra asked. She seemed concerned at the thought of a squad of Trateri soldiers moving in for the foreseeable future.

"It is as much for your protection as ours. I had not considered the possibility that my enemies might latch on to you as an avenue to infiltrate my ranks or use your home as a platform to launch an attack from above. I will take steps to correct that oversight."

Eckbert cackled. "Too true. I will have our people prepare a place for them to sleep. Perhaps some of your men will like to visit the oasis with our women."

Ilyra gave him a disgusted look before casting her eyes up to the ceiling with a beleaguered expression. "Our women aren't broodmares for you to trot out to tempt men with, you old fool."

Eckbert looked affronted. "I never said they were, but if the opportunity presents itself and the two parties would like a little alone time, I'm not one to stop them."

Chirron and Van looked a little startled at the exchange, neither one looking like they believed what they were hearing. Even Shea was a bit startled at the extent of Eckbert's desire to see the women of his village impregnated. It just wasn't a view typical to the Lowlands where they guarded their women's virtue with a rigorous zealotry. They treated them by turns like precious treasure or valuable livestock whose bloodlines needed to be preserved. The Airabel villagers did not seem to prescribe to that same thought process. Judging by the way a few women were eyeing Fallon and his generals, Shea was willing to bet Eckbert's wishes would be honored at the first opportunity.

Fallon opened his hands and gave them a fierce grin. "Now, shall we enjoy this feast you've put together for us?"

CHAPTER THIRTEEN

H as he said anything yet?" Fallon asked Caden upon arrival. Caden had had the foresight to move the man to a different part of the camp. One where Shea wouldn't easily be able to overhear her former companion when he screamed.

"Yes. The man won't shut up." Caden gave the tent where their captive waited a disgusted look. "Nothing he says seems to be of any consequence, however."

Darius snorted. He'd invited himself along to the interrogation. Braden had remained behind in the treetop village with Chirron and Van. Fallon hadn't been happy leaving Van up there, knowing the other man tended to be brutal to those the Trateri conquered. There were also rumors of how he treated the opposite sex. Nothing concrete, however.

Despite that, Fallon had faith the general would keep him in check.

"Let's see if we can jog something loose, shall we?" Fallon gave Caden a wolfish grin. It had just a hint of brutality to it.

Fallon stalked past him and into the dark space inside the tent. There was a small brazier lit on one side; it was the only light now that night had long since fallen. The Airabel villagers knew how to throw a feast and had kept Fallon and the others long past sunset. Coupled with the long journey down the tree in the dark, it was well past midnight.

"Look who has returned. The conquering warlord, master of all he sees," Reece said upon seeing Fallon. He had a sly smile on his face, the expression that of a fox who thinks it's cornered a mouse. Only Fallon was as far from a mouse as one could get.

He didn't respond to the greeting, choosing silence as he crossed his arms over his chest and settled a dark look on Reece.

"Oh, scary. Does that look often win you confessions?" Reece refused to be cowed.

The man was foolhardy. Cocky and arrogant when surrounded by danger. Fallon couldn't bring himself to respect him. He was a showboat. Fallon didn't see much resemblance in the skill and poise Shea possessed and this boy's cocky assumption that no harm would befall him.

A small movement in the corner drew Fallon's attention. Witt stood behind the captive with his arms at his sides and a considering expression on his face.

"What can you tell me?" Fallon asked.

"What kind of question is that?" Reece asked. "Do you think I'll just answer?"

Fallon leveled a calm look on the other man. "I wasn't talking to you."

Reece blinked in confusion.

A slight tug at the corner of Witt's lips spoke to his amusement. "He's definitely a pathfinder. My guess is he's not been assigned to a specific post. He's skilled, but his arrogance keeps him from advancing further in their ranks. It's probably why they put him on this assignment. He's expendable."

Reece face nearly turned purple with insult. "I'll have you know that I'm considered one of the best in my age group, and they don't consider me expendable in the least."

Fallon raised an eyebrow. "Oh? Is that why they sent you on a suicide mission?"

Reece snorted. "Hardly. Shea won't let you kill me."

"Do you see Shea anywhere near here, boy?" Darius asked at Fallon's back.

Fallon hunkered down getting in Reece's face. "Shea does not make the rules in my army. I do. She might be upset about your death, but by then it will be too late."

For the first time Reece looked a little uncertain. Good, the little shit finally understood just how serious this was. It wasn't a game. There would be no calling a halt if Reece decided he didn't want to play anymore. Fallon was deadly serious and there was nothing he'd like more than to relieve this man of his head.

"I'm her cousin. She'd never forgive you."

Fallon stood up. Hm. That might put a wrinkle in things. He didn't let that stop him though. "It might take a long time, but I have a feeling she'll eventually come back around."

Reece snorted. "You don't know Shea very well, then. That woman holds a grudge like no other."

"It might be worth it just to shut you up," Witt said, poking Reece in the back of the head.

Reece shrugged and tried to duck away from Witt. He didn't get far, restrained in the chair as he was.

"What is it that you want?" Fallon asked. He was tired of the games. He wanted to be in bed holding his woman, not here interrogating a fool.

"Didn't you get the note?"

Fallon's jaw ticked. "You mean the note you invaded my space to leave on Shea's pillow."

"Yeah, that note."

Caden scoffed. "This boy is an idiot."

Darius's expression made it clear he agreed. "How is he a pathfinder? I'm beginning to revise my opinion of them after meeting him."

"He is not typical to their ranks," Witt said, never taking his eyes off the other man.

"What's the big deal? The note was very clear. Shea can come back home and even bring the little friends she's made." Reece's expression made it clear he had no idea why they found the note so offensive.

Fallon snapped. He'd crossed the space in seconds and grabbed Reece's shirt, jerking him and the chair he was still tied to half off the ground. "The big deal is you trespassed in my space. You violated the room I share with my Telroi. Worst of all, you seek to take what is mine. I have killed men for less. I have destroyed villages and salted the earth they rested on so nothing could grow again for offenses not even half as grave as the insult you gave. That is the big deal."

Reece's head flopped around on his shoulders as Fallon shook him with every other word. Fallon's voice rose until it was a thunderous roar in the small space. The other three made no attempt to separate him from his victim, looking on with bored expressions.

Fallon took a deep breath and opened his hand. Reece fell, his chair wobbling before falling on its side. Reece coughed several times before craning his head to glare up at Fallon.

"I don't know what she sees in you. You're not her normal type at all."

Fallon bared his teeth at the man on the ground and chuckled. It was the laugh of a dragon faced with someone so far beneath him that he couldn't even be classified as a threat anymore. Reece would have to work harder if he wanted to get to Fallon. It didn't matter if he was Shea's type or not. She was his, and he was hers. The end. What came before was unimportant. Besides, it wasn't like he'd been a monk before he'd met her.

Reece eyed him warily. "Didn't work, huh? Perhaps you're smarter than you look."

Fallon reached down and set the chair and Reece upright. "Start talking. My patience for you is wearing thin. Once it's gone, my men will kill you and put your body somewhere no one but the beasts will find it. We'll tell Shea you went back home."

"She'll know. They'll send others until they get what they want."

Fallon cocked an eyebrow and shrugged. "By then, our bond will not be so easily broken."

Reece sighed and tilted his head back to look up at the canvas. Fallon watched with interest. It was a trait Shea had demonstrated on more than one occasion—usually when she was frustrated or had to consider a problem. Perhaps it was a family trait. After a long minute, Reece tilted his head slightly and directed his eyes so he could see Fallon.

"The pathfinders want Shea to come home."

"No."

He sighed and kept going. "They want her to come home and bring you and your army with her."

Hmm. That was interesting. And unexpected.

"Why?"

Reece shrugged. "They didn't tell me that. I'm just a pawn—isn't that what you said?"

Fallon grabbed a finger of the other man's and twisted just far enough to put pressure on the joints but not enough to break it. "Why?"

"Because something's wrong!"

Fallon released the finger and stepped back. "Wrong how?"

"You've seen it. The mist. The beast attacks, aggressive beyond anything we've seen in generations. We've lost four settlements over the past three months. Established settlements that shouldn't have been destroyed so easily."

"And what is it that they're hoping Fallon will do for them?" Shea's cool voice came from the tent's entrance. She shot a look at Fallon before turning her attention back to Reece.

Caden sent a questioning look to Fallon, asking without words whether he wanted her removed. Fallon gave a slight shake of his head. No, he wanted to see what she'd do. Then he wanted to ask how she'd followed him.

"What do you think they want, Shea? They want his army. They want his help in beating back the beasts."

"That doesn't make sense, Reece. The guild never asks for help. Fallon and his army wouldn't be content to deal with the beasts and then leave the Highlands to go their merry way. They'll want payment. Why would the guild chance it?"

Reece sat back and shrugged. "Why don't you ask them for yourself?"

Shea made an angry sound of frustration.

Fallon leaned forward grabbing Reece's hand and bending it back at an unnatural angle. "We're asking you."

Reece glared into Fallon's eyes for a long minute. Whatever he saw there made him blanch and look away.

"This isn't like normal. When's the last time the mist reached this far into the Lowlands?"

"Not for centuries," Shea answered.

Witt looked interested in the conversation and stepped closer.

"Exactly. There's something at work here. Something the guild can't explain."

"That's a good excuse and all, but the guild has never bothered itself to care about the villages of the Highlands before unless their tithe went missing. What's the real reason?" Witt asked.

"That's not true," Reece said. "They care. They're just limited in what they can do."

Witt's snort made it clear what he thought of that response.

"They've faced this before," Shea said. "Why risk it?"

Reece's sigh was angry. "Because of you. Because of what you did. You woke something when you went into the Badlands, and now everything has been placed in jeopardy. This is your fault and it's your job to fix it."

Shea stared at him, her face paling in shock. "That's not true." She shook her head and took a step back. "That's not possible. We barely made it past the first demarcation. There's no way we caused this."

Reece's shrug was tired. "I don't know what to tell you. Everything I've seen or been told says the problem originated in the Badlands and it's just getting worst. If you don't want another cataclysm on your hands, you'll do what you can to help. Go home, Shea. Bring your friends, because you're certainly going to need them."

Shea had a stunned and broken expression on her face. The fight had run out of her.

"Keep him alive," Fallon ordered Caden. "I'll want to speak to him again."

"Understood."

Fallon took Shea by the arm and walked her out of the interrogation room. She didn't say anything to protest, letting him lead her where he would. He noted with grim satisfaction that Trenton stood in a pool of shadows next to the tent and Wilhelm was a silent presence across the way. He'd have words for them later, but their severity would be mitigated by the fact that they'd remained with her.

The walk to their quarters was silent and seemed much longer than normal. Fallon was content with the silence, not wanting their words to be overheard by any of his men. He had questions and Shea was going to answer them for once. He'd let her get away with some of her non-answers regarding the Highlands and the pathfinders' guild, understanding what it meant to be loyal. He liked that her loyalty wasn't something so easily replaced, but his patience with it had just run out.

*

Shea's mind whirled at the information Reece had given her, and the accusation that everything currently wrong could be laid at her feet. It was a ridiculous claim. Wasn't it?

Yes, it was. There was no way that expedition had managed to create this level of discordance. They'd never made it anywhere close to the Badland's heart, most of them dying before they'd even gone a week.

Still, something was wrong. The mist, the increased attacks, the frostling Shea had run into previously. All pointed to something being amiss.

They swept into their quarters. Fallon released her arm and made a beeline for the carafe of wine that was always kept filled. He poured himself a chalice and drank it down before pouring himself another.

Shea was too consumed by her own thoughts to notice immediately how agitated he was.

"Fallon, we need to talk about this. I think Reece is right. I need to go. I need to go back to the Highlands."

He slammed his cup down; she jumped as her widened eyes landed on him. He advanced on her, only stopping when she took a step back.

He eyed her with determination. "You're not going anywhere."

"You don't understand."

"I understand that the first time your precious pathfinders beckon, you hearken to their call like a dog to their master."

"That's not fair."

"Isn't it? Shea, half the time, you act like you'd rather be anywhere but here. You're always going on about becoming a scout again, but isn't that just an excuse to hide, to pretend that you're still one of them?"

She glared at him, her throat tight. "I want to be a scout because it's what I'm good at. It's your insecurities that keep me from it. Your fear that holds me back."

"There are other options than just being a scout. Why can't you see that?"

It was the same argument, just a different day. "You never asked what I wanted. You just assumed you knew what's good for me. Well, you don't. Only I do."

He shook his head, his face stubborn. "Not in my army you don't."

That was the kicker. Everything was his. Not theirs. Shea gritted her teeth. This wasn't important right now. What Reece had revealed was. "We're not going to agree on this."

"We don't have to. I've already made my decision. I'm not changing my mind."

Shea took a deep breath. "Reece brought up several good points. There is something wrong. The pathfinders might be able to help us."

"We've gotten by until now. No reason we can't continue doing so."

The sound that came from her throat was angry and full of frustration. "And you call me stubborn. Fallon, there are things in this world you don't understand. What you've seen so far is merely a pittance of what waits to be unleashed at the heart of the Badlands. If they're right and the heart is waking, it will be a second cataclysm. You said the last one drove your people from their homes. These lands were once populated with ten times the people. You could walk from one end of it to the next on great roads. The cataclysm changed all that. It destroyed everything. If there is a chance that it's happening again, we have to do all in our power to stop it."

Fallon shook his head. "All the more reason to stay out of it. I don't know these people and I certainly don't trust them. For all you know this is a trap. You've said before how ruthless they are."

"It's a chance I'll have to take."

"You're not going. That's final."

"Fallon," Shea protested to his back.

He shook his head and walked out of the tent before she could say more. Stubborn, stubborn man. This wasn't over.

Shea followed and was brought up short when Trenton stepped into her path with an apologetic look.

"Get out of my way."

"I'm sorry, Shea. The Warlord has given orders. You're to stay in the tent for now."

Shea's eyebrows climbed nearly to her hairline, and she stared at him with a shock that quickly turned to fury.

"Oh, did he?"

Trenton drew a deep breath. "Yes, and he's authorized us to use force if necessary."

Shea was quiet for a moment, her shock and anger filling her with ugly feelings that wanted to burst out. She couldn't let them. She needed to retain control.

"And you'd do as he asked?"

His nod was somber even as the look in his eyes were apologetic. "I would."

Shea looked away. There was a tight feeling behind her eyes and a prickling at the bridge of her nose.

"He is my Warlord," Trenton said in a soft voice.

She nodded, not saying anything for a long moment. When she'd gotten her emotions under control she looked him in the eye. "And here I thought we were becoming friends."

There was nothing to say to that. Shea turned and walked back into the tent, not acknowledging the soft apology that followed in her wake.

Back in the tent, she moved quickly through the communal area to the bed chamber. She went directly to a trunk at the foot of the bed, kneeling to open it. The trunk held most of Shea's things—clothes, odd knick-knacks she'd picked up here and there and wanted to keep, including the green jacket that was part of her scout uniform and a knife she'd stolen when she'd appropriated that jacket.

She plucked the knife out of its scabbard and stood. If Fallon thought he was going to keep her locked up in this tent, he had another thing coming. This wouldn't be the first time she'd escaped from one of these tents. Admittedly, last time she'd been fleeing because she'd thought her life was in danger, but this worked to.

She walked to the opposite side of the tent and set the knife against the canvas. She hesitated, her arm tensed to push the knife's point through to the other side. This was the action of a child. One who didn't get their way and threw a fit to punish everyone around them.

Her arm dropped. It would be so easy to vent her frustration by going on walkabout. So easy to disappear right from under their very noses. To punish Fallon for being an obstinate, stubborn and unreasonable man. That didn't mean it would be right. Just because you could do something didn't mean you should.

He was right. He had enemies that would love to take him down through Shea. Despite being in the middle of the encampment, it was still dangerous to be walking around at night. All sorts of beasts, both four legged and two, came out at this time. She was only lightly armed and tired.

Still, she didn't want Fallon to think he could get away with this kind of behavior. She was his partner. Not his prisoner. It was time he understood that.

She raised her arm and cut into the canvas. It was easier than the last time she'd done this—the knife sharper. She stepped through and looked around, half surprised no one had thought to put guards on the back of the tent given her history.

She shook her head and stepped back into the tent, going over to her bed and laying down. She didn't need to go anywhere. Her point had been made. Besides, her comfortable bed was right here.

*

"I must say I'm a little surprised you're still here." Darius's voice came from the broken partition. They would have to get that fixed before much longer. Shea was a little surprised it hadn't been already.

Darius stood a foot inside the personal quarters. He was alone and dressed simply.

Shea sat up. "What are you doing here?"

He shrugged and held up a bottle of wine. "I thought you could use the company, considering Fallon is pacing the camp like a wild animal."

Shea considered him through narrowed eyes. They were not friends. Darius had never gone out of his way to engage her before. When Fallon was gone and had left Darius in charge, she'd barely seen the other man. It made his presence here a tad suspicious.

He looked around and noticed the gaping hole Shea had cut in their tent. "I see I spoke too soon. Did you desire another entrance?"

Shea didn't answer, giving him a stone-faced stare.

He sighed. "Well, at least you're still here. That's something. Why don't you come out here so we can talk? I doubt Fallon would appreciate my presence in his private chambers with only his Telroi for company."

"You assume I care what he thinks right now."

"Of course, you care, or you would have taken the exit that you so diligently made and taken off into the night. Come, I have wine."

Darius didn't wait for her response, disappearing into the other room. There were small sounds of movement as he rustled around trying to find glasses.

Shea gave a heavy sigh and got up.

Darius had made himself at home in the short time Shea had taken to follow him. He reclined on one of the pillows that had a chair back attached. He'd nabbed two chalices from the long table and set them next to him on one of the low tables next to his pillow chair.

"Please. Help yourself." Sarcasm tinged her voice.

He gave her a lazy grin. "I always do."

Her huff held a note of laughter in it. She took a seat beside him and reclined into the backrest, nabbing the glass of wine. She took a sip and made a surprised expression of pleasure. It was pretty good. Much better than she would have thought. Probably from one of the south-eastern cities. She thought she remembered wine being one of their main exports.

"So. Why are you here?" Shea asked, cutting to the chase.

Darius took a sip and made a pleased expression. "Lowlanders are so different from us. They can't fight worth shit and they fear their very shadows, but they do make some amazing things, don't they?"

Shea gave a shrug of agreement. "They do seem to excel at the trades."

"What about your people? They have anything like this where you come from?"

Shea shrugged noncommittally. She didn't want to get into another discussion about the Highlands and what it had to offer. One of the reasons it had never been conquered was because most people were convinced there wasn't anything up there worth conquering. It was hard to go to all that trouble, if there wasn't going to be a reward worth having at the end of it.

"You do that well," Darius said, pointing his goblet at her.

"What?"

"Deflect. Pretend to be less than you are."

She gave him a questioning look, not quite understanding his point.

"When it comes to anything but your abilities with scouting, you downplay what you can do."

"I don't do that." That was ridiculous.

"Oh?" He took another sip of his drink as he studied her. "The beast board. Why haven't you taken more of an active role? More than scouting, that idea has the

151

greatest potential to effect real change by educating and training our soldiers in the dangers they face every time they step out of camp."

"That's Clark's thing. Him and Charles. They came up with that and they're doing a great job."

"They've asked for your help several times now."

"They don't need it. They're doing fine as is."

"That's your problem. Fine isn't good enough. You have a unique set of skills that we could take advantage of. I know you know that. Your work trying to prepare Eamon's men for the mist proves that. You're good at it too. Surprisingly so."

Shea didn't have a response to that, electing to take another sip of her wine.

"You're a leader who doesn't want the responsibility of leading," Darius said after a long pause.

Shea nearly choked on her wine. There were many things that could be laid at her feet. That wasn't one of them.

"How much of this wine have you had?" she asked Darius.

"Enough to know that I'm right. You'll see."

Shea peered at him from the corner of her eye. He didn't look drunk, but perhaps he hid it better than most.

"Fallon's changed since he met you," Darius said after a long silence. "You probably don't see it, but the rest of us do."

Shea set her goblet down and leaned back, fixing Darius with a long stare. They were finally getting to the reason he was here.

"What makes you say that?"

"There were plans to invade the Highlands immediately after we conquered the Lowlands." Darius's words were a boulder thrown into a still pond.

Shea went still, her heartbeat reverberating in her ears.

"He put that aside." Darius pointed his goblet at her. "For you. He wouldn't have done that before."

"How do you know? I thought you had decided that it was unconquerable because of Bearan's Fault."

Bearan's Fault was a string of cliffs hundreds of miles long. The Highlands sat on the shelf above the Fault and below them was the Lowlands. It was if some giant had ripped the two lands apart and then tried to tape them back together, the resulting pieces not quite lining up again.

Though they weren't unsurpassable, it would be next to impossible to get an entire army with supplies and horses up them without completely giving up any element of surprise. Such an endeavor would take weeks if not years.

"Not if we went through the Badlands." He gave her a sly smile. "But you knew that, didn't you?"

She knew much more than that, including a way through the cliffs that would allow Fallon to take his men and horses in half the time and half the danger.

"What's your point?"

"My point is that you've changed him. He's different now."

"Let's say you're right, and he is. Why are you telling me this?"

He shrugged and poured himself another glass. "Maybe I'm hoping you'll take pity and not take that exit you made. That you'll have patience with him. Change takes time. He might seem unreasonable and autocratic, but he has softened with you. More than any other person in this world."

"And do I just give him a pass in the meantime? Let him walk all over me. Keep me prisoner in the place we call home? How long do I give him to change?" Anger coursed through Shea's voice. He wasn't putting this all on her shoulders. She didn't know a lot about relationships, but she knew they were a partnership, each person responsible for the well-being of the whole. She couldn't do it on her own nor did she want to.

"No, of course not. Hold him responsible. Let him feel your anger. Just don't run away. Don't shut him out." This last was said with a meaningful look.

Shea flushed and looked away, knowing she was at fault for that last one. Had already fallen back on it the night before.

He made a slight huff of acknowledgement seeing his words had scored a point. "We're warriors and not often given to soft words, but he cares for you. Probably more than any other person in this world. All I'm asking is that you give him a chance to find his way back before you do anything drastic."

There was a small sound at the entrance of the tent. Shea looked up to find Fallon standing there, his eyes shadowed and his face expressionless.

Darius aimed a smile at Fallon and raised his cup. "We're drinking. Join us."

Fallon's eyes went to Shea and then back to Darius. He advanced, grabbing a goblet from the long table and then settling on a pillow across from Shea. Darius poured him some wine and sat back.

Shea sipped hers while avoiding looking at Fallon. She held herself stiff and straight.

"How many of our men do you think will have stories of this oasis tomorrow?" Darius asked. "Some of those women were eyeing us like they were preparing for a feast. I've never seen the like in Lowlanders. If I didn't know better, I would say there is Trateri blood in their past."

"The Airabel are few, and the isolation of their home and events in the past have led to the danger of inbreeding. They are most likely hoping your men can give them new bloodlines," Shea said.

Darius aimed an affronted look her way. "You mean they plan to use us as broodmares."

"In this instance, I think it would be more like stallions."

"Well, don't that just beat all. This land gets stranger and stranger all the time." He leaned forward. "Do they actually think we'd leave our children behind?"

Shea gave him a quizzical look.

Fallon answered her unspoken question. "The Trateri love children. Our lives are hard and dangerous. Every life is a precious gift. If my men were to sire children, they would take them with them when we left."

Shea shrugged. "Only if they knew about them ahead of time. They're betting that by the time the women show, your army will have moved on. It's unlikely that you'll be in this area again anytime soon, and by the time they circle back the women will have given birth and claimed their own people sired the children."

Both men stared at her with twin looks of distaste.

"I will let the men know to be careful with the women. We'll leave a detachment behind to keep an eye out for any births," Darius told Fallon.

Fallon shook his head. "Of all the things I thought we'd face, I never thought we'd be in danger of Lowlanders making off with our unborn children."

"It's an ever-changing world, my friend." Darius drained his wine and stood, leaving the half-finished bottle behind. "Well, I'm off."

Shea looked up, a little surprised at the abrupt departure. Fallon, with his typical granite facade, didn't even twitch. He took a slow sip of the wine and acknowledged Darius's departure with a nod.

"Before I go, I suggest you take a look at your personal chambers." With that last remark, Darius made his departure.

Fallon's head tilted as he stared into his wine. Suspicion dawned on his face and he stood, making his way to their personal quarters without a word. Shea let him go as she calmly sipped her wine.

Three, two, one.

There was a crash in the other room and a stream of curses reached her ears. She trained her eyes on the front entrance and was only mildly surprised when no one ventured in to see if they were in any danger. Darius must have warned them. Smart man.

"Would you like to explain why there is a new entrance to our bedchamber?" Fallon's silky voice came from behind Shea.

"You're smart. I'm sure you can figure it out." Shea took another sip of her wine.

He prowled closer, his movements containing a lethal edge.

"You were going to leave me." He sounded like the very idea that she would contemplate such an action enraged him.

She raised an eyebrow. "Now why would I want to do that?" She gave him a long minute to answer. His eyes narrowed, taking on a dangerous glint "Ah, yes. Perhaps that's because you treated me like a prisoner, having your guards keep me here whether I wanted to or not."

He looked away. She felt a spurt of grim satisfaction. He knew he was in the wrong.

"That was for your own safety."

"Bullshit. That was because you were angry and wanted to take it out on me." She waited for him to correct her. When he didn't, she continued, "I'm here because I want to be here. The next time you do something like that, expect me to be gone."

She set her glass down and stood. Shea walked past an unmoving Fallon to their chamber, saying over her shoulder, "I suggest you station one of your men at our new entrance so that we're not murdered in our sleep by one of your many enemies."

CHAPTER FOURTEEN

Shea woke to an empty bed. Again. She rested one hand on the indent from Fallon's body before rolling over and facing in the other direction. It had been several days since their argument, and neither of them had made any effort to make amends. Their exchanges had devolved into a series of icy greetings.

She'd busied herself with helping Clark and Charles and their beast classes. Something she enjoyed more than she wanted to admit. They had taken her proposal of teaching tracking and recognizing the different signs of beasts to the next level. The class size had doubled in a few short days and they were having to put people on waiting lists.

Shea knew that would change once patrols started back up in full force. A few had been sent out, but Fallon hadn't lifted all restrictions yet.

She heaved herself to her feet and shuffled over to her trunk, pulling out a clean set of the scout uniform she'd taken to wearing when she taught. It was really just a pair of pants and a linen shirt missing any patches that would have signified her unit, division and clan.

She ducked out of the tent, using the entrance she had made in her fit of anger. Wilhelm waited for her. He gave her an easy smile and handed her a roll filled with spicy meat, the Trateri's version of a quick breakfast. The smell tantalized, causing her mouth to water and her stomach to rumble.

"Here, I thought you might need this since you always skip breakfast," Wilhelm said.

Shea grunted. Her relationship with her guards had been damaged by that night, and she wasn't quite willing to forgive them for following Fallon's orders. She accepted their presence, but she made no attempt at friendly overtures. The same couldn't be said of them.

"Are you heading for the beast class again today?" Wilhelm asked, falling into step beside her.

She nodded, her mouth full of the roll he'd brought her.

"What's the name of that beast you were talking about yesterday? The one with three horns?"

"A trihorn boar."

The trihorn boar got its name from its three horns, two on its forehead and one on its nose. It had a muscular body and easily reached to Shea's waist. It was carnivorous and extremely aggressive when its territory was threatened. It also hunted in packs.

"Yes, that's the one."

"What about it?"

"How big did you say those packs were?"

Shea shrugged. "It depends. Most are between ten or fifteen, but I've seen packs of twenty before."

"And they eat people?"

"They can, but we're not their main prey. They're very territorial and will attack anything that trespasses, including people."

"That is very interesting."

Not really. It was actually pretty typical of a beast.

They continued for several steps, each left to their own thoughts.

"You haven't shown up for training for the last few days," Wilhelm said after a moment.

Ah, there it was. The reason for his questions. Shea had been wondering when that was going to be brought up.

"I've been busy."

"Be that as it may. That training is just as important as the instruction you give in the beast classes. You should make time for it."

Shea didn't respond, choosing silence as her answer.

Wilhelm didn't let that deter him. "It would also go a long way towards making amends with Trenton."

This time Shea couldn't help her snort. "It is not my job to make amends with you two. Fallon has decreed that I have to have guards, so I have them. I do not need to be friends with either of you, and your emotional well-being is none of my concern."

"You know he had no choice but to follow Fallon's orders," Wilhelm said softly.

Shea stopped and turned to face him. "Perhaps not. However, he made it quite clear that Fallon—and only Fallon holds his loyalty. That's fine, both of you are Anateri. I know that means something to you, and I can respect that. You do your job, and I'll do mine."

Shea meant every word she said. She understood that their first duty was to their Warlord. That was fine. She'd been the one to confuse matters by thinking they had a quasi-friendship going. That was on her. She wouldn't make that mistake again.

They'd arrived at the place where she would conduct her class for the day. She gave Wilhelm a nod before turning and heading to the front of the class, picking up a list so she could note the names of those in attendance. Wilhelm let her go without trying to engage her again.

"Alright, let's get started," she told the men and women assembled. "Yesterday we went over what trail sign to look for to track a trihorn boar. Today, we're going a little deeper into the forest and you're going to practice looking at their tracks. Any questions?"

A woman raised her hand. Shea gestured for her to speak.

"When are we going to learn about the mist?"

Shea heaved an internal sigh. That question had been asked in every class she'd taught. "That's a different class. Your division leader needs to recommend you for placement. Any other questions."

There were a few rumblings, but no one else raised their hand. Good.

*

Fallon stifled his impatience with his council, which was made up of the various clan heads that were in camp. The clan leaders and their betas for Horse, Lion, Earth, Rain, and Ember were all present. Rain and Ember were clans who had recently made the long journey from the Outlands to join the rest of the clans.

He'd had reports that their members were causing minor disruptions throughout camp and had been less than willing when their warriors had been assigned to the other divisions. There had already been several fights that had landed the offenders on punishment duty.

"All I'm saying is there is no reason to sit here and do nothing," Joseph, the beta for Rain, said. The rest of the clans looked disgruntled that a beta was being so outspoken in a formal session. Normally only the heads spoke. The betas were there simply to know what was going on in case they ever had to step into the position of leader.

"You and your clan have not been here the past few months," Henry, the leader of Horse clan, explained. "You do not understand the deeper strategy or the dangers afoot. Your plan would see many deaths."

"We're Trateri, not Lowlanders. We do not let fear of death dictate our actions," the clan leader of Ember said. Zeph was a tall man with dark skin and dark eyes. He was one of the few Trateri to grow a beard. He was also known for his skill with bow and arrow and spear. His people were great hunters in their homelands and were second only to the Earth clan in creating weapons. "Your time here has made you soft, old friend."

"There is a difference between courage and foolhardiness," Fallon said before there could be any more argument. "Every hunter learns their prey and its habits before they strike. It is the same concept here. You are used to fighting the south-eastern cities. This is a different scenario, one that requires patience and learning a different set of tactics."

Ben spoke, his eyes solemn. "Our enemy here is not the Lowlanders. We lose more men to beasts than we do in battle."

Zeph grimaced. "There is no honor in such a death."

Many in Fallon's army agreed. It was causing dissent. The forced inactivity was making the discontent more vocal. Fallon needed to give them a direction for their frustration.

"My people are getting restless with all this sitting around and doing nothing," Van said. He lounged in his chair with all the grace of a feline.

"What about a tournament?" Henry's face was thoughtful.

That could work. It would give his soldiers an outlet and let them compete against each other for the glory of their clans.

The other clan leaders looked like they were considering the idea.

"There could be a prize for the winner," Ben said. "My blacksmiths have several expert caliber swords that could be offered up."

"Perhaps a prize from all the clans depending on the event," Zeph said.

There were several murmurs of agreement.

"This still does not solve our problems," Gawain said. He was the head of Rain, a short man that had a permanent scowl of dissatisfaction on his face.

Van's exhale was angry. "All Rain seems capable of is complaining. Perhaps he is afraid that the months that he languished in the Outlands have made his people soft while the rest of us were conquering the Lowlands."

Gawain glared at the other man. It was a sore point to him, since the clans who remained behind would not share in the war spoils. Those who had followed Fallon had reaped the rewards in tithes and would continue to do so now that the Lowlands were all but conquered. It was why Rain and Ember were so vocal about invading the Highlands.

"I don't see why we haven't made our move on the Highlands," Gawain said. "We've captured one of theirs. From what I've heard, they all but gave us an engraved invitation."

Fallon's body went still, and his eyes narrowed to dangerous slits. Darius stiffened beside him.

"And where did you hear that?" Fallon's voice was silky as he leaned forward, every muscle in his body tensed to pounce. This was the Warlord speaking, and every one of them knew it as they looked at him with guarded expressions.

Gawain's face was tight, but he didn't back down. "Are you saying it's not true?"

Fallon tapped his finger on his thigh, considering very carefully what tactic he wanted to take with this. Loyalty was a fickle thing. Doubly so when dealing with the clans. He had the backing of the soldiers and many in the lower castes. However, the clan heads and their betas were used to power. Some were with him because they wanted a reprieve from the infighting and thought consolidating the powerbase would keep them in their positions longer and prolong their life. That didn't mean they wouldn't turn on him at the first opportunity. How long could he hold the Trateri without their backing?

"I do not answer to you," Fallon said. He looked at each clan head in turn. "To any of you. Your presence here is at my discretion. When I have news that I think pertains to you, I will share it. Until then, attend to your people. Rain and Ember— you are new to this camp, yet your people have caused many problems since arriving. I would be careful if I were you not to become too big of a nuisance. You would not want what happened to Snake clan to be repeated."

More than one person looked away from Fallon. News of what he'd done to that clan had become a cautionary tale. Their leader had sought to assassinate Fallon and had even come close a time or two. When he'd caught up with her, he'd returned the favor and then executed her and all of her advisors. The rest of the clan, he'd disbanded. Some became outcasts, forced to the edges of their society where they still struggled to eke out a living.

Fallon stood, his point made. He might need the council's good will but he wouldn't be controlled by it.

"Henry, since the tournament was your idea, I'll leave the planning to you," Fallon said. The more he thought about it, the more he liked the idea of a tournament, of a chance to pit the skills of his men against each other. He might even find time to join in on the events.

*

"Shea, Shea," Clark's voice called over the crowd. Shea looked up to find his curly hair bobbing up and down as he jumped and waved to her. He was shorter than most of the men surrounding him and disappeared as soon as he landed, only to pop back up again.

"He's certainly an energetic guy," Trenton observed with a wry voice next to her. He'd relieved Wilhelm at the midday meal.

They'd stopped at one of the cooks' campfires to pick up something to eat before the afternoon classes that Shea was teaching on the mist. Daere was supposed to join them shortly, as was fast becoming her habit.

Shea ignored his comment and focused on Clark's arrival. The younger boy looked excited as he finally made it to them.

"Did you two hear? There's going to be an all-clan tournament in three days."
Trenton whistled. "We haven't had one of those since we began this campaign."
"What's an all-clan tournament?" Shea asked.

"It's a series of contests designed to test the different skills of a warrior,"
Trenton explained.

"But anybody can compete. Even an Outclan can compete. The only requirement
is that you are Trateri. Some compete to gain recognition. A lot of the mentors will
pick an apprentice based on how they do in the different skill sets."

"So, the throwaways can't compete," Shea said. Figured. For all Fallon's
speeches on how he wanted to unite the Broken Lands, it was still very much the
Trateri against everyone else.

Clark's brow furrowed as he frowned. "We haven't had an all-clan since we took
on the throwaways. I wonder if they'll modify the rules so they can take part."

"They probably wouldn't acquit themselves well even if they competed," Trenton
said. His gaze was fastened on Shea as if he was expecting a rise out of her.

Shea lifted an eyebrow. Nice try, but she wasn't that easy.

Clark ignored Trenton. "That's not even the best part. Every division gets to
come up with three events. Eamon's asked us to put together an event."

Shea stared at him with a blank expression. That's it? She didn't get why he was
so excited by this.

He rolled his eyes at her lack of enthusiasm. "Do you know what an honor this
is? The event planners are nearly as famous as those who win the events. This is our
chance to put the beast class on the map for the other divisions. If we plan
something that they remember, they might consider implementing our model in
their own divisions."

"Hm." Shea still didn't get it since it sounded like a pain in the ass to her, but
she was happy for him anyway. "Sounds like you and Charles have a lot of work to
do."

"Not just us; you're part of the team too. We couldn't do this without you." He
put a hand out. "Unless you wanted to compete. In which case, you couldn't take
part in the planning. That might work even better. This way you can prove you're
the best."

Shea's eyes widened and she was shaking her head before he'd even finished.
"No, I don't think so. I'll help you plan, but competing isn't really my thing."

"I'm going to tell Charles the good news. He's going to be stunned." Clark didn't
wait for their goodbyes, hustling off in search of his friend.

Shea turned back to her food, noting with a frown that Trenton was resting his
chin on his hand and grinning at her. He fluttered his eyes at her when he noticed
her attention.

"Not even a Trateri a full year and you already have followers."

161

"Clark's my friend."

He made a hmm sound that failed to denote agreement.

"What?"

"I see through you. For someone who likes to pretend they're an outsider, you sure have a lot of friends in your corner. Not everybody gets asked to design an event. The Trateri take their tournaments very seriously. It's one of the few activities we can gather for without intentionally shedding blood but still compete for the honor of our clans."

Shea took a bite of her food.

"And this is something Fallon didn't give you either. You got it all on your own merit," he observed.

Shea looked at him in question.

"If you were wondering, that is."

She hadn't been, but she was now. Just how much of her life was Fallon responsible for? Was he the reason Clark and Charles were so interested in having her help with the Beast Board? And despite Trenton's assertion, was he the reason they were getting this chance?

She took a slow bite of her food. It was something to think about.

*

Shea walked towards the tent she shared with Fallon with a slight limp, looking forward to washing off the thin coating of grime she was carrying around. One of the classes had startled a pair of wylde pigs, the slightly smaller cousin of the trihorn boar; Shea had played decoy while they brought the pigs down. Unfortunately, not before one had rammed her leg, leaving a nice sized bruise.

Trenton had not been happy when he found out. He may have even cast aspersions on Shea's intelligence and muttered about hard-headed women who didn't know their limits, before he stalked off after leaving her in front of her tent.

One little bruise and he was acting like a child. He'd left worse injuries on her during some of their training sessions.

Shea gave the two guards a resigned nod, not registering their surprise at her acknowledgement. Wilhelm and Trenton hadn't been the only two to suffer from her withdrawal. The rest of the Anateri had been treated to the same remoteness.

She limped inside the tent and drew up short, noticing that Fallon and several men were seated around the table discussing plans. They quieted at the sight of her, and she found herself the center of attention.

"Oh, I didn't realize you were busy. I can come back," Shea offered.

Henry stood, aiming a friendly smile her way. Shea hadn't realized he was there until now. "Nonsense, our matter is unimportant, and we were almost finished anyway."

Shea looked at Fallon in question. She really hadn't meant to interrupt.

He nodded, his face guarded and remote. "Henry's right. This can be continued later."

Taking that as their dismissal, the rest of the group filed past Shea and out of the tent. Henry was the last to go. There was a slight hitch to his gait as he moved towards her.

He patted her on the shoulder as he reached her. "He's a difficult man, but I think you'll find the rewards worth it in the end."

Shea gave him a confused look as Henry chuckled and made his exit, leaving Fallon and Shea alone for the first time since their argument.

Fallon busied himself, pouring another glass of wine as Shea moved closer.

"I really am sorry to have interrupted. If I'd known, I would have waited," Shea said, feeling awkward. She hated the distance she could feel between them, but she didn't know how to bridge it.

"It's fine. This is your home too. You should never feel that you have to wait to enter it."

He poured her a glass of water and slid it her way. She took it and sipped, relishing the cool feeling as it hit her parched throat.

"I hear there's an all-clan tournament," she ventured.

He arched an eyebrow. "Do you know why they're excited for one?"

She shook her head ruefully, "Not a clue. Clark couldn't wait to tell me, but I have no idea what the hubbub was about."

Fallon chuckled and Shea felt the weight on her shoulders lighten. "An all-clan is rare. It's a holdover from when we were divided. When one was called, any clan in attendance declared a truce with the rest of the clans."

Made sense. No one would want to show up for a tournament if they would face an ambush at the end of it. Of course, with the Trateri, that might have been part of the fun.

"It was a chance to gather and pit their skills against one another without bloodshed." He thought a moment and then revised that statement. "Without much bloodshed. Now, it's a way for young warriors to showcase their skills in the hopes of raising their status or securing a position in my elite units. The clans also stake their pride on the outcome."

"Eamon's asked Clark and Charles if they would design an event."

Fallon looked surprised. "That's a pretty big complement. The organizers are very particular about who they allow to arrange the individual events since all are open to anyone who wishes to compete."

Shea shrugged. "Clark seemed to be very excited about it."

"He should be. They don't let just anyone help. Will you be involved?"

"He seemed to think I would be. Not too sure though."

His gaze sharpened on her. "Why?"

She lifted one shoulder. "I've never been to one of these. I wouldn't know the first place to start, and shouldn't the credit go to a Trateri?"

He scowled. "You are Trateri."

She looked away and shrugged again.

He took a deep breath. "Do your people ever have tournaments like this?"

Shea thought about it. "I don't think so. They're mostly focused on training. Once an apprentice passes the last test, they're assigned to a village or their next posting. It can be years before they circle back to the keep again." She tilted her head. "Some of the towns have festivals where there are occasional competitions, like who can toss a rock the farthest."

Shea had never been very interested in attending those, not understanding the interest in comparing whose throw had the longest reach.

"There are events like that, but most test a skill. My favorites have always been hand-to-hand combat or tests of horsemanship."

Shea would have liked to see him compete in one of those. "And how many of these have you won?"

He gave her a wicked smile. "Every single one."

She lifted an eyebrow. "Every one? Even your first?"

"I'm a legend. Haven't you heard?"

She snorted. "You're something all right."

He had a crafty expression on his face when he asked, "Shall I prove it?"

She tapped her glass with one finger as she considered him.

He leaned forward, setting his wine aside. "Let's make things even more interesting with a bet. I win, and you owe me a boon."

"Fine, but turnabout is fair play. If you lose, you owe me one."

"Deal." He held his glass out for her to toast.

"Alright, deal."

They drank to seal the deal.

Fallon finished his with a long gulp. "It's too bad you'll be considered an organizer and ineligible to compete. I would have liked to have seen you victorious."

Shea's drink went down the wrong pipe kicking off a storm of coughing. "In what event? There's nothing I could beat the Trateri at."

"I don't know. You have shown a surprising resourcefulness over these past few months. I'm sure you could have brought my men to their knees."

His statement struck her as funny, Shea snorted and threw her head back to laugh. "In what world are you living? Have you not seen me these last few months practicing with Trenton? Last week I nearly fell off my mount. I make toddlers seem skilled."

He pointed at her with his glass. "You forget these tournaments test more than just skill with a weapon. They're designed to test your mind and body and mental fortitude. There will be endurance courses, even navigation courses. Also, Trenton is considered elite. You can't judge your skills by his. Most of my soldiers would have similar difficulties. You are better than you believe."

"Hm." Shea wasn't quite convinced.

"I have faith in you. I will be here to push you until you have the same belief in yourself," he told her.

She gave him a sideways look before dropping her eyes and taking a sip of her drink. He lifted an arm. She shifted over, turning her back and leaning against him.

Fallon pressed a kiss on the side of her forehead. "My world is grey and cold when you're not in it."

"Mine too."

CHAPTER FIFTEEN

I still think we should be spending this time going over last-minute preparations," Charles complained.

"Shush your worrying. We've already gone through things ten times," Clark said. "The Warlord is riding. He hasn't competed in years. This might be our last time seeing him."

Shea ignored the exchange, watching the contenders on the field. Evidently, Fallon's inclusion in the race was a bigger deal than she had previously thought. Since news of his entry, the audience for the event had swelled to four times the size of other events.

Even the Airabel villagers had turned out, lining the branches and rope bridges above the audience. Shea had offered to take Clark and Charles up there where the view was undoubtedly better but had been refused. Emphatically. Both men had looked at her like she was crazy, so she'd dropped it. She kind of regretted that now, with the press of Trateri on all sides.

Fallon, like the rest of the competitors, was barechested, his hair knotted back from his face, with a streak of black darkening his eyes and temples. He looked over at Shea and smiled, the expression causing some of the women around her to titter in a way she hadn't heard since she lived in Birdon Leaf. She knew that sound. It was the sound of women admiring a good-looking man that they would like to have. A man that was Shea's.

This feeling of possessiveness was new to her. She didn't know if she liked it or the accompanying jealousy.

"What are they doing?" Shea asked as two riders lined up on either side of the field.

The riders began a slow trot toward one another. In the next moment, the horses opened up to a full-on gallop, thundering headlong towards each other. The riders leaned over, one managing to get his hand around the other's foot and yanked, unseating his opponent. The man crashed to the ground and rolled, arms up to protect his head.

A thunderous roar of approval came from the crowd as the victor rode past, his arms held high above his head as he whooped.

Shea's mouth was open as she stared wide-eyed as the next pair squared off. "Please tell me I didn't just see that."

"I don't know what you're so upset about. This is pretty tame so far. Once they get past the qualifying rounds, it gets a lot more violent," Charles said, his face bored.

She turned to look at the other two with wide eyes. "How do you not consider this violent? If he'd fallen under the horse, he would have been trampled."

Clark nodded. "That is a danger. There are rules to keep the competitors from targeting each other like that, but it happens by accident every once and a while."

"And you still do this?" Shea couldn't help the way her voice rose at the end.

The two looked at each other, their expressions saying they didn't understand why she was so aghast. They looked back at her and nodded.

"Why?" she asked with wide eyes. "That is the action of a crazy person."

She looked back at Fallon. What kind of madman would do this? What kind of madman would do this after making a bet? Why had she agreed to the bet?

Her palms started sweating and her stomach roiled. If he died, it would be because of that stupid bet. She leaned her head against the wooden fence the Trateri had erected to keep the audience from swarming the field.

"Shea, what's wrong?" Clark asked.

"She just realized exactly what Fallon volunteered himself for." Eamon's voice came from overhead.

"There's nothing to be worried about, Shea," Clark assured her. "He's competed in this event many times and always walked away with only minor injuries."

That did not make her feel more comfortable.

"Give it up, boy. You're not going to talk sense into her. This is something you only understand with time and when you have a stake in the outcome," Eamon told him. He clapped Shea on the back. "Steady on, lass. You wouldn't want any of these layabouts seeing you flinch, would you?"

Shea raised her head. No one was looking at her now, but if she kept it up long enough, she would soon draw attention. Daere would have her head if gossip spread that the Warlord's Telroi cowered during these tournaments.

As soon as she looked, she wished she could duck and hide again. Fallon was up. He waited until she looked his way before raising a fist in salute. She dawned a cool expression and gave him a regal nod.

His opponent said something that had Fallon's face darkening. They split apart and took their spots on either side of the field. Fallon picked the side that faced Shea.

He sat still as the call was given. His opponent exploded into movement, his horse racing furiously down the field as Fallon waited, arms crossed over his chest and a stony expression on his face.

"What's he doing?" Clark asked. "He needs to build up momentum or his opponent will barrel right into him."

A pair of forearms landed on the fence next to Shea. Trenton watched the action with an intent expression. "Watch carefully."

Shea did.

Fallon waited until his opponent reached a third of the way down the field. He dropped his arms. Between one second and the next his mount lunged into a full-fledged gallop, its hooves churning up the dirt as it strained for every ounce of speed. In an almost lazy movement, Fallon leaned over, hooked his opponent's foot, and yanked—sending the other man crashing to the ground.

The crowd roared, their sound drowning out the small prayer that Shea offered up.

Fallon's reined his horse to a stop next to his opponent who had gain his feet and stood looking around with disbelief. Blood ran from a cut on his forehead. Fallon leaned over, touching the wound with two fingers as he said something to his opponent. He didn't wait for a response as he touched his heels to the horse's sides and sent it trotting toward Shea and her companions. Clark bounced up and down, nearly giddy with delight.

Fallon's eyes were somber, though they held a small piece of wickedness as he rode up to Shea. She tilted her head to look up at him. The crowd had fallen silent, just the two of them staring at each other.

Fallon leaned forward and smeared his hand down her cheek and neck. His teeth flashed white and he let out a war holler as he gave his horse a signal that had it rearing onto its hind legs before it hit the ground running.

The crowd roared, the sound deafening under the forest's canopy. It took a moment before Shea realized they were chanting "Hawkvale" over and over again, the words almost indistinguishable in the din.

She touched her cheek. Her fingers came away with red.

"Is that blood?"

Eamon understood her despite the noise. He nodded.

"It's considered an honor to be anointed with the blood of his enemy."

"This is just a competition, right?"

Eamon shrugged. "To a Trateri, every opponent is an enemy."

Shea gaped up at him. She had blood on her. There was actual blood on her skin that her Warlord had put there, and Eamon was talking to her about enemies and honor.

"You people are a little crazy," she said. "I mean, gone 'round the bend–not coming back-crazy."

He shrugged. Then he nodded. "You're the one who picked us."

She scoffed. "We remember things very differently. I seem to remember a certain someone grabbing me by the arm and telling me I was late."

Eamon's smile flashed before he gave a whoop as one of the contestants accomplished a daring feat.

"You could have left at any time. In fact, I seem to remember at one point you did leave."

Shea shoulders rounded until they almost touched her ears. "Yeah, but someone had to go and get themselves almost eaten by a shadow beetle, didn't they?"

Buck's hands landed on Shea's shoulders. "And I for one am very glad you came back to distract that beetle."

"When'd you get back?" Eamon asked him.

Shea looked back at him in question. She hadn't realized his team were one of the few who'd picked up patrols again.

"Last night. There are some freaky, scary things out there right now." Both men's faces turned a little grim.

"Did you turn your report in already?"

"Hm." Buck made a sound of affirmation. "Your annoying assistant is already going over it and making copies to be distributed among the command teams."

"Good, I'll want to review it with you tonight."

"Perhaps after I've enjoyed myself a little." Buck gave Eamon a roguish grin as his eye caught that of a Trateri woman with a heart-shaped face next to them.

Eamon waved his hand, letting Buck go. He wasted no time in pursuing the other woman, whose smile at the sight of him heading her way put the rest of them in no doubt how Buck's night was going to end.

The contestants on the field had narrowed to half their original size. Several Trateri walked onto the field dragging large items.

"What are they doing?" Shea asked.

"They're setting up obstacles. The second round is a little different than the first. They still have to unseat their opponent, but now they have to do it while dodging the items in their path."

Yes, because it just wasn't dangerous enough before. Crazy barbarians.

Charles pushed away from the fence. "We have to leave to get setup for our event."

Clark protested. "Just a few more rounds."

Charles looked hesitant, the pull of watching the Hawkvale compete just as much of a temptation as it was for his friend. His jaw firmed. "We need to make our final arrangements. The Wind Division commander showed his trust in our abilities. We can't let him down now."

Charles gave Eamon a nod of acknowledgement. Eamon pressed his lips together as if he was fighting to hide a grin.

Charles pulled Clark away, giving Shea and Eamon a determined look.

"I'll catch up in a few minutes," Shea told him as he left.

"If you must," he told her, leaving before she could say anything in response.

"Grumpy," Eamon said, looking after Charles and Clark. "He's probably just stressed about things going well today."

"It was nice of you to give them that opportunity," Shea told Eamon.

He shrugged off her words. "It wasn't me. I did offer their names as an option, but it was the elders who picked. What you all are doing is resonating with a lot of people."

Shea was glad he hadn't given them the opportunity just because of their previous relationship.

"You should watch this event until the end," Eamon said. "You want to see who wins the bet, right?"

Shea's jaw dropped and she hissed, "How do you know about that?"

Trenton straightened from his position next to them. "Everyone knows about that. It's the talk of camp."

Eamon chuckled as Shea's face turned beet red. "Don't worry. I'm sure he'll go easy on you when he wins."

"You're so sure he'll win?" Shea asked with an arched eyebrow.

He shrugged. "Of course. He's the Warlord."

"And about ten years older than the rest of the competitors," Shea said with a challenging expression. She should have known better. It was what had led to the ill-placed bet with Fallon.

"Not everything is about age," Trenton said, waggling his eyebrows. "Sometimes experience wins the field."

The crowd roared as Fallon unseated his opponent in a graceful movement at odds in such a big man.

Trenton leaned close. "I think he's a little more motivated than usual."

Shea blushed. Her color deepened when Fallon threw her a darkly significant look. Next time she would have to be more careful with her challenges. They always seemed to get her in trouble with this group.

*

Shea moved through the crowds as quickly as the press of bodies would allow. She vibrated with impatience, as she waited for an elderly woman accompanied by a child to move out of her way. She'd stayed later than she should have, watching Fallon compete. He'd won, to the surprise of no one but Shea.

The bet was lost. She owed him a boon. Shea could only imagine what he would request, the tricky warlord. To top it off, she was now late for the event she'd helped plan. The slow-moving crowd didn't help matters.

A pair of grubby hands tugged at her pant legs. Shea looked down into a pair of bright blue eyes and a gap-toothed smile belonging to a sweet looking girl. One that was wearing a thin, threadbare shirt, and holding a bright yellow flower up to Shea.

"Is that for me, sweetheart?" Shea asked with a smile. It was hard not to be charmed by the little girl.

The urchin child nodded and offered it again.

Shea felt in her pockets, hoping for something to give the child, who looked no more than four or five. Shea hadn't seen overt signs of poverty among the Trateri. The clans, for all the feuding and infighting they brought, looked after their own. If a child was orphaned, they were absorbed into the clan and provided for. Same when someone lost a partner. She knew of no instances where someone had been turned out, not to say that there weren't any. This child looked like she hadn't bathed in weeks, and her clothes looked like they were one strong wind from disintegrating.

"I have nothing to give you," Shea admitted.

The girl's face drooped in disappointment, the expression tugging at Shea's heart. She looked at Trenton for help. Her guard avoided her eyes and scratched his neck. Shea frowned at him. Useless man. Always around when he wasn't needed, and absolutely worthless when he was.

She looked back at the little girl and held up her wrist. "Do you like my bracelet?"

The girl looked at it and nodded.

"How 'bout we trade then? My bracelet for the flower."

The girl gave Shea a gap-toothed grin full of innocence and nodded.

"Shea, that bracelet is valuable," Trenton said, his expression uneasy.

"All the more reason she should have it. Maybe it'll bring her good fortune." Shea pulled the bracelet off and handed it to the little girl. She thanked her when the little girl handed her the flower.

The little girl took the bracelet and petted it. She oohed and awed over it and ran her fingers along the graceful lines, before looking back up at Shea.

"Goodbye, thank you for my flower," Shea said. She began walking away even as the little girl's eyes tugged at her heart. She didn't make it far before a small hand slid into hers and Shea looked down to find the little girl hurrying to keep pace with her little legs.

"No, no, sweetheart. You need to stay here where your mother and father can find you."

The little girl looked up at Shea and cocked her head, not seeming to understand. Shea looked at Trenton again for help. He looked back at her and shrugged. No help there.

"Mist is alone in this world." Gala shuffled toward Shea and Trenton, her arms clasped behind her back. "From what I understand, she has been mute since her parents died. There is no one for her to wait for."

"Elder Gala." Shea inclined her head to the other woman.

The girl child, Mist, let go of Shea's hand and ran to Gala. She danced around in front of her while holding up the bracelet for the other woman to see.

Gala bent down and made the appropriate sounds of appreciation. "That's a fine bracelet you have there." Gala looked up at Shea. "One would even say the giver was very generous."

Shea looked away and gave a shrug.

Gala stood up and observed Shea with canny eyes. The kind that saw right through a person down to their very core. Shea had never been very fond of people who could do that. There were too many things she wanted to keep to herself, keep hidden.

"I've got to get going. My event starts soon," Shea said, giving an excuse for her hurry that also happened to be true.

"Yes, you and the other two responsible for the beast board are in charge of the hunt, if I recall."

"That is right." Shea didn't ask how Gala knew. The other woman struck Shea as the sort to know everything about everyone around her.

"That is an unusual honor to be given to a group so young and untested."

So Shea had gathered. It made her wonder just why her little team had been chosen.

"I will walk with you as far as your staging area," Gala said. Before Shea could protest, she looked down at Mist. "Shall we?"

The little girl nodded enthusiastically before looking at Shea with bright, excited eyes. Shea didn't have it in her to deny that face.

She mustered an uneasy smile for the two, then turned and set off, keeping her pace slow so her companions could keep up. Mist rambled in front of them as Gala walked with a measured pace beside Shea.

"You have not attended the last two sharies," Gala observed.

A sharie was a meeting attended by many of the elders in the clans. Usually each clan held their own sharie every month. She'd made it a point to be busy doing something else the last few times one had been called.

"Yes, I've been very busy of late with the Hawkvale's return and planning for this event."

Gala gave her a sideways look that said she knew exactly how much of an excuse that was. "When I was your age, I also found it difficult to attend the sharie as well. So many people looking to me for answers when I had none."

Shea felt a tinge of surprise. "I thought most who attended were elders."

That was what she had seen. She was the youngest by several decades in those gatherings.

Gala made a sound of agreement. "I was like you, the Telroi to a powerful man. Do you know the purpose of a sharie?"

Shea thought a moment. "To share your grievances in a neutral setting."

"That is one purpose. The other is to have our grievances heard by our leaders."

"How is that? I've never seen the Hawkvale attend one."

Gala gave a graceful nod. "In the past, he would send one of his top advisors to hear our complaints."

"Daere?"

A smile tugged at Gala's lips as she confirmed Shea's guess. "Indeed. We may not speak to him directly, but he ensures that our voices are heard and acknowledged in one way or the other."

They walked several more feet in silence.

"And my presence helps with that?" Shea didn't see how. Fallon hadn't even been in the camp for the few sessions she attended. There was no possibility that she would have conveyed their messages to him. "How?"

"Every person in our clans contributes to its overall well-being and the greater Trateri people as a whole. We each have our role to play. The warriors, the craftsmen, the healers and hunters. Without just one of these roles, our society would collapse."

Shea could see that. Highlanders had similar roles, though they assigned worth to those roles. Merchants, and those that grew and harvested food, were often at the bottom of that tier. She still didn't see what that had to do with the sharie.

"I have found throughout my many years that a person needs to feel valued for their contributions. To do otherwise breeds resentment. That has no place in a clan. Those little feelings can grow into big ones that threaten a clan's safety and well-being."

"I understand. My people have a similar view."

"Would that be the pathfinders?"

Shea nodded. "The Highlanders have a similar structure to their society, but they often look down on those they see as performing less meaningful roles. There is often a schism in such instances. However, one village's ways are different than another's."

They were as varied in their beliefs and society as the Lowlanders. Perhaps more so because of the inherent isolation of the Highlands.

"I would find it interesting to visit with some of these Highland villages."

Shea didn't know about that. While she called the Highlands home, its people were hard and unwelcoming to strangers of any type.

"They see me as an extension of the Hawkvale," Shea said, trying to understand the meaning behind Gala's words.

"Very good. Perhaps there is hope for you yet."

They'd arrived to where Shea's friends had set up their event. Clark waved at her frantically from the outside of a large crowd.

"You should join your friends. The young one looks like he might burst out of his skin any moment," Gala said.

Shea looked at them and then back at Gala. She wanted to continue this conversation.

"We will talk later." Shea made the phrase an order rather than a question.

Gala inclined her head.

Shea turned to go and stopped when there was a tug on her pants. She looked down to find Mist standing behind her looking up at her with a worried expression.

"No sweetie, you can't come with me."

"Mist, stay here with Grandma Gala for now." Gala looked down at her with a kind expression.

Mist frowned unhappily but let go of Shea's pants. Her shoulders drooped as she wandered back to Gala.

Shea gave her a small wave before turning and heading for Clark.

"Are you ready for this?" Clark asked.

"Do I have a choice?"

He laughed. "Not at this point."

"Then I guess I'm ready."

Charles stepped up and waved for attention. "Excuse me. Excuse me, can I have your attention?"

The gathered Trateri continued to speak among themselves. Only a few noticed Charles's attempt at getting their attention and even those went back to their conversations when it was apparent the rest wouldn't quiet.

"Oi, the game master has spoken. Shut your gobs and pay attention." Trenton's shout made Shea jump.

Charles cleared his throat and nodded an acknowledgement of Trenton's help. Trenton stood back and folded his arms across his chest to fix the rest of the crowd with a glare. Faced with the wrath of one of Fallon's Anateri, the group quieted and turned their attention to Charles.

"Yes, well. Let me explain the rules. See the three white squares drawn on the ground. You'll be placed into one of those depending on how many answers to a set of questions you get right."

A set of hands went up. Their owners spoke before they could be called on. "Who decides the questions?"

"We do." Charles's answer was matter of fact.

"Who decides if we're correct?"

Shea lifted an eyebrow. Who did they think decided that?

Charles's answer was a little more tactful. "We do." He waited a beat to see if there were any more stupid questions. "As I said, you'll be placed into one of the three squares depending on your answers. There will be two 'beasts' that you'll chase once we release you from your square. One is a decoy and the other is your quarry." Charles gestured at Clark and Shea. They each lifted a hand to show they would be playing the beast. "Your objective is to follow the path they lay out and catch the beast. The first one to catch the correct beast wins."

"How do we know which is the real one?"

"They will be laying tracks down to indicate what beast they are. The other will lay down different beast signs. It will be your job to determine which is which."

There was a commotion from behind that distracted Charles from his explanation. Shea shifted so she could see better. Fallon, still clad as he was during his tournament event, stepped to the front of the group and folded his arms across his chest. He must have come directly from winning his last match.

Clark and Charles looked at Shea with amazed and questioning expressions. She shook her head.

She bit her lip and narrowed her eyes on him. What was he doing here?

He cocked an eyebrow at her and turned his attention to Charles. His patient expression said he was waiting for Charles to continue with his explanation of events.

Charles looked at Shea one last time, his face guarded and just a bit frustrated. He hesitated before going on to explain the rest of the rules. Shea and Clark would stick to the outer perimeter of the encampment so they didn't lose people in the forest beyond. They'd debated for a long time about the boundaries, and it was decided it was too dangerous and unpredictable to take the group past the final sentry line. They also didn't want a bunch of competitive Trateri running through the inner camp among crowds trying to capture Shea and Clark. There was still plenty of space to hide and track on the outer perimeter.

She snuck a look back at Fallon. His eyes were fastened on her. When he caught her peeking, he gave her a wicked smile. She sighed. Somehow, she didn't think Fallon cared who was the decoy and who was the beast. There was only one person he planned to hunt.

The question portion of the exercise went quickly. Only those who were frequent attendees of Charles's beast class landed in the first square. They would hold a distinct advantage over the rest as they would be the first to be released to track

Shea and Clark. A handful were placed in the second square with the majority ending up in the last square. There were some grumbles as they ordered themselves into the proper square.

Charles gave Shea and Clark a nod. Trenton straightened and followed them into the forest beyond.

The three made their way to the stash of tools they'd placed in the knot of a tree earlier in the morning. The tools should help them mirror the tracks of a red back, a revenant and a hularna.

Clark would be the red back for this exercise and Shea would be the decoy.

"Good luck," Shea told Clark.

"You too. Somehow I think you're going to need it more than me."

Her grimace said she agreed.

They each pressed the stamp in the ground and then set off in opposite directions. The sign they left would be the trackers' first test.

"Why did you make Clark the red back?" Trenton asked as Shea left some scratches waist high on a tree.

"Who do you think they'll assume is the real target?" Shea asked.

"You."

"Exactly. Clark is perfect. If they try to read our foot prints, those who aren't sure will pursue me. Those who do know how to read signs will pursue Clark." The object of this game was to test the competitors' knowledge and tracking skills, in addition to their endurance. Most Trateri knew how to track, it was something they were taught as children since much of their diet consisted of what they hunted. There was no way Shea and Clark would be able to completely erase their presence. This was their way of evening the odds.

Shea set off at a run, heading to the next place where she'd leave another sign. Trenton kept up with her easily. Together the two of them moved through the forest, stopping only when they needed to set the next sign. Shea alternated between the revenant's tracks and the hularna's. She broke off stems and bent branches, sometimes laying a false trail before backtracking.

An hour had passed before she heard the first sounds of pursuit. There was a loud curse as one of the contestants stepped into a briar patch she'd led them through. She grinned. That would teach them to pay attention to their surroundings.

She moved off at an angle from them, not wanting to be caught just yet. The game was still early and Clark hadn't blown the horn to say he'd been caught.

"You are diabolical," Trenton remarked after Shea left a false trail pointing into a nest of stinging thistles. The flower's petals would leave welts and rashes on any unsuspecting victim that chose to brush against them.

Shea shared a smile with him as she backed away from the nest, careful not to brush up against any of the yellowish, green petals.

"I learned from the best."

"This may end up backfiring on you," Trenton said with a skeptical glance at the stinging flowers. "He will not be happy when he catches up to you if he has welts and a rash all over. He might even find a nest to throw you into."

She shot Trenton a grin. "If he's arrogant enough to get caught in this, he deserves what he gets."

She'd decided she liked this game. Liked outwitting Fallon and making him chase false trails. The only way it would be better is if she could ditch Trenton and do this alone. He made their trail a little too easy to spot.

She stared at him in thought.

"Oh no, don't even think it. You're not ditching me."

She sighed. Such a stickler for the rules.

She wiped her hands on her pants and gestured for him to continue. He started to turn and Shea bent to grab her print-making tool. A whistle sounded in the air. Shea threw herself to the side. An arrow sailed over her head and thunked into the trunk of a tree barely a handbreath from Shea.

Trenton spun, drawing his sword at the same time. Another arrow whistled through the air. Trenton deflected it with a swift movement. "Get up. We need to run."

Shea leapt to her feet, darting past Trenton and behind the cover provided by upraised roots that were as tall as she was. They raced through the trees, giving little thought to where they were going. Shea ran, knowing any moment an arrow could land in her back.

She weaved through the trees, zigzagging to and fro. Trenton crashed through the underbrush beside her.

The sound of pursuit followed them. Shea tripped, falling down a bank and rolling into a stream bed. She pushed herself half upright in the water.

Where was Trenton? He'd been right beside her. She was alone now. They must have gotten separated.

She took her time getting up, keeping her movements soft and silent. There was a rustle in the bushes behind her. Shea slid through the water, keeping low, until she could press herself against the bank. She waited with bated breath as footsteps came closer and closer.

They paused right above her head. She didn't dare move for fear that it would attract attention. After a long moment, the footsteps retreated.

Shea released the breath she was holding and leaned forward. Her game of hunting had suddenly become all too real.

She'd have to apologize to Trenton and Fallon the next time she saw them. After all the grief she'd given them regarding their insistence of having a guard on her at all times, she finally saw what they had been saying.

She pushed herself away from the bank, pausing to glance over it. Nothing moved in the forest around her. She'd have to chance it. She couldn't stay here. Eventually her hunter would backtrack and find her. Her only chance was making her way back to the encampment and finding help.

She didn't even have a weapon to defend herself with. She'd been stupid and left it behind, thinking that it was unnecessary for the game. Trenton was probably going to have a lot to say about that when they met back up.

For now, she needed to be quick and quiet. She could do this. It was no different than evading a beast. Granted, this beast walked on two legs and was highly intelligent, but he didn't know the forest like she did, and he lacked the superior senses of a true beast.

Yes, she could do this. She refused to be ended by a coward with an arrow, shot in the back like prey.

She ran down the stream bed, hiding her foot prints in the water in case her hunter did come back. After a fair distance, she scrambled up the bank and across the forest floor.

She stopped on an exposed boulder and listened. The human senses were powerful if one knew how to use them. Shea had been taught to listen and feel with more than just the tangible.

Her senses told her something was off in the forest. The animals had gone silent and the air had a menacing, oppressive feeling to it. It was still and quiet, not even the branches in the trees rustling with wind as the world waited, watchful. Shea's back itched as if someone was watching her.

It could be her attacker, or it could be someone from the game. That had been the purpose, after all—hunt the beast until they caught it. She hadn't heard any sign of pursuit in the last few minutes, but Fallon, in particular, could be tricky. Either way, it was probably best to avoid whoever was after her. She couldn't be sure if they were friend or foe.

She slipped off the boulder and moved silently over the ground, her senses tuned to the world around her.

There was no movement, but the forest felt ominous—like there was something waiting in its depths, something that meant Shea ill.

She rolled into some underbrush and slithered across the ground on her stomach.

A rustle in the branches alerted her that she wasn't alone. Something was behind her. If it was the shooter, she needed to get out of his line of sight. Regroup and see if she could slip away unseen.

She waited, every sense tuned to spot her hunter. There. The branches of a small tree just barely moved. Could be the wind but the branches around it weren't moving.

Shea moved away, careful to keep her movements silent and not disturb the bushes around her. She needed to find a way to deal with this. She slithered into a natural indent in the land and under an upraised tree root.

Her hand landed next to a vine with purple tracery on it. Shea froze, eyeing the vine with a hint of fear. As she watched, it slithered across the ground, much as she had, weaving back and forth as it sought its prey.

She held her breath as another vine slithered next to her, up and over one of her hands. A sleeper vine nest. Of all the luck. Her assailant wouldn't need to do anything to her. She was going to get herself killed all on her own.

She carefully turned onto her back. Above her a deep purple flower opened and closed. There were other flowers intertwined with it, each a varying shade of purple. Some were tightly closed, the bud bulging in odd places on the side. She had a guess as to what was causing that, and it was enough to make her break out into a cold sweat.

Voices reached her. "I think she came this way."

"Are you sure? It could be another false trail. She's been laying them all afternoon."

"She didn't have time to lay one this time. She would have been fleeing for her life."

"If you say so."

The vines perked up at the voices. They snaked across the ground, barely causing a rustle against the dead leaves, their movements as sinuous as they were graceful.

Shea held her breath as one moved across her stomach. They must be attracted to sound and movement. Otherwise she'd be dead already.

All she could do was wait as her hunters came closer. They could be part of the game, hunting her as the beast. Something told her to wait. Something in the way they spoke made her think they were the ones who had shot at her.

She waited.

Two men stepped around a tree and exclaimed when they saw her on the ground. The smaller of the two raised a bow and arrow and started to point it at her. Guess that answered that question.

All the while the vines crept closer. From above another vine dropped down.

Shea waited.

The man drew the arrow. The vines attacked. Shea moved, exploding from the ground and sprinting away from the men.

There were twin screams behind her as she fled. She didn't hesitate. There was nothing to be done anyway.

She ran until she couldn't run anymore. By sheer instinct, she had managed to run toward camp instead of away. The forest around her began waking up again and the air lightened as if a cloud had passed.

Finally, she slowed and then stopped. She needed to catch her breath and figure out where she was. A twig cracked behind her.

Shea froze and then sprang away.

Her hesitation cost her. Arms wrapped around her before she could even take a step.

CHAPTER SIXTEEN

Shea landed on the ground with a body on top of hers. She twisted and turned, using her elbows to strike at the person behind her. She kicked back, gratified when she heard a grunt behind her.

"Shea, it's me. Fallon. Quit fighting."

Shea stilled. She turned her head to see an irate pair of whiskey colored eyes looking down into hers.

"Fallon." All of the fight left her. She collapsed onto the ground, her body boneless with relief. Her limbs had a fine tremble in them, a remnant of the adrenaline that had driven her body until now and the fear from when Fallon had grabbed her.

He looked down at her with puzzlement and then looked around them. "Where's Trenton? Tell me you didn't ditch your guard again."

"We got separated after someone shot an arrow at us."

Fallon's attention swung back to Shea. His body went from relaxed against hers, to hard as granite. His gaze swung to the forest around them, taking on a watchful look.

He grabbed her hand and pulled her to her feet before setting off into the woods with her towed behind him. One hand rested on the long dagger at his waist.

"How long ago was this?"

Shea tried to think. Time had gotten away from her while she'd been playing cat and mouse. "An hour maybe. I'm not sure."

"Did you see them?"

Shea winced as his words reminded her of the last time she'd seen those two. With sleeper vines wrapped around them, screaming in pain and fear.

"You could say that."

His stride didn't hesitate, covering the forest floor quickly. Shea kept up easily. He still hadn't let go of her hand.

"They're probably dead right now. They followed me into a nest of sleeper vines. I don't think they made it out." Because of Shea.

"Good." Fallon's words were curt as they moved through the forest at a quick clip. "That saves me from having to kill them. When we get back, you can give us a general idea of where you left them, and I'll send some men to retrieve their remains if there are any. It would have been nice to be able to interrogate them."

Shea's reply was faint when it came. "I'll endeavor to remember that next time."

Fallon looked back and flashed her an amused look. "You do that, and Darius will worship at your feet."

"What every girl dreams of."

"More women than I can count have expressed that desire," Fallon said. "He's considered one of the best catches in my army by man or woman."

"No wonder he's so arrogant," Shea said. She was beginning to feel better. Stronger and less shaky. She felt more herself again.

If she remembered correctly, they were close to where Clark and she had stashed the tools to make the beast tracks. They shouldn't be more than a few minutes from the field where the game had started.

They entered the clearing at a near run. Several of Fallon's Anateri, including Caden, waited in a clump next to the table of refreshments that had been set up for the end of the game. Trenton was among them, his clothes disheveled and stained with dirt and blood. He had a bandage wrapped around one arm.

The Anateri were armed and looked like they were organizing a search party.

Fallon hailed them as he and Shea came out of the forest. Caden whistled and his men surrounded them, providing a barrier. Anyone attempting to shoot an arrow would not find Shea an easy target.

"Get men into the forest to perform a search," Fallon ordered as soon as he was in hearing distance of Caden. "Shea said her attackers disturbed a nest of sleeper vines, but there may have been others. I want everyone still out there rounded up and questioned."

Caden turned and made a few gestures to his men.

Trenton stood straight, relief in his eyes at the sight of Shea. "When I realized we'd been separated, I returned to organize a search. It's my fault she was in danger. I'll accept any punishment you deem fit."

Shea rolled her eyes. The gods save her from arrogant nitwits who wanted to fall on their swords.

Trenton saw her and frowned, his expression stern.

"Oh please, you were in no way responsible for us getting separated. If anything, I know you stayed behind to try to cover my escape," Shea told him, ignoring the frown he aimed her way.

Trenton ignored her and straightened his shoulders and lifted his chin. "Nevertheless, she was my charge and I failed her."

Shea narrowed her eyes on him. The stupid idiot was going to get himself into unnecessary trouble for something he couldn't control. If anyone had been at fault, it was Shea. After those first few arrows, she had run without paying much attention to anything but escape. It was a stupid mistake that a daisy would make. She should have kept her head and wits about her.

"That's a ridiculous claim," she said. "Stop being noble. It wasn't your fault we got separated or that a couple of lackwits with arrows put me in danger."

Fallon looked between the two of them with a thoughtful expression on his face. "I agree with Trenton."

Shea scoffed and turned to him with anger dawning on her face.

He held up a hand to forestall her coming words. "His punishment will be to train you to prepare for all sorts of situations that might come up so that next time you can react with more skill. I also think continuing as your personal guard will be punishment enough for his transgressions."

Fallon gave her a pointed look. Her mouth snapped shut as she frowned at him. She resented the fact that he had made it seem as if guarding her was a punishment, but she couldn't argue with him without putting Trenton's neck back on the chopping block. Fallon had unreasonably high expectations for his guards. She didn't want to be the one responsible if anything happened to Trenton.

Tricky, tricky Warlord.

She'd like to argue against the need for more training but the events of today had shown a huge gap in her skills. She'd survived because she was lucky. There was a good chance she wouldn't be the next time an enemy came for her.

She turned to Trenton. "I guess we'll be spending more time in the training arena once you're healed."

"There are people she can train with until you're cleared for duty again," Caden told Trenton. He turned his head towards her. "I will take over your training until Trenton can work with you."

Great. The only person worse than Trenton was Caden. She'd seen him train with Fallon. The man was a dictator. One who was relentless and tireless. She nodded her agreement. Arguing was useless, and a little time spent with him could make a difference down the road.

"I've dispatched several teams to sweep this section of the forest. They'll report back when they've finished," Caden told Fallon.

Before Fallon could respond, a large shadow blotted out the sun streaming through the forest branches as screams rose from the encampment. Shea looked up to see golden feathered wings as large as a house.

"Golden eagle."

Shea hit the ground, pulling Fallon down with her. Caden and Trenton followed, landing with a thump.

The eagle swooped down, overshooting Shea and the rest to pluck a horse from an enclosure. The horse screamed with fear, its legs kicking before it went still as the eagle's claws broke its neck.

Another eagle dropped from the sky. This time rising with a person in its clutches.

Shea's heart thundered in her ears. The leftover adrenaline that had been in her system earlier flooded through her, erasing any fatigue.

This wasn't right. How were the golden eagles here? Their territory was the mountains and plains, where pickings were easy, and their movements unhampered by the giant vegetation of the forest.

Shea watched as one of the eagles tried to lift off and had to drop its prey when it couldn't extend its wings because of trees hemming it in on either side. The person it dropped crawled toward an upraised tree root as the bird hopped awkwardly after him. Its talons carved deep grooves in the wood.

"Attack its wings," Fallon ordered Caden. "Don't let it back into the air."

Caden let out a roar. The Anateri followed him. Some held spears and others bows and arrows. They circled the bird and worked on bringing it down while it mantled its wings at them and gave a screech of warning.

Shea grabbed Fallon's arm before he could run to help. "Its eyesight is incredibly sharp. It can spot prey from a mile away. Don't let it back in the air. It can be out of the range of your weapons in seconds and dive on you before you can blink. Stay close to the trees as much as possible. It'll make it harder to maneuver there."

Fallon nodded. He brushed her cheek with a gentle touch and then was gone.

A hand fell on Shea's arm. Trenton's expression was grave. "We need to go."

Shea nodded. Yes, they did. The second one would come back for its mate.

As she stood, she glanced back at the forest and paused. A figure stood in its shadows. She could have sworn she recognized him. His shape was familiar, the way he carried himself. Though the distance made her second guess herself. There was no way it could be him. He was dead. Had been since their trip into the Badlands.

An eagle screamed, just as it dived into the camp. The Trateri split, some racing to meet the coming danger while the young and non-warriors raced to find shelter. Shea followed along, knowing that she'd just get in the way. She wasn't trained for combat and had not trained to be part of a team.

She ran beside Trenton, trying not to get swept along with the press of humanity.

There was a war cry above her and a villager from Airabel flung a spear at one of the eagles. Another leapt through the air, freefalling until he landed on the back of an eagle, taking a knife to the beast's neck until blood dotted its feathers.

The eagles were swarming. Shea had only seen the like one other time in her life. The Badlands. This scene was as bad as any she fought there. Terror was a wild beast in her chest.

Another eagle dived, while its companion fought off the man from Airabel. This time there was no scream as it rose, blond curls draped over its talons.

"Mist! Trenton, it has Mist." Shea pointed at the eagle that struggled to flap its way to safety. It turned as villagers shot a hail of arrows at it.

Trenton looked up and cursed. "Shea, wait."

Shea didn't wait. She ran along the ground keeping the eagle in sight as it careened through the forest, its wings too big. They brushed the sides of the trees as it fought to rise.

Shea found a ladder leading into the trees and started to climb. One hand over the other as fast as she could. Reaching a rope bridge above, she pulled herself up and ran along it, shadowing the eagle below.

She leapt into empty space when she ran out of bridge and barely landed on another tree's oversized branch. They were in the mid canopy. The branches weren't as tightly woven as they were in the world above. She had to pay attention to where she placed her feet. It would be easy to fall here.

The eagle flapped as it fought through the dense forest and gave a battle cry as Trateri soldiers forced it back. Shea turned, following a branch.

There. That was her chance.

She leapt, grabbing a hanging vine and swinging out into air. She let go and fell, her heart in her throat and utterly focused as the eagle grew in size beneath her. She landed on its back, sliding down until her hands managed to grip tight onto its feathers.

The wings flapped, hitting her on the side of the face. She bit her tongue but held on.

Mist whimpered from where she was clutched in the beast's claws.

Shea clung to the bird. She hadn't thought this plan through before she implemented it. Impulsiveness was really going to get her killed one day.

She couldn't kill the beast with Mist clutched in its claws. It would mostly likely result in Mist's death as well as Shea's when they all went crashing to the ground.

Shea waited, drawing the dagger she'd grabbed when the beasts first attacked. She'd need to time this very carefully.

An eagle could open and close its claws at will. Right now, it held Mist lightly enough that the girl hadn't been killed. Probably because the eagle wanted its prey alive for whatever reason.

Shea waited until they were over a soft-looking copse of tangled branches and vines, interwoven, thin and flexible enough that they might slow Mist's fall but not be as hard as the ground.

Shea struck, sinking her blade into the eagle's side again and again. The beast thrashed beneath her. There was a short gasp of breath as it released the girl. Shea buried her blade one last time before pushing off.

Her freefall was cut short as she crashed into the branches, lacerations forming where her skin dragged along the sharp wood. She fell through the first layer, each branch flipping her a different way as they broke under her. She came to a stop, hanging upside down, her leg caught between two branches.

That was such a bad idea. On the scale of bad ideas, it was probably one that would go into the history books.

Shea groaned. Every bone in her body felt that fall. "Let's never do that again."

There was a rustling in the branches next to her and then blond curls coupled with watery blue eyes peered out at Shea.

"Hey, sweetie. Are you hurt anywhere?"

Mist shook her head.

Shea closed her eyes. "That's good."

"Shea! Shea, where are you? Answer me." Trenton's voice came from below. He sounded frantic.

"Here, we're over here!" Shea yelled back.

Curses sounded from below them and then the sound of a man grunting and hacking at the branches they were incased in.

They'd landed in a copse of boughs that grew tightly together with very little space between. It looked like a prison made of very thin wood.

Shea used her abs to lift up, grabbing a branch near her foot with one hand to redistribute her weight as she wiggled her foot free. There would be no living it down, if Trenton discovered her stuck upside down. She yanked her foot once more and then fell, landing hard on her back. A sword cut through some of the boughs next to her.

Trenton peered in, taking note of Shea sprawled on her back and Mist above her.

"Help Mist, first," Shea ordered.

He didn't argue, turning his attention to the little girl. "Come here, child. Let's get you to safety."

"It's probably safest here," Shea said, sitting up with a grimace.

"The soldiers drove off the eagles they didn't manage to kill. It should be safe for now."

That was a relief.

Trenton held the girl as he and Shea worked their way back down to the forest floor. They weren't as high up as Shea had thought. Her previous calculations had been off.

It was a relief to reach the ground, though she kept one eye on the forest above them. The fear of another attack was ever present. She wasn't the only one feeling it either. The Trateri they passed were preoccupied with the world above. Much more so than she had ever seen them before. Several soldiers kept watch on the canopy as others tended to the destruction on the ground. Healers assisted the wounded.

Trenton, carrying Mist, opened a path before them. The Trateri moved out of their way as they walked, some giving Shea a bow, others clasping their fist to their chest. Shea gave a small nod in acknowledgement before turning her eyes ahead. The attention made her skin itch.

"Why are they bowing?" she whispered to Trenton.

"They saw what you did for Mist. They're paying you their respects."

"I thought she was an orphan, not worth anything to the clans."

"You put your life on the line for the least of us. It means something."

She disagreed with the thought that Mist meant less than the rest of the Trateri, but she could see what he meant. She fell silent as they made their way to Fallon's tent.

"Send a healer inside, now." Trenton gave the order as he walked past the two Anateri standing guard. Both men looked at Shea, their eyes widening and shock turning their faces pale before one took off at a run to do his bidding.

She touched her forehead, her fingers coming away with blood. Judging by their reactions, she must have looked pretty bad.

She followed Trenton inside. He set the child on a chair in front of the table. He picked up a handkerchief and tossed it at Shea. "If you ever want to leave this tent without a full escort, I suggest you get yourself cleaned up before Fallon sees you."

She took that to mean she was right, and she looked as awful as she felt.

He turned back to the child as Shea pressed the cloth against her head, wincing at the sting. Head wounds were the worst. They always bled way more than they should.

Chirron entered the tent while Shea was still mopping up the blood from her forehead and neck. It had dripped onto the collar of her shirt, and her pants were ripped and bloody from the scrapes on her legs.

Chirron's face was carefully blank as he cataloged Shea's injuries with a glance.

"Help the girl first," Shea said when it was clear he planned to attend her first.

He spared a glance at the girl as Trenton gently lifted her arms and pressed against her ribs. Mist jumped, making a whimpering sound as she yanked her arm out of his hold and folded it against her side.

Chirron looked back at Shea. "All due respect, but the girl's injuries, or even death, would not affect the Trateri as much as yours would."

"Not to mention your Warlord is apt to throw things if he learned I was delayed in receiving a healer's attention," Shea observed.

Chirron inclined his head. "I'm glad you can see my view on this."

Shea nodded. She hoped he could hold onto that feeling.

She held up a hand as he reached for her. "As much as I can empathize with your position, I still insist you see to the girl's injuries first."

She gave him a friendly smile. He didn't look particularly moved by her smile. Perhaps it needed work. She touched the cloth to her forehead, or maybe it just needed less blood.

"Telroi. Fallon would not be pleased to learn I treated another before you."

Shea snapped the cloth down. "I know very well what Fallon would want. Can you honestly tell me he wouldn't wish one of his men treated before him?" She raised an eyebrow expectantly.

He met her stare with a stubborn one of his own. She took his silence as agreement.

"My injuries aren't critical and hers might be. The sooner you check her out, the sooner you can move on to me." She gave him a stony look, the one she gave Fallon when she wasn't going to budge on something. "If you hurry, you might even be able to finish her examination before Fallon tracks us down."

His lips firmed, and he treated her to the glare she was more used to. "As you wish."

Good. She'd finally won one battle.

Trenton stood back, setting his hand on Mist's shoulder as Chirron took a knee before her and gave her a friendly smile.

"Let's get you checked out, shall we?"

She gazed at him solemnly, her lower lip sticking out just slightly. Mist watched as he felt along her legs and arms. When he reached for her ribs, she jerked away and looked at Shea.

"It's alright, Mist. He's not going to harm you. He just needs to see where you're hurt," Shea told her. "Can you show him where you're hurt?"

Mist nodded, the dirt on her cheeks making her seem even younger than she was. She lifted her shirt and pointed to the already purpling band appearing around her midsection. There were also signs of older bruises lower on her stomach and small burn marks that definitely hadn't been created when the eagle picked her up in its claws. In addition to almost being killed by a beast, the girl had been abused in the not so distant past.

There was a low curse above her as Trenton took a deep breath. Shea didn't let any of the horror and pity she felt show on her face.

"Thank you, Mist. You did a good job." Shea gave the little girl a smile and turned her eyes to Chirron whose face had settled into a grim mask. Wrath was in his eyes as he helped the little girl lower her shirt.

"Stay here with Trenton while I speak with the healer." Shea jerked her head to indicate he follow her. She stood, her body protesting the movement, and led the way to the other side of the tent, far enough that Mist wouldn't overhear their conversation.

Shea waited as Chirron joined her. He took several deep breaths, visibly trying to calm himself, before speaking, "Her injuries from the attack by the eagle are minor, all things considered. I will need to keep an eye on her for the next little while to make sure there is no internal bleeding and create a poultice to address some of the bruising."

Shea watched him carefully. Despite his measured words, she got the sense he was seconds away from snapping. She liked him better for the obvious anger he felt over the apparent abuse the girl had suffered.

"And the rest?"

He took another deep breath and busied himself adjusting the bracelet on his wrist. Shea let him, knowing he needed time to compose himself.

"There are signs of long-term abuse. I can't be sure, but I believe at least one of her arms has been broken in the past. There is also scar tissue from being burned."

It was Shea's turn to seek her composure, even as her blood sung for vengeance against whoever had hurt that sweet child. She had never sought violence, but she thought she might finally understand Fallon a little better. It took her considerable discipline not to tear out of this tent to hunt down the perpetrators. The only thing keeping her in place was the knowledge that it would be difficult to find those responsible.

That's not to say that if she ever did uncover who hurt Mist, she wouldn't relish leading them into a spinner nest or a pack of revenants. She might even get creative and track down some of the more vicious beasts, the ones that would make the person suffer before eating them.

"I thought the Trateri protected their young," Shea said, unable to bite back the words.

Chirron's nostrils flared. "They do, but we have our bad seeds, just as everybody else. Those that did this will be found and dealt with. The Warlord will make sure of it."

Fallon moved into view, his eyes coming to rest on Shea and Chirron. He had a streak of blood on one cheek and a cut on his arm. He looked like he'd been in a battle, his body tense, and his posture poised for an attack at any time. His expression darkened at the sight of Shea, still bloody, her wounds untreated.

"I had not realized I had given you permission to make promises on my behalf," Fallon said, his tone silky.

Chirron watched him with caution, like one would a large mountain lion that you were pretty sure saw you as its next meal.

"May I ask why my Telroi is standing with her wounds untreated and blood covering her while you make such claims?" he asked, his voice rising with every word.

"Perhaps because there was someone here who needed help first," Shea told him, shooting a meaningful look in Mist's direction. The girl cowered in her seat, her chest heaving up and down as she looked at Fallon like he was a wolf about to pounce on her. "Or would you like to tell me that her needs are less important than mine?"

Shea's expression told him there was only one right answer to that question.

His jaw flexed, and he lowered his chin to send her a look that could have shorn boulders in half. Chirron and Trenton looked like they were trying to make themselves invisible during the silent showdown between Shea and Fallon.

"My mistake. Of course, the child should receive attention first. They are our future." Fallon conceded his loss with a graceful incline of his head. "Now that she has been helped, perhaps Chirron can get on with tending to your injuries while you update me on who I am supposed to find and kill."

Shea's shoulders rose and fell as she took a deep breath. That was probably the best apology she was going to get. The implacable look on Fallon's face told her he wasn't budging from his spot until she let Chirron tend to her.

"They're superficial wounds," she told Fallon.

"Then this should go quickly so Chirron can tend to the more gravely injured among my people."

Or he could drop this and allow Chirron to get to more important duties now. That wasn't going to happen though.

Shea's sigh was gusty as she held the cloth she'd used to blot away some of the blood out to Chirron. He took it and pointed her to a seat.

She sat and held still as he pressed against the skin around the cut on her forehead. A cool, almost numbing sensation spread from the places where he touched. It wasn't enough to dim all the pain, however. Fallon hovered over them looking like he wanted to shed Chirron's blood every time Shea winced.

She needed something to distract her from Chirron's probing fingers or else she feared he wouldn't live through tending to her wounds.

"How are your men?" she asked.

"Fine. There were a few casualties, but we managed to bring down several of the eagles."

Several. She still found that strange. It was damn near impossible for that many to gather.

"We were lucky they attacked here, where their movement was hampered. On the plains or in the mountains we would have faced much greater losses."

That was another thing. Why had they attacked here? This wasn't their natural hunting grounds. She'd listened to many stories told by the Airabel villagers, and they had almost no references to the golden eagles that plagued much of the Highlands and Lowlands.

"How did the Airabel villagers fare?" Shea asked.

"They suffered some losses. Many of their warriors fought honorably from above to keep the eagles from carrying off their victims. Their actions have won them much favor from my generals. Eckbert has volunteered his healers to help assist the wounded," Fallon said.

"I need to talk with Eckbert." Shea pushed Chirron's hands away. Something about this didn't sit right with her.

"I'm not done," Chirron snapped, slapping a hand onto her shoulder and pushing her back down. "You'll go nowhere until I've cleaned and put stiches in this cut."

Shea glared up at Chirron. She had places to be and people to question. There were more important things to take care of than treating her superficial injuries. Chirron raised one eyebrow, his expression saying he wasn't impressed with her glare. He gave Fallon a pointed look.

Fallon stood watching them, with his arms folded across his chest and a frown on his face. He looked seconds away from throwing things.

Shea saw his point. "At least send someone for Eckbert."

Fallon gestured and one of the men in the room with them left. Shea presumed on the errand of summoning the village elder.

"Now that that's taken care of, perhaps you can hold still." Chirron didn't wait for her agreement, pressing a cloth he'd soaked with a liquid to the cuts on Shea's forehead. She hissed as it stung.

"The pain will do you good," Chirron said, bending closer to get a better look at what he was working with. "The liquid will keep you from getting an infection and reduce signs of scarring."

"Your bedside manner leaves a lot to be desired," Shea told him.

He picked up her hand and pressed it to the cloth on her head. She kept it there as he turned and busied himself with his satchel of supplies.

"I treat warriors all day. Men who think they are immune to such common ailments as infection. I've learned to be direct."

Shea snorted. She could believe that.

"If this can reduce scaring, it's a wonder your soldiers have so many of them," Shea told Fallon.

Chirron paused in what he was doing and looked up. "His men can't be bothered with such things. They believe scars are a sign of strength."

Fallon's eyebrows were just barely lifted, and his mouth curved down with just the slightest hint of disdain. He gave them a long stare that said he had no interest in this conversation.

"Warlord, I've brought the village elder," one of Fallon's Anateri said from the entrance. He stepped aside to allow Eckbert to enter.

Eckbret was clad in leather armor and carried a quiver in one hand and a bow across his back. His face had been painted so that he would blend in with the forest and his eyes held a fierce light. One that she had seen many times in Fallon's. This man was a warrior—old and past his prime, but he still held that spirit, and his garments and weapons said he was prepared to defend his people to the death.

Shea blinked at the odd vision. Eckbert had always seemed like a harmless old man.

"I've positioned my men in the trees surrounding this area. If there is another incursion by the eagles, they will sound the horn so our vulnerable can take cover." Eckbert's eyes landed on where Chirron was tending to her cuts and softened. "I am glad to see your adventures haven't left you too worse for wear."

Shea stiffened as her eyes slid to Fallon. She'd been hoping he wouldn't hear about her jumping onto the back of a golden eagle while it was in flight. The downward turn of his mouth said that was a futile hope and probably had been since the beginning. The Trateri gossiped as much as any group of old wives she had encountered in the Highlands.

"Thank you," she told Eckbert. "Your men's assistance saved my life and Mist's. I don't think I would have been able to get the eagle to drop us if they hadn't attacked it from above."

"Yes, you have my gratitude," Fallon said, his voice a deep rumble. "Your people have shown honor and bravery. I will be glad to have them in my army."

Eckbert eyes got that familiar crafty gleam. "Perhaps my men will bring back Trateri wives and cement our bond by combining our bloodlines."

Fallon's lips twisted in amusement. "Perhaps.

"Did you lose many?" Trenton asked.

Eckbert's eyebrows lowered and his cheeks sagged. Sadness coated his face. "Any loss cuts deep. Our people weren't prepared, many of our most vulnerable fell to these creatures."

"Has there ever been an attack of this nature before?" Shea asked, leaning to the side so she could see Eckbert better. She received a cuff to the head from Chirron. She glared up at him but sat back and let him clean the wound.

"I've asked my elders to review our oral history. I can say they haven't attacked in so many generations that they've faded from our collective memory. It seems many things that were once myth are returning to this world." His face turned grim. "I fear my people are not prepared for this."

Shea feared the same. The Airabel knew the dangers of their forest and could slip through it like ghosts. With the outside world encroaching on their lives, they would have to adjust quickly or fall into the void like so many villages before them.

"Have your men get in touch with the Wind Division commander, Eamon," Shea said. "He can give you some basic information about what you might be facing."

It wasn't much, but it was all she could give right now.

"What about your people?" Eckbert asked. "I know they have much knowledge that can be shared, and we have been on friendly terms in the past."

Shea's gaze turned inwards. The pathfinders, for all their knowledge, were loath to help others seeking guidance. They hoarded what they knew like dragons on a pile of gold, viewing any who had not taken their oaths as being unworthy.

"They are far from here. It would take months for any message you sent to reach them and be returned." Shea settled on her response.

"And the pathfinder Reece?" Eckbert lifted an eyebrow, intelligence shining in his face. This was no befuddled old man. There was a reason he'd gotten to his position. Shea was willing to bet he used the persona of a kindly old man only intent on procreation to lure many off their guard. "I assume he is still alive. He could have much to share with us."

Fallon unfolded his arms. "He is alive, but he will stay with us. I still have business with him."

Yes, the pathfinder Reece. A man who had shown up mere days before this attack.

Chirron held up a needle and thread. "Hold still."

He pulled the skin taut.

Something didn't sit right with Shea. There was more to this. And she was betting Reece had some of the answers.

Shea pushed Chirron's hands away, ignoring his squawk of protest. "I want to see Reece."

She popped to her feet without waiting for a response.

"Where do you think you're going? Sit back down. I still need to stitch up your wounds." Chirron's voice was angry as it followed her out of the tent.

Fallon was beside her. "Shea."

"Where is he?" Shea waited a beat, holding Fallon's eyes. He frowned at her, his eyebrows lowering.

She turned away. Fine. If he wasn't going to answer, she'd find him herself even if she had to search every tent in this place.

CHAPTER SEVENTEEN

Y ou're going the wrong way," Fallon informed her.

Shea stopped, her shoulders tightening before she did an about face. Fallon waited for her with an expression that was both expectant and amused. She swept by him and stalked along the tents.

"Do you know where you're going?"

He knew she didn't.

She'd stormed out of the tent when he failed to answer, and now she was wandering around the encampment with no real clue as to where to find Reece. She was faced with admitting her hotheadedness or committing to this course of action.

Fallon paced along beside her, his large form shadowing hers. "How long do you intend to waste your time when you could just ask for help?"

Shea took a deep breath and stopped, turning to meet Fallon's eyes. He lifted one eyebrow expectantly. Nope. She couldn't do it. She turned on her heel and kept walking.

He grabbed her arm and pulled her to a stop. His lips covered hers before she could form a protest.

Need rose in her—a torrential feeling threatening to subsume her beneath its fury. The pure gratitude that they were both alive to fight, and love, and everything that came with it.

The fury of their passion eased, and she pressed several kisses to his lips before she pulled away and pressed her face into his chest. His arms were a warm weight around her as he rested his chin on top of her head.

Together they breathed, Fallon's hand smoothing down the back of her head.

Seeing him race into danger had given her new insight into how he must feel when she did the same. She was just grateful that he'd come out the other side unharmed. There were some among the Trateri who had not been so lucky.

She sniffed and stepped back, her eyes holding his for a long moment. Understanding was there. Understanding and a somber realization that the day could have very easily ended differently—that it very nearly had.

Shea had been lucky with that stunt with the eagle. By rights she should be dead or at least gravely injured. If it hadn't veered toward that copse of branches when it had, she and Mist would have hit the ground with nothing to break their momentum and probably have broken every bone in their bodies.

"He's this way," Fallon said.

He took her hand and led her through the camp. A thin coating of sadness covered the people Shea saw. The Trateri moved with a grim purpose as they prepared for a second possible attack from the eagles.

They'd fortified several of the tents and had set upraised sentry posts at regular intervals in the camp. Several of Fallon's soldiers manned them, their eyes turned to the skies and long-range weapons held in their hands. She even thought she saw a boomer or two among them.

Fallon noticed where she was looking. "I authorized the use of the boomers should the golden eagles attack again."

"I thought you'd decided not to put those into circulation because of your limited access to the bullets."

Fallon's men had confiscated several of the weapons from villages throughout the Lowlands, but never in the numbers he needed to implement their use in his army. That, coupled with the fact that the maintenance, and the bullets used to fire the weapon were in short supply, had meant that they were an oddity the Trateri found interesting but ultimately useless.

"These circumstances have required a special response. Witt has been training several men in the use of the boomers—none quite measure up to your friend Dane yet, but he's confident that they can acquit themselves well." Fallon stepped around a clump of Trateri who were holding an impromptu briefing. "Caden is working directly with their commanders to make sure the weapons are handled with the appropriate respect and aren't used for personal vendettas."

Shea wouldn't want to be one of them should a weapon go missing or be used inappropriately. Caden was a scary ball crusher when he wanted.

They stopped in front of a tent guarded by one of Fallon's Anateri, one that was familiar from last night. Shea's anger rushed back to the forefront. She didn't wait for Fallon's permission before she stalked toward the Anateri. He spared a glance for Fallon, asking without words for his permission, before he pulled back the tent flap so Shea could step inside.

"Was this you?" Shea didn't wait for an answer before she was in Reece's space, her hands clasped on his shirt. "Did you do this?"

Reece's hands came up to grab hers as he tried to pull away. There was a cot in the room and he was unbound. They were nicer accommodations than Shea would have guessed, considering how angry Fallon had been with his presence when he first showed up.

"Shea, what are you going on about? Let go of me."

She shook him again before Fallon was there, pulling her away. "Did you do this, Reece? If you did, so help me I will make you pay."

Reece adjusted his shirt, pulling it straight with a dirty look aimed at Shea. "I'd call my present situation punishment enough, but I have no idea what you're talking about, Shea."

"The golden eagles, Reece. Did you call them?"

Fallon went still beside her. She didn't spare him a glance. He wasn't going to be happy when he learned how much she had with-held of the pathfinders' capabilities.

Reece's face went cold, his eyes icing over and his mouth turning down. His gaze went from Shea to Fallon's. "I have no idea what you're talking about."

She scoffed. "You know exactly what I'm talking about."

"No, I don't," he said through gritted teeth as he gave her a warning look.

She ignored his warning. If he'd done this, he'd gone too far. "Bullshit. There were children, Reece. One of those beasts tried to take a child."

"Shea, stop."

Not this time.

"You and I both know you have the ability to do something like this. Do you have a beast call? Does the guild know about this?"

"What is a beast call?" Fallon asked from behind her.

Reece shook his head as Shea lifted her chin. She didn't care who knew. If her people had done this, if they had set the beasts on the Trateri and the Airabel villagers, her loyalty to them would be at an end.

"Don't."

Shea looked at Fallon. "A beast call is rare. There are only two that I know of and it's exactly like it sounds. It can call beasts. The ones I know of both date back to the cataclysm."

"Can it control them?"

Reece threw up his hands and sat back down, shaking his head.

Shea ignored him. "No, at least not that we've found. As far as we've seen, it simply summons whatever beasts are in the area. If there was a way to control them with it, that knowledge has been lost to us since the cataclysm."

"Share all our secrets while you're at it, why don't you?" Reece said.

Shea glared at her cousin, words coated her tongue but didn't spill out. She had many things to say but couldn't get them through the anger that had taken hold of her.

"They would have eventually forgiven you for abandoning your post, you know," he informed her. "But not now. You've gone too far, Shea."

"I already knew." Fallon's words fell between them like a blast of cold water. Shea paused and looked at him. He'd known? How?

Reece scoffed. "So, you've already told him. I shouldn't be so surprised."

"I didn't tell him anything," Shea said, not taking her eyes off Fallon, who appeared calm and composed.

"No, she didn't. Your secrets aren't as well-guarded as you assume, pathfinder," Fallon said with a quirk of his lips.

Reece's face was arrested as he studied Fallon. "Impossible. Only pathfinders know about the call, and only a few of them at that."

Fallon lifted one shoulder in a shrug. "Secrets have a way of coming out. For instance, if a single child survives after his town is inundated with beasts shortly after a fall out with the pathfinders, certain conclusions are drawn."

Witt. Had to be. He was the only other person from the Highlands that Shea knew of. He and Fallon had some type of weird relationship that she still didn't understand. The other man was sharp and observant. It didn't surprise her in the least that he'd put that together. It made her wonder what other conclusions he'd managed to draw about the pathfinders' guild and the secrets it held.

Reece's expression smoothed out as he studied Fallon and Shea. His gaze shifted to Shea. "This doesn't change things. You will find it very difficult to come back after this."

She stepped closer to him and leaned down. "You assume I want to come back. My home is here. My people are the Trateri. There is no going back. I wouldn't even if I could."

Fallon's eyes seared a hole into the side of Shea's head. She didn't look at him, keeping her gaze focused on Reece.

"You don't mean that," Reece said. His expression said he thought she was bluffing, that he couldn't fathom a world where she didn't want to return to the fold.

"I do mean it." She let him see she was serious, because she was. She'd built a home with the Trateri, found a place to belong. As much as she'd tried, fitting into the Highlands was a lost cause. Even among the pathfinders.

His eyes widened slightly before his guard slammed shut. He looked away.

"Did you do this?" Shea asked again in a calmer voice than before.

"No, I've been here the entire time, and your friend there made sure I was thoroughly searched for weapons. His guards mentioned something about a relation to a ghost."

Shea's lips twitched. That would have been her fault. She'd surprised the Trateri when she first met them by her resourcefulness a time or two.

197

Shea looked at Fallon and received a nod saying that what Reece said was true. Her fingers tapped against her thigh. That didn't mean he wasn't responsible. She'd only seen the beast call once and wasn't sure she could identify it if she saw it again. The Trateri who'd searched him could have very well missed it.

"I'll have my men search him again," Fallon said coming to the same conclusion Shea had.

"He could have left someone outside the perimeter as well," Shea said, observing Reece carefully.

He'd recovered from his earlier surprise and was back to his smart-ass self. He made a gesture at his chest, as if to ask, 'who me.'

She gave him a meaningful glance that said she wasn't buying it. She knew her cousin, and he was as tricky as the day was long.

"It's just me, Shea. Our elders thought you would be more inclined to listen to someone related to you."

"I'll have my men do a sweep of the surrounding forest," Fallon told Shea. "See if there are any signs of his companions."

It was unlikely they would find anything. Pathfinders could be ghosts when they wanted.

"You know something about this," Shea told Reece, her eyes narrowing. It was there in his eyes, a slight tightness that gave him away. She would have missed it if she hadn't grown up with him, if she hadn't spent many a time falling for his tricks.

Reece met her eyes.

"We can always use force to get what we want," Fallon offered, his voice a lazy threat.

Reece's eyes flicked to Fallon. "Go ahead. See where that gets you."

"It doesn't make sense that the elders sent you to bring us back, to let Fallon into the Highlands," Shea said, thinking out loud. There was something there, something just outside her reach that would make everything fall into place.

He groaned. "I told you why they wanted you and your barbarian Warlord."

"There's been an uptick of beast activity before. Forty years ago, we lost five villages to a surge of beasts and the pathfinders did nothing. This is different. You're hiding something."

What was it?

Reece was quiet, watching Shea carefully.

The beast call. Somehow everything came back to the beast call.

"You think another beast call, one not controlled by the pathfinders, has been found."

It would explain many things, the increased sightings, the way some beasts were being found far from their normal hunting grounds. What it wouldn't explain was how the golden eagles had been called into an environment so at odds with their territory. Beasts were ruled by instinct. This forest with its tight and twisting spaces would have set off every instinct the eagle had—unless whoever called it had a way of controlling it.

That should be impossible though. There had never been any evidence of a call exerting any control over a beast beyond summoning it, and that only if it wanted to come. Their normal territory was far from here. A call never should have been able to reach them and pull them so far off their normal course.

"You think I had something to do with what's been happening," Shea said, coming to a realization. He didn't just think her previous mission had sent the beasts far from their normal territory. He thought she had deliberately and maliciously been calling them to her.

Reece's watchful gaze didn't move from her. So that meant she was right. Her former people thought she'd been, what, summoning beasts in her spare time. For what purpose? The only thing a beast ever brought when it intersected with people was death and destruction. Did they really think her capable of such a thing?

"Where would I even have gotten a beast call?" she asked, hurt tingeing her voice.

His eyes were steady on hers.

There was only one place.

"You think I picked one up in the Badlands."

Fallon stepped closer to Shea, sensing the hurt behind her flat words. His presence at her back bolstered her, telling her she didn't face this alone.

"You are the only one who survived. We don't know what you picked up while you were wandering around that place. Our ancestors left many dangerous things there."

"You know how I feel about those things."

His shrug was careless, though his eyes were intense pools of dark. "You were lost there for over a month. The Badlands have a way of twisting people, and we both know that you're not the same as when you went in."

She drew back, his words as effective as a slap. She shook her head and walked out of the tent. She didn't stop walking once she was out, continuing along her path for several minutes.

In some ways, he was absolutely right. The Shea before the Badlands had been very different, softer, and someone who had believed in herself and her dreams. The Shea of now was older, wiser, and knew that life wasn't going to give her anything. If she wanted something, she needed to keep her head down and work at it, and even then, life had a way of snatching what you wanted right out from under you. Internal scars littered the inside of her mind from the things she'd lost—the things she'd given up.

"What happened in the Badlands?" Fallon asked from behind her once she'd slowed to stare at a blanket of giant mayflowers. They towered above her, their blue flowers nestled under the broad, flat leaf that shielded them from above.

Shea didn't look at Fallon. She tilted her head up and stared at the maze of branches overhead. Today, the trees felt like giant sentinels that time had frozen, their branches rustling in the wind as the sounds of the forest rose around them.

"Thirty of us went in; only I came out." The words were said to the world above her.

"You blame yourself." Fallon's words were a statement not a question.

"There's no one else left to blame."

They were quiet for a long minute.

"It was my idea. No one had ever successfully explored the Badlands. Just an excursion here and there on the edges." Shea felt the need to explain. "Over a thousand years and we only have the barest glimpse into the world before the cataclysm. I wanted to see. I wanted to explore and make life better for everyone. The Badlands are one of the few untouched places; the chance to make a name for myself was ripe for the picking."

"Until everyone died."

Shea made a sound of agreement. "Until everyone died."

That was the kicker. So many friends. People who followed Shea. People who trusted she knew what she was doing. Their voices still haunted her dreams.

"Why do they blame you for the current turn of events?"

Shea was quiet, not able to put into words the thoughts coursing through her head. "We have stories of what lies at the heart of the Badlands. They're stories passed along for centuries. I thought they were myth, something made up by our elders to explain the unexplainable."

Turned out she was wrong. Those stories were just the barest glimpse into what waited there.

"The elders think we penetrated the heart—that we were in danger of waking what slept there."

"But you didn't."

Shea took her time answering. "I told them that we barely made it past the first marker. There are five total."

"And the truth?"

"The group fell apart long before that. There was dissention almost as soon as we crossed into the Badlands." Shea didn't like thinking about that time. She'd prefer to bury what happened and move on. "Shortly after reaching the first demarcation, the golden eagles descended. We'd already lost several people. They carried off half of our number, leaving the rest to fight among ourselves."

Fallon rested a hand on her shoulder and gave it a squeeze, saying without words that he was here. That she wasn't alone.

"Some of us wanted to continue on; the rest wanted to go home."

"You split up." Fallon sounded sure of his answer.

She nodded. "Not at first. We tried to stick together and agree on a course of action. There were too few of us to have a good chance of surviving if we split up, so I made the decision to pull us out. I told the rest they'd follow, or I'd have them excommunicated from our guild."

Shea had told the elders she was the only one to survive the eagles, that by some miraculous turn of events she had survived where the others had not.

"A few days later, three of our number decided they weren't coming home, that they had come too far. They got up one night and disappeared into the mist that had descended while we were sleeping. I sent those who remained home while I went after the three."

She should have left them to their fate. If she had, maybe things would have turned out differently.

"I tracked them several miles before finding two of their bodies. The third was too damaged to identify. The mist must have affected their senses, or maybe they just lost their caution, because they'd wandered into a bantum nest."

The bantum was a beast whose smell, that of rotting flesh and garbage, preceded them. It was very easy to know when you were close to a nest. The pathfinders should have been able to easily avoid it.

"I don't remember too much after that. Everything blurs together. I remember being afraid and constantly running from something. My people found me several weeks later, delirious and raving."

"What about the men you sent back?"

She shook her head. "They never made it. We don't know what happened to them."

They'd probably gotten disoriented much as Shea had or been overtaken by the mist and been unable to find their way out. She never should have left them. It had been stupid of her.

"You blame yourself for their deaths." It wasn't a question. Not just theirs; everybody who went on that mission. "You must know that you would have probably suffered the same fate had you stayed with them."

She lifted one shoulder. "Maybe, maybe not. I do know that none of us would have been there, if not for me. I planned that expedition, everything that happened can be laid at my feet."

He arched one eyebrow, his expression understanding and chiding. "That's an arrogant assumption."

She scowled at Fallon.

"Did you force them to come, or were they volunteers?"

Shea's quiet was answer enough.

"They chose to be there then. You can't take their fate on your shoulders. That way lies madness and is an insult to who they were."

Shea scoffed. "You can't tell me you don't feel the same responsibility for your men. I've seen you with the battle reports. You feel every death."

"Of course. That is part of a leader's responsibility, but I never make the mistake of shouldering the blame for their deaths. They chose to be here. They chose to follow me. I feel their deaths because they laid them down to defend my vision, but I don't assume the guilt for them. That would desecrate the sacrifices they made."

Shea looked away. She'd never considered it in that manner before. Always before, the deaths of the thirty men and women who had followed her into the Badlands was a weight dragging her down. A reminder that the last time she commanded people she'd failed them in every way possible.

"I've learned that sometimes, despite all your planning and training, things go wrong. Plans fall apart, and people sometimes die. That doesn't mean we give up. It means we fight harder for what we want, that we take life by the throat and force it to surrender."

It was an inspirational speech, but Shea wasn't sure how much inspiration she could draw from it. The end result remained the same. Others died while she still lived.

"This beast call they're concerned about. Is it possible that you picked one up and didn't realize it?" Fallon asked.

Shea shook her head. "I don't remember picking anything up, and I didn't have a pack when I was discovered."

"You said you were disoriented and delirious when they found you. It could very well be that one of those that first encountered you took the beast call without you being aware of it."

"Anything is possible when it comes to the Badlands, but it's highly doubtful." She'd known every person on that discovery party for years. Many of them related to her in some way. It just didn't seem likely.

"Either way, this beast call sounds like it's the reason for the problems my men have been having in recent months."

She was afraid of that. It meant she could guess the next words out of his mouth.

"We're going to answer the pathfinders' summons," Fallon said, his mouth a grim line. There was a fierce light in his eyes as if to say he was looking forward to it. "If what they think is true and there is a mastermind setting the beasts on my men, I want to know."

"It's not going to be that easy," Shea tried. The last thing she wanted to do was to send Fallon and his men into the Highlands. She didn't think that would be good for them or the Highlands.

He gave her a fierce smile. "It never is. That's what makes it so fun."

"You're not going to let me talk you out of this, are you?"

She really wished he would. He had no idea what was in store for him there. Nothing good would come of this. She was almost sure of it.

*

Fallon waited until Shea had set off to check on the friends she had among the Trateri before turning back to the tent containing Reece.

He stopped next to the Anateri guarding the entrance. "Let no one inside. Not even Shea."

The Anateri shared a glance before giving a nod to show they understood.

Fallon ducked inside, his eyes immediately drawn to the prisoner. Reece had moved from the chair to the cot where he reclined with his hands folded behind his head as he stared up at the ceiling as if he could see beyond it to the sky above.

Fallon had caught Shea staring at the sky on more than one occasion but had never asked what so fascinated her. Seeing Reece do something similar reinforced the relationship between the two—a relationship Fallon found himself mildly jealous of, a feeling he wasn't comfortable or familiar with.

"I've noticed Shea always looks to the sky in moments of rest or when she needs reassurance. It seems you do something similar. Why is that?" Fallon asked with a casual voice.

Reece didn't stir from where he lay, simply turning his head slightly to keep Fallon in view. "Does she now? That's interesting. I hadn't realized." He fell quiet again. Fallon waited with all the patience of a hunter, one accustomed to letting his prey set its own trap. "It's probably a remnant of our training. The sky is an ever-changing canvas, but for those who know where to look, you can find set points that can tell you your location."

"Like the West and East stars," Fallon said. His people used the night sky to navigate as well. There was a star in the east and a star in the west that never changed its position in the sky. Using them, you could always be assured of the direction you were traveling.

"Just so."

Fallon studied the other man, noting the microexpressions in his face and the way his eyes slid away from Fallon's.

"You're lying." Fallon was sure of it. "I have no doubt that she and you can navigate by the stars, but that's never her first choice. They're good for a general direction check but useless during the day."

Reece stared at Fallon for a moment, his thoughts hidden. "You're not as stupid as you look."

Fallon crossed his arms, not perturbed in the least by the insult. He'd endured much worse things said about him. If the other man thought to gain information from Fallon's loss of temper, he'd have to work much harder at his insults.

Reece sat up. "When we were children, Shea spent much of her time training in the various pursuits her parents deemed worthy of a pathfinder. She took it very seriously. Even back then she was focused and driven. It left little time for play."

"Were you not in the same training?" Fallon asked.

Reece's smile was humorless. "More or less, but my parents didn't expect the same level of excellence of me. They used to send us out into the wilderness, with little more than a compass and knife for survival. Shea and I would entertain ourselves by watching the clouds and telling stories using the shapes we found there."

Fallon found himself fascinated by this rare glimpse into Shea's childhood. He'd noticed when she told him stories of her journeys, that they were always about the places she'd visited and the things she'd seen. There was rarely much insight into her as a person. He was charmed by this bit of whimsy Reece had revealed. It made him wonder if she would tell their children stories set in the clouds when it came time.

"But you didn't come here to hear more about our childhood," Reece said, with a canny look.

Fallon arched an eyebrow, grimly amused. "Guess you're smarter than you look as well."

Reece's quirk of the lips was less than humorous. "Let's get down to business, shall we?"

Fallon grabbed a chair and pulled it over so he could sit facing Reece. He settled into it and observed Reece, letting the other man feel the full weight of his regard.

"I want to talk terms," Fallon said, letting the other man see his resolve.

Reece's lips broadened into a smug smile, the kind the cat gave a mouse that had just played into its paws. Fallon felt a small tug of amusement at the other man's assumption that he had everything under control. Many men had thought similar things before, yet the Warlord was always the one to come out ahead. Reece and his fellow pathfinders would soon learn the full meaning of what it meant to poke a warlord.

CHAPTER EIGHTEEN

It was nighttime before Shea made her way back to her tent after checking on her friends. They were lucky. They'd come through the attack with minor injuries. Clark and Charles had been in the underbrush tracking down those Trateri who hadn't made it back to the starting point at the assigned time. Once they'd heard and seen the attack, they'd led those with them to shelter under the web of roots from the soul tree. Neither one had suffered any injuries.

Eamon and Buck had been less fortunate. Both had been in one of the fields competing when the attack began and instead of taking cover had rallied those around them into small groups to harry the birds. Both had taken minor injuries. Buck would have a scar from his shoulder to the middle of his chest from the eagle's claws as a reminder.

She was just glad they were safe. She didn't need even more deaths to feel responsible for. Though according to Fallon, she had assumed a responsibility that wasn't hers to begin with.

Both Trenton and Wilhelm were a silent presence at her side throughout. She was too tired to resent their presence.

She stepped inside her tent after murmuring a greeting to the Anateri standing guard. Trenton, her ever present shadow, stopped to have a discussion with them as she pushed her way inside.

Darius, Braden, and several of the clan leaders were gathered around the dining table, maps spread out before them. Everyone was still dressed in their battle armor and armed with weapons.

Fallon looked up at Shea from where he leaned against the table. He nodded his head at the plate by his side.

Shea was tempted to just keep walking. The events of the day had drained her. She didn't know if she had it in her to sit through whatever this was. Her stomach rumbled, reminding her that she hadn't eaten since the morning meal.

She walked to Fallon's side. He nudged the plate piled high with her favorite foods her way as Darius gave a status report.

"We lost twenty during the attack," he said, looking around the table. "Most of those were unable to defend themselves—the old or the very young. A few warriors but mostly noncombatants."

"A relatively minor amount, considering some of the battles we fought down south," Van said, his face pulled into a frown.

"The problem is the blow to morale." Braden's serious gaze touched on Shea before moving on. "Our people take attacks aimed at our heart seriously. They will be out for blood once they've recovered their equilibrium."

"My men are already threatening to lead a war party to these eagles," an unfamiliar man said. Shea guessed he was the clan leader for Ember or Rain. She wasn't sure which.

"They'll have to travel quite a ways," Shea inserted, after swallowing the piece of meat in her mouth.

"And you are?" The man's gaze was cold as he observed Shea the way one might a bug.

She didn't let his tone deter her, used to it by now. "Someone familiar with the golden eagles' territory and habits."

She pulled one of the maps closer to her. They'd chosen one that represented most of the Broken Lands, though the spaces where the Badlands and the Highlands should have been were mostly blank. Just a few mountains drawn in, with the Trateri sign for danger interspersed throughout.

"They make their nests in the mountains near here." Shea pointed to a spot at the top of the map, well past their known landmarks; it was just blank space. In reality, their home was further north than she'd indicated, but she thought this made her point quite nicely. "To get to them, you'd have to climb Bearan's Fault before walking a few hundred miles over extremely rough terrain until you reach the passes that make up the Dragon's Tooth mountain range—it spans three hundred miles—and then cross the plains of Eire. You'll be easy pickings for the eagles on those plains, but perhaps you'll get lucky."

The other man's gaze was even more remote and cold when she finished. She didn't let that bother her, preferring to keep him and his men alive rather than make a friend.

"The golden eagles are not the enemy," Fallon said, his gaze challenging the other man. "They are just the weapon our enemy has chosen to wield."

"It seems our enemy has many weapons to choose from," the other man returned. He lifted his chin in challenge.

All he needed was to flare his nostrils and stomp his feet and he'd look exactly like a bull male skarrygh facing-off with another for the right to rut with his chosen female.

"Gawain." Henry's voice held a warning.

The man's eyes shifted to Henry, but held no less challenge. "I am simply making an observation. The Hawkvale promised us riches and spoils to make up for abandoning our ancestral lands. Since coming to this forsaken place, I have seen little evidence of either."

"Perhaps, had your people joined us sooner and not waited until we were already victorious, they might have taken a piece of the wealth the rest of us split for ourselves," Ben said. The head of the Earth Clan's voice was calm and even. He didn't spare a look for Gawain and instead remained focused on the maps in front of him.

"So we could face dishonorable deaths?" Gawain arched one eyebrow.

Shea stiffened at that assertion. She did not like the insinuation that dying at a beast's claws was dishonorable. She'd known many men and women who fell to beasts. This man with his superior attitude wasn't going to disparage them. Especially when he probably had little to no experience with beasts.

"What's dishonorable about it?" Shea asked, her gaze direct. He wasn't the only one who could be challenging. The clan heads glanced at her, some with disdain, as if to say she had no place talking in these meetings. She continued before anyone could stop her. "Tell me. What is so dishonorable at dying at the claws of a beast?"

His response was a derisive stare.

No answer. That was alright; Shea had plenty to say.

"When's the last time you fought off a revenant pack with nothing but your sword and a few good men?" He didn't answer. The table was dead silent. "How many eagles did your men bring down? Because the Wind Division brought down two, but not before three men gave their lives to protect women and children. What's so damn dishonorable about that?" Shea's chest heaved as she shouted the last words. She refused to look away from Gawain, whose expression had soured as she continued.

When she had made her point, she looked around the table, noting those who met her eyes and those who looked away. Henry, Darius and Braden weren't afraid to hold her gaze. Ben gave her a small nod of respect. Van looked away. The last man, one of the new clan leaders she'd yet to be introduced to, looked mildly interested.

Shea's hands shook ever so slightly where they rested on the table. She hated losing her temper. It always felt like she'd overreacted, and she was left dealing with the fallout.

Fallon's hand slid over one of hers and he gave it a slight squeeze. She glanced at him to find him regarding his clan leaders with an impassive expression.

After a long moment in which no one spoke, Fallon said, "I have a pathfinder in my custody, one who has had much to say about the recent increase in beast activity and the emergence of the mist."

All eyes turned to Shea, suspicion in several of them. She gave them her best Fallon impression, channeling an impassivity that she didn't feel. Her stomach was tight with nerves and a sense of dread.

"How convenient that you've found one of these people so soon after the attack," Gawain said, carefully avoiding looking at Shea.

She narrowed her eyes at him. He might not have overtly indicated her as the architect behind this, but she got the point.

Fallon ignored his words. "This person has indicated the pathfinders may have knowledge to share about these attacks."

Shea kept her surprise off her face. He hadn't said anything about the beast call or the possibility that the pathfinders might be the ones behind this.

"I've decided to take a force into the Highlands at their invitation to see what we can uncover and if there are any weapons we might take advantage of." Fallon's tone invited no dissent.

"Why can't she tell us what we need to know?" the strange clan leader said, jerking his head at Shea.

"Shea has already shared her knowledge," Fallon said, the words little more than a growl.

"Rather freely, in fact," Braden said, surprising Shea. "Ember, you should send some of your vanguard to the beast class she started. They could do with picking up a few pointers."

If he was Ember, then Gawain must be Rain.

"I will keep that in mind," Ember said with an interested nod.

"If you ladies are done trading secrets, could we get back to the point at hand?" Van complained.

"I am not sure I see the purpose in leading a force into the Highlands," Ben volunteered, his mouth pulled into a somber line. "You've already stated previously that there is no easy way to get the men, mounts and supplies we need into the Highlands."

"That's true." Fallon braced his hands against the table. "I've recently learned there might be an alternate route."

Shea stiffened and her gaze swung toward Fallon to find his eyes resting on her. She held his gaze for a moment. Surely Reece hadn't told him about the caverns.

The knowledge was there in Fallon's eyes. Shit, he had. How serious was this for the pathfinders to let that knowledge fall into the hands of outsiders? And how likely was it that they would let those same outsiders live once they'd fulfilled their role?

Fallon pulled the map towards him and pointed to a spot fifty miles west of the Badlands. "This pathfinder claims there are caverns that lead right up into the Highlands. It's supposed to be considerably easier to navigate than the cliffs, and we'll be able to take the mounts and supplies."

The men stared at the spot he pointed at.

"Why weren't we made aware of this before?" Ben asked.

Fallon's council leveled gazes heavy with accusation on him. There was the feel in the air that Shea sometimes sensed right before a storm. The mood was about three breaths from violence.

Van's eyes narrowed, and he looked about ready to issue a challenge, one that Fallon would be forced to fight. Normally, she would bet on Fallon any day of the week. She'd seen him fight. The man possessed an almost supernatural skill with the blade. But she knew he was tired and bruised, having fought with his men to bring down the eagles as well as participated in the tournament.

"He didn't know about them," Shea said, before any more accusations could be thrown. "I never told him."

She'd probably just made her life a thousand times more difficult, but better that, than seeing Fallon's people turn on him. Not when she could prevent it.

Shea found herself the center of attention once again.

"And why is that?" Braden asked, his forehead wrinkling with a frown.

Judging by the anger on some of the clan leader's faces, Braden's question was the more civilized version of what others wanted to say.

She met his stare with a calm expression. "My people do not give that information out lightly, for reasons I'm sure you can imagine."

"How are we supposed to trust this woman when she continues to harbor secrets?" Van asked. The look he leveled on Shea made no secret of his distrust.

She forced herself to meet his gaze evenly. Not letting him intimidate her despite the tight feeling in her belly. Worse, was the thought that Fallon might be harboring some of those same thoughts. She couldn't even fault him if that was the case. She did keep secrets—things that could drastically turn the tide for his people.

Sometimes she felt like a piece of meat caught between two ravenous wolf packs, tugged back and forth, until she threatened to rip right down the center.

"I agree with Lion Clan," Gawain said, watching Shea with an avarice that didn't suit the present discussion. "How do we know that anything discussed here will not reach our enemies ears?"

Fallon's brows lowered into a dark scowl. "You question my honor."

"Not your honor, just your choice of bedmates," Gawain said.

"Gawain, you will respect your Warlord," Henry's voice was a whip of sound.

The skin at the corner of Gawain's eyes tightened and his shoulders rose as he took a deep breath. "How can you defend him like this, Father?" Gawain asked, finally turning to address the leader of the Horse clan.

Shea fought to keep her surprise off her face at the revelation that Gawain and Henry were related. She glanced between the two. They looked nothing alike. Gawain was easily a foot taller than Henry and the bones in his face were much finer, giving him an almost delicate appearance.

"His Telroi has already admitted to withholding relevant information from our armies." Gawain gestured at Shea.

"My armies," Fallon corrected, his regard dagger-like in its sharpness.

Gawain paused in what he'd been about to say. Fallon waited until the rest had focused on him.

"Not your armies. Mine." He looked at each clan leader in turn. "In case any of you have forgotten."

The clan leaders dropped their eyes from the challenge in his, and an awkward silence descended. At least awkward to Shea, since she was the cause of the dispute.

Braden met Fallon's gaze with a stubborn one of his own, while Darius had a thoughtful expression on his face. Shea suspected that any ground she might have won with Braden had disappeared with her admission that she'd withheld information regarding the Highland's defenses.

She kept her sigh inside.

Fallon returned his gaze to Gawain, giving him his full regard. It was like watching two titans square off, prepared to do battle. Only, one of these titans held all of the weapons and was assured the win.

Gawain bared his teeth in a fake smile. "Of course, Warlord. I never dreamed otherwise."

Fallon let it go, his body relaxing next to Shea's. "As I said, I will take a small force into these Highlands and meet with these pathfinders to see if there are any weapons that we might use in this battle."

"We could go back to our lands," Ben said. "We've gained our spoils from the Lowlands. Our people have never lingered this long after conquering our enemy."

There was a rustle as the others murmured varying degrees of agreement.

Fallon looked at Braden and bowed his head. The other stranger, the one they'd called Ember, shifted, his big body appearing discomfited for the first time.

Braden took a deep breath. "That's not an option."

"For more than one reason." Fallon's words didn't invite questions.

Ember and Braden looked like they might say more, before settling back at a warning look from Fallon. Neither appeared happy.

"I'll be taking an element from all of the clans. Darius will work with the division commanders to identify those who will follow me into the Highlands. The rest will stay here and maintain the progress we've already made." He waited a beat as the rest of the clan leaders absorbed this information. "That is all. You are dismissed. Tend to your injured and comfort your people."

The group dispersed. Shea was interested to note Gawain and Van leaving together, their heads close as they murmured together.

"That's going to turn into a pain in the ass," Darius said coming to stand next to her.

She made a sound of agreement before glancing up at the normally genial-looking man. Today, his face had grooves carved into his skin, his eyes tired with a hint of sorrow behind them.

They weren't close—he was more Fallon's friend than hers and had been responsible for essentially kidnapping her from her former life—but she couldn't help the empathy she felt for him. She had friends here, but he'd grown up with these people. He probably had family and friends that were put in danger.

"Did you lose anyone?" Shea asked.

He nodded, grief leaking through his normal shields.

She hesitated before laying a hand on his shoulder. Words always felt so inadequate in situations like these. She remembered people voicing platitudes after her return from the Badlands. They brought little comfort and usually made her want to punch something.

Sometimes the only thing to do was offer silent commiseration.

After a long moment Darius said, "Eamon and his team are among my first choice to head into the Highlands." His eyes were shrewd as Shea looked away. "Their time spent with you will serve them well, I think. They're uniquely qualified to face the dangers of your homeland."

Shea couldn't argue with that. Of any in Fallon's army, Eamon and Buck were the two who were most prepared for what lay above the fault. Their time spent with her meant they'd learned more than most about beast sign, not to mention the campfire stories she'd shared on occasion. Nothing that would have pointed to her origin, just stories meant to caution about what lay in the dark places of these lands.

"You're going to have to make a choice, you know," Darius said when Shea was quiet. "Between us and who you used to be. Someone who splits their loyalty between two gives their loyalty to none."

"It's not that easy," Shea said. "I may wish to keep my life here but that doesn't mean I can ignore what has gone before."

Darius nodded. There was understanding in his eyes. "You're in a difficult position. One I don't envy. Do me a favor; at least consider my words. For Fallon's sake, if nothing else. Your actions affect not just yourself. A question of your loyalty is a question of his as well."

Shea didn't have a response. Seeing that she was considering his words, Darius gave her a respectful nod before taking his leave.

Fallon kept to his side of the tent as the rest of the people who'd attended the council left. Caden stopped beside him, waiting until the rest had emptied out.

"Do you have the report?" Fallon asked.

Caden gave a sharp nod. "With the eagle attack, my men were delayed starting the search for her attackers. They found no one in the forest."

"And the remains of those caught by this sleeper vine?"

"Only a few bits of metal were left. There were no distinguishing marks on the pieces, so we have nothing."

Fallon gave a grim nod and waved his hand in dismissal.

Shea waited until Caden left before approaching Fallon. She wiped sweaty palms on her pants. For the first time in a while, she wasn't sure of her welcome.

He hadn't seemed angry when he'd revealed the caverns, but that could have been for the benefit of his council. She knew that had the situations been reversed, she would not have been so forgiving.

There was a rustle from the partition and then a head topped with a riot of blond curls appeared about a foot off the ground as Mist peeked under the cloth hangings one of Fallon's servants had hung in place of the old partition.

Seeing that the coast was clear, Mist disappeared back into Shea and Fallon's sleeping quarters. Her rear appeared as the she crawled backwards through the partition. Shea watched with a tinge of amusement as the child dragged a fur that was easily three times her size across the floor and then under the table Fallon leaned against. There, Mist mounded her fur, creating a nest at Fallon's feet.

For the first time in hours, Shea felt a lightening to the feelings of seriousness and near hopelessness the eagles had brought with them.

She walked to the table and knelt down. "What are you doing down there?"

Mist's eyes appeared over her fur, their blue depths dancing with the mirth only a child could summon. She was silent as she ducked back under her furs. A giggle tinkled up from her nest.

Fallon crouched down, observing the child-sized lump under the furs before he looked to Shea. His lips curved the barest bit at the corners before he stood. Shea took that to mean he didn't mind Mist's presence.

Shea set a hand on what she thought was the lump's back and shook it gently. She was rewarded by the sound of a faint giggle.

She smiled as she stood. The smile remained even as she met Fallon's eyes over the table.

He had several maps and reports spread out before him. "Are you planning to keep the lostling?"

"Lostling?"

"It's what we call those who've lost their families or been abandoned to the mercy of the clan."

Shea supposed it was a better term than throwaway, but not by much.

Her gaze was pensive as she stared at the table under which Mist had bedded down. She wasn't sure how to have this conversation. To be honest, she hadn't thought much beyond saving the little girl and had never considered what would come after.

"What would happen to her if we didn't keep her?" Shea asked in a cautious voice. There was no way she could send the child back to the people who had abused her.

"She wouldn't be given to the people who had her before if that's what you're asking," Fallon said. Seeing the question on her face, he continued, "Chirron told me about the bruises and scars you found on her. Some old and showing signs of healing."

She nodded, her face grim at the reminder. She rolled her lips between her teeth, not sure whether to ask about what should be done about the people who'd abused her.

"Do you know what clan she came from?" Shea asked.

"Chirron plans to ask around to see if he can find who was supposed to be caring for her. It will be more difficult than I'd like with all of the newcomers. It would help narrow the search if you can get details from her."

Shea screwed her face up into a grimace. She wasn't sure she was the right person for the task, not having extensive experience with children. They were cute, but she'd never interacted with them for more than a few minutes every couple of months. She had a feeling the conversation with Mist could go very badly, very quickly. The last thing she wanted to do after the traumatizing experiences of this afternoon and the trauma of her past abuse was further scar the child for life.

Fallon lifted an eyebrow, guessing at Shea's thoughts. "Children are not as fragile as you seem to think. You've got her trust, and I'm betting she considers you a hero after you saved her from the eagle. Just talk to her and see what you can find out."

He made it sound so easy. Too bad she had a feeling it would be like trying to walk a tight rope through a nest of hornets.

"How do you know so much about children?" Shea asked.

"I've spent many hours with the children of the various clans, playing, and getting to know them when I can."

Shea felt surprise at this admission. It wasn't that she thought Fallon an ogre incapable of dealing with children, but she had never pictured him going out of his way to spend time with the mini beasts.

It explained so much. In the first mission she'd embarked on when Eamon mistook her for a scout and forced her to join his squad, they'd come across a village that had sacrificed their children to a revenant pack. Even day-old babies had not been spared. Fallon had executed every man and woman in that village with the exception of two, whom he charged with telling everyone they met of what he'd done to their village. And if that wasn't enough, he also burned down every building until they were fine ash before burning the fields of crops and then salting the ground they stood on.

The Trateri didn't mess around when it came to vengeance. They took honor very seriously. Cross them and it wouldn't be just one person paying the price.

The incident had been the start of Shea seeing the Trateri as more than just people she needed to escape from.

"What will you do when Chirron locates those responsible for her care?" Shea asked, suspecting she knew the answer already.

"Children are the clan's future. Neglect them and you neglect the heart of your clan." Fallon's brows lowered, and his expression darkened. "Anybody who could abuse a child of their clan is not someone I want among my people. They will be dealt with in the way I deal with all of my enemies."

Death. And probably not a very nice death at that. She still had nightmares sometimes about the manner in which Fallon had put his brother to death. It was a slow, torturous, way to go. She sometimes heard the pleading and sobbing in unguarded moments. His death had been justifiable, given he'd tried to have Fallon killed several times. That didn't mean she rejoiced in it.

Shea tapped the fingertips of one hand against the table as she delayed the next thing she wanted to ask.

"I did not need you to protect me from my council," Fallon said, bringing up the topic Shea dreaded.

She jerked one shoulder up in a shrug. "I told the truth."

"The truth is a weapon best wielded carefully."

She cocked her head. "The truth is the truth. It doesn't change."

He arched an eyebrow as his lips quirked. "Doesn't it?"

"What do you mean?"

His face was thoughtful as he considered his next words. "When you are leading an expedition, how do you make your decision on what course to take?"

"I consult any maps I might have of the area. If it's a route I'm familiar with, I take into account what beasts may be close, the physical capabilities of those with me and the likely obstacles we will encounter on any given path."

"How much of that do you share with those you lead?"

She saw his point. The answer was very little. Some because they wouldn't care, but mostly because she didn't trust those type of decisions to committee. She'd always operated under the assumption that what they didn't know couldn't hurt them. They couldn't argue with her if she just gave them the answer she thought best.

She thought a moment and then conceded, well they could, but it was a lot easier to ignore them or get them to do what she wanted, if she didn't explain how she had arrived at that conclusion.

She frowned at Fallon. "That situation is different. I didn't trust the ones I led to make the right decisions or to keep themselves alive. Your council should be different."

Right?

"Why? Because they're Trateri?" His smile was humorless. "Or is it because you think clan leaders should be above such things. I trust them as much I would a viper at my throat. Perhaps less. They are my allies because it serves their needs, but make no mistake, they would turn on me in a moment if it served their purposes and they thought they could survive."

"I thought you trusted Darius and Braden."

He nodded. "They are among the few. I consider them brothers." An echo of pain entered his expression. "Perhaps more so than my actual blood. I can trust that they and my Anateri are unlikely to betray me."

Her gaze sharpened. That sounded like he allowed for the possibility for anyone to have the potential of betrayal. That was a distressing thought. Did he feel the same about her? Was he waiting for her to turn against him? She didn't know if she could live her life constantly having to prove her love and loyalty.

"Your army is loyal to you."

He nodded. "Yes, and many of the clans as well. The difference is they love a legend—the Hawkvale, the warlord to unite all of the clans under one banner. It is both harder and easier to lose their trust and loyalty."

She understood what he meant. An idea was both easier and harder to discredit. It was ephemeral, something intangible. As Shea had discovered when she was a scout, everyone had a story about the Hawkvale. He was this larger than life character that they only knew by what they'd heard.

It would only take a few well-placed rumors and whispers to get the ball rolling. If Fallon's actions then fed into that rumor, it wouldn't be long before the morale in his army turned nasty. For instance, if the loyalty of his Telroi was called into question, his men might not be so willing to back him against the clan leaders.

She looked down at the table, drawing a pattern against the wood as she pondered his words.

His hand touched hers. "Our enemies are numerous, and they are looking for a chink in our defenses. They are hungry for blood. To everyone else, we are partners, united against all comers."

On the surface, she believed his words wholeheartedly, but there was an undercurrent to them that left her feeling their time together was running short. She covered his hand with her own and leaned into him, resting her forehead on his bicep.

How was she going to balance the two forces in her life without losing sight of who she was and the promises she'd made?

His other hand cupped the back of her head. He smoothed her hair before touching his lips to her ear.

He tugged on her, scooping her up and dragging her into his lap. She wrapped her arms around him and hugged him, setting her chin on his shoulder.

"You know they're going to try to kill you," she said softly into his ear. She wasn't talking about his council.

His arms tightened around her for a brief moment. "They may try, but better men than them have failed."

She sighed and pressed her face into the side of his neck.

"They'll seek to divide us. They'll strike while we're not looking."

"They will not be successful."

She wanted to believe him. She really did. She just didn't know if she could. He didn't understand her people like she did.

"This is not a good idea."

"You said it yourself. There is something wrong. We must do everything we can to find that problem and destroy it." He moved a piece of hair away from her face. His thumb ran up and down the side of her neck in a caress that sent shivers coursing through Shea's body. She leaned into his touch. "Besides, wasn't it you who advocated for going up there to see what was happening?"

She pulled back, her eyes snapping fire at him. "I'd planned to go by myself, and you damn well know it."

He lifted an eyebrow. "How is that less dangerous than what I have planned? At least I will be taking an army to protect my back."

She rolled her eyes. "More like present a nice big target. I could have slipped in and out before anyone was the wiser. You can't kill what you don't even know is there."

"Now who's cocky?"

She gave him a sharp grin. "It's not arrogance if it's true."

His smile when it came was dark and wicked and hinted of things done in the dark. He leaned forward, pressing his lips to hers. She met the fury of his passion with a storm of her own.

There was a small giggle from the ground.

Shea and Fallon pulled apart, looking at each other with equally surprised looks. They turned in unison to find an imp with a mass of blond curls and blue eyes staring up at them in innocence.

"I forgot she was here," Fallon said in bemusement.

The statement struck Shea as funny and she buried her face in his neck as she shook with laughter.

His chest rumbled as he chuckled. He leaned back to stare at the ceiling. "We'll have to figure out other living arrangements for her tomorrow. She can't stay in our room at night."

The thought of a child's presence forcing the Warlord to abstinence made Shea laugh harder.

"You're the one who wanted children," Shea said after she'd gotten her laughter under control.

He stared at the child with a put-out expression. "I'm beginning to rethink that decision."

She pressed a kiss against his jaw and stood. "Come on, sweetie. Let's find you a place to sleep for the night."

Mist scampered out from under the table and ran up to hug Fallon before latching onto Shea's hand.

CHAPTER NINETEEN

D oes she speak?" Daere asked, her gaze fastened on Mist as the little girl investigated the tangled ivy growing along the trunk of the tree. Mist's gaze was fascinated as she bent closer to peer at something among the vines.

"Not much. Not yet," Shea answered.

"Is she mute?"

Shea shook her head. "Chirron didn't think so. I think she just needs to get comfortable before she opens up."

Daere's gaze was pensive as she stared at the girl. To Shea's surprise, she hadn't protested Mist's presence when she'd arrived to speak with Shea about preparations for the upcoming journey. In fact, the woman had seemed all too eager to have the girl join them.

Shea had expected at least some protest, maybe Daere pointing out how it wasn't seemly for the Warlord's Telroi to have appropriated an orphan. Again, the other woman had surprised her.

"Have you explained that you're leaving yet?" Daere asked.

Shea shook her head. That was why they were out here. It wouldn't be long before Fallon and his men were ready to depart—maybe days. Shea didn't want to disappear on the little girl, but there was no way she could bring Mist with her into the Highlands. Not when she still didn't know what they were walking into.

Daere's expression reflected understanding, and she turned the conversation to other matters. "With her name, I suspect she may have originated from the Rain Clan. Some among our people will give their children names that honor their clans and show solidarity with them."

Shea nodded. She'd thought that too, but hadn't wanted to say anything until she had proof. She had to move carefully or risk alienating certain sects of the Trateri even more than she already had.

"She won't speak of what came before," Shea said. "It is making things difficult."

Daere nodded. "I'm sure you'll track them down. You are nothing if not resourceful."

Shea raised an eyebrow, amused. "That almost sounded like a compliment."

Daere met her eyes with a sardonic look of her own. "Don't let it go to your head."

Mist drifted toward a white ivy. It wasn't deadly, but it would leave the child uncomfortable and with a nasty rash for a few days.

"Mist, don't touch that," Shea said. The little girl jerked her hands back, her shoulders hunching. Her wide, frightened gaze swung to Shea. Everything about the little girl shouted fear, from the crumpled expression to the way she held her body. It made Shea's chest hurt to see that expression on her face at just four little words.

Daere cursed softly enough that the little girl wouldn't hear them. She kept her face arranged in a pleasant expression—a feat that Shea envied—as she said words that made even Shea's ears burn. "When we find the people who hurt this little girl, I am going to enjoy visiting some of the tortures of the afterworld on them."

Shea couldn't agree more.

"I'm not mad at you, Mist," Shea reassured the little girl. She came and knelt beside her and pointed at the cluster of leaves Mist had been about to touch. "See the white veins in the middle and the darker green on the edge."

The fear didn't fade from Mist's eyes even as she looked where Shea was pointing.

"There're usually three leaves that come to a point; like this. Do you see?" Shea used a stick to point out the different features, softly touching each feature as she described them. Mist frowned as she looked where Shea indicated. "It's white ivy. It's not really poisonous. At least not in the way we think of poison. There is a sticky oil on the leaves that most people are highly allergic too. That's how it causes a blistering rash. If you see three, leave it be."

Mist nodded solemnly after Shea finished, her eyes so serious as she mouthed the last phrase to herself.

"You know, Mist, Fallon and I will have to leave on a journey soon."

The little girl's head shot up, and she looked at Shea with horrified eyes. Shea's heart clenched at the fear she saw on Mist's face.

Mist gestured to herself and then Shea, her hopeful question clear.

Shea shook her head. "I'm sorry. You cannot come with us. Where we're going is too dangerous to bring you along."

Mist's face fell, and she directed her attention down at her feet.

Shea saw that she was losing the girl and tried to console her. "My good friend, Daere, will look after you while we're gone."

Daere smiled at the little girl, her expression warmer and softer than anything Shea had seen before. She came and knelt beside Shea. "Hello Mist. I am very happy to meet you."

The little girl looked unconvinced and sent a reproachful look Shea's way. It would have been funny if there hadn't been desperation behind Mist's eyes.

Seeing it, Daere said, "Shea said as a treat she would teach us a little about the forest before she left, and when she gets back she will teach us about more of the Lowlands. Isn't that right, Shea?"

Mist looked between Shea and Daere with suspicion before finally giving Shea a hopeful expression.

Shea smiled at her. "My mother used to take me on trips when I was your age, and she would teach me everything about the world around me."

She really had. Even twenty years later Shea still remembered those trips and the patience her mother had displayed. Shea had been a curious child. Always trying to wander off and explore.

"I can teach you a little before I leave and then more when I return," Shea said, looking around at the forest. They wouldn't be able to go far, but to a girl who'd grown up in the Trateri homelands, this place would seem plenty wonderous.

Mist's hand touched the back of Shea's hand. She waited until Shea looked at her again to point to another plant, this one with a yellow flower that looked like a spiral inside.

"Do you want to know what that is?"

Mist nodded, her eyes still solemn. Shea's mouth quirked in a half smile. "Very well."

Daere drifted closer as Shea explained the various properties that she knew for the flower the locals called a golden spiral. An hour passed as Mist and Daere found more and more things for Shea to describe. Before long Shea was holding an impromptu beast class as she sketched out different beast footprints in the dirt.

Shea was completely absorbed in the descriptions as the three of them put their heads together to look at the current beast print Shea had pressed into the ground.

She didn't even notice how they had become the center of attention until someone asked, "How do you distinguish between the revenant and the cackle dog? The two prints look almost identical to me."

Shea looked up to find several Trateri dressed in clan colors that she didn't recognize, gathered around watching. The men and one woman were all bigger than the other Trateri she'd met. Their features broader with a fierce look in their eyes that made Shea think that they weren't used to playing nice with others.

Ember's clan leader stood among them, his clothes much plainer than yesterday. He was missing the leather armor and the bloodthirsty look. Surrounded by those Shea assumed were his kinsmen, he almost seemed relaxed.

Daere stood up, brushing her hands against the seat of her pants. "Zeph, I had heard your clan finally joined us."

Zeph inclined his head, a smile pulling at the corner of his lips. "It is good to see you again, little cousin."

Shea's eyebrows lifted. Cousin? This man was related to Fallon?

Seeing the question written on her face, Zeph addressed Shea, "We're related on the paternal side, whereas Hawkvale shares a connection with my lovely cousin on the maternal side."

Shea nodded, not knowing what else to say. The Trateri family bonds were important to them and resembled a thorny thicket. Though Fallon had no immediate family, he seemed to have many extended relations.

A tall man, his blond curls tamed into a bun on top of his head ventured close and crouched next to Mist. "Are you learning about these beasts that we've heard so much about?"

Mist ducked her head and edged closer to Shea, not stopping until she was behind her.

The man looked up a Shea, his eyes sharp and suspicious. Mist stayed where she was, her head pressed into the back of Shea's leg.

Shea stared back at the man and his friends with no clue as to what to say. Mist's reaction was extreme, and she didn't know quite how to explain it to strangers. Or if she even should, given the fact that Fallon planned to find the person behind the child's abuse.

Daere stepped into the silence. "What brings you here?"

Zeph and his man didn't look away from Shea and the girl, their eyes focused and intent.

The blond leaned forward, trying to peer around Shea. He gave Mist a charming smile "It's alright, little one. I won't harm you."

Mist burrowed deeper into Shea.

"It doesn't look like she wants to talk to you," Shea said, not liking how much interest he showed in the child.

She still wasn't sure how abrupt she should be, not with Ember's clan leader standing right there. The last thing she wanted to do was alienate another potential ally of Fallon's. What she wanted to do was scoop Mist into her arms and leave the area as fast as possible. Perhaps set Chirron on them to investigate. The chances were the little girl had associated the man from Ember with someone she used to know, but it wouldn't hurt to have him checked out.

"Bax?" Zeph asked, his gaze watchful.

"There are bruises on the little one's arms and the back of her legs." The blond's voice remained pleasant as he relayed that information, though there was an edge to it hinting at his unhappiness.

Zeph gaze moved to Shea as the last semblance of friendliness faded from his face.

"I don't care who you spend your nights with, but if that child has suffered abuse at your hands, I will see that you are punished to the fullest extent of our laws." Zeph gave her a look that said he'd very much enjoy taking her apart with his bare hands. That he might not wait for justice.

Shea's jaw dropped. Why did they immediately assume that she was the one to hurt Mist?

The blond lunged forward, attempting to grab Mist. His hand barely grazed her shirt before Shea swept her away with one hand while blocking his attempt with the other. He spun, his arm reaching up to grab her, going for her shirt. It was a technique that Trenton had used on her more than once in their self-defense training.

This man was a shade slower than Trenton and didn't have Trenton's creativity. Shea responded, her body reacting through sheer muscle memory. She fell back a step, grasping the hand gripping her shirt and applying pressure to the wrist while kicking at his knee. She pulled him forward, breaking his hold and pulling him off balance. He landed on his back with a grunt.

She thought she'd managed to evade him until his hand shot out to grab her ankle and yank. She hit the ground with a grunt. She kicked out, connecting with the blond's head as she scrambled backwards. If he got ahold of her, her chances of escaping were seriously reduced.

"Leave her alone!" a small voice screamed. A small form flew at Bax. Mist attacked him with furious fists, screaming her head off the whole time. Shea was taken aback at the fury on the little girl's face and didn't move for a long moment, watching the unfolding violence with wide eyes and an open mouth.

Bax, to his credit, didn't offer the girl any violence in return. He struggled with keeping Mist from hurting herself or him with only mild success. Shea winced as the little girl landed a blow above his eye.

Trenton appeared like a shadow behind Zeph, his blade a threat against the clan leader's neck. Seeing the situation devolving to a place they wouldn't be able to recover from without shedding blood, Shea darted in, grabbing the little girl under the arms and dragging her back as Mist kicked and squirmed in her arms. She tried like mad to attack Bax where he lay on the ground, his hands open and spread as if to say he was unarmed and harmless.

Shea soon saw why as Wilhelm appeared from Shea's other side, blade drawn and his face an implacable mask.

So much for not offending another clan leader. Her guard had his blade at Ember's throat and her other one looked like he was seriously considering stabbing the man lying on the ground through the stomach.

Daere stepped forward, her face flushed and her eyes glittering furiously. "Explain the meaning of this."

For a minute Shea thought she meant Trenton.

"Ember will not tolerate the abuse of a child," Zeph said, his face reserved as he ignored the blade at his throat. He looked with interest at Shea trying to sooth Mist by rocking her back and forth. The child's chest heaved with the force of a bellows. "But perhaps we were hasty in our assumptions."

Shea gave him an incredulous look as if to say 'ya, think?' The woman beside Zeph smothered a smirk.

Zeph's expression was wry as he acknowledged her unvoiced point.

"I met Mist right before the eagle attack," Shea said. She chanced straightening, not wanting to have this conversation while she was on her knees. "It wasn't until afterwards when a healer was examining her for injuries that we discovered she'd been mistreated."

"She's the child you saved," the blond on the ground said. Wilhelm shifted forward, his movement a threat. Bax held his hands up higher and gave the other man an apologetic look.

"Yes."

"My apologies, Daere," Zeph told the other woman. "I should have known you of all people wouldn't serve a woman who abused children."

Shea looked between the other two, feeling like she'd missed something. This wasn't the first time someone had referred to Daere and a child. It was on the tip of her tongue to ask a question. She swallowed it back when she noticed the grief on Daere's face. Shea had a feeling this story had a very sad ending. She didn't want to subject Daere to having to explain such a thing in front of all these people. She'd tell her if she wanted to, eventually.

"Yes, you should have known better," Daere said, not giving Ember's clan leader an inch of understanding.

Zeph inclined his head as much as the blade Trenton held at his throat would permit. "You're right. This was an unfortunate assumption."

Daere's face was implacable. "I'm not the one you need to apologize to."

Zeph nodded, his gaze shifted to Shea. "Please forgive our jumping to conclusions."

"You're all idiots," Shea declared before she could think better of it.

A choked sound came from the woman at Zeph's left. Shea ignored her and the slightly surprised look on Zeph's face. Did he really think she'd let this go so easily?

"You frightened Mist and damn near created an incident that could have left several dead. Even if you'd been right about me abusing her, there are a dozen different ways you could have handled it that didn't lead to bloodshed."

"We're Trateri, darling. Bloodshed is what we do," the man lying on the ground drawled.

Shea lifted an eyebrow, utterly unimpressed with his charm. "And scaring little girls until they cry, is that also what you do?"

Bax frowned, his blue eyes flicking to the little girl and then back to Shea. "That wasn't my intention." To Mist, he said, "Little one, I meant you nor your protector any harm. Please forgive me."

The smile he flashed her would have decimated anyone over the age of sixteen. It was charm personified. Shea was willing to bet Bax had ladies lined up just begging for his apologies.

Mist peeked at him before burying her head back in Shea. "No."

Bax's smile faded and he looked slightly irked. Shea had to fight against a smile. It would be many years before a smile like that would work on the little girl.

The woman at Zeph's side broke into peals of laughter, the sound cutting through the gathering tension faster than a knife. "Finally, someone capable of ignoring that oh-so-slick charm that you're known for."

"Shut it, Holly. No one asked you." Bax shot the woman a glare.

"No one needed to. As the only other woman in this camp who ever saw through that phony façade of yours, I must show her my appreciation." Holly came forward, taking a knee in front of Mist. Shea didn't move, watching with interest this other woman dressed in the same simple garb as the men. While the Trateri allowed their women to serve in the army and carry out tasks traditionally seen as duties only suited to men in Highland and Lowland society, it was still rare to see one who actually fit in that world.

"Hello, little one. On behalf of the numbskulls behind me, I sincerely apologize for the fright you took."

Mist hands squeezed Shea's pants a she regarded the other woman with a frown.

"They didn't mean any harm in it. They really thought they were trying to help." Holly's face was open and kind, her expression soft and her eyes warm.

Mist looked up at Shea as if asking permission. Shea smiled back at her. The little girl looked back at Holly and gave a nod, her eyes focused on the ground the entire time.

If nothing else, this incident had at least gotten Mist speaking again. Shea was grateful for that, even if she would have wished the circumstances were different. She kept her happiness at Mist speaking to herself, not wanting the little girl to become self-conscious and retreat back into her shell.

Holly slapped her thigh and stood. "That settles it then. The idiots back there will refrain from any more heroic actions that don't suit them, and you and I will become friends." Holly looked at Shea. "So, you're the Telroi I've heard so much about."

"My name is Shea." She wasn't quite sure what to make of this woman who looked friendly and had charmed Mist where her friend couldn't. "Not Telroi."

Shea didn't enjoy being referred to by the role she played in Fallon's life. She was a person, damn it, with dreams and struggles of her own. If they'd called her scout or pathfinder, that would have been one thing. The term Telroi made her feel like an appendage of Fallon's.

The skin at Holly's eyes crinkled as her smile lit up her face. "Very good. I will remember that for future."

Holly turned to Daere, offering her right hand in a warrior's greeting. Daere took her arm, clasping it right below the elbow. "It's been a long time."

"A few years at least," Daere said with a smile.

Their body language said they were friends and had been for a long time.

"Can you tell your watchdog to ease up?" Zeph asked, his expression set to rueful.

Shea eyed Trenton where he still stood with his blade pressed against Zeph's neck. He met her eyes with unhappy ones of his own. She jerked her head. He frowned but obeyed, withdrawing the blade and stepping away. Zeph pressed a hand to his neck, his fingers coming away with blood.

"You were a little overzealous, don't you think?" he asked.

Trenton gave him an implacable look Shea swore was part of the training the Anateri had to go through. She'd seen the exact same look on more than one Anateri's face.

"What are you doing here?" Shea asked before anything else could be said that might jeopardize Fallon's relationship with the Ember clan. Shea was already trying to figure out how to explain to him why Trenton had held a knife on their clan leader and why she'd kicked one of them while they were down.

"Darius's suggestion. My vanguard and I will be accompanying you and Fallon on your trip into the Highlands. Darius thought you could set us up with a few lessons so we'll be better prepared," Zeph explained with a slight quirk to his lips.

Shea arched an eyebrow. "I don't know why. Clark and Charles usually host the classes on beasts. I help out sometimes but that's really more their thing than mine."

"But you're the expert on all things beast and Highlands related," Zeph said smoothly. "My men and women deserve the best training they can get. You're the best so you'll train them."

Shea gave him an incredulous look. Did he really think he could order her to train his men? Especially after the whole affair with Mist?

"Am I now?" she asked.

"The class is also full," Holly said, with a reproachful glance at her clan leader. "Clark said you might be able to help us."

Shea shut her mouth and stared at the other woman in thought. Clark and Charles would have to be overwhelmed with new recruits for them to pass off this lot to Shea. They'd been trying to grow the concept of the beast class and get more clans participating in it under the assumption that more people meant more information, which meant a more complete picture of what they faced. For them to pass people off to Shea, things had to have gotten out of control.

Shea stared at the five Trateri from the Ember Clan standing before her. It would be so easy to turn them away. Despite their apology, Shea had to wonder if they would have leapt to the same conclusion had she been Trateri. It was one thing to know you were an outsider and another to have it thrust into your face.

Still, could she afford to turn them away knowing that their deaths due to ignorance would be on her head? When such a simple thing as sharing a little of her knowledge would keep them alive? Could she justify withholding that knowledge for any reason?

The answer was no. She couldn't. Even if they had been enemies she would feel compelled to help them. It might not be the pathfinder way or even the Trateri way, but it was her way. If she could give such a simple thing, she would.

She sighed. "I'll see what I can do. You do know that it took me almost an entire lifetime to gather this knowledge. There's no way I can impart all of it in just a few hours."

"Give us what you can. You never know when something will come in handy." Zeph sounded distracted as he noticed several men heading their way. The head of the Rain clan was at the front of the group.

They all eyed the newcomers with varying levels of suspicion and distrust.

"Ember," Gawain said with a nod so slight that Shea wasn't sure she'd imagined or not "I see you had the same idea as us."

"Rain." Zeph's face relaxed into smooth lines, all suspicion wiped away.

Bax climbed to his feet and stood with his legs spread and arms held slightly bent at his sides. He looked relaxed, but Shea suspected he could explode into movement at any time.

Gawain finally graced Shea his regard. "The Hawkvale's Telroi. I have been looking for you."

Shea didn't miss the dismissive glance that Gawain swept over Mist or the way the child wedged herself tighter behind Shea as if afraid to draw more attention to herself.

"It seems you've found me."

The smile he gave her was amused and polite and held the kind of goodwill that almost made Shea question her previous impression.

"I believe we got off on the wrong foot," Gawain said, stepping closer. Wilhelm tensed at her back and even Trenton eyed him with a degree of suspicion usually reserved for Lowlanders. "I will admit I lost my head yesterday and said some regrettable things. We lost some good people. I'm afraid I let it get to me. I apologize for any words that may have offended."

Pretty words, but Shea wasn't sure how many of those were sincere. He seemed earnest, his expression open and containing a friendliness that had been lacking yesterday.

She just didn't quite believe it. Something kept her from trusting him entirely.

She could see how the confusion and attack might have led him to being a tad more hostile than he would be normally. For that reason, she was inclined to give him the benefit of the doubt despite her reservations.

"I understand. Yesterday was a trying day for all involved."

He held his hand out to her to clasp. "I hope we can put this behind us for Fallon's sake, if nothing else. We were as close as brothers growing up. I would hate to have harsh feelings between myself and the woman he has chosen to have by his side."

Shea stared at his hand, not liking how he was forcing her into accepting his apology but also not seeing a way to gracefully decline. She clasped his hand, grasping his forearm in much the same way Daere had clasped Holly's. Her nod was grudging.

"I'm told you have much to share regarding the beasts and terrain we might encounter in the Highlands," Gawain said stepping back. "My men and I would appreciate any guidance you might be able to give."

Both Ember and Rain were accompanying Fallon into the Highlands? Shea would have thought he'd want some of the men who were familiar with the Lowlands. They at least had some idea of what to expect.

She eyed both sets of Trateri, wishing not for the first time that she had undertaken this journey alone. Keeping all of these people alive was going to take a miracle.

"Of course, I'd be happy to share what I know." Shea looked down to where Mist was still burrowed into her. "Perhaps we can pick this up tomorrow. There are a few things that need my attention today."

Gawain looked at the girl attached to Shea. "Hello, lalu. Could you spare your friend for a few hours today?"

Mist didn't answer, though Shea could feel her body shaking.

"She must be shy," Gawain said, aiming a smile at Shea as he stood.

"Something like that."

"I'm afraid we'll need your help today," Gawain said. "As the Hawkvale intends to ride out tomorrow."

What? Shea hadn't heard that.

Gawain looked sympathetic to the surprise clearly written on her face. "You hadn't heard? He made his decision this morning. Those with orders are preparing even as we speak."

She'd seen Fallon at the midday meal. He could have told her then. Why hadn't he? Was he afraid to trust her for fear of the information getting to the pathfinders? That couldn't be it. He may have just been distracted. There could be a million reasons for why he hadn't told her.

"I'm sorry if this is a surprise. I assumed you knew." Gawain really did look apologetic.

Shea's smile held a thread of tension. "I'm sure he just got caught up in preparations. Anyway, if that's the case I will need to prepare as well. We have several weeks of travel before we reach the Highlands. I can start teaching Ember and Rain the basics on the trail."

It'd give her more time and also real-world examples to draw from.

Gawain clasped his hands. "Perfect. We will find you then." He turned to Zeph. "Is that an acceptable plan to you, Ember?"

Zeph eyed him with an odd expression on his face, one Shea couldn't quite decipher. Holly, at his side, also looked displeased at Rain's presence.

"That is an acceptable compromise for Ember," Zeph said. "We will find you on the trail."

Shea gave them all a look that said she looked forward to it. Or at least that was what she hoped it said. In reality, she was dreading the encounter already.

"It is good to see you again, my fierce one," Gawain told Daere as she fell into step with Shea.

Daere was reserved as she gave Gawain a nod. "And you as well."

"I had hoped to spend more time getting reacquainted with you," he said to her back.

"There will be time for that later," Daere said. Her smile was awkward. She clasped Shea's elbow and steered her away from the group, reaching down with her other hand to tug on Mist's arm.

"What was that about?" Shea asked.

"Nothing."

Shea snorted. She wasn't that dumb. "Nothing, my ass. Why did I sense a vague threat behind his words?"

"Because you did," Daere said.

"Is he a danger to you?" Shea asked, her eyes locked on Daere's face. If he was, Shea didn't care who he was or how much Fallon needed him. She'd put a stop to him herself, even if she had to lead the man into a beast's nest to do it.

"Not in the way you mean." Daere didn't look at Shea, her gaze turned forward.

"What do you mean?"

"Gawain is mostly harmless. He's always been jealous of the attention Henry gives Fallon. It's one of the reasons he broke off to form his own clan."

Shea shot a look at Trenton and Wilhelm who kept pace with them. Their attention was directed to the area surrounding them, but Shea would have bet anything that they were listening to every word.

"And how is he not harmless?"

"He's very good at manipulating people. His ambition has a way of blinding him to everything but what he needs to get what he wants. That ambition has hurt many people along the way."

Shea took her words to mean that Daere was one of those who fell victim to Gawain's ambitions.

"So, I shouldn't trust him."

Daere huffed out a laugh. "You shouldn't trust anyone but Fallon and your guards. Haven't you learned anything in the weeks with me?"

"I don't remember that being one of the lessons."

Daere gave Shea a sideways glance. "It was in the subtext."

"Ah, well. There's your problem. You're relying on me to catch the subtext. I'm a straightforward kind of person."

"I'm beginning to understand that."

CHAPTER TWENTY

S hea looked up at the grey cliffs that towered over them, the Trateri warband Fallon had gathered stretched for half a mile behind her. It had taken two weeks to get to this point. Saying goodbye to Mist had been difficult. The little girl had seemed so alone and small when Shea had told her she would be staying behind with Daere. It was one of the few times Shea had regretted leaving.

Now, they stood at the base of Bearan's Fault looking up at cliffs that would be impossible to climb unless they left the mounts behind. Even if they did, it would be a difficult and time-consuming journey since the cliffs towered over them by several hundred feet.

She took a deep breath as she stared up at all that separated her from home. When she'd first thought of coming back here, she hadn't realized how nostalgic she would be or how much she'd missed the Highlands. It was like an old, crotchety friend that probably hadn't even noticed she was gone. Still, it felt like a piece of her that had been missing was suddenly back in its rightful place.

"You came down that?" Clark asked, his voice hushed and shocked.

Shea nodded.

"I always knew you were crazy," Buck said, his mount coming up on the other side of Shea's horse. "No wonder you have no problem jumping off things." He had a look of consternation as he looked up at the cliffs.

"I'd like to say it's not as high as it looks, but it really is," Shea told them. "On the Highland side, approaching the fault is like walking off the edge of the world— scary, and exhilarating, and oh so fun."

Buck gave her a look that said she was proving his point.

"Since meeting you, I feel my life has gotten increasingly more interesting," Eamon said from the other side of Buck. "I'm not sure if that's a good thing or not."

"Have any of our people ever been up there?" Clark asked. "I don't remember anyone claiming raider's rights."

"I've never heard of any stories," Buck said, still staring at the cliffs like they were something that had been put there to purposely thwart him. "All of our tales deal with the Lowlands and the Badlands. I don't think our oral history even acknowledges this place."

Shea wasn't really surprised. Highlanders kept to themselves. Their home's inherent isolation made that easy. The only time they came down the fault was when they were trading, which wasn't often. The trading expedition where Shea had gotten caught by the Trateri was one of the few.

"How are we going to get up there?" Clark asked the question everyone was thinking. "How are we going to get the horses and our supplies up that?"

"There's a way." Shea spurred her horse on, steering it toward where Fallon and Caden had stopped.

She pulled on her reins, bringing the horse up beside them. Both men spared her a glance before turning to observe the cliffs blocking their way.

"It looks bigger than I imagined," Caden said, his face set in a frown.

Fallon grunted. He'd faced the cliffs before when he'd calculated the chances of a successful campaign in the Highlands. Edgecomb, the town where he'd first met Shea, wasn't far from here either.

"What's the plan?" Caden asked.

Fallon held up his hand and gestured. From the ranks behind them, two Anateri rode forward shadowing the figure that walked between their two horses. Reece looked up at the three of them.

"How do we get up it?" Fallon asked, authority ringing in his voice.

Reece smirked at Shea. "What's the matter, Shea? Don't you remember the way?"

Shea took a deep breath. "It's been over eight months since I left. I assumed your superiors would have changed the code in that time."

There was also the small fact that she couldn't exactly remember the location of the entrance. It would take days, if not weeks, for her to locate it. Then she would have to figure out the key to get inside. Somehow, she didn't think Fallon's army would wait around patiently for her to take the time to do that.

If she'd still had her maps, she might have been able to cut that time in half. The pathfinders had them coded for a reason. It would have had a hint on how to decipher the code should it have been changed.

"What happened to your map?" Reece asked with a sardonic expression. "Everything you need to know is in there."

Shea gritted her teeth as she looked away. "They're gone. I burned them."

In part because Fallon's brother had very nearly been successful in decoding them and she didn't want their secrets falling into the wrong hands. The other reason, the main reason if she was being perfectly honest, was because she didn't want the temptation of an easy escape from the Trateri and the warlord she called her own. It also took care of ever allowing love to cloud her judgment.

Reece let out a low whistle. "That takes some guts. I'm surprised he let you."

Shea's brows snapped together as she leveled Reece with a glare. "Answer his question. How do we access the cavern shortcut?"

Reece looked like he was going to continue needling Shea but a slight shift from the man at Shea's side changed his mind. Fallon looked like he'd expended all the patience he was willing to give. Shea thought he might try to strangle her cousin if he didn't get to talking, and fast.

"Fine. You've turned into such a spoilsport, you know that?"

Shea fixed him with a gaze that said she was not amused. She had always been the spoilsport among the two of them—the voice of reason in whatever insane plan that struck him.

Reece turned to walk towards the cliffs. Caden stiffened and let out a sharp whistle. The Anateri guards Fallon had posted reacted immediately. They kicked their horses into a gallop and circled Reece, weapons drawn as they herded him back towards Fallon.

"What the hell are you doing?" Reece asked, his face flushed as he glared at the guards as they used their horses to force Reece closer to where the three of them waited. It was move or be crushed, the horses snorting and bobbing their heads any time Reece looked like he planned to stand his ground.

"Shea, will you ask that musclebound idiot at your side to call off his lackeys? I don't know how you expect me to find a way into the caverns, if his men keep acting like a bunch of newbies jumping at the least provocation."

"You can tell us the location of the entrance. We will do the rest," Fallon said. He eyed Reece like he was a bug he wanted to squash.

"That won't work," Reece said, finally addressing Fallon directly.

Shea could have told him earlier that pushing Fallon was the best way to not get what you want, but she figured she'd let him dig his own grave. He was her least favorite cousin, after all.

"As your lovely friend over there could tell you, if she planned on being the least bit helpful, these entrances can be a bit tricky. If you don't know what you're doing, you could walk right past it, best-case scenario. Worst-case, you trigger something that leaves a lot of people dead, including yourself."

Caden scoffed. "You want us to believe your people have some sorcery to enable you, and you alone, to access this place. Next, you'll want us to believe that the sky might fall unless you're there to hold it up."

Reece looked at Shea. "How did you allow yourself to be caught by these dunderfucks? And why have you stayed this long?"

The guard behind Reece kicked him in the back of the head. Reece fell to his knees. He glared over his shoulder at the guard.

Shea regarded the Anateri with a wry look before addressing Reece, "That's how."

Amusement crossed Caden's face, tugging at his lips, and was gone before Shea could do more than blink at him.

"The Trateri can be very persuasive as you've just experienced," Shea said before turning to Fallon. "He does have a point though. The caverns aren't entirely natural and have been rigged with traps should they be breached by the enemy."

"I'm beginning to believe your people are the real force behind the Highlands," Fallon told her.

Reece snorted. "You're just figuring that out? Guess she does have some loyalty after all."

"Enough, Reece. Stop picking and prodding to see how he reacts," Shea said, fed up with him. "Or I'll let Fallon do to you what he's been wanting to since you snuck into our home."

"I don't know how you can call that piece of cloth held upright by a few sticks a home."

The faces of the two Anateri behind Reece darkened, neither man liking the insult. The horse of one stepped forward and shoved Reece in the back with its nose, the force almost toppling Reece back to the ground.

Shea regarded her cousin, unimpressed. "Stop saying shit you don't mean to get a rise out of them. You and I both know we've called much worse accommodations home in the past."

She knew he remembered the time they'd lived out of a cave for three months when they were teens and apprenticed to a master pathfinder. Their master thought it would be good for them to experience what it was like to be lost and alone in the Highlands, so he'd left them stranded hundreds of miles from the nearest village. They'd been lucky for that cave too, or they would have had to sleep exposed to the elements and any beast wandering by.

Reece dipped his chin as he stared up at her with a frustrated expression. She raised an eyebrow.

"If you two are done fighting, I'd like to get back to the matter at hand," Fallon said in a mild voice. The only hint of impatience was in the way his horse shifted under him and pawed the ground, picking up on its master's emotions.

"I told you a pathfinder has to find the entrance, or you risk getting a lot of people killed."

Fallon bared his teeth in a semblance of a smile. "Good thing you're not the only pathfinder here, then."

All eyes turned to Shea. Reece looked at her with a considering expression.

He shrugged. "That could work."

Shea sighed. "Tell me what I need to know so we can get this over with."

Reece crouched and picked up a rock lying next to him on the ground. "Fine, get down here so I can show you what you're looking for."

Shea dismounted and handed her reins to Fallon before walking over to where Reece was drawing a symbol on the ground.

"You're looking for this symbol."

Shea recognized the swooping circle with the squiggly line bisecting it. "This is Lodi's cavern."

"Yup." He gave her a cheeky grin.

"Why would you bring us to Lodi's pass?" she asked in a scandalized voice. "You know this place is dangerous." Not to mention unlocking it was a giant pain in the ass.

"What's Lodi's pass?" Fallon asked, coming to stand beside her so he could look over her shoulder.

Shea exhaled a gust of air. "It's the least used of the caverns. No one takes it unless they're desperate. There are things in there that don't take kindly to strangers. It's a real bitch to find, too."

"And there's your answer right there." Reece stood and tossed the rock up, catching it as it came back down. "It's nearly impossible to locate even if you've been through it before and the denizens don't even allow pathfinders access all the time. Your Warlord and his army will have an impossible time trying to get back through it after this."

"We'll have a devil of a time getting through it this time too," Shea snapped. "That's if I can even find it."

"Aww, does the great and wonderful Shea have a little self-doubt?" Reece sneered. "Too bad your Warlord refused to be reasonable, or I'd help you out."

They both looked at Fallon. He stared back at them with a ruthless expression. Shea knew without asking that he didn't plan on bending. He didn't trust Reece as far as he could throw him, and Shea couldn't say she blamed him. Reece wasn't trustworthy under the best of circumstances. His role within the pathfinders almost demanded a bit of shiftiness, and since he'd first appeared, he'd seemed to be doing everything in his power to antagonize everyone around him.

"Can you do it?" Fallon asked, his gaze direct.

Shea pinched the bridge of her nose and sighed. "I don't know. I've never come through here before. I doubt Reece even has, for all that he wants to make you think otherwise. All I have are the old stories to go by."

Fallon nodded. "That'll have to be enough."

She sure hoped so.

*

Shea pulled herself up onto a rocky outcropping. She was dirty and sweaty, her shirt a different color in places. And she felt no closer to finding that damn symbol.

"See anything?" Trenton called up to her.

She leaned over the edge of her ledge. "Nothing yet."

"Horse lords, girl. Stop leaning over things." Trenton mumbled to himself, his voice carrying on the wind, "You'd think she had a death wish or something."

After walking along the edges of the cliffs for a good hour, Shea had given up on finding the entrance below. Fallon's men had continued to look while she decided to climb, hoping to spot something from above. As her guard and one of the few with experience climbing—something he'd gained while chasing Shea all over Airabel over the past few months—Trenton had been tasked with following Shea up the cliffs.

Shea leaned back and looked up. The clouds today were light and puffy, creating shapes that shifted and changed with every breath. It would have been the perfect cloud watching opportunity.

She sighed and looked back down. The Trateri were spread in a long line up and down the cliffs. She could just make out the faint sounds of voices below as they called back and forth to each other.

If they couldn't find this entrance, Shea had a feeling Fallon would face a lot of opposition from the other clan leaders for dragging them on a wild goose chase.

They needed to find it.

She turned back to looking. This thing could be anywhere. Reece had gotten them in the general vicinity, but that didn't help much. This entrance hadn't been used in decades. It was entirely possible the symbol marking it would be covered up or weathered away. Shea doubted it had been maintained over the years once the guild decided it was more trouble than it was worth.

That brought her back to why Reece had brought them to this particular entrance. She believed him when he said it was to keep Fallon and his men from invading once the pathfinders had gotten what they wanted from him, but there was this hunch buried deep inside her gut that said there was more to the story.

She used the wall to stand, clinging to one handhold as she hung away from the edge.

"Will you please quit doing that? I know you're half spider, but there's no reason to test fate," Trenton yelled from below.

Shea allowed a small smile to cross her face before she started searching again. There was nothing that stood out in the cliffs close to her. She turned and looked up. Could the original keepers of this entrance have placed the symbol higher up in the hopes that those not worthy would be unable to locate it?

Other entrances were concealed in small crevasses at the bottom of the cliffs or hidden under the long grasses that came right up to the edge in some places. This entrance had plenty of rocky outcroppings and crevasses to search but no vegetation that came close to the cliff.

What did she remember about Lodi's Pass?

For starters, the cavern was the closest to the Badlands so its original keeper would probably have been doubly paranoid about keeping unwanted visitors from trespassing. They would have done a very good job of hiding the symbol.

If Shea had been the keeper, she would have hidden it somewhere high and not easily seen from the ground.

Trenton finally reached the small outcropping Shea had taken advantage of to rest on. His breath was coming in pants and his skin was soaked in sweat.

"Why is this so hard?" he asked, catching his breath. "I don't remember the sky villages being this hard to get to."

"We're at a higher elevation. It makes breathing and physical activity more difficult. Also, the soul tree had easy hand grips that could be used to climb. This requires a different kind of strength. It can be taxing on the body."

Trenton nodded. "Wait, where are you going?"

"Up. I think we need to get higher."

Shea concentrated on her next hand grip, hauling herself up and placing her feet carefully. They really should be doing this with ropes and anchor points, but she was too impatient to wait, and they weren't going that high.

"I'm going to remember this the next time I have you in the training ring," Trenton shouted after her. When she didn't answer, he used the wall to stand and started up. "I'm beginning to think Fallon and Caden have a grudge against me."

Shea paused where she was, brushing at an oddly shaped rock in front of her. It wasn't the symbol, but it was something. It was oval with a raised etching on it. Using one hand to anchor herself, she placed her feet carefully on the side of the rock before she set her other hand on it and brushed away some of the moss that had grown over the years. It turned just barely under her hand.

"I think I may have found something," Shea told Trenton.

"Good. Then maybe we can get down off this cliff."

Hm. The symbol was a series of lines that pointed up, but if she turned it as far as it would go, the lines pointed to her right. She looked where they pointed and saw another knob very similar to this one.

"Go back down to the outcropping we were just on. I want to check something out."

"You know I'm supposed to go with you."

"I have to climb sideways, and I don't know where this leads. You sure you want to do that?"

Trenton looked where she motioned. A low curse reached her.

"Just do what you have to do and don't worry about me," he told her.

Shea rolled her eyes. Men and their stupid egos. If he fell off this cliff because he reached muscle failure, she wouldn't bother to care.

"Suit yourself," she said before making her way, hand over careful hand, to the knob she thought might point them in the right direction.

It wasn't until several knobs later, after climbing and then descending several feet of the cliff that she found what she was looking for. The knob she'd turned pointed directly down. Shea moved so she could get a good look.

There below her, on a rock outcropping, the top of which could only be seen from the spot Shea currently clung to, was the circle with the wavy line inside of it. The outcropping in question was sandwiched between two other rocks that jutted out from the cliff sheltering the one with the symbol. She would have to descend between the two mammoth rocks to get to the column with the symbol.

"Found it," she shouted back at Trenton where he was resting on a ledge several feet away.

"Finally."

She began her descent. She was almost to the first rock when there was a shout from below.

"Eagles. The eagles are coming."

Shea looked up, her heart in her throat.

Trenton leaned over the side of his ledge. "Get to the symbol and open the cavern."

She clung to the side, her face upturned. He was a sitting duck where he was. The eagles could snatch him right off that ledge.

"Go, I'll be right behind you."

There was nothing Shea could do but listen. She climbed faster, stopping only for the briefest second to make sure that Trenton was following her. His face was a mask of concentration as he descended as fast as he could.

Shea was in the shade of the two rocks, her handholds suddenly cool under her hands. She was still several feet up when the sun was blocked by a giant pair of wings. An eagle's head thrust between the crevasses, the beak closing inches from Shea's face.

A loud squawk sounded and then the head withdrew only to be replaced by another bird's, this one smaller with a cream-colored head that shaded to gold near the neck. It had several brown spots around its neck and chest. Using its smaller size, it darted inside, its beak growing larger and larger as Shea watched in horror. She yelped and jerked back as the hard beak brushed against her. That jerk was what saved her, the bird snapping at air as Shea fell the last few feet to the rock pillar.

She landed hard, the breath exploding out of her. No time to hurt. She needed to get moving and protect herself. Rolling to her side, she crouched as she looked above. The eagles both tried to thrust their heads inside, only to get in each other's way. The bigger eagle flared its wings and let out an ear-piercing shriek. The smaller one answered its challenge with a full-throated cry of its own. It dived to the side, the bigger one following with another shriek. They circled above, intent on a furious battle as they dived at one another.

Shea didn't question her luck, grateful that the two were more concerned with defending their territory than picking her off.

She turned back to the symbol below her—a circle filled with another circle and bisected by the wavy line. She'd found what she was looking for, now she just needed to make it work.

The eagles above broke off their aerial battle, disappearing as they dove at the ground below. Shea hoped the Trateri out there managed to evade them long enough for her to figure this out.

According to the story that Shea could remember, the entrance responded to the fire of the great eye and the blood of the chosen children. The second part should be easy enough. Whatever made her a pathfinder should open this thing. The first part though—what in all the Broken Lands was the fire of the great eye. Was it fire? That had to be too easy.

"You figure this out yet?" Trenton shouted down at her, his head peering over the side of one of the stone monoliths.

"You're alive?" The question popped out of Shea before she could censor herself.

"Not for long if you don't get this thing open."

"I'm working on it."

"Work faster."

Shea dragged her foot across the stone, brushing away any debris that had accumulated over the years. The symbol itself was in pretty good shape, the white paint showing no sign of erosion or damage.

"Shea, you need to get this open."

"I told you I'm working on it."

She looked up. Trenton's face was tilted away from her, but something very close to fear covered the part she could see.

"No, you need to get it open now. There's a black cloud in the sky coming from the Badlands, and I'm pretty sure it's not the kind filled with rain."

Shea grumbled to herself. A bright flash of light near where Trenton crouched caught Shea's attention.

"What's that?" Shea pointed.

Trenton looked down, blinking as his eyes adjusted to the dim interior. His gaze went to where she was pointing. "It looks like a mirror or a glass of some sort."

"Of course, that's it."

Fire. What was the sun but a massive ball of fire creating heat and light? Shea wasn't really sure where the eye portion came from, but this place was built right around the cataclysm. There could have been all sorts of weird sayings or religions to explain the world falling apart.

"Trenton, I need you to climb down to that mirror and aim at the middle of the circle."

"Do you see where that mirror is? How do you expect me to cling practically upside down and then move it? Not all of us are descended from spider people," he shouted back.

"I need that light to get this entrance open. You're the one that can see what's coming; you tell me if it's possible."

There was a growl from above and then he threw a leg over the edge, lowering himself over the side. Shea hoped his arms weren't spent during their impression of mountain goats earlier.

She bounced lightly on her feet as Trenton made his careful way down the side of the monolith he'd been crouched on and across to the mirror. Time was of the essence, and every second he took felt like grains of sand sliding through an hourglass—inevitably bringing doom closer with every breath.

"Come on, come on," she muttered under her breath. She didn't want to distract him or cause him to fall, but he was taking so long.

"I'm here. What do I do?" he asked, not looking back at her.

"You need the mirror to catch the light and shine it down here."

He nodded and reached over to tilt the mirror to catch the sun that shined down at an angle, the beam never touching the pillar on which Shea stood.

"It's stuck," Trenton grunted, wrestling with the mirror. He moved over, finding grips in the rock face for his hands and using a leg to kick at the mirror.

"We need that mirror, so don't break it," Shea warned.

"I've almost got it. Almost there." With one last kick, the mirror turned with a screech to rival the eagles' cries.

It glittered as the sun caught it, rotating and reflecting down into the crevasse. Its beam dragged across the rock, closer and closer to where Shea stood.

"There! Keep it right there." It was pointed directly at the middle of the circle. Shea saw why they'd called it the eye of fire in the story. From this angle, with the mirror reflecting the light it looked like an eye had caught fire.

"Time for my part," she said in a soft voice. She pulled out a knife and looked at her hand.

"Shea, what are you doing?" Trenton asked in a calm voice. He'd paused in his descent when Shea withdrew the knife.

"It needs sun and blood to work. Don't worry; I know what I'm doing." Sort of. She hoped.

"The Warlord is not going to be happy about this," Trenton muttered.

He was right. Fallon was going to be very upset if he got in here and found Shea bleeding, even if it was from a self-inflicted wound. That was to say, if he survived the eagles and whatever black cloud Trenton had spotted.

She set the knife against the palm of her left hand. Hesitation stayed her hand. She moved the knife to her forearm. She might have need of her hands before this journey was through, and a cut on the palm was an absolute bitch to heal when you used it constantly. Not to mention painful.

"Here goes nothing."

Shea drew the knife across her skin, biting down to keep the sound of pain inside. Cutting yourself on purpose was totally different than a wound you received while going about your life.

She knelt and held her arm over the eye. The story hadn't said where the blood needed to fall, so she figured the eye was as good a place as any.

"Work." She willed the thing. If it didn't, she didn't know what else to try.

For a long moment, the cavern was silent. Nothing happened. Then there was a rumble—one that was felt more than heard. The ground under her started to shake.

Trenton cried out as the wall he'd been descending started moving. He lost his grip and tumbled off, missing the monolith Shea stood on and falling to the ground below.

"Trenton!" Shea cried, throwing herself to her knees on the side of the platform. The area he had fallen was shadowed, and she couldn't see his form to know if he was alright. That was all the attention she could spare for him as the rock around her began to move. She clung to her perch as it shook and quaked.

Perhaps this hadn't been her best idea.

Rock and dust cascaded from above, the monoliths closing in on each other and sealing out the sun, leaving Shea alone and in darkness.

CHAPTER TWENTY-ONE

The eagle swooped for another pass. Fallon leaned close to his horse, its legs pumping as it ran for all its worth. The eagle grew larger and larger, falling from the sky faster than anything Fallon had ever seen. At the last second its wings snapped out, catching the wind as it sailed over Fallon's head.

Fallon reined in his horse, slowing its gallop and watching as the eagle bypassed his men and headed to the cliffs. It was joined by a second eagle, both preoccupied by something tucked away and out of sight.

Shea. They were going after Shea. She'd been climbing near there before they appeared. Fallon didn't want to think a beast could be that smart—to bypass easy prey in favor of a much more difficult quarry—but he didn't know how else to explain why the golden eagles were acting so counter to their nature.

He saw Reece up ahead, looking at the eagles the same way Fallon had.

"Could this beast call be the cause of this?" Fallon shouted, reining his horse to a stop next to the pathfinder.

Although there were plenty of mounts with each of his men bringing four to enable them to switch off when their first mount got tired, Fallon had not given Reece one. He'd wanted the other man tired and irritated from the journey.

Reece looked lost as he stared at the eagles as they pecked at something in the rocks. Fallon took heart, seeing their continued preoccupation as a sign that they'd been unsuccessful in their hunt.

"I don't know," Reece finally said. "I've never seen them act like this. It's against their nature."

"So, it's the beast call."

He shook his head. "A call shouldn't be able to control them. Its sole purpose is to summon a beast. It doesn't pick the beast and certainly doesn't guide its actions."

Fallon thought they needed to revisit that assumption. What he was seeing contradicted that statement. It was the only explanation.

"We need to get those eagles away from the cliffs." The words 'and Shea' went unspoken. To the men who still stood guard over the pathfinder, Fallon said, "Put him on a horse and get him to the cliffs."

There would be some protection afforded by tucking in close to the cliffs. For a short time at least.

Fallon let out a war cry, summoning his men as he galloped towards Shea. Half of his army was still strung out along the cliff, looking for the entrance that Fallon was half convinced didn't exist. Those that heard him galloped towards him, forming a wave around him, Fallon at the tip of the spear. He slowed the gallop. They needed to distract those birds.

In the distance, Braden had formed the men that couldn't answer Fallon's call, creating a square, archers inside, spearmen on the outside. The men fell into line easily, having practiced the movement several times during the journey to Bearan's Fault. They'd learned from the first attack. The golden eagles would not find them such easy prey this time.

"What's your order?" Caden shouted next to him.

"Have Braden's men harry the eagles. The rest ride with me."

Fallon whistled and the men around him broke off, following him without question or doubt as he rode back out onto the wide-open plains. The cliffs receded behind them, but not quickly enough for what Fallon had planned.

They were bait. Harrying the eagles would only do so much. Moving bait would pull them off their victim.

A bugle sounded behind them. It was the signal Fallon had been waiting for. He let out another cry and the ranks split, groups breaking off to form a large square, spearmen on the outside edge and archers on the inner edge of the square.

Fallon took a position inside the square on the side where the eagles would attack. He shouted his order. "Archers to the ready."

His men reached for their bows.

"Nock arrows."

Only the sound of heavy breathing and horses shifting was heard.

"Hold."

The eagles grew in size until Fallon could count the spots on one.

"Draw."

That was close enough.

"Loose arrows."

The arrows released with a series of twangs. In a smooth movement, his archers knocked their next arrow and drew back their strings.

"Loose."

Another volley of arrows flew.

One eagle screeched and pulled back, the powerful beat of its wings taking it higher into the air. Its companion kept coming, attempting to snatch a man off the line. Fallon was there with spear in hand, jabbing up into its stomach. Other spearmen joined him, some glancing off its protective feathers, a few finding their mark.

It peeled off to join its companion in the air. Together they circled.

"Archers!" Fallon shouted. Bows lifted. "Loose."

A storm of arrows sailed toward the eagles. They swooped and dived to avoid the worst of it.

"Loose."

The eagles beat their wings and climbed.

Thunder sounded from the cliffs and the ground shook. Such a loud noise that Fallon was half convinced the world was about to meet its end as the horses tossed their heads as their eyes rolled.

They were too well-trained to rear and toss their rider, but they pranced in place. Eagles didn't concern them, but the ground moving under their feet was enough to upset years of training.

"Look," one of Fallon's men shouted. To Fallon's eyes he looked not much older than a boy. He was familiar. Fallon thought this might be one of the men Shea was friends with.

A small opening appeared in the cliffs. One not visible before.

"She did it," Buck shouted.

Of course, she did. If anybody could, it was Shea. In the nick of time too.

"One hundred meter sprints," Fallon said. "On the next pass."

There was a chorus of battle cries acknowledging his command.

The eagles passed over head, shying away from the volley of arrows the archers sent in their direction.

"Now."

The lines broke as the horses thundered back toward the cliffs and the safety they now represented.

They reached their hundred meters, the horses wheeling to form the same square they had before. Archers on the inside, spearman on the outside so their backs could be protected.

The eagles separated in mid-air, one swooping in from the left while the other angled to attack from the right. Fallon remained focused on the closest, concentrating on shouting commands and trusting that one of his commanders would take care of the other side.

Eamon shouted, "Loose," a beat before Fallon.

There was a cry as one of the eagles closed its talons around a man, trying to drag him from his saddle. The spearmen next to him closed ranks, thrusting with their spears. An arrow found its way into its eye, the boy Shea had befriended giving a triumphant shout.

Its talons opened, dropping its victim. The man fell to the ground, blood gushing from a stomach wound as the eagle climbed into his sky above him.

"Get him back on his horse," Fallon ordered. "We move now."

Two of Fallon's soldiers threw the injured man onto his horse before leaping onto their own. The group took off at a gallop.

"Fallon, look," Eamon shouted, pointing to the west and the Badlands.

"I see it." Fallon's face was grim as he bent closer to his horse and flicked his reins, trying to summon more speed.

A black cloud—moving in an unnatural way as it changed direction and speed against the wind—was heading in their direction. Fast. It was close, much too close. The eagles had distracted them from the danger amassing in the distance.

Eamon turned, calling over his shoulder. "Ride! Ride as if the hounds of the underworld are nipping at your heels."

The cavern entrance was close now, looming larger with every hoof beat. Fallon didn't dare call his men to stop to face the eagles bearing down, knowing that if they did, that black mass would be on them.

He just bent lower and let his mount have its head, trusting that it would make it.

He could hear the beat of wings on the air, coming ever closer. Feel the air on the back of his neck from those wings.

Braden stood at the head of several lines of men that had formed on either side of the entrance. Fallon met his eyes as he charged closer.

Braden's mouth moved, shaping a word. "Loose arrows."

Arrows flew once again. Aimed at the sky and the creatures bearing down on them.

Then he was past, his horse plunging into darkness. His men followed close behind.

*

A cough echoed around Shea.

"Trenton, are you alive?" she asked. She didn't dare move, unsure of how much room she still had on her perch.

"Barely."

She let out a sigh of relief. As much as the man was a pain for his insistence on shadowing her even when she felt it unnecessary, she would have missed him if he'd died.

"How badly are you hurt?" she asked.

A groan echoed up to her. "Battered and bruised, but otherwise okay."

Shea debated whether to trust that assessment, knowing he'd probably say the same thing even on his deathbed. "Nothing broken?"

It would have taken a miracle for him to have survived that fall without a broken bone or two.

"I'll be fine."

In other words, yes, but he didn't want to admit it.

"I'm coming down to you," Shea said.

Her eyes began to adjust to the dim light. There must be an opening somewhere. True darkness in a cave is a black so deep and pervasive, that even the best eyes in the world wouldn't be able to see a hand in front of their face. No light meant no sight. Since Shea could see, dim though it was, it meant light was filtering through.

She slung her leg over the edge and carefully felt her way down. It was slow going and left her muscles clenched at the anticipation that the next grip would be her last.

"Almost there," Trenton said as Shea inched her way down. "Few more feet."

His voice sounded close. Shea descended until one foot touched the ground. She turned to find Trenton propped against a wall. He looked terrible, cuts and bruises on his face, one hand clasped against his ribs.

She knelt beside him, looking him over. The way he held his arm to the side of his body and kept his breaths light and shallow made her suspect he had broken, or at least cracked, a few ribs. Not surprising given the height he'd fallen from.

"I'm fine, Shea."

She ignored his words. "Can you move your arms?"

She gave him a serious look that said she wasn't moving from this spot until he humored her. He rolled his eyes but moved each arm, demonstrating that they were working.

"What about your legs?"

He shifted, bending one leg then the other.

At least that was something. It didn't mean he hadn't cracked a bone, but he should be able to walk out of here at least. The more pressing concern was internal bleeding. For now, he was mobile, which was good because carrying him out of here would be very difficult. Not impossible, but it would probably take everything in her to accomplish it.

"Do you think they found the entrance?" Trenton asked.

"I hope so."

Neither one wanted to think what would happen if they hadn't.

Trenton looked up to where the sky used to be. "I don't think we're going to be able to climb out the way we came."

Shea agreed. "I don't think you'll be climbing anywhere in the shape you're in."

His chuckle cut off in a wheeze of pain. "Somehow I think you're right."

She eyed him with worry. She didn't know if she'd be able to carry him out of here and leaving him behind wasn't a choice.

Trenton understood what she didn't say. "You should go on without me. You'll move faster."

"That's not happening."

"You're letting sentiment cloud your judgment. You and I both know we won't make it out of here if you wait on me. Go, find the others and then come back for me."

"I do that and there's no guarantee I'll find my way back. For all you know, this place is a maze."

"It's a risk you have to take." He looked up at her, his eyes fogged with pain.

Shea met his gaze with a steely one of her own. She wasn't leaving him behind.

"Did I ever tell you about the oath all pathfinders have to make once they pass their ceremony?"

He shut his eyes and huffed. "You rarely talk about that part of your life and then only with Fallon."

He had a point. She had been closemouthed when it came to life before her adoption into the Trateri. She had been so focused on not inadvertently revealing something that might tempt the Trateri in the direction of the Highlands that she now wondered whether that energy might have been better spent elsewhere.

"Once we pass our last phase, we take an oath."

Trenton closed his eyes and leaned his head back, his face one of resignation. Shea smiled knowing he could guess where she was going with this.

"We vow that those we lead into the wilderness will not be left behind—even if it costs us our lives. So, you see, I can't leave you behind. It would violate my oaths."

He snorted. "You're not a pathfinder anymore. You're Trateri remember? And we do what we need to survive."

"I'll always be a pathfinder. It's not a piece a clothing you can put on and take off at your convenience. It is the bedrock upon which I am built. Just like now I am Trateri. Both form who I am, for better or worse. Split loyalty or not." Shea needed to find a way to reconcile the two pieces of herself. It was the only way to survive with her sense of self intact. The only way she could live with herself.

"That still doesn't change the fact that our resources are limited and our time is short. You can't afford any delays," Trenton said, his face a grimace.

"Then I suppose you'd better dig up some of that Trateri stubbornness and get your ass moving."

Trenton aimed a glare her way. "I was trying to be conscientious of you."

"Well don't," Shea snapped. "I can take care of myself."

"You know Fallon is going to be livid if you don't make it out of here," he groused.

"Well then, I suggest you get your ass in motion, so we can avoid that turn of events."

She grabbed him by the arm and helped him stand. He grimaced as he gained his feet, his weight leaning hard against her.

"Let's get out of here," he said.

*

"Do you hear that?" Shea asked.

It was faint, the bell-like sound falling and rising as if wind were playing a symphony.

"What is that?"

"I don't know." She listened and walked a few steps further, keeping one hand on the smooth rock of the passageway and the other in front of her. Trenton held onto the back of her pant loop as she tested the ground before her with every step.

She'd managed to make a torch out of scraps before they began their trip but had chosen to conserve its light until they really needed it. It had left them wandering blind and necessitated a slow and steady progress.

The sound now felt like it filled the chamber, vibrating in her bones as it rose and fell. There were tones that rippled and tangled together. It sounded very similar to the wind chimes the Airabel hung outside their wooden hunts, only here, the sound was purer.

"There's a breeze," Shea said as wind tickled the hair on her neck. "Could be a natural phenomenon."

Wind rushing over a natural hole in the rock could create a similar sound. However, given the number of tones, she would say there were several holes of varying sizes for the wind to play. It gave her hope. Where there was wind, there was usually a way out.

"Come on, let's keep going," Shea told Trenton.

As they traveled, the music-like sound became louder and louder, echoing off the rock until the air vibrated with it. Shea could feel it in her chest as her entire body tuned itself to the sound.

She bumped into something and took a step back. The chimes came to a discordant halt. She reached out to feel for whatever had brushed against her, but her hand met air. With no sight, she couldn't tell if what she felt was a danger to them or not.

Fumbling with the torch that she'd created and then stuck in her belt, Shea brought it around front before fishing the flint and steel out of her pocket where she'd placed them so she could find it easily.

"I'm going to light the torch," she told Trenton.

"I thought you wanted to wait so you could preserve it in case we need it later."

She had. "There's something in front of me that I can't make sense of. I'll light the torch, figure out what's blocking our path and then douse it again."

Shea sensed the shrug he gave her and took his lack of argument as agreement.

With a few strikes of the flint, she got the torch going and held it up. The way in front of her was unobstructed.

Her eyebrows drew together in a deep frown. How was that possible? She had run into something. She was sure of it.

She stepped forward and her foot brushed against something. Shea brought her foot back and crouched down next to the object.

On the ground in front of her was a branch of some old tree, much like the one she held in her hand. Wrapped around the end was a wad of white fabric. She thought she even detected cobwebs, which made lighting torches simple because they acted as kindling would for a campfire.

She picked up the torch and held it close to her face. The smell wasn't familiar, but Shea would bet everything she had that it was some sort of slow burning accelerant.

"Is that a torch?" Trenton asked from behind her.

Shea made noncommittal sound.

"How did a torch happen to land right in front of you?"

That was a very good question. One she suspected she knew the answer to.

"So, the stories were true," she said in a soft voice.

"What stories?"

Shea stood and dusted off her pants. "The ones that say we're probably not alone in these caverns."

Trenton's hand went to the knife sheathed at his side as he looked around the passageway with a sudden suspicion. She shook her head. Whoever had left this was long gone.

Shea looked at the torch for a moment before tucking it into the belt of her pants. She lifted her other torch high above her and looked around. The passage they were in was narrow with no offshoots that another person could hide in.

How did their gift giver get so close without making a sound? As the chimes picked up again, Shea conceded that it was likely that the person's approach had been masked. But how had they known where to set down their gift so that Shea would find it? It was far more likely that she would have walked right past it.

Shea gave up on solving the mystery. It was far more important to get back to the group than to go hunting for the denizens of these caverns.

She knew whoever had left this was likely long gone by now, but still she didn't feel right without giving thanks. Shea was pretty sure that they would have been in a lot of trouble without the gift.

She bent her head and said a silent prayer of gratitude, before lifting it and humming a melody that rose and fell with the chimes. It sounded rather nice, if she did say so herself.

"What do you mean we're not alone?" Trenton asked.

"Let's get going," Shea said, not wanting to lose any more time. That sense of urgency was still riding her hard. "I'll explain as we move."

Trenton hobbled after her as Shea prepared to tell him a story—one she barely remembered since it had been so long since she'd heard it herself.

"I don't remember what started it or why it came to be, if I ever knew in the first place, but it's said this place is named after a man called Lodi. He was said to be a great protector in the old world, someone who led his people with strength and wisdom." Shea held the torch so Trenton could see where to duck. "I'm not sure if this happened during or after the Cataclysm, but it's said that he and his people were attacked by a great army. To save them, he retreated to this place. That plain we were on—a great battle waged there as he and his men made a last stand to give his people time to retreat and seek shelter in the Highlands. It's said that after that battle finished, Bearan's fault grew by several feet and the entrance was smoking rubble."

Shea paused to catch her breath. Spelunking through a small passageway was more physically demanding than she remembered—all of the twisting and bending.

"If the entrance was reduced to rubble, how were your people able to uncover it," Trenton asked as he took a break.

Shea shrugged, the dim light making the movement more dramatic than it was. "I don't know that part. All I can tell you are the parts I remember, which aren't many."

"How does that story relate to what left us that torch?"

Shea unfolded from the bent over position she'd had to use to get through that last section. The tunnel before her opened up, allowing her to stand upright and proceed without having to turn sideways. She was grateful for that fact because Trenton's progress was getting slower each time he had to bend over.

The torch she held flickered. It was close to being spent. She pulled out the one that had been left for them and held it against the guttering flame. It caught fire easily, the flame brighter and steadier than it had been on the torch she'd created.

"Well, Lodi's battle was waged with magic and sword. When it became clear that he was going to lose, his magic users cursed his men to become terrible beings that would haunt these caverns, keeping those that meant his people harm from passing." Shea looked over at Trenton, concerned about his labored breathing. She might have to leave him somewhere after all.

"Magic?" he scoffed. "I'm surprised to hear that from you. You've always struck me as too practical to believe in such things."

"I'll admit that most events that are ascribed to magic have perfectly logical and natural explanations." Shea tilted her head in thought. "But I also know that magic is very real. I've seen it. Some say magic, or rather the war over its use, is what caused the cataclysm and the world as we know it today."

Trenton's face was skeptical as he made his painstaking way through the cave. "I've never seen anything but a few tricks that could easily be explained by sleight of hand."

Shea shrugged. "The major magics have been gone for a long time, but echoes still remain. Even among the Trateri. Take Chirron for instance."

"His healing isn't magic," Trenton said.

"You are correct. Most of what he does isn't magic, but have you noticed how his patients seem to heal faster than they should? I bet people prefer him over another healer. Even when he does the exact same thing as others, it is more effective when coming from him. Take the wound on my head for instance; that should have taken weeks instead of days to heal and left a scar." Shea touched the spot in question. "Instead, it's all but disappeared."

"Maybe it's all in your mind."

"Maybe." Entirely possible, but Shea didn't think so. There had been a brief moment when he'd had his hands on her head where she could have sworn a numbing coldness had spread through her. "No one is sure if it's the original soldiers, their descendants, or beings that had nothing to do with Lodi and his battle, who haunt this place."

"Great. Another mystery. Is there anything in these lands that isn't mysterious and deadly?"

Shea shot him a grin. "What would be the fun in that?"

CHAPTER TWENTY-TWO

F orm a line. Spearmen at the front, archers to the rear," Caden ordered. "Don't let any of those creatures inside."

The cavern they had sought shelter in protected them from aerial attacks, but any of the beasts could follow on the ground. Several of his men had already lit torches to see what might be lurking inside that could attack their rear. The light illuminated a chamber so big and vast that Fallon could fit his entire army in it and still have room leftover. The ceiling was so high above them that the torches did little to penetrate the shadows.

They needed to keep the winged beasts out or they'd have similar problems as before.

One of the torches' light reflected off wooden panels carved with strange symbols.

"Stop," Fallon told the man holding the torch. He advanced toward him, taking the torch and holding it up to the wood. It was a door, one nearly as tall as the chamber they stood in. Caden, seeing what Fallon was interested in, grabbed another torch from one of the men and crossed to the other side of the entrance, illuminating a similar wooden panel.

"They're doors," Witt said, his voice surprised and full of wonder.

"That they are," Fallon said.

Braden called a retreat from outside and the Trateri that had covered Fallon's escape poured in. Fallon grabbed several men.

"Get these doors closed," he ordered, putting his shoulder to the one closest to him. Braden fell into place beside him. Gawain and Zeph put their shoulders to the door on Caden's side.

With a scream of protest, the wood slid forward.

"Again," Fallon shouted.

His men heaved at the doors, as the archers filled the mouth of the cave with volleys of arrows, the pikers defending the line from any creatures that got too close.

The heavy doors resisted for a long moment, the centuries they had stood in the same position making them stubborn, but Fallon's men persisted. With a groan they began to slide shut.

Eamon called for the men to retreat as the opening narrowed. They backed up in an orderly fashion, the last few slipping inside as Fallon and the others got the doors closed. He stood back, grabbing the metal bolt next to him and sliding it into the loop on the other door. Caden repeated that with the bolt above him. There was a third bolt below that Fallon shoved forward.

The doors secured, they stepped back, prepared to jump forward should the locks fail. The wood bulged inward once, dust cascading down, before settling.

There was a whoop as his men realized the battle was over and they'd come out victorious.

Zeph stood beside Fallon and gave the doors a cautious look. "This is a very odd land. I have never seen creatures acting in such a manner. I counted at least five winged species out there."

Fallon grunted. He had seen the same.

"Since when do these beasts attack in a coordinated fashion? If your Telroi hadn't opened this place when she did, we would have been slaughtered," Zeph said.

The Ember clan leader made a very good point.

"Bring me the pathfinder," Fallon ordered one of his Anateri. He needed to locate Shea. Every moment that passed without seeing her safe while giving him her grumpiest expression tied the knot in his chest tighter.

Van and Chirron approached, the two men giving each other a wide berth. Fallon fought the oath that he wanted to spit out at the sight. The two had never gotten along. Chirron, a man who spent his time healing and saving people, was the exact opposite of Van, a man who used his skills to keep Chirron busy.

Fallon had need of both in his army. Though he preferred to deal with each separately and not when he had more pressing matters on his mind then their ongoing feud.

"We need to get moving," Van said without any preliminary conversation. He gave the doors Fallon stood by a look of distaste. "There's no telling how long these will hold, given how old they probably are. The beasts could break through at any moment. It would be best if we were far from this place when that happens."

"We can't leave," Chirron said, giving the other man a scathing look. "There were many wounded. I need time to stabilize them, or you risk them perishing on the move."

Van turned to fix Chirron with an exasperated glare. "Chi, we can't risk these doors breaking. You'll have way more patients than you can handle at that point. Sometimes you have to make hard choices; this is one of those times."

Chirron scoffed. "Don't give me that load of horse dung. There's been no sign of the doors weakening. There's no reason not to take the extra time to ensure these men get the care they need."

"If you and your healers haven't been able to stabilize them by now, the chances of them surviving this journey are slim," Van returned, his face drawn into grim lines. "We can't leave them here nor can we accommodate their pace going into the Highlands."

"You want me to give them mercy," Chirron accused.

Van's expression didn't lighten or offer quarter. "You do them no favors by prolonging their deaths."

"I'm not going to do that just so your life can be a little easier," Chirron hissed.

It was easy to forget that the smaller man had gone through the same training as the rest of the Trateri. The same training that produced some of the best warriors in the Broken Lands. His interests might have turned to healing instead of killing, but in many ways Chirron was just as deadly as any other man in Fallon's army.

"Enough," Fallon said, breaking up the brewing fight. He couldn't afford to have two of his highest officers break into fisticuffs over a disagreement. The blow to morale would be crippling. Not to mention, he had more important things to turn his attention to, like finding Shea, and then finding a way out of here. "How many are beyond even your skills?"

Chirron expression turned stubborn, his mouth turning down and his body tightening as if in preparation for battle.

Fallon gave him a warning look, in no mood to humor his principles.

Chirron relaxed, his expression smoothing out, though some of his unhappiness showed. "Three are in a bad way. I am not sure they will survive until sunset."

"And the rest?"

"Two might pull through, if given adequate rest and care. The rest have minor injuries that, if treated immediately, shouldn't pose a risk to their health as long as they keep the wounds from getting infected."

"Offer mercy to the three. If they choose not to take it, we'll give them a week's worth of rations and water and find them a place with decent cover to remain. Stabilize the rest. We'll leave as soon as that's done." To appease Van, Fallon told Zeph, "Gather several men and have them stand watch at these doors. At the first sign that they're failing, we'll leave, regardless of whether the injured are ready or not."

Seeing his Anateri approaching with Reece in tow, he dismissed the other men and summoned Caden and Braden with a flick of his hand.

"Where is she?" Fallon didn't waste any time cutting to the heart of the matter.

"I don't know."

"Don't lie to me," Fallon said. He was ready to rip this man's head from his shoulders. "She opened your damn caverns. She should be here, so where is she?"

"I'm sure she'll be here. She's probably just delayed." Reece didn't look too concerned about Shea's fate. A fact that had Fallon clenching his hands to keep from attacking the other man. He still had need for Reece, which was the only thing that saved him. "We should get going as soon as possible. I'm sure she'll catch up when she's able."

"We're not going anywhere until I know she's safe." He took a step closer to Reece. "You'd better pray she survived, or this trip and your life are going to be very short."

Reece sighed. "I'm growing weary of all of these threats."

"Are you now?" Had Shea been here, she could have told Reece that the amusement on Fallon's face was a dangerous sign. She wasn't here, so her warning went unspoken.

"If you'd planned to kill me, you would have done it by now."

Fallon's hand landed around Reece's neck. He squeezed, relishing the gurgling sound the pathfinder made. "Perhaps I should make good on some of my threats then. Since you are so weary of them, of course."

Reece's voice came out in a babble, not making much sound.

Fallon drew him forward, turning his ear towards Reece. He shook his head. "Nope, sorry, I'm afraid I still can't hear you."

Fallon released him. Reece staggered back, his hand to his throat as he glared. Fallon regarded him with amusement. The pathfinder looked like a stray pup debating whether to go for its master's throat. Fallon almost wished he would. It would give him pleasure to put the pup down.

"You're crazy, you know that?" Reece croaked.

Fallon didn't respond, knowing silence was sometimes the best weapon.

"I'm going to remember this," Reece said.

"We hope you do," Caden said, amusement on his face and in his voice as he walked up. "Perhaps it will serve as a reminder not to antagonize the Warlord."

"Now that we've established that my threats contain some bite, perhaps you would care to share your theories on what might have happened to Shea." Fallon's voice was silky. His time playing with this man was almost at an end. If he didn't learn what he needed to know, he'd be all too happy to kill him.

"I don't know. She should be here." It was a bold thing to admit, given how clearly Fallon had demonstrated his feelings for the other man. It almost made him respectable. Almost.

Witt's presence behind Reece drew Fallon's attention. "Warlord, you're going to want to see this."

Fallon cocked his head as he considered the other man. He hoped for Witt's sake, that he'd interrupted for a good reason, and not just some misbegotten assumption that he could redirect Fallon's wrath.

Fallon headed for Witt, telling his men, "Bring him."

They followed Witt into the gloom, the torch he held the only light revealing their way.

Fallon didn't miss the way his men eyed their surroundings with a deep unease. It was a feeling he shared. Men weren't meant to exist underground. It felt like he was walking in a tomb, one Highlanders had created for their forgotten dead. The Trateri didn't believe in burials, thinking that interment underground trapped the spirit in the decaying body. They usually left the dead to the elements, or burned the corpse, so the person's soul could return to the world, closing the circle of life.

"There." Witt pointed the torch down into a deep trough that had been dug into the dirt. In the trough were skeletons, many of them. There were half-gnawed bones and discarded weapons, the metal rusted and brittle with age. Whatever garments these poor bastards had worn to their deaths were preserved by the cool air in the caverns, denied the chance to decay and fall apart.

"Horse lords protect us," Caden said.

Witt knelt next to one of the bodies, using a stick to raise the arm. "The flesh was stripped from their bones, otherwise I suspect the climate in here would have preserved the bodies. I can't tell if whatever beastie ate them was also the one to kill them."

"Either way, I'd say we're not the only things in here," Caden said, giving Fallon a look.

No, Fallon would agree. Which meant the pathfinder had a lot of explaining to do.

All eyes followed Fallon's to Reece where he stared down at the remains with a fixed expression.

"Would you like to explain?" Witt asked, his voice calm.

"He's had his chance to explain," Fallon said from where he crouched near the trough. He jerked his head. Reece was seized from behind, the faces of the Anateri implacable masks.

Caden unsheathed a knife at his waist, turning to Reece with a hard expression.

"Are you sure that's wise?" Witt asked.

Fallon cast a sharp glance at the other man. Witt held his hands up in supplication.

"I'm not questioning you. It's just he's the only person besides Shea who has any hope of guiding us out of here. He may very well be the only person who can find her."

"Those are good points, both of them," Fallon conceded. "But if we can't trust him, there's no point keeping him around. He's had many chances to earn our trust and failed at all of them."

"This place is a maze," Reece said. "You'll never get out of here without me."

Fallon smiled, the movement lacking any warmth or amusement. "I'm not convinced you can get us out of here either way. Shea is the one that found the entrance if you'll recall."

"I brought you here." Reece struggled against the men restraining him.

"I would not brag of that, if I were you," Caden observed, his face coldly amused. "Since we've listened to you, we've been attacked by eagles and a whole lot of other beasts. The Telroi is now missing, and we are stuck in a place that reeks of death."

"What do you care for some woman who's fucking your master?" Reece's expression was watchful, as if he was testing them. It was the only reason Fallon refrained from striking him down where he stood.

The men holding him tightened their grip to a painful point. Reece didn't make a sound, a determined expression taking over—one Fallon had seen on Shea's face on more than one occasion when she'd felt like she'd been backed into a corner or when she was testing the waters for one of her bigger stunts. It made him question Reece's motivations. Enough that he decided to watch and observe before deciding one way or another.

"I'd be careful if I were you," one of the men holding Reece warned.

"That's our Telroi you're insulting," the other said.

Both men had been with Fallon for many years. Their loyalty was unwavering, and it seemed it extended not just to Fallon but to Shea as well. A curious and welcome development. The first sign of acceptance.

"My men take insults against the Telori rather personally," Caden warned. "She's saved our Warlord's life on more than one occasion. That, if nothing else, commands your respect."

Reece's mask fell for a moment, and Fallon thought he saw the faintest shadow of relief on the other man's face before his emotions were hidden again. It was enough that he was willing to take a chance on the pathfinder. A small one.

"You say you don't know where she is. What's your best guess?" Shea often said she didn't know, but she usually had a guess that turned out to be right more often than not. Fallon had to wonder if it was a family trait or part of the training these pathfinders underwent.

Reece turned guarded. "It's possible that there is another entrance to these caverns that she would need to take once she found the symbol. It looked like she was pretty high in the cliffs when the eagles descended."

"And can you find this other entrance?" Fallon queried with a lift of his eyebrow.

"No." Reece hesitated a moment. "But she should be able to find her way here. She has an uncanny way of getting out of scrapes."

"I'm well acquainted with that trait."

Reece's chuckle was brief. "You should have grown up with her. She turned both our parents' hair gray before she took the pathfinder mantle."

He almost sounded like a cousin should. It made Fallon tempted to respect him, but he was loath to drop his guard with this man who represented everything he could lose Shea to.

"Looks like we have no choice then, we'll wait for her to find us," Fallon decided.

Caden's sigh was weary. "The clan leaders are going to have a shit fit over this."

Fallon allowed real amusement to touch his eyes. "They are welcome to bring me their grievances."

"Yeah and be eviscerated for them." Caden's words were dry, even as his mouth quirked in a half-smile.

*

Shea heard a distant rumble of sound. She stopped and listened. Voices. She thought she heard voices. She rounded the corner and nearly fell over an edge, the drop of which was shrouded in complete black. Shea grabbed the wall as her steps sent rocks skittering over the edge.

She counted. One. Two. Three. Four. She'd hit twelve before she heard the clatter of it landing. That fall would have probably killed her.

She looked around, searching for what she'd heard. It was possible it was nothing but the wind playing tricks. With the way this place echoed, it wouldn't surprise her.

Bright, flickering light in the distance to her right drew her attention. She squinted. Those were torches.

She started to shout out, but hesitated at the last second. It was possible those lights didn't belong to Fallon. Alerting them to her presence could be a death sentence, if it was an enemy. She bit her lip and looked back the way she'd come.

Trenton was waiting. After all her talk of not leaving him behind, she'd eventually had to make the tough decision, knowing she could summon help faster than if she tried to carry him. She suspected that if she took much longer to find a healer, she would be returning to a corpse.

She squared her shoulders. Time to take a chance.

"Fallon! Anybody there?" she shouted.

She waited a moment. No reaction from the torches. She didn't let herself give up hope. It was possible that her voice hadn't reached them or that the echoes had made the words indistinguishable.

She tried again. "Fallon, help! Fallon!"

*

"Do you hear that?" Witt asked. He stood and walked a few paces from the fire Fallon's men had started to ward off the chill of the caverns.

"What are you talking about?" Eamon asked.

"That."

They all listened. A voice reached them, the words almost indistinguishable except one. A name. Fallon.

Caden looked at Fallon. They both came to the same conclusion at the same time.

"Shea." Fallon popped to his feet, grabbing a torch and rushing to where he thought the voice was coming from. "Shea!"

"Fallon!" Her voice was getting stronger and clearer.

"Where are you?"

"Up here! I'm up here," she shouted.

Fallon looked up and saw a dim light high above.

"Of course, she'd be somewhere high," Caden said in a sour voice.

"Any idea how we get her down?" Fallon asked.

Witt's expression was doubtful as he observed the cavern wall. Eamon looked just as lost but equally unsurprised. Both men were well acquainted with Shea and her penchant for finding herself in high places.

Eamon nudged some wood lying broken on the ground. There might have been stairs at one time connecting the passage above to this great chamber, but they were long gone.

"Trenton's hurt. He needs help." There was a long pause. "I think he's bleeding internally."

"I can probably get up there," Witt said. "It wouldn't be the first time I've had to make a climb."

Caden frowned at him. "Do all of you Highlanders make a habit of climbing cliff faces like mountain goats?"

Witt gave a careless shrug. "Those who spend any significant time outside the villages. Eventually, everyone comes to something impassable by normal means. It helps to know how to climb."

Caden made a sound that prophesized the grumpy old man he'd eventually become, if he lived long enough.

"I'll need supplies though. Between me and Shea, we should be able to fasten some sort of device to lower him down."

Caden waved a man over to take note of everything Witt said he needed. Once the supplies had been delivered, he stood back with his hands on his hips to observe the wall.

"I'm coming with you," Fallon said.

Witt gave him a skeptical look, one that was at home with the weather-beaten lines around his eyes. "No offense, Hawkvale, but I doubt you know what you're doing. Best to just stay down here and wait."

The expression Fallon fixed on Witt was the sort that had caused grown men to nearly piss themselves. It made his feelings on Witt's statement very clear without a word having to be spoken.

Witt sighed and then shrugged. "Suit yourself. It's only me who's going to catch the sharp end of her tongue if you end up with a broken arm."

"While you guys are debating who's coming up here, I'm going to go back and get Trenton," Shea called from above.

"You're to do no such thing," Fallon yelled back. "Stay right where you are."

There was a grumble above and the distinct words of bossy, arrogant, and ass drifted down. The rest of the men carefully didn't look at Fallon, whose eyes narrowed as Shea continued. He would enjoy exacting his revenge when he caught up to her.

Eamon, Buck, and Witt turned away to hide their grins, each having been on the end of a similar tirade before. Sometimes for having told Shea what to do. Sometimes for doing something she considered stupid.

"Question," Buck said once her voice had died down. "How are you going to climb with no light?"

Witt looked at the other man and then back at the wall. The lights from the torches created harsh shadows. It would be difficult to discern hand holds in it. "This is going to be a problem."

"Is there another way, maybe another passageway?" Eamon asked, looking at Fallon.

He shook his head. "If there is, there's no guarantee that it won't triple the journey or end in a maze of tunnels."

"Guess the only way is up," Eamon said, stepping back.

"You could always try holding the torch in your mouth," Buck volunteered.

Witt snarled. "I'm not letting fire that close to my face."

"Afraid you'll scar your pretty mug?" Buck taunted with an arched brow.

"Enough. We'll take our chances," Fallon said. "Let's start."

"I'd like to go with you, Warlord," Eamon volunteered. "Shea has taught me a few things about rock climbing so I might be an asset."

Fallon nodded.

"I'll lead," Witt said, waiting for Fallon's agreement before starting up the rock face. Fallon and Eamon followed soon after.

*

Shea waited as the men below made their ascent. It was tempting to disregard Fallon's order and go back for Trenton. The only thing stopping her was the knowledge that she wouldn't be able to move him very far without their assistance. Given his wounds, she suspected she might do him more harm than good if she tried to drag him through these tunnels.

After what felt like an eternity, Witt reached her. She bent down to help him over the ledge, and then stepped back as he offered the same help to Fallon and then Eamon.

Fallon stepped past the other two, his hand coming out to haul Shea into his arms. Once there he clung to her, his hold tight. She buried her face in his shirt and inhaled, grateful to have a moment like this. For a minute, she had feared such things would be part of her past.

They didn't waste breath on voicing the fear that had lived with them since the eagle attack, content to hold one another and just be. Eamon and Witt directed their attention out into the cavern, letting the two have a private moment.

Finally, though it hurt her to do so, Shea stepped back. They had important things to do. First among them—getting Trenton help.

"I'll lead you to Trenton." Her eyes met Fallon's in the flickering light of the torch, their warmth conveying how glad she was to see him alive and well, before she turned toward where she had left her guard.

Hopefully, he would still be there when she returned—alive and threatening her with more training. Gods, she hoped he was still alive. She didn't want to have to live with having left him to die alone.

CHAPTER TWENTY-THREE

H ow long have we been down here?" Clark asked, keeping pace with Shea. "It feels like an eternity."

Shea looked to find him craning his neck back to give the rock above them a dissatisfied glare. He looked back down with a huff, the small patches of visible sky, where the ceiling above had collapsed in places, seeming to have put him in an even more morose mood.

It was a sentiment many in their party shared as their time underground stretched to days.

"I told you; this way is longer because we have to go under the cliffs. Be grateful for the horses. If we were walking, it would take us a few weeks to make the journey. As it is, we'll probably be back aboveground in a few days," Shea told him.

Trenton had been recovered and treated in time. Shea had been right. He'd been more injured than they had first assumed and had been bleeding internally. Luckily, Chirron was able to stabilize and treat him.

For most of the first day, Chirron had kept him heavily dosed with Trateri medicines that caused him to sleep. After that, they'd had to allow him to be awake for travel. The daft man had tried to ride before both Chirron and Shea had come down on him, threatening to finish the job the fall had started, if he didn't get off the damn horse.

It wasn't until Fallon had ordered him off that he'd listened, though. Shea was still a bit sore about that. A fact she would make known to him once he was back on his feet again.

"Hold," someone called from the front.

Clark stood in his stirrups, trying to gain enough height to see what had caused the command.

Buck rode back down the line, his eyes bright with excitement. "Shea, you need to see this."

He wheeled his horse and sent it bolting back towards the front of the line before she could even question him. Clark looked at Shea for two beats, before crying, "Hiyaw."

His horse followed Buck's. Shea nudged her mount into a trot. She crested a slight incline and pulled the horse to a stop, it turned in a circle as Shea looked down the slight decline in awe.

"It's a city," she said in wonder.

A very old city, one that looked like it had been here for centuries. Perhaps millennia. Dead and buried down here. Buildings as high as the cavern stretched as far as the torches illuminated. She squinted above them. She thought they weren't as tall as the cavern, so much as their tops were embedded in the ceiling of rock, as if the cavern had formed around them and not the other way around.

"How is this possible?" Eamon asked in a soft voice.

"I don't know. I've never heard anything about a city being down here," Shea replied.

She wondered which one it was, if it stemmed from the cataclysm or before. Had to have, right? Who else was capable of such marvelous workings besides their ancestors? Even from here, even given the state of ruin it was in, she could tell the excellent craftsmanship—far beyond that of the last few centuries.

The buildings loomed like elegant giants, with as many broken windows as there were intact. Material the likes of which Shea had never seen, holding the weight of their frames up, even after these long years. The cavern's cool climate had probably helped with that, but still. It was incredible.

"It gives me the creeps," Gawain said, looking at the city with suspicion.

"Same," Zeph said. "It feels like the dead wait inside its borders."

"Really? I can't wait to explore," Clark said, watching the city with fascination.

"No one asked you, boy," Gawain said. "Get back with the other soldiers."

Clark flinched, his shoulders climbing to his ears and his face falling. His gaze darted to Fallon and away as he took the dressing down.

"I asked him here," Shea said, staring Gawain down.

He snorted but didn't say anything, Fallon's presence keeping him from voicing his opinion.

"I'll just go, Shea. It's alright. I should probably report back to see if they need any scouts." Clark didn't wait for a reply, turning his horse and sending it galloping back to the line.

She watched him go before taking a deep breath. She turned back around. Eamon and Buck watched her for a moment before giving the Rain Clan's elder hard glances. He didn't pay them any attention, probably deciding they were no more worthy of being here, than Clark had been.

"You do the boy no favors by making him think he can break the chain of command," Gawain said, his tone patronizing. "You won't always be there to protect him."

Shea's hands tightened on the reins of her mount. It took considerable effort to bite back the words that wanted to escape her. Only the knowledge that Fallon might have need of this man kept her from the scathing retort she had forming.

In a coordinated movement, made all the more comical for it, Buck and Eamon stuck their tongues out and rolled their eyes before assuming their normal stone-faced expressions—the ones they wore around Trateri expedition leaders whom they found obnoxious.

Shea smothered the brief giggle the sight caused her. She schooled her face and gave them a nod of gratitude. She looked up and blinked, as she found herself pinned under the enigmatic gaze of Fallon. His eyes flicked to her two friends then back to her.

She held her breath, sensing a chastisement coming. He lowered one eyelid in an exaggerated wink before sticking just the tip of his tongue out and wrinkling his nose. This time she didn't quite contain her laugh.

Fallon's face was cool and implacable as Shea lost the battle and her chortles rolled out. The rest of the party besides Fallon, Eamon and Buck eyed her with concern, not seeing what she found so funny.

"If the Telroi could compose herself, perhaps we could get back to the business at hand," Braden said.

"My name is Shea. I suggest you remember it."

Braden's forehead wrinkled as he frowned at her. She held her breath waiting for the rebuke. He turned back to Fallon, ignoring her command. "We can send the scouts in first to learn more before the main body moves."

Eamon nodded his agreement. "My scouts can recon the area and then report back. I think small teams of three to five would be best given our lack of knowledge."

It was a good plan. One Shea would have recommended had she been in charge.

"I will be on one of the teams," Shea said. She lifted her chin and met Fallon's gaze. "Of all of us, I have the most experience with places like this. It would be a waste of a valuable resource to keep me back."

"I think we can manage without you," Braden said in a dismissive voice.

Shea ignored him, knowing that Fallon's was the only opinion mattered.

Eamon voiced his opinion. "Her skills are some of the best I've seen, and she does have more knowledge of this place. It would considerably boost our odds."

"I think she should go," Gawain said, unexpectedly siding with Shea. "Shea," he said, stressing her name, "might be able to see something our men overlook."

Shea fought to keep the shock off her face at Gawain's support. He'd made no secret his suspicion of her and her loyalties. The fact that he'd be in support of her addition to the scouting teams wasn't only surprising, it was suspicious as well.

She gave him a sideways look but only saw an expression of concentration on Gawain's face. There was no evidence of deceit or ulterior motives. She gave a mental shrug, setting aside his motivations for now. Perhaps he thought by letting her go, he could expose her for a traitor, or perhaps he thought she'd perish while scouting. Since either scenario wasn't going to happen, she decided it would be a waste of energy trying to dig below the surface. Time would eventually bring his real motivations to light.

"You should send me as well," Reece said, inserting himself into the conversation. "I have just as much experience as Shea. Furthermore, I'm the one who led you to this place."

Eamon snorted. "Yes, the ambush by golden eagle has inspired such confidence in your skills and loyalty."

Reece's shoulders bunched, and he gave Eamon a cold look. "The eagles were no fault of mine. I don't control them. Perhaps if your men had been a little quicker, they wouldn't have drawn the eagles' notice."

"We don't trust you," Buck said, stating the truth in a matter of fact manner. "People we don't trust aren't typically sent out with the scouts."

Reece lifted an eyebrow. "And yet you trusted Shea to lead you. Your scout team was the one she was part of for the past few months, wasn't it?"

Shea narrowed her eyes at him. He was up to something. While that information was widely known among the Trateri, it wasn't the sort of thing they would share with a prisoner, someone they barely trusted. Where had he gotten that little tidbit?

"Best be careful, boy," Buck warned. "We don't take it lightly when someone slanders one of our own."

"Shea has long since proven her loyalty," Fallon said when it looked like Buck was about to throw discipline to the wind and attack Reece. "The same cannot be said for you."

Reece lifted his hands, backing down with one last glance around the group. He heaved a sigh but didn't argue.

Fallon looked at Shea. "You may go with the scouts." Shea took a deep breath and started to smile. "I'll be going with you."

She debated whether to argue but decided not to take his stipulation as a slight on her skills.

"Fallon," Caden protested. "That is unwise."

Fallon gestured for quiet. "I've made my decision. You can send two of the Anateri with us if that makes you feel better, but we will be part of the scouting party."

Caden shut his mouth, his lips tightening as his eyes shot to Shea in a glare that should have singed her eyebrows. It was clear he laid the blame for Fallon's decision at her feet. If Fallon came back with so much as a scratch, she suspected Caden would find a way to take it out of her hide.

Guess she just needed to make sure they didn't run into any trouble they couldn't handle.

*

Shea stepped lightly among the rubble of the long dead city. She'd made the decision to leave the horses at the edge, feeling that it would be easier to make their way quickly and quietly if they were on foot. The horses the Trateri trained were hardy and perfect for war, not spooking at the scent of blood and vicious on the battlefield. She still didn't trust that they wouldn't get it into their little horsey brains to panic at the first sign of a beast.

That tight feeling in Shea's chest that she'd been carrying around for the past few months as she tried to find her place among the Trateri started loosening as she slipped seamlessly back into the role she'd worn for most of her life. It was so easy to be this person, the one that always knew what they were doing.

She stalked along the deserted streets of a city that hadn't seen humans in many generations, careful to keep her footsteps silent as she kept her head up and on the swivel looking for any sign of beasts or other things that could present a danger to Fallon's army. Fallon, Eamon and two of the Anateri made their equally silent way, following behind her at a distance of about ten feet between each.

When she'd explained her reasoning for the distance, Fallon had given her a look like he wanted to demand she stay safe behind him but had taken a deep breath and then let her proceed as she'd wished. She'd been a bit surprised at the easy capitulation to be honest. She thought he would argue a lot more with her and that she'd have to point out she had way more experience in such matters. The fact that he had listened and ceded control to her gave her hope.

She held up her hand, fist closed, signaling a halt. The men behind her froze in place, their hands dropping to the swords at their waists as they watched the city around them with suspicious gazes.

Something was off. Something beyond the feeling that the city was watching, waiting. As if it was some great entity with a consciousness. One that was not entirely welcoming to these strangers.

Fallon didn't waste time asking what was wrong or questioning what was there. He made two sharp gestures, signaling his men to spread out, leaving Shea to figure out why her instincts were telling her there was danger all around them.

People see so much more than they realize. Sometimes, especially when you've had years of training, something that you might not have consciously noticed, pricks at your subconscious inspiring those gut feelings. Shea had learned to listen to those feelings. They had rarely led her wrong. Right now, they were practically screaming. She just had to figure out what had set them off.

The city was quiet around them, the only noise that of other scouts far off in the distance. No movement in the buildings around them. Shea sniffed at the air. No smell either.

Still, she waited. Better to be slow and cautious then fast and dead.

Eamon, used to this behavior from her, edged into her view and gave her a nod, letting her know without words to take her time. He knew about her feelings. He'd learned to trust them. Fallon was equally content to wait.

After a few more minutes, Shea straightened, though she kept a wary eye around them. Whatever was there was gone.

Fallon made his way across the ground, careful not to make any sound. "What was it?"

"Not sure," Shea responded. "It almost felt like we were being watched."

"Are you sure that it's not just this place causing that feeling?" There was no judgment in Fallon's voice. He was simply asking a question anyone might ask.

For that reason, Shea gave it some thought. It was possible. Everyone was on edge. Zeph's observation that this was a city inhabited by the dead wasn't far off. It certainly felt that way, with its oppressive air and the feeling that it was waiting for something that would never come.

Shea looked up at the sky. Certain parts of the cavern ceiling had crumbled, crushing the buildings below and leaving rubble strewn all over. It had created gaps through which sun could pierce. The roots of vegetation grew through small spaces, as if reaching for the city below.

Shea shook her head. "I think this is separate from that. It's the third time I've felt that we're not alone here. It feels like something is following us, though I don't know what, or who, or if it's dangerous." Frustration colored her voice.

Fallon laid a hand on the small of her back, giving her support without saying a word. She took a deep breath and met his gaze. He gave her a firm nod of approval.

She smiled at him briefly before turning back to the city in front of her. She took a step only to stop abruptly. This time it was no secret what had caused her caution. Low voices echoed off the deserted stone buildings around them.

Fallon let out a quiet whistle. His Anateri dropped to a crouch, running on swift feet to take position at the front of their party where the sound was coming from. Eamon found a spot and hid behind it, unsheathing his dagger.

Shea stayed where she was, knowing that Fallon would lose his mind if she tried to get closer or inserted herself into the middle of danger. She was willing to give him this. When all was said and done, she wasn't a fighter. Not like the Anateri and Fallon. She would defend herself from a beast, but she would prefer not to.

There was a soft clatter as whatever approached sent a small pebble skating across the cobblestone street.

Shea held her breath.

A figure appeared around the building, followed quickly by another then a third—this one Shea recognized. She released her breath and straightened, calling out softly, "Buck."

His gaze shot to hers, taking in the Anateri crouched and waiting and the tension in the rest of her party's bodies. He raised his hand and waved.

The Anateri put their weapons up and straightened. Their bodies were still alert, but they didn't look like they were going to spring into attack at any moment.

Buck was followed by Clark, Fiona and a man Shea didn't recognize.

"Fancy meeting you guys here."

Eamon snorted before laying a censorious glance on Buck. "I thought you had the western quadrant."

Buck grinned and shrugged. "We finished our sweep and thought we'd help another group with theirs before we headed back to the rendezvous point."

"I'm sure." Eamon expression was wry. He was well acquainted with Buck's curiosity. "I should have known you wouldn't have been able to resist exploring further."

"How'd you get stuck with this guy?" Shea asked in greeting as Clark and Fiona approached.

"Punishment." Fiona's voice was dry.

Buck pressed a hand to his chest in mock hurt. He turned and looked at Shea. "You want some company? We'd be happy to tag along."

"Speak for yourself," the tall man at Buck's side said, looking around with suspicion. "It feels like these buildings are biding their time—waiting to consume us. My grandmother used to warn me about places like this."

"Stuff it, Johnny," Buck snapped back. "Put on your big boy breeches and act like a Trateri instead of a mealy-mouthed Lowlander."

Shea gave Buck a meaningful frown at that insult.

"Hey, you're not a Lowlander. You can't take offense to those insults anymore," Buck said, pointing a finger at her.

Shea sighed. "I don't have an objection with your presence." She looked at Fallon after her answer. He might feel otherwise.

He lifted an eyebrow and folded his arms, making it clear this was her party. It was up to her.

"It'll be like old times," Shea told Buck.

He grinned back at her, "Hopefully not entirely. I doubt the Warlord wants to see you swinging off any buildings."

Fallon's response was swift. "Yes, this Warlord would prefer your feet to remain firmly on the ground for the foreseeable future."

Shea shook her head with a wry smile. She didn't say anything, but it was a sentiment she shared. She'd had enough sailing through the air to last for a lifetime. There were only so many times a person could freefall before their luck ran out and there wasn't something to catch them.

"Before I forget, you didn't happen to notice anything while you were looking for us?" she asked.

Buck cocked his head as he frowned in thought. After a moment, he shook his head. "No, nothing of note. How 'bout you guys?"

Fiona spoke, "Nothing but empty buildings and silent streets. Not even the hint of the inhabitants who used to live here."

Shea figured as much. Whatever, or whoever was out there, was doing a good job of disguising their presence.

Shea took the lead, letting the others fall in behind her.

"What do you think happened here?" Johnny asked.

"Whatever it was must have been pretty bad," Fiona answered. "Most of these buildings look like they're pretty intact even after however many years. The inhabitants wouldn't have abandoned them without reason."

"You mean besides the fact that they're in a cavern?" Clark asked.

"I don't know. A cavern doesn't seem so bad," Buck said. "You're protected from most nasties and since no one knows you're down here, it'd be hard to invade."

"I don't think I could give up the stars and the sun," one of Fallon's Anateri volunteered.

Shea agreed. Humans weren't meant to survive in total darkness and isolation. There had been plenty of stories through the years of people going mad when living in either. Perhaps that was what had happened here. Perhaps the inhabitants did try to live down here and had gone crazy and killed each other. Stranger things had happened during that time period.

There was a creak, a sound at odds with the quiet of before. Shea halted and looked up. Fallon, attuned to Shea's every move, stopped and glanced at her. The rest of the group continued forward a few steps before noticing Shea's preoccupation.

Her instincts clamored at her—stronger than before. Something was wrong. There was another sound, like that of stone fracturing. The wall for a building, one that had partially crumbled under the last cave in, shifted. Not much, but it was enough.

Shea watched in horror as it slowly tilted. It hit the point of no return and began toppling.

"It's collapsing, run!" she shouted. The men watched for a frozen moment before scattering, trying to avoid the stone as it rained down from above.

Fallon grabbed Shea's arm and hauled her behind him. A small rock struck her shoulder, making her cry out. Fallon held one arm above his head, protecting it from the smaller rubble.

The wall toppled into another building. With a loud groan, it buckled and began to give way, falling toward them as they fled. Shea and Fallon dodged, running for all they were worth as another building in front of them began to fall, this one three stories high and much bigger.

They were trapped between the collapsing buildings.

Shea cast around for a place that would provide cover. All she saw were more buildings, each as likely to fall as the next. There was nowhere to go.

Fallon leapt, taking her to the ground and covering her body with his own. She didn't protest, knowing if a building landed on him, she would be crushed underneath as well. She looped her arms around his neck and waited. Her eyes screwed shut as the stone rained down around them.

After a long moment, when the dust had settled, Shea opened her eyes. Fallon had both arms around her head, further protecting it. She'd done the same to his. His eyes stared into hers from an inch away, the intensity of feeling in them nearly taking her breath away.

"We're alive," she finally observed.

"For which I am thankful."

He dipped his head and placed a soft kiss on Shea's lips.

"Fallon!" a voice cried in the distance.

He sighed against her lips and she gave a soft laugh. "It just never ends with them."

He sat up and held out a hand to pull her to her feet. They were dusting themselves off, as they were covered by a thin layer of dust that had been displaced when the buildings had fallen, when their scouting party found them. They were joined by Caden and several other Anateri.

"Are you alright, Warlord?" Caden asked as he approached at a rapid pace.

"Somehow." Fallon didn't seem surprised at his presence.

Shea gave the two a suspicious look. She had a sneaky suspicion that the feeling of being watched all day hadn't been in her imagination and that the man at her side had been the one to order it.

"What is Caden doing here?" Shea asked.

Neither man spared her a glance. Shea gritted her teeth. Figured.

She stalked off. If they wanted to keep secrets and play games, then that was fine. She would go be useful somewhere else and leave the plotting to Fallon and Caden.

Shea looked around, counting heads. Her group was all here.

"Buck, do you have everyone?" she asked.

He turned and counted. "We're missing two."

She saw that. Fiona and Clark.

"Anybody have eyes on them during the fall?" Shea asked.

"They got cut off and ran the other way. I lost track of them after that," Johnny said.

"Let's split up and look for them," Shea said. "Eamon, you're with me. Buck, you can decide the pairings for your team. Be careful of further collapses. We don't know if their structure is compromised as well. Yell if you find something."

She stalked off, not giving the Anateri or Fallon time to argue. She had no doubt he would order someone to follow her, but in the meantime, she would do what needed to be done. That included finding Clark and Fiona.

"Hold up, Shea," Eamon said.

Shea bit back the sharp retort that wanted to spring to her lips. She was angry about the building collapse, frustrated that she'd felt something was wrong and hadn't listened, upset that Fallon had once again kept secrets from her, and worried about the two who were missing. None of which was Eamon's fault and yelling at him wouldn't help anything.

Seeing the frustration on her face, Eamon held up a placating hand. "Look I understand you're in a rush, but you need to slow down and go carefully. You could trigger another collapse."

Shea took a deep breath. He was right. Worse, she'd rip someone's head off if they had acted as recklessly as she just had.

"You with me?" Eamon asked.

She gave him a sharp nod before turning back to the search. This time she was more careful as she went, blocking out the anger, frustration, and desperation that tried to urge her faster.

The other men called out Clark and Fiona's names as they moved. No voices returned the calls.

Shea moved further in the rubble, careful not to step anywhere that might start a secondary collapse. If the worst had happened and Clark and Fiona were buried under there, they might still be alive. Another collapse could kill them.

"Clark," Eamon called at Shea's side.

They made their way slowly over to the other side of the rubble. Shea wasn't surprised when Fallon and Caden joined them. The Anateri were a silent shadow at their backs. Shea wished they would spread out and look too, but knew voicing that opinion would be a waste of time. They had the look of men intent on protecting their Warlord.

"If the boy and woman came this way, it is doubtful they would have survived," Caden told Fallon.

Shea looked up from where she crouched and fitted Caden with an implacable expression. "Until we have their bodies in front of us, I won't write them off."

He nodded. The slightly sympathetic look in his eyes made Shea uncomfortable. It was easier when she could be mad at him. Without the heat of her anger, she had nothing to focus on but her increasing sense of hopelessness at Clark's odds of surviving.

"Warlord, I found something," Wilhelm said, nodding at something at his feet.

Shea and Fallon crossed over to where he stood. Shea crouched and brushed her fingers lightly against the ground. A footprint. Only half of one, but it was something.

She moved away and hunted for others. "Here's another one."

This one was a full print—the stitching from the person's footwear making a distinctive mark on the outer edge of the track.

"This means he could have survived," Shea said.

Eamon crouched beside her. "No, it's not his. It's too big, and these aren't the marks that his boots make. See where the stitching is? Clark wears leather soled boots with treads on them. These are different."

He was right. Damn it.

"Then, are they Fiona's?"

Eamon shook his head and looked up, meeting Fallon's grim expression. "No, these don't belong to anybody in the Wind Division."

Caden bent over them. "They look like something Rain might wear. Gawain's men are used to the plains and haven't switched to hard bottomed shoes."

"Rain shouldn't have been searching anywhere close to here." Eamon stood and put his hands on his waist as he looked down at the print.

"What does that mean?" Shea asked.

Fallon bowed his head before looking up and pinning her with a fierce expression. "There's a traitor among us."

CHAPTER TWENTY-FOUR

Shea caught up to Fallon as he left his war council. They'd reported back after finding the print. Clark and Fiona were nowhere to be found. Since it was getting late, Fallon made the decision to meet up at the rendezvous to regroup and send a larger search party out. Shea had wanted to go but had been vetoed by more than one person.

"When were you going to tell me?" she asked in a low voice as they walked. She didn't want everyone listening. Fallon and Caden had decided that the possibility of a traitor was only to be kept among them until they decided how to proceed.

"And what is it that I was supposed to have shared?" Fallon asked, his voice equally quiet.

"That you had decided to seed those who might mean you harm into this mission," she said through gritted teeth.

It was the situation with his brother all over again. Fallon had decided to draw his brother out into the open by leaving the appearance of weakness so those who plotted against him would be tempted to strike, giving him the chance to turn the tables on them.

"I always have enemies. It is best you assume they are always present."

The sound that escaped Shea was very close to a growl. "That's not what I'm talking about and you know it. Gawain, Rain. Why did you bring them? It's obvious even to me that there is no love lost between you."

Fallon's chuckle slid against her like velvet. "Very few of the clan leaders have any soft feelings towards me. I threaten their power. Any one of them would be overjoyed to have my head."

"Then why do you keep them alive?" She didn't understand it. He was the Warlord. An all-powerful conqueror genuinely loved by his soldiers. If he didn't want them in power, why didn't he do something about it?

"Because we need stability. As much as I dislike the majority of the clan leaders, they fill a useful role. Most genuinely care for their people and want the best. Without them, the clans could splinter more than even I could control."

"So, you let them plot against you?"

"Yes, I let them plot, until their scheming presents an actual danger."

"And meanwhile they're free to go around putting others at risk, including Clark," Shea shot back, her eyes spitting fire.

"What would you have me do, Shea? Kill all those I suspect of disloyalty. Become the monster your pathfinders see me as?"

Shea was brought up short. No, that wasn't what she wanted. Not at all. It made her hesitate. There had to be some happy medium. A way to protect those they cared about without becoming merciless beasts.

Fallon sighed. "You are partially correct. I did let some of those troublesome elements secure a spot on this journey, but not for the reasons you are thinking. At least not entirely."

They began walking again. The men were setting up campfires since they had decided to stay here for the night. Shea checked the cavern ceiling. The gaping spaces in it and the general size of the cavern should make fire relatively safe. At the very least, they were unlikely to asphyxiate on the smoke.

"So, this isn't a ruse to lure out your enemies. Again."

He gave her a crooked grin. "That hadn't been the original intention, but who am I to argue with this opportunity?"

Shea snorted. She bet. Fallon was the sort of man to take advantage of every chance life presented. The possibility of eliminating more enemies while consolidating his power base was probably too tempting to pass up.

"What was the original intent?" Shea asked.

"You said it yourself. The Highlands are dangerous. Your people are dangerous. There's no reason to think that that danger won't take a toll on my men. Better to sacrifice those whose loyalty is in question then my best."

Shea raised an eyebrow. That was diabolical, and not the main reason, if her knowledge of Fallon was anything to go by. She fixed him with an intent stare, saying without words that she knew there was more.

His grin flashed. "More importantly, I couldn't chance leaving them behind where their rot might spread to the other clans."

"Keep your friends close, but your enemies closer?"

He inclined his head.

She shook her head. Figured.

She walked through the orange glow from the fires to the ridge that overlooked the abandoned city, Fallon a solid presence at her side. When she stopped, he came up behind her and wrapped his arms around her chest, tugging her gently until she leaned back against him. She did so with a sigh.

"I never thought I'd see the like," Fallon said into her ear. "It's beautiful, in a desolate kind of way."

Shea made a sound of agreement, content to look out over the city. Worry about Clark out there, alone and possibly hurt, tried to take hold. She pushed it back. Worry was a wasted emotion. There was nothing she could do right now, and Fallon had already sent men to search. She wasn't so arrogant as to think she was the only one with the skills to find them.

"What wonders your Highlands must hide."

Shea's grin was fleeting in the dark. "Even for me this is new. While I have seen ancient cities before, I've never found one underground. It must hold some interesting secrets."

Fallon drew back slightly, and she could sense his eyes on her in the dark. "You almost sound like you want to explore."

Shea was quiet for a moment. Her guild would have frowned on such a yearning, but this was Fallon. If she couldn't reveal her innermost thoughts and desires to him, then they were wrong for each other.

"Not today—we have much ground to cover before I can indulge my curiosity— but someday I'd like to return, find what brought it to this place," Shea confided. "There is so much to learn from a place like this."

"Perhaps when we've settled things with your pathfinders, we can return to this place and take a few weeks to plumb its depths."

Shea tilted her head back, struggling to make out Fallon's features in the dim light. "I'd like that."

Even in the dark she could see the tender expression that settled on his face. It did funny things to her stomach, sending it fluttering all over the place.

His arms gave her a last squeeze before falling away. "Come, dinner should be nearly ready."

She took his hand as they headed back to camp. It was a rare pleasure, since Fallon generally preferred to keep his hands free in case of attack. He must have felt relatively at ease to allow it. They walked hand in hand until the campfires came into view, then he gave her hand a last squeeze before pulling his back.

They found a spot at one of the campfires. Shea was happy to see Eamon, Buck and a few other familiar faces she recognized gathered around the fire, each holding bowls filled with hot food. Fallon indicated she take a seat before breaking off to get food for both of them.

"Any luck?" Shea asked Eamon, her voice hopeful.

Eamon shook his head. "We swept that entire area and found no sign. We're going to conduct another search in the morning."

"However, if Rain has anything to do with it, they'll have us moving on before we find anything," Buck muttered. It was clear by the hard tone of his voice, his thoughts on that.

"That will not happen," Fallon said, handing one of the bowls he held to Shea. "We owe young Clark and Fiona our best efforts. You have my word that we won't shirk our duties to them."

Both Eamon and Buck bowed their head, respect and relief on their faces. "We appreciate that, Warlord."

Reece wandered over from wherever he'd been biding his time, shadowed by two Anateri.

"I hear you ran into trouble out there," Reece said, his eyes focused on Shea.

Shea twirled her fork in the bowl Fallon had given her and didn't answer. Her cousin didn't let that phase him as he watched her. He took a seat across the fire from Shea and Fallon.

"You've gotten rusty," he said, making himself comfortable. "Losing someone on a mission. What would our elders say?"

Shea bit her tongue.

"There was nothing she could do," Eamon said, his voice light.

Shea's eyes shot to him. She knew that tone. He might sound easygoing, but the way he focused on his bowl and the careful way he moved said he was one wrong word from exploding.

"The buildings just collapsed," Buck volunteered. "Even Shea couldn't have predicted that."

Reece raised an eyebrow. "I'm surprised you let them enter the buildings. You know how old those things are."

"I didn't. We weren't anywhere near them when they collapsed."

Reece cocked his head, puzzlement on his face. Shea knew he found that strange but kept the possible chance of sabotage to herself. One, she didn't know if the buildings were sabotaged. This place was old. Two, Fallon wanted to keep knowledge of the possible sabotage to a select few, so as not to cause panic, and to keep those plotting against him unaware he knew of their schemes.

Reece's eyes were thoughtful as he stared into the fire. "Isn't that interesting?"

Fallon's thigh touched Shea's, his warmth was welcome given the chill in the cavern, and she let herself lean into his side.

"So, you're Shea's cousin?" Buck asked as the fire crackled and popped. "You must have known her when she was young. Got any good stories?"

Shea lifted her head and glared at Buck. "What kind of question is that?"

He spread his hands and shrugged. "What? I'm just trying to make conversation. Get to know the other pathfinder in our midst. You're always such a mystery. You can't blame me for being curious."

"I'd be interested to learn whether she's always been this grumpy," Eamon said.

"Grumpy? I'm not grumpy."

"Oh yes, you are," Trenton said. "You get this frown on your face, and then the next thing you know, you're questioning how someone has survived in the world this long. To their face."

"Wait, wait," Buck said. "My favorite is when she asks if they were dropped on their head as a baby."

"She still does that?" Reece asked.

"Yup, and this was when she was masquerading as a man and a scout. Asked the leader of a war party that, and then when he said no told him that was a pity, because maybe being dropped on his head would have knocked some sense into him."

The rest of the group laughed.

"Did you really do that?" Fallon asked in a low voice next to her ear.

Shea's shoulders tried to reach her ears as she looked away. That was answer enough. A warm chuckle feathered through her hair. Shea rolled her eyes. Yes, laugh it up. In her defense, that man had wanted to take the warband right through a nest of gravers when she had specifically told him it was a bad idea. It wasn't her fault that he'd gotten so upset at her words that he'd tried to prove her wrong and nearly ended up dead in the process.

They laughed about it now, but at the time Eamon had been furious over her insubordination. The only thing that had saved her tail, was that the man had been so shaken he had forgotten all about her insults. The nice thing was that he hadn't questioned any of her advice for the rest of their journey.

She frowned. She could kind of see why they thought she was grumpy.

"She learned that from our master," Reece said when he stopped laughing. "He was even worse. Everyone he met was an idiot, and he never failed to tell them as much."

"Old Winchell," Shea said with a fond smile. "He was an ornery old man, but he was the best pathfinder I've ever met. Taught us everything we knew."

"Including how not to catch hoppers," Reece added.

"Hoppers? What are those?"

"It's this salamander-like creature that lives in some of the mountain streams. They like to lay their eggs in spring and then burrow deep in the mud to survive winter. They're very tasty and their scales make fine jewelry."

"But they're tricky to catch," Shea added. "Winchell said if we caught one, we could spend a month in one of the Highland villages sleeping in a real bed."

"Did you catch one?" Buck asked.

"No, but not for lack of trying," Reece said. "You see, they're very hard to find. Shea and I spent an entire month just trying to catch sight of one. When we finally found them, Shea decides to cover herself with mud in hopes of making herself more appealing to the hoppers."

"Did it work?"

Reece's face broke out into a wide smile. "Oh yes. A little too well. You see it was mating season and they like to lay their eggs in mud banks. Since Shea had covered herself with the stuff, the hoppers swarmed her and began laying eggs. The thing about hoppers is that they secrete this sticky webbing that enables the eggs to stay stationary even when the streams flood."

"How'd you get the eggs off?" Eamon asked Shea.

Her face turned bright red. She mumbled, "I didn't."

Reece barked out a laugh. "She ended up walking around with little eggs attached to her for almost a week because she couldn't bear to kill all those babies."

"I was just covering for you," Shea returned. "You started sobbing when Winchell told you that you had to be the one to yank the eggs off, since you didn't stop me from covering myself with the mud in the first place."

"Sounds like an interesting person. He might have a few good pointers. I'd like to meet him one day," Eamon said.

Reece and Shea's faces sobered. Shea turned her eyes to her food.

"That'll be difficult as he's dead," Reece said, looking into the fire and avoiding looking at Shea. His jaw flexed.

The rest of the group stared at each other across the fire.

Buck was the one to broach the silence. "How'd it happen?"

Reece stared across the fire at Shea. The shadows flickering across his face made it hard to decipher his thoughts.

After a long moment, he said, "He followed his apprentice into the Badlands and didn't come out again."

Shea's hands clenched around her bowl of food. Her appetite was gone.

Eamon looked across the fire at Shea, his face sympathetic. He didn't ask the question she knew was on everyone's mind. For that she was grateful.

Fallon's arm brushed hers. "You never talk about that place."

Shea shifted but remained quiet.

"No, she doesn't, does she?" Reece said with a humorless smile. "Even with those of us who deserve an answer."

Shea hunkered down. She wanted to answer. She did, but somehow her words always got lost.

"I don't even know why you went there. With him of all people. He wasn't even one of us."

Shea flinched, knowing exactly who he was talking about. "How can you say that? He grew up with us. He was just as much Winchell's apprentice as we were."

"He didn't pass the test. He wasn't a pathfinder, no matter what went on before."

Shea scoffed. "One test doesn't negate all the things he learned."

"It does when it means he can't navigate the mist," Reece shot back. "I don't know what you even saw in him. He was always weak, always using you to make himself look good, stealing credit that should have gone to one of us."

"It doesn't matter now, does it? He's dead." There was sadness in Shea's voice at those words.

Reece's mouth snapped shut, but he didn't say the words that looked like they were begging to explode from him.

Fallon watched the two of them with a considering expression. "Who is he?"

Shea's gaze shot to his, she looked stricken and slightly guilty.

Reece shook his head at her in disgust. "You haven't told him?"

"You know I haven't," she snapped back. "That's why you brought it up."

She knew her cousin. This trip down memory lane had a purpose. He could pretend otherwise all he wanted, but this was exactly what he'd been hoping to discuss when he sat down. She only wished she had guessed sooner, so she could have found anywhere else to be.

Shea gave up glaring at her cousin and faced Fallon. She took a deep breath. Too late to hide this now. She only wished she'd had this talk with him sooner when there were less people about. "His name was Griffin. We three grew up together."

"What she hasn't said is he was also her first love. The man who led her into disaster and ruin and got her demoted to a rank and file pathfinder serving a village no one would touch," Reece added.

Shea shot her cousin another dirty look, wanting to strangle him when he returned her glare with a smirk and a shrug.

Fallon's face was thoughtful as he studied her. His silence pulled other revelations from her.

"He couldn't pass the final test. He couldn't navigate the mists. It devastated him. When you fail the tests, you're sent away from the keep. It doesn't matter if you grew up there or if your entire family lives there. They don't allow those who fail the test to remain."

There was a low whistle from Buck. "That's pretty harsh."

Reece shrugged. "It's our way and has been for generations. There have been problems in the past. The rejected are given the choice of settling in one of the villages nearby or they can make their way further afield. Some choose to join the caravans and chance the wilds to travel from village to village. Griffin chose another path entirely."

Shea took up the thread of the story. "He knew, like we all did, that the pathfinders had never led a successful expedition into the Badlands. He thought that if he could find one of the ancient cities and come back with something big that the guild might make an exception for him."

"Translation, he convinced Shea to do all the hard work so he could reap all of the rewards."

"I'm not the only one he convinced," Shea said in a soft voice.

Reece shrugged one shoulder. "You're right about that. You're the one they trusted though. Thirty men and women went in; one came out. Winchell followed Shea because she was always his favorite and because he felt responsible for Griffin. It's not often a child of the keep fails the test. He took it as a failure on his own part. I'm sure Griffin helped form that outlook."

He had. It was something that Shea didn't like thinking about. Speaking ill of the dead didn't sit right with her. They were unable to defend themselves.

"I thought it was your idea to go into the Badlands," Fallon said with a thoughtful expression on his face.

"Might as well have. He never would have gone there if not for me. You know the rest," Shea told Fallon. She'd told him the ending of this story. "We lost several people before we were even a week into the Badlands. After the eagles attacked, the group lost morale and broke apart. Eventually I was the only one left."

"Which was why she took the entirety of the blame for Griffin's stupidity," Reece said. "It didn't help that none of you bothered to get permission for your little excursion before you left. Shea was demoted to Birdon Leaf, who sent her to the Lowlands, and here we are."

The group was silent for a long moment after that. Shea found she was unable to meet anyone's eyes. She stood. "I'm going to go check on something."

She moved off without waiting for a response.

Fallon watched the shadows swallow Shea. He looked across the fire as her cousin watched her leave with an expression that was both combative and defeated at the same time. Fallon had to wonder what the man had hoped to get out of that little exchange.

"I'm the one who went searching for her when her party disappeared. Three weeks I looked, and all the while, the hope of finding her alive got smaller and smaller each day." Reece looked across the fire at Fallon. The emotion had drained out of his face, leaving him looking tired. "When I found her, she was delirious. You could count the number of ribs; her skin was sunken, and her bones stuck out like sticks. She hadn't eaten or had anything to drink for days. I thought she was going to die."

"But she didn't. Because of you," Fallon said.

Reece ran a hand through his hair. His sigh was heavy. "No, she didn't, but for a long time it felt like she had. You called her grumpy," he said to Buck. "She wasn't always like that. Once upon a time she was sunny and enthusiastic, always believing the best of anybody and any situation. She was still acerbic, her tongue could leave a man bleeding, but it was rare for her to let loose. And curious. So damn curious. She used to drive her parents crazy, always disappearing into the wilds to study whatever beast was nearby. He changed that."

Fallon stood, collecting his bowl and Shea's mostly untouched one.

"I've seen more of the old Shea with you than I have in a long time."

Fallon didn't react as he carried the bowls back to the cooks and their apprentices.

He tracked Shea to the rise overlooking the city. He didn't know if she realized it, but she always headed to a high place when she needed to think. He thought observing the scene below gave her some measure of calm, but he'd never asked.

She was right where he thought she'd be, staring angrily down at the abandoned city, though there was little to see with the low light the fires behind them provided.

"I was stupid," she said without looking at him.

He stopped, not finding himself surprised that she knew he was here. She always seemed to know. Sneaking up on her was rare.

"About what?"

"I knew he was using me. I knew he didn't care as long as it meant he'd be a pathfinder in the end."

Fallon joined her on the ridge. He made a 'hmm' sound.

Shea sighed. "I was fine with it. I figured once he was a pathfinder, he'd finally settle down and finally see me."

"I'm glad he's dead. It saves me the trouble of killing him," Fallon said.

The laugh that escaped Shea seemed to surprise her. She dropped her head and shook it. "Me too. What does that say about me? That I'm glad the person I thought I loved is dead?"

"It says you're smart, and that you know I'm infinitely better than some boy unable to pass a simple test."

"It's actually pretty hard."

Fallon waved a hand and made a disgruntled noise. He didn't care. "You're mine. You've always been mine. You were just a little slow figuring it out."

Shea looked over at him. He didn't have to see her face to know that it was full of skepticism.

"This from the man whose army kidnapped me, and then who threatened to hurt my friends if I tried to run away."

Fallon grinned into the night. He loved it when she pushed back. It made him want to chase. To conquer.

He sidled closer, his larger form dwarfing hers. He laid his lips against her neck, then smiled against her skin at the breathless sound that escaped her. He feathered his lips along her jaw, breathing in that indelible scent that signified Shea. A scent that reminded him of the combination of wildflowers and the chill bite of mountain air.

"We can't. There are too many people around." Shea's voice was filled with regret even as she tilted her head to give him better access.

Her modesty always surprised him, given how little privacy a nomadic life of expeditions offered. The knowledge that she'd preserved this part of herself was another piece of the puzzle that he never got tired of assembling.

"My men can keep the others away from us."

"And what about them?"

He pulled back, cupping her face in his large palms. "I'm the Warlord. If I tell them not to listen, they won't."

Her snort of disbelief might have offended a more sensitive man. He found himself delighted, playful in a way that he had never had the chance to be.

"Fallon."

Her resolve was weakening; he could sense it. He held himself still, a predator knowing when to wait out his prey. Pressure would make her choose the opposite—just because she could.

"We can be quiet." His hand found its way under her shirt to rest against her waist, one thumb moving in a gentle caress against her skin. He'd missed the feel of her during this journey and he consoled himself with that single caress.

She sighed. That was all the permission he needed. He swept her into his arms finding a spot on the ground as his lips found hers. Together, they consumed each other—their passion burning through them with a fury fed by their abstinence over the last week. The knowledge they were surrounded by his men and could be interrupted at any moment lent urgency to their movements.

This time he didn't have the patience for gentle, his hands rough, as they pulled her shirt over her head and bared her to the dim light. It was a shame he couldn't see her better, only able to see the slight glow of her flesh. Her hands yanked and pulled, urging his tunic over his head.

He ripped her pants off, dropping his lower body between her legs and pressing hard against her, glorying in the pressure, the warmth between her thighs. He hissed as she sank her nails into his back, trying to bring him closer.

Her movements became frantic as he moved one hand between them, his fingers gliding through her folds to dip into her center for one pump, two, before withdrawing to circle that delicate bundle of nerves at the top of her sex.

Her hips tried to follow him as he withdrew, and he chuckled even as he pressed one palm on her belly to keep her still. She made a sound of protest, even as her legs rose and clutched at him, trying to force him back. Her slight frame belied her strength, one that was built over numerous mountains climbed and miles traveled.

Her movements were sinuous and full of power as she tried to take control and flip him onto his back in a move he knew one of his men must have taught her. It was only because of endless hours of practice countering that same move that he managed to quell her attempt at domination.

His chuckle was warm in her ear as he pinched her nipple between his fingers and gently pulled. It was her turn to hiss at the pleasure pain.

He kissed and nipped his way down her body, soothing the sting of his bites with gentle kisses. Reaching the spot at the apex of her thighs, he ran his nose down the side where the thigh joined with her torso and inhaled, glorying in the scent of her arousal. It was a sensitive spot. One he'd found quite by accident and had taken advantage of ever since.

Her gasp drove him on as he tempted and teased, her almost silent cries urging him as he licked and sucked. He thrust one finger into her channel then joined it with another, the strangled gasp she gave letting him know she liked it. Her thighs clenched around his ears even as he gave her no quarter, the muscles tensing and flexing as she tried to resist, to fight her climax as she always did. It was always a battle, one he took pleasure in winning.

Her inner muscles clenched and gripped at his fingers as she neared the point of no return. He was as hard as a rock, her soft gasps acting as an aphrodisiac.

Right as she was poised to hurdle over the cliff, he withdrew. He sat back on his heels and wiped his mouth, looking down at the beautiful mess in front of him. Her chest heaved and eyes he knew were spitting blue fire glared up at him. The fury was almost tangible in the air, feeding his own lust.

He placed his hands on either side of her and leaned forward. His cock hovered at her entrance. He couldn't help it as it twitched, the randy bastard eager to dive into her warmth. He waited until her breathing had calmed, until she looked at him, until she had opened her mouth to blast him with her sharp tongue. He drove forward, slamming home in one thrust, rejoicing in the sharp cry of need that rose from her.

His control teetered, then fell when her knees rose to clutch at his sides. His rhythm picked up—his muscles tightening and his teeth clenching as he pounded into her.

Her cries rose around them. He snarled, "Mine."

Her entire body tensed as her womb quivered and then her release was upon her. Her voice raised in a soft wail that he caught with his lips as she bucked against him. His release followed, and he pressed hard into her. He could never get close enough.

He collapsed against her, careful to keep most of his weight off her as they caught their breath. Of all the women he'd lain with, Shea was the one who made him lose control. Who inspired twin feelings of possession and tenderness. Sometimes he felt like he would be torn apart by the conflicting needs each feeling brought.

He pushed a lock of hair out of her face, his elbows and forearms framing her head. Bending, he pressed a gentle kiss to the corner of her mouth.

"So much for ordering them not to listen," she said. "I think the whole camp couldn't help but have heard that."

He felt a spurt of amusement. "Maybe we should try again. Just so you can practice being quiet."

A fist came up to thump against his side.

"Ouch," he said covering her fist and pressing it against his skin. He pressed a kiss behind her ear. "That hurts. I think you should make it up to me."

Already he could feel himself stirring against her. She was a drug he couldn't get enough of.

"Oh, you do, do you?"

His kisses moved along her jaw in answer. Her legs moved restlessly against his.

"I do," he said, before his mouth covered hers.

It was a long moment before their lips parted enough for him to say, "Try to be quieter this time."

There was a long moment, one where her eyes were slightly glazed, before they widened in realization. Then his lips were back again, and he was putting her fury to better use.

CHAPTER TWENTY-FIVE

Shea guided her horse around another pile of rubble, careful not to venture near any of the buildings hovering over them like hulking beasts. Fallon's army was nearly through the abandoned city. He'd made the choice to have them move out this afternoon when no sign of Clark or Fiona had been uncovered. Several of his men had also disappeared during the search.

Shea had tried arguing. She'd even gone so far as to suggest Eamon, Buck, and a few others remain behind with her to continue the search. Both Fallon and Reece had vetoed that idea. She understood Fallon's reasoning but couldn't guess what was in her cousin's mind.

He'd grown increasingly tense the further they ventured into the city. Any other man she would have called jumpy. Reece, however, just seemed on edge, like a sudden noise might be responded to with extreme violence.

There was an itchy feeling on the back of Shea's neck, like they were being watched. It had started while they were still camped and gotten worse as they traveled deeper and deeper into the city.

The men in Fallon's army had started whispering of ghosts, eyeing the buildings around them with suspicion born of fear. Shea didn't often find herself falling victim to such a mentality but even she was on edge.

If not for Clark and Fiona being missing, she would have advocated leaving this place far, far behind.

Fallon was just ahead of her, his Anateri forming a shield between them and the rest of the city. She knew from the pinched look on Caden's face that he distrusted the buildings around them, probably only slightly more than he did the men following them. He and Fallon had decided that the clan leaders would ride with them. That way they could keep an eye on their potential saboteurs.

Shea had been on edge for the entire ride, watching for the slightest sign an attack was imminent. So far, the clan leaders seemed perfectly normal if a little tense, but that could be attributed to the current surroundings.

A scrap of cloth hanging from a stray post caught Shea's attention. It was located behind two buildings and only visible because she passed by what could have been an alley between them in some long distant past. She pulled on her reins, forcing the horse to step in a tight circle.

Trenton slowed his horse, his face a grimace of pain as his ribs protested. Chirron might have kept him alive, but he had several broken ribs that reminded him every time he moved of how close a call he'd had of it.

"What is it?" he asked.

She didn't answer. She stood in her stirrups to get a better look. That jacket was a familiar green. It was one she might have worn once upon a time. Clark had been wearing his as protection against the chill of the caverns when he'd gone missing.

Her first reaction was to rush for the jacket as if it might tell her where he'd gone, if she could just reach it. She quelled that urge, knowing that it could be a trap. Probably was a trap.

It seemed too simple for his jacket to turn up here—miles away from where he'd disappeared.

"I see something," she said.

Trenton's head snapped around, looking in the direction that seemed to draw her attention. He was quiet as he searched. It didn't take him long to spot the jacket.

"Don't do anything stupid," he cautioned before giving a sharp whistle.

Fallon and the Anateri came to a stop. Fallon looked back. Noticing Shea and Trenton, he urged his horse toward them.

"What is it?" His words were sharp and abrupt, but Shea didn't take it personally. He was on alert like all of them. This was the Warlord speaking, someone expecting a report.

Shea tilted her head to the jacket.

His sharp eyes fastened on it and he frowned. He'd seen the same thing she had. Such a nice present. It was practically wrapped with a bow.

Eamon rode up on her other side, his gaze already fastened on what held her attention. He let out a low curse when he caught sight of the jacket.

"What are your orders?" Trenton asked.

Fallon was silent for a long moment, his body tense.

Shea urged her horse forward, bypassing the alley between the buildings to ride around front.

"Shea!" Fallon called.

She ignored him. The building to her right held her entire attention. Movement in one of the windows high above had her hands tightening on the reins. They were being watched. Definitely a trap. The question was who had set the trap? And why?

She steered her horse to give the building a wide berth as she made a circle around it and the abandoned jacket. She had no intention of getting close, but they needed more information before they made any decision. The only way to do that was to do a little reconnaissance—something Fallon would have ordered had she not been here.

Men. They could be so smart sometimes but also dumb.

Shea was careful to keep her distance from the jacket and any nearby buildings when she was on the opposite side of it; Fallon watched her with a darkly intense look as she stopped and observed. It was quiet on this side of the square.

Fallon and a few of his men had stayed on the other side. No doubt he'd stopped anyone from following her for fear they would set off any traps that she might have bypassed. Again, smart man.

She glanced back up into the building. There was no movement that she could see from this side. She looked back at the jacket. It was nailed to a stone post. There was no wind down here, so it was utterly still, just hanging there.

The ominous air of the abandoned city lay all around her. The weight of fear and tension seemed to press in on her, ratcheting up her adrenaline. She took a deep breath, not letting the need for action lead her to a rash impulse.

A cool breeze stirred her hair, lifting it from her neck as it swirled around her, bringing with it the faintest sounds of voices, indistinct and indecipherable. She frowned. There should be no way for air to flow in this place. Any air that might have made it through the cracks in the rock above would never have reached this far down.

The voices carried by the wind grew more distinct. A murmuring, fueled by a thousand individual voices, rose. It was difficult but Shea though she heard one phrase being repeated over and over.

Enemy of my enemy, you are betrayed.

Betrayed?

Her eyes shot to the building. Some of the men had not come back last night. Perhaps the ones responsible for the collapse of the buildings before?

Her eyes went to the base of two buildings, but she didn't see anything amiss. Still, that feeling was there in the pit of her stomach. The one that said something bad was coming.

Fallon looked like he felt it too as he stepped closer to the alley that would lead him to the square and the jacket.

"No, stay back," Shea shouted. Her horse responded to the urgency of her voice by prancing in place. It was the only thing that saved her. An arrow flew by, piercing the air where she had just been. Shea ducked in her seat, hanging off the side of her horse as she tried to shield her vital points.

Almost at the exact same moment, an explosion rent the air and the buildings they would have been riding through, had Shea not gotten distracted by the jacket, began to fall, collapsing in a great wave of dust and rubble.

The commotion proved too much for her mount. It reared, dumping her to the ground before taking off in the opposite direction of the collapse. Shea stayed low to the ground, not knowing if the bowmen in the building planned another shot at her or had already disappeared.

"Shea!" Fallon roared.

Shea coughed and lifted her head. The cloud of debris from the explosion and collapse had not yet dissipated. She couldn't see him through the alley, nor he her.

She could hear him though. She could also hear Caden ordering his Anateri to keep him back.

"Stay there. We don't know if they've set up secondary traps," Shea shouted, or tried to shout, since the air made it hard to speak without coughing.

She sat up cautiously, hoping the poor visibility would keep her from being shot.

"There are archers in the buildings. Find cover," she ordered.

There was a low murmur as Caden ordered his men into the buildings to search for their ambushers.

The world had turned a dusky gray. Shea climbed to her feet and limped forward. The jacket and post rose out of the gray, the only familiar landmark.

She grabbed the jacket and pulled it from the post, figuring that since she was here already she might as well get what she came for.

"Clear," one of the Anateri yelled. It sounded like his voice was coming from high up in the building she suspected the archer had been in when she'd been shot at.

"Here as well," another called.

Shea was glad because the dust was clearing from the air. She could see Fallon now, Caden at his side.

His eyes sparked with relief at the sight of her. She waved letting him know she was alright. His shoulders relaxed and he took a step toward her. She put up a hand and shook her head. No, she didn't want him between those two buildings. Chances were they weren't posed to collapse, but it never hurt to be careful.

He nodded, understanding her concern. Impatience drew his brows together. He turned on his heel, disappearing from view. Shea figured she had only a few moments as he took the same route she did to this square.

She turned the jacket over in her hands, noting the rips in the arm and one on the back. A few dark spots down the front had her stomach clenching with worry. It could be blood, but there was a chance it was something harmless. Though her mind was having a hard time coming up with an alternative.

There didn't look to be enough of it to indicate a severe injury, but it was hard to tell. Shea couldn't imagine Clark abandoning this jacket lightly. He took great pride in being a scout, and this jacket declared his status to other Trateri.

She bent and examined the cobblestones around the post. The cool climate of the cavern had preserved much of this place, even wood that should have long rotted away. That didn't mean it was entirely untouched by the elements. The thick clay dirt that littered much of the caverns had accumulated here too. Shea could only guess that an underground river had originally carved this space out before drying up. She knew if the city had been exposed to continuous flooding, it would be in much worse shape.

Despite the dirt and debris on the cobblestone, there was no evidence of any footprints besides her own. What sort of man could walk the square, pin the jacket where someone would see it, then set several traps without leaving behind a single print as evidence of their existence?

Perhaps the Trateri assertion that ghosts lived here wasn't too far from the truth.

There was a slight sound as Fallon made his way around the buildings. Shea stood, glad to see him alive and breathing. Had they not stopped to check out this jacket they could all very well be dead by now.

She took a step toward him and then froze as the ground shifted under her. She held up a hand. Something on her face must have warned him because he stopped, his guard instantly up.

The ground crumbled under her. She let out a sharp cry as she tumbled down into the darkness.

"Shea," Fallon roared, charging forward. The terror in her eyes giving him speed. Even then, he wasn't quick enough.

She fell, the ground disappearing from beneath her. There was nothing he could do, besides watch. The sound that left him then should have sent the rest of this decaying city crashing to the ground. A sound that held the pain and desolation of a man who held the power to conquer the world. There was no pain like watching the one you lived for, the one who gave color to the world and put breath in your lungs, die right in front of your eyes.

It was something he'd vowed to never have happen again. Yet here he was, watching Shea fall, helpless to do anything. Again.

Caden dragged him back from the edge when he would have gone in after her. "There's nothing you can do. You won't help anybody by following her down."

Fallon fought against his friend, the man who had vowed to lay down his life in defense of his. He fought and raged against this man who kept him from the woman he loved.

"Fallon. Fallon," Caden said, defending himself against his blows. "Grab him."

Several other arms found their way around Fallon. His Anateri hanging onto him as he strained and fought to the edge of the hole Shea had fallen into. All the while roaring.

Eamon and Buck appeared, their faces a mask of shock. There wasn't enough of Fallon present for him to wonder whether their reaction was because of his utter loss of control or the fact that another of their friends had been claimed by this cursed place.

Eamon jerked and then looked from Fallon into the darkness that had claimed Shea. "I hear something." He watched the pit for a long moment, before calling, "Wait, let him go."

Caden glared at the other man, his expression telling him without words how much he disliked that idea.

"I don't think she's dead," Eamon said. "Let him go so he can see for himself."

Fallon went still—hope a wild thing in his chest.

Caden's movements were cautious as he loosened his grip on Fallon. When Fallon didn't rush the spot where Shea had fell, he nodded at the others.

Fallon didn't spare his men a glance as he took one hesitant step and then another. It wasn't like him to experience uncertainty. He was a conqueror. A warrior. He made a plan and he implemented. There were no wasted actions. Everything he did had a purpose.

At the moment, his only purpose was making sure Shea still breathed. He'd give his entire army for that one thing.

He stepped to the edge, knowing if Eamon was wrong, the darkness inside of him, the one Shea had managed to beat back with her sly smiles and stubborn hardheadedness, would consume him and nothing in this world would ever be safe again.

"Anybody up there?" a voice called from below. "Fallon."

His chest rose in a deep breath, and the cold that had gripped him since the sight of her fall began to thaw.

"Shea, how badly are you hurt?" he asked.

There was a long pause.

"I'm bruised but otherwise unharmed."

He didn't like that pause. Shea was the kind of person to hide how badly she was hurt to protect him. Especially if she knew there was nothing he could do and didn't want to worry him.

"We're going to get you out, just hang tight."

He turned to Eamon, his voice a whip of sound. "Find me some rope. Now."

Caden stepped forward. "Warlord, your men have cleared the two buildings and have found no sign of the archer."

Fallon held up his hand before Caden said something Fallon would not be willing to forgive him for. "I'm not leaving her down there."

"There could still be those waiting to ambush you. You're exposed here."

Except they hadn't attacked him. They had attacked Shea. Why was that? It was the third time she'd been directly targeted. It was enough to make him doubt that he was the one they were after.

"I'm. Not. Leaving. Her." Each word was precise.

Caden had been with him long enough to recognize that tone and bowed his head. Good. Fallon didn't want to have to replace him. He'd been loyal for many years, but even he didn't get to tell Fallon what to do. Fallon went back to glaring at the hole.

"Where is that rope?" he shouted. Impatience a living thing within him.

Other parts of the square caved in. His men shouted and backed up in alarm. Fallon crouched as the ground shook and shook, like a dog trying to dry itself off.

When it had finished he stood, "Shea, are you still there?"

There was a long moment of silence. "Yeah, but this place isn't too stable right now. I'm not sure I'll survive another cave-in like that one."

Eamon ran up, a coil of rope around his shoulder.

"We've found rope. We're coming for you."

"Don't. The ground's not going to hold much longer. I can see how unstable it is. I'm actually surprised the entire square hasn't collapsed already."

"I'm not leaving you."

"I can see another way out."

"You're lying."

There was a rusty laugh from below. "I'm actually not. There really is a way out, and I think I'm supposed to take it."

Fallon frowned. What did that mean?

"I'll meet up with you when I can. Follow Reece out. He should know the way."

Fallon's expression turned thunderous. The Anateri close to him took a step back. Caden, who had been with him from nearly the beginning, just barely flinched. Fallon ignored them all.

"That is not happening," he hissed.

How could she even suggest something like that? Something that went against the core of who he was?

"I'm not really giving you a choice. I'll see you up there."

His eyes narrowed to slits. She would not. He forbade it. There was a rustle below as if she really was trying to make her way to this exit.

He lost what little reason he had left. Fallon leapt forward, an explosion of movement that took him over the edge and into the pit Shea had fallen into.

He landed with legs crouched and arms spread, the impact reverberating up his limbs. Shea turned to look at him, her eyes wide and her mouth open.

"What are you doing?" she shouted. "Have you gone insane?"

He straightened, his legs and back protesting, and strode over to her. He ignored her as she tried to wave him off, grabbing her and wrapping her in a tight embrace

She let him hold her for one long moment, her arms coming up to clasp him, before she shoved him away.

"You idiot. What were you thinking?"

"I was thinking you could use my help."

One eyebrow rose in an incredulous expression. "How exactly does you being down here help us? Now both of us are stuck in this hole instead of just me."

He folded his arms over his chest and fixed her with his best arrogant expression, looking down at her with a look that said she should be thanking him instead of giving him a hard time.

"I'll lift you out," he said.

She gave him a skeptical look before glancing at the hole above them. "And what about you?"

"Caden has rope. He can use that to get me out of this place."

Shea's face reflected her uncertainty. She looked to the side and Fallon saw that she hadn't been lying earlier. There really was a tunnel that appeared to lead away from this place.

"We could go that way."

He shook his head. "No, we go up. I don't want to chance it leading somewhere worse."

She nodded. He'd told her about the bones near the entrance. Neither one of them wanted to meet the denizens of this place if they could help it, especially alone and lightly armed.

Fallon walked around the small space. It only took a few strides to meet the wall. He found a spot that looked relatively stable and cupped his hands. "Here you go. I'll lift you out."

She stared up at the hole and then back down at Fallon. "I don't like this. We should wait for the rope. Then we can both go."

"There's no point. Let's get you out of here, and then there will be one less person to hoist out later." His tone left no room to argue.

He felt a wave of relief when her mouth firmed, and she stepped towards him. What he hadn't told her, the reason he was so insistent that she go now, was because she was right. This place was very close to falling. Every moment they waited was another one where this place might collapse. He wanted her above, where it was safe before that happened.

The fall must have unnerved her more than she'd let on for her not to pick up on any of that or call him on his autocratic orders. For that he was grateful, even as a thread of worry touched him.

She placed her boot in his hand, and he lifted her easily until she was standing on his shoulders.

"Shea!" Buck's head appeared over the edge. He looked like he'd lain down. Seeing Shea so close, he extended his hand. "Here, I'll pull you up."

Shea reached, catching hold of his hand easily. He lifted her out, pulling until she was over the lip of the ledge. Fallon stepped back, watching the place where she'd disappeared.

Shea crawled several feet from the edge wanting to keep her weight as distributed as possible so as not to collapse everything. Buck was right beside her. When she turned and sat, he clasped her on the shoulder, patting her arms and legs.

"I'm fine, Buck."

"Just making sure, crazy lady."

"Does Caden have the rope?" she asked, looking around. Eamon and Caden were making their way towards them.

Before he could answer, there was a crack. Half the courtyard caved in.

"Fallon!" Shea lurched forward. Eamon and Caden grabbed her and dragged her back. "Fallon!"

There was a gaping hole where the post had been. Even the spot where Shea had been lifted out was gone.

An ugly feeling rose up inside her—one that threatened to grab her by the throat and spew venom and darkness.

Fallon was down there. Fallon was down there. Fallon was down there.

Shea didn't realize she was repeating the words over and over until Eamon stepped in front of her and grabbed her face.

"I know, lass. I'm sorry."

Shea made a choked sound. She couldn't cry, her eyes were dry. This couldn't be happening.

"Was the Warlord down there?" a voice shouted.

There were running footsteps as several people spilled into what remained of the courtyard.

"I told you to keep them back," Caden snapped, his voice coming from a distance. All Shea could do was stare at the hole where Fallon had been.

"They used one of the buildings to slip past us," another voice answered.

Fallon was gone.

"You didn't answer me. Was the Hawkvale down there when it collapsed?"

"I don't answer to you, Rain," Caden snarled.

"I'd be careful, outcast, in how you speak to the clan leaders. I don't care if he did make you Anateri. With the Hawkvale dead, one of us stand to take his place," Van said.

Dead.

There was a scuffle as Caden lunged at the other man. Only the quick reaction of his men kept him from landing a blow. Eamon and Buck surrounded Shea, their eyes on the others even as they protected her.

"Do you see a body?" Shea's voice sounded like that of a stranger.

The other men paused, all eyes coming to her. She didn't notice, staring at the dark abyss of space.

No one answered her.

She finally looked up, her eyes calm and her face composed. "Well? Do you see a body?"

"Will somebody shut her up? We don't have time for histrionics."

Shea bared her teeth. A fight. Good. She needed one.

"How 'bouts I show you histrionics?" Buck threatened, stepping forward.

Van looked at him and curled his lip. "I can see the first order of business will be ensuring discipline in the ranks."

"There will be no first, second, third, or any other order of business," Shea said, her eyes flinty. She lifted her chin when the other men glanced at her. "Because the Hawkvale is not dead and you will *not* be taking his place."

Van gave a derisive laugh as he looked around the rest of the group. Zeph had joined Van and Gawain. His face was guarded and remote. None of the other men laughed, just looked at Shea with varying levels of intensity.

Van looked at Shea with scorn. "What are you going on about?"

Shea spread her hands to encompass the area. "Do you see a body?"

They all looked at the collapsed square. No body presented itself.

"What does that matter? No man could have survived that collapse."

Shea lifted an eyebrow, "No one said Fallon was down there at the time of collapse."

Van made a sound that was half-huff, half-laugh, like he thought Shea was jesting. Her face remained serious, her eyes winter cold. "You're serious."

"She is," Caden said before she could answer. "There is no proof that the Hawkvale was down there."

"We all heard her screaming," Gawain said.

"You don't really expect us to believe this fabrication," Van inserted.

"No body, no death," Shea told him. She allowed a humorless smirk to grace her lips.

"This won't stand," he hissed. "You will not rule in his stead. Our people will not allow a throwaway to lead us."

Shea didn't allow emotion to touch her. "We'll see."

Van gave her a look of derision before whirling and stalking back the way he'd come. Gawain looked at the rest of them. "He's right. Eventually the men will demand answers."

Zeph was the last to go. He looked at the rest of them before departing without a word.

When they were gone, Caden looked at Shea. "I hope you know what you're doing."

She leaned forward and rested her palms on her thighs. The confrontation had left her shaky. "So do I."

"Is there reason to hope he lives?" Caden asked.

She took a deep breath and straightened. "There was another way out. I wanted to take it, but he thought it was too dangerous—that we'd get lost. If he was in the passage when the courtyard collapsed, he could still be alive."

"But you're not sure?" Eamon asked.

Shea didn't answer.

"Horse gods, protect us," Caden muttered.

CHAPTER TWENTY-SIX

Y ou two know Fallon best. Where would he go? What would he do if he survived?" Shea asked Caden and Braden, keeping her voice low so they weren't overheard.

Besides Darius, the two men had the most experience with Fallon. They knew his habits. They could probably guess the thoughts in his mind right now. While Shea had grown closer to Fallon in the past few months, she didn't have the same level of history with him.

She'd drawn them aside, into a small area away from the main group. She wanted their thoughts before the rest of the Trateri caught wind of what had happened in that square.

The two men stared thoughtfully at her. Caden's forehead had several frown lines in it, while Braden firmed his lips and narrowed his eyes.

"He would try to make his way back to the main element."

"Would he expect us to remain here?" Shea asked.

Braden shook his head. "No, he would want us to keep moving, especially in light of the collapses. He'd try to meet us at the rendezvous point. Otherwise he would trail us until he could catch up."

That answered the question of stay or go.

"What kind of opposition can I expect from the clan leaders?" Shea asked. She had a sense of what was coming but wanted their feedback as well to see how much it differed from hers.

"You already know Van of Lion will be a problem," Caden said, his arms crossed over his chest. "Gawain of Rain shouldn't be trusted either. Fallon and he have a troubled relationship."

"I would have said Zeph from Ember would be a good ally, but he has been rather close with those two of late. He could be a trusted supporter, or he could stab you in the back," Braden said.

Great.

"What can you tell me about the buildings that collapsed?" Shea asked, moving on.

"Probably sabotage again."

If she hadn't stopped for that jacket, they would have ridden right into the kill zone. Then they might all be dead instead of just possibly Fallon.

She rubbed at the pain in her chest.

"Lock down the camp. No one in or out," she ordered. "If the perpetrators are still here, I don't want them to have the chance to go after Fallon while he's alone and possibly injured."

"I agree," Caden said with a firm nod. "I've already given my men orders to get a head count. They'll bring us the names of anybody who was missing at any point."

"Good. I want to hear what the clan leaders are saying as well. Bring me anything you find," Shea said in dismissal.

Both men took their leave.

Shea took a deep breath and closed her eyes. Panic threatened to spring up from that knot in her chest. She forced it down by sheer willpower.

Fallon wasn't dead. She believed that. She had to.

A wind blew from behind Shea, rustling her hair. She stilled but didn't turn. Whatever lived down here, she had no desire to see it.

Remember, enemy of my enemy. Choose your path wisely. Cold breath hit the back of her neck and then was gone.

*

Shea couldn't sleep while Fallon was out there. She'd made the decision not to chance trying to go into the collapsed courtyard, but it didn't mean she didn't want to. Instead, she'd done the smart thing, the right thing, and had moved Fallon's army further into the city and towards the path leading out of this place.

First things first, she needed to get his men out of here. The warning from whatever lived down here couldn't be ignored. She had a feeling if they stayed past their welcome, their bones would be the ones decorating the entrance way. She'd kept them on the one street that seemed to meander in the direction they needed. She didn't know if that path was the one the being had spoken of, but it felt right.

Murmurs caught her attention. Shea lifted her head just slightly. She'd chosen a spot away from the fires, not wanting to be around anyone right now.

Braden conferred with a couple of men. The furtive way they moved warned Shea it wouldn't be a good idea to be seen watching them. She put her head down just as Braden looked in her direction. She held still, waiting until there was no movement before looking up again. Just in time to see Braden disappear into the city.

Now, where was he going at a time like this? Especially given no one was to leave camp. He might be a trusted general of Fallon's, but that didn't mean he could disregard orders. Right?

Shea sat up. Someone would just have to see what he was up to.

Mindful of the guards roaming the perimeter, Shea followed Braden. Careful to keep her movements swift and silent.

Following someone in a cavern with little light was not easy—especially when you didn't dare risk a torch for fear that you would be seen. The crevasses in the ceiling let in a little light from the moon and stars, enough that she wasn't totally blind.

She stumbled on unseen obstacles more than a time or two. Each time her heart leapt into her throat.

As they moved further and further from the camp, leaving the perimeter behind, Shea became convinced that Braden was up to something. Why else would he have left? Especially when he'd agreed with her that they should lock down camp.

It dawned on her that she was following a Trateri general, a man as trained as Fallon in the art of warfare, without backup or having even told anyone where she was going. She wanted to kick her own ass for her stupidity.

This wasn't smart. She should have told Caden or at least brought someone along.

A figure loomed out of the shadows. Shea made an undignified sound—a cross between a squeak and a scream—as hands grabbed her. Her training kicked in. She swept one arm up trying to break his grip. Her assailant countered by grabbing her hand and bending it sharply backwards.

She gasped, her body bowing to keep the hand from breaking.

"Shea?" The grip on her hand relaxed. A torch flared, illuminating their surroundings. Braden stared at her in disbelief and suspicion. "What are you doing here?"

Shea stared at him for a long moment. No lie came to mind. She had nothing prepared.

"You're following me." It was a statement; not a question.

She nodded.

He gave an angry sigh. "Why?"

Because he'd been very suspicious skulking around the camp. Because she was curious.

She doubted he'd be happy with either of those answers.

"Why are you out here?" she asked going on the offense. "Caden said no one was to leave."

He gave her a grim look. "I'm a general."

"Does the Trateri version of that word mean someone who doesn't have to follow orders?" Shea asked before she could think better of it. She was out here alone, and he'd already proven he was better at combat than she was. The last thing she wanted to do was antagonize him.

His gaze said he was not amused.

"I think you're right. I should head back." Shea tried to step around him and was brought up short when he lifted an arm and blocked her way.

"No, I think you should accompany me." The smile he gave her didn't quite reach his eyes. "So I can ensure your safety, of course."

Shea kept any skepticism she felt inside. She didn't want to antagonize him. "I'm sure that won't be necessary. Camp's not far."

It was a subtle reminder that someone might hear her scream and come running.

He looked over her head and then ran his eyes over her. "And how do you plan on finding your way back without a light? I see no torch on you."

Shea glanced back. There were enough buildings standing between them and camp that any light was blocked. Only darkness waited behind her.

"I'm sure I'll be fine. I just need to find my way around one or two buildings."

"Nonsense. Fallon would never forgive me if something happened to you on the way back." He waited a beat. "Unless there's some reason why you don't want me around?"

The implacable look on Braden's face said he wasn't going to let this go. Shea was left with two choices—resist and try her luck on making it back with an angry general hunting her or go along and wait for her chance to escape.

She gave him a smile that didn't reach her eyes. "No, you're right. Trying to find my way back in the dark is madness. I'll stay with you."

He gave her a slow nod, looking less than convinced of her words. He turned, saying over his shoulder, "Stay close. We wouldn't want you falling into any sinkholes."

Shea strides stuttered before she forced herself to calm. It was hard not to see that last comment as anything but a subtle threat given what had happened to Fallon.

"You never did say what you were doing out here," Shea said after a long moment of walking through the abandoned city.

"I'm looking for something."

"Something or someone?" Shea didn't know why she was pushing him. She didn't really want an answer right then, especially given there were plenty of places to hide her body with no one being the wiser. They would think she'd just wandered off. Maybe looking for Fallon, though she was sure some would say she was abandoning them.

The gaze he cast her over her shoulder was hard to decipher. After a pause, he said, "You are very curious."

Shea shut her mouth. They walked past several smaller buildings, many of which might have been houses in the city's long ago past. She slowed down, letting the space between them widen.

"I couldn't understand what Fallon saw in you. There he was telling me how he wanted to strengthen his hold on the Lowlands, that he wanted to put any thought of conquering the Highlands on hold." He looked at her and stopped. "What are you doing?"

She feigned an innocent expression, her heart thundering in her chest. "I don't know what you're talking about."

"Am I walking too fast?"

She shook her head.

"Then keep up. I want this done before the army awakens."

Shea's hands shook as he gave her his back and continued walking.

"I'd planned to kill you, you know?" He gave her a casual look over his shoulder. Shea almost tripped before righting herself. "I thought you'd done something to him, somehow. Something to make him forget his ambition."

"What changed your mind?" Shea's voice was thin.

He tilted his head thoughtfully. Before he could speak, the clip-clop of several horse's hooves reached them.

Braden stiffened and doused the light from his torch. It was all the distraction Shea needed. She darted into the shadows and away from Braden. Rushing headlong into the darkness, praying she didn't trip.

There was a muffled shout behind her, but no sound of pursuit.

She slowed to a quick walk, fearing if she continued running she'd kill herself faster than any enemy ever could.

Alone, darkness pressing in on her, she looked around in the pale light. She hadn't noticed it before, but the stones glowed ever so slightly when there was no other light around. As her eyes adjusted, the green blue glow became more pronounced. She lifted her hand to touch a stone wall next to her.

"Bioluminescence."

In nature, there was evidence of some animals—mostly bugs and microscopic organisms—that glowed in the dark. She'd heard tales of entire lakes that took on an otherworldly glow on the darkest of nights, but only during certain periods of the year. She had never been lucky enough to see such an event herself.

Her fingers came away with a slight glow. If she had to guess, she'd say there was some type of algae or plant growing on the stone of the city. The light from the torches must have made it impossible to see. No light, and suddenly she could see each building, softly glowing before her.

It was a breathtaking, utterly unique experience.

She wished Fallon was here to see it, but perhaps he was noticing something similar right now wherever he was.

The clip-clop of horse's hooves reached her. The rider had been partially responsible for helping her escape Braden. She'd have to give them her thanks later.

Right now, she had to decide if she wanted to call this person's attention to her. She was still in the same situation as before. Alone, lightly armed, and with the knowledge that no one was supposed to have left the camp.

The glow of the city beside her dimmed as the rider drew near, a torch in hand. Shea stepped back into the shadows, hoping to get a glimpse of the person. Perhaps that would help her make a decision.

She didn't have long to wait as a trio of riders came into view. The first two men tugged at her memory, but she still couldn't place them. The last one, however, had her stepping out of her darkened corner.

"Charles."

He, at least, she recognized. He was probably out here looking for Clark. While still against orders, it was understandable he wouldn't want to abandon his friend. The men with him were regular attendees of the beast class.

The men looked around, their eyes searching in the dim light. Shea walked closer to them, her movement calling their attention.

Charles eyes widened in surprise. "Telroi, what are you doing out of camp?"

Shea gave him a sheepish grin. "Would you believe I got lost?"

The three men gave each other a long look.

"It would be very difficult to believe that," Charles said. His two friends steered their horses in a wide circle to either side of Shea, until the three stood one in front and two on either side.

Shea watched them carefully. Perhaps Braden had her paranoid, but the actions struck her as vaguely threatening.

"What are you and your friends doing out here?" Shea asked, looking around. "I thought Caden ordered no one to leave camp."

She knew he had, because she was the one to give the order.

Charles tilted his head, the look in his eyes flat even as he regarded her with little expression.

Now that she thought about it, Charles had always been Clark's friend. Not hers.

"Yes, he did, didn't he?" Charles said, unsheathing his sword from where it was strapped to his saddle. Shea took a careful step backward, her eyes checking on the two other men. "I suppose lying at this late stage would just be a waste of energy. You wouldn't believe me anyway."

"Not now that you've drawn that sword," Shea told him.

A grin flashed across his face and then was gone, leaving his expression as dead and lifeless as before.

She didn't bother asking him what he was doing. That much was obvious. He and these men planned to kill her. Braden was seeming more like the better bet.

"You're the one responsible for the assassination attempt during the tournament," Shea said.

"Took you long enough. You really are dumb, even for a throwaway."

Right now, she didn't disagree with him. She'd called his attention to her, knowing no one was supposed to be out of the camp, because she thought he was a friend. More evidence that her people skills were no better, even after all these months.

"You never even suspected I was anything other than a friend," he said. He seemed very like a stranger in that moment. Not the kind person willing to help scouts learn a beast's habits. "I must admit to some anxiety after the first attempt on your life failed, but then you just kept coming back and even recommended me for more responsibility."

Shea kept a cautious eye on the other two. They watched her with small smirks.

"I do have to thank you for this opportunity though," Charles said, drawing her attention. "I had hoped to kill you. The Warlord will be just a bonus."

Shea didn't bother to keep the contempt off her face. "As if you could."

"You were right; he isn't dead," Charles said in a soft voice. Shea felt her heart lurch. "One of my men spotted him earlier. I'll be sure to send him to you shortly."

Charles struck out with his blade, a clean, crisp movement that was startling in its speed. Shea barely jumped away, a thin slice of pain opening on her shoulder. The wound wasn't deep. Given the lack of concern as Charles watched Shea retreat until her back was against the wall, he had little worry that she would escape this encounter alive. He was toying with her.

Desperation and panic fought for space in her head. She struggled to remember what Trenton had taught her, what he had drilled into her time and again during training.

Her opponent had both an extended reach with his sword, and a horse that could trample her to death. She was also outnumbered.

One hand slipped behind her to withdraw the short dagger she kept on her at all times. She'd prefer a sword, but she hadn't thought to bring hers when she slipped out of camp. When Trenton found out, he would skin her.

She held it close to her side.

"She's armed," the man on her right said. "End this, so we can move on."

There was a small thump as an arrow embedded itself into the throat of the man who had just spoken.

Shea didn't wait, taking advantage of their surprise and darting in the direction of the fallen man. His horse stamped and whirled. Shea dodged it as Charles and the other man kicked their horses after her.

She ducked past the horse, noting Braden standing bow in hand, notching another arrow.

She'd never make it to him before one of the other two ran her down. Her feet turned toward a gap between two buildings. She ran along the small space even as the sound of hooves pounding against cobblestone followed her. She burst onto the next street.

"Shea, follow me," Braden said from several yards down the street. He'd guessed her route and followed on a different path. She hesitated, her suspicions of before no less valid. "Don't be stupid. I just saved your ass."

He had.

They'd stand a better chance if they were together.

Her decision made, she ran towards him and followed when he turned and made his way through the city. It wasn't long until the sound of pursuit followed, chasing them through the city—gradually herding them in a certain direction.

"How are they doing this?" Shea asked, leaning against the side of a building. She was out of breath and beginning to think there might not be a way out of this.

Braden shook his head. "They must have more men out here."

"How many people missed head count?" Shea asked.

"Ten."

She dropped her head back and looked up at the inky darkness. Only small patches of a starry night sky could be seen. Ten. He might as well have said a hundred.

"We're making a lot of noise. Eventually Caden and the rest of the men will hear and come investigating," Braden said.

Shea preferred not to rely on ifs and shoulds. There was no guarantee they'd hear all this racket, and even if they did, chances were Shea and Braden would be dead long before then.

"You shouldn't have run off and called attention to yourself." Disapproval colored Braden's tone.

Shea shot him dark look. "I'm sorry. When someone threatens to kill me, I tend to try to remove myself from the situation."

"I never intended to kill you."

Shea scoffed, letting the sound speak for her.

"I didn't. I just said at one time I had planned to kill you. You know, before. It's been a while since I've actively plotted your death."

Shea opened her mouth with a sharp retort but was prevented from speaking as a horse and rider clattered around the corner, torch held aloft. Seeing them, he called over his should, "Here, I've found them."

"Time to go." Shea bounded away from the building, Braden on her heels. Another rider cut them off at the end of the street as the first closed in behind. They started for an alley but pulled up short when another horse and rider trotted out of the shadows.

They were surrounded.

Braden put his back to Shea's, notching an arrow and holding his bow at the ready. He'd given her his sword so at least she wasn't completely unarmed.

Charles turned the corner, letting his horse walk towards them at a leisurely pace. "General, what a surprise. I had not thought to see you out here."

"Who is this?" Braden asked Shea, not taking his eyes off the armed men approaching them.

"Charles. You met him. He was in charge of the beast board."

Charles smile was ugly. "I suppose I shouldn't be too surprised he doesn't recognize me. It would be too much to expect a general to know those that serve under him."

"I know the name of every man and woman in my command. You're not one of them," Braden said, still not looking at Charles. His attention was wholly focused on the two riders behind them.

"Of course not. You wouldn't want a cripple getting in the way." Charles hands tightened on the reins.

"Is that what this is about?" Shea asked. "Misplaced anger over your lot in life?"

Charles snorted. "Maybe a little, but it's not the only reason."

Scorn showed on Shea's face.

Charles smiled. "You don't believe me."

She shrugged.

"At first, I only intended to get you out of the way. As I'm sure the general here can tell you, you're a distraction to the Warlord. His men have noticed, and they don't like it. This idea of conquest. It is ridiculous. We take, we pillage, and then we return home. That's how it's always been."

"Fallon always intended to claim the Lowlands," Shea said. "I'm not the one who convinced him to stay."

"But you are the one who made it possible. Your beast board. Your ideas. Even this place. Do you think he'll let this end once he reaches your homeland?" Charles shook his head. "No, he'll take, and take, and take until there is nothing left."

A shadow flickered in the light behind Charles.

"Your lands are rotting," Shea said. "There's nothing left there except madness and death."

"You're lying."

"She's not," Braden said. "I've seen it with my own eyes. Our healers are trying to figure out what's wrong, but they have been unsuccessful. Many have succumbed to the madness."

The man next to Charles shifted. "The men from Rain did say something wasn't right."

"Quiet. Nothing they say matters. She's still an outsider. A throwaway. We do our people a service getting rid of her," Charles said.

He dug his heels into the horse's sides and spurred it towards Shea. She held the sword in a guard position, watching closely.

"Stop," a voice yelled from the building.

Charles pulled his horse up sharply as Clark climbed out of a window and dropped to the ground.

"Clark, stay back," Shea called.

"It's alright, Shea." Clark held out a hand as he made his way over to stand between the two of them. Charles watched him come, a guarded expression on his face.

"What are you doing?" Clark asked him.

"I'm standing up for people like us."

"By killing Shea? She's never done anything to you. If anything, she's helped us gain status."

Charles almost looked like he might listen. He parted his lips to speak when one of the other men said, "Enough chitchat. Kill them."

"I'm afraid he's right. We've come too far to turn back now." Charles unsheathed the sword at his side.

Clark took a step back, placing himself between Shea and Charles.

"Clark, move."

Clark shook his head. "I refuse."

"I'm doing this for us. For what we went through."

Clark shook his head. "I want no part in this. If you do this, you'll have to go through me first."

"Very well, then."

There was a sharp cry as the man to Shea's right slumped off his horse and fell to the ground. Fallon stood next to him, bloody sword in his hand.

A dark figure leapt from the building next to them, landing on Charles and taking him to the ground. Braden took advantage of the distraction and let his arrow fly. It found its target in the shoulder of the rider behind them.

Charles and his assailant rolled, their limbs a furious blur as they fought.

More of Charles's men poured out of the street in front of Shea. Even with Fallon, Clark, and the person Shea assumed was Fiona, they were outmatched.

There was a woman's cry of pain. Charles rose to his feet, the sword in his hand bloody. He aimed a kick at his attacker.

"Fiona," Clark cried, running for the other woman.

"You can't win," Charles shouted at Clark, who ignored him.

Shea's eyes rose to the buildings beside them, shadows lurking on top of them. Bright eyes flashed from above.

"No, I think it's you who can't win," Shea said in a soft voice, her focus still on what waited above.

A frigid wind picked up around them, rustling Shea's hair and plucking at her clothes with harsh hands. She could almost hear voices in the air. A tingle skated along her skin, a sensation very similar to that of the mist.

Betrayal. Weapons. A path.

All the ingredients were there.

"What would you know?" Charles said, ignoring Shea. His voice was ugly, no hint of the shy, studious man of before in it. "They treat me worse than the throwaways simply because of a birth defect. He's the worst of them."

Charles pointed at Fallon, his face a mask of disgust. "Patting me on the head, saying good job with that stupid beast board. Elevating your little friends who lied to him, lied to us all, to protect you. When meanwhile, I exist on the scraps of the kindness of his elite."

"You need to stop this," Shea said, edging towards Clark and where he knelt by Fiona. "You won't like the consequences of what comes next."

He scoffed. "Big words from a throwaway who is about to die. There are changes coming. We've already got the backing, people willing to support us when you and he are gone."

"Whose backing?" Fallon asked. "Who has been whispering in your ear?"

Charles regarded Fallon with narrowed eyes. Shea couldn't believe she had never seen the snake at his heart. It was obvious now, here at the end. How had she not seen it before?

"Shea, Fiona needs immediate help if she is going to survive," Clark said in a soft voice as she neared.

She knelt at his side and pressed her hand to Fiona's wound. The other woman's skin was pale, but her eyes fierce. One hand snapped up to grasp Shea's in a tight grip.

"Do your worst, pathfinder. Don't let him get away with this," Fiona panted around a bloodthirsty grin.

Shea returned that grin with a fierce one of her own. "I will. You stay alive."

Fiona made a choked sound and nodded, pain making her eyes go vague for a moment.

"What are you doing?" Charles asked as she stood and walked to the middle of the street.

She ignored him as she knelt and brushed her bloody hand against the stone. "I've made my choice and chosen my path."

"Get up before I order the rest of you killed," Charles called. Shea could hear the scrape of his limp as he shuffled closer.

Shea stood, leaving a bloody handprint as evidence of her pact. She turned, her eyes meeting Fallon's. She gave him a soft smile, putting all the love she had for him into it. Her eyes moved to Charles and her smile faded, leaving nothing but grim determination behind.

Charles and his men moved toward her, leaving only the other two horsemen to guard Fallon and Braden. Not that it mattered. Soon, nothing they did would matter.

She met Charles' gaze, repeating what she had said earlier. "You shouldn't have done that."

Charles made a disgusted sound. "What are you talking about?

"You shouldn't have hurt Fiona. You shouldn't have betrayed your Warlord. They don't like people who break faith. Now you will pay."

"Who is she talking about," one of his men asked.

"Perhaps she's gone loopy," said one of the others.

"You're all going to die," Shea said with a small smile.

The four traded uneasy glances.

Charles rolled his eyes. "Don't listen to her. She's trying to scare you."

"I don't know. It's felt like someone has been watching us ever since we entered."

Charles slapped the man who had spoken in the back. "It's a trick. She's trying to divide us."

Shea watched the interactions with a blank expression. Her eyes moved to Fallon and Braden as their captors herded them closer. "Do nothing. Show no violence, and you may live."

"That's enough out of you." Charles backhanded Shea. The blow turned her head and opened a cut on her lip. She lifted her head and smiled, her teeth bloody.

A spine-chilling moan echoed from above them, the sound rising until it turned into a cackle.

Charles and his men jumped, brandishing their weapons at the city.

"What was that?" one shouted.

Shea watched them with an implacable expression.

One of the men stepped toward her, "You heard him. What was that?"

She looked at him for a long moment before saying one word, a smile twisting her expression. "Death."

A wall of wind hit, blowing Shea's hair into her face and obscuring her vision for a moment. She was grateful, especially when a great presence, one that held the chill of the coldest winter on the longest day in the darkest night passed her. There were some things not meant to be seen by human eyes.

"Fallon, shut your eyes," Shea ordered.

Screams filled the air, the kind that came from the soul as the body was ripped apart. Shea knew she would hear their death screams in her nightmares until the day she left this world. Screams filled with agony and fear, ripped from the gut, every person's worst nightmare given voice. There was the sound of running before more screaming came. Shea kept her eyes tightly shut, even as the presence in the air strengthened.

The screams ended, the silence left behind scarier than anything that had gone before. Shea's pulse thundered in her ears and the sound of her breathing overwhelmed her.

Very good, daughter of my enemy's enemy.

"Are you going to kill me now?" Shea asked.

The presence hesitated, filling the air with—was that surprise?

Would you like us to?

Shea shifted and frowned. She hadn't thought she had a choice in the matter.

Ah, we see. You thought a blood sacrifice would be necessary.

She had. Otherwise, why had they waited to act? If they had attacked sooner, Fiona wouldn't have been injured.

The sacrifice has already been paid, and you and the other four hold no weapons and no ill intentions. Besides, that would have defeated the purpose of saving you now and before.

Before? Shea couldn't help it. She opened her eyes, a bluish haze spread across the ground, thick in some places, sparse in others.

"You're the one who left the jacket on the post," Shea said in realization. She sensed rather than saw the beings nod of agreement. "Why did you help us?" Shea asked so she wouldn't be tempted to argue with the presence. She sensed if she pushed, they might decide she and her friends were fair game as well.

Curiosity. Necessity. We have a vested interest in your continued well-being.

"What do you mean?"

The air swirling around her stilled, a sense of weight coming from it—as if it was sentient and the matter at hand required much contemplation.

Even as removed as we are, trapped here away from the sun and the world, we can feel it. Feel as the heart awakens bringing with it the old ones. Right now, they are testing this new world, but soon, soon they will rise and seek to finish what they once started. It will be a new order, one based on their warped vision of perfection.

"I don't know what you mean."

Did you think you could walk into the heart of where it all began and come out unchanged? No, my dear, you stared it in the face, listened to its voice. It's not a question of if you've changed, but how much you've changed.

"I don't understand."

There was a great sigh, one sound coming from a thousand voices. *No, I suppose you don't. You will soon. Take your people and leave this place. You have until the sun hits the doors above the fault. After that, we consume all that has remained.*

The wind brushing against Shea died down, leaving nothing but emptiness behind. The blue haze faded. Shea thought she saw the faintest outline of forms.

Fallon and her group were the only living beings that remained.

He crossed the space between them at a run, grabbing her in a hug that threatened to crush her.

"Fallon, we need to get out of here."

"I know. I heard."

Shea drew back. "How did you even find us?"

"I took that tunnel you had pointed out and found Clark and his friend wandering down there. We've been traveling together over the past few hours. Your chase through the city caught our attention. When we saw what was happening, we waited until the right moment." He brushed a piece of hair behind her ear and cupped the back of her neck. "That was close."

She nodded. "Yeah." Even closer than he knew. The denizens of this place could very well have decided to take them along with Charles and his men. The fact they hadn't was a curious blessing.

"If you two are done, perhaps we can leave. You heard what that thing said. Anyone down here come sunrise is a walking meal." Braden looked at the cavern ceiling. It was still black, no evidence of light filtering down from the cracks and holes, so there was no way to tell how close to sunrise they were.

Fallon looked at his general. "I'm looking forward to the story of how you two came to be wandering around out here without any protection."

Shea grimaced. He was not going to be happy when he heard that story.

His expression softened when he looked back at her. "Until then, let's get Fiona patched up and then get moving."

She nodded her agreement.

Fallon gave her neck one last squeeze before he stepped back. Braden gave Shea a considering expression before moving to help Fallon with Fiona. Shea took one last look around, paying attention to the buildings' roofs before turning her attention back to the matter at hand.

CHAPTER TWENTY-SEVEN

Shea watched the last of Fallon's men pass through the small set of doors that would give them entry to the Highlands. On each door, a set of runes was carved. Shea didn't need to know the language to know that it was probably the reason why the denizens of the caverns remained where they were.

They were just in time. The sky had darkened to a deep midnight as the stars and the moon shuttered their faces in preparation of day. Soon, threads of color would begin eating away at the darkness as the sun rose.

Clark stared at the doors with a slightly lost expression on his face. He'd been silent on the way out. None of his normal chipper personality showed. The only time Shea saw a glimpse of the old Clark was when Buck and Eamon had tackled him when they'd appeared.

After the reunion, he'd withdrawn again.

Shea approached him, not knowing what to say. His friend had betrayed him in one of the worst ways imaginable. That tended to leave a mark on a person. No platitude she gave him would make that better.

She settled for standing beside him as the sun began to rise, letting him know without words that she was there for him. That he wasn't alone. Sometimes, that's all you could do for a person.

When his head bowed and his shoulders shook from silent tears, Shea took a step closer and wrapped her arm around him. She kept a grip on him even after Eamon came up on his other side. His eyes met hers in understanding. She'd told him what had happened with Charles on the journey out.

Long after the dark had ceded dominion to the light, Clark straightened and gave them each a small, hesitant smile.

"Oh, that reminds me," Shea said. She withdrew a green jacket from her pack. "We found this while in the city. I believe it belongs to you."

"My jacket." Clark reached out to touch it. Shea handed it to him. "How did you find it?"

"It was just hanging from a post in the city. Actually, stopping to retrieve it probably saved Fallon's and my lives. How'd you lose it?" she asked.

"I don't know." Clark's face was perplexed. "I woke up to find it gone after the first time Fiona and I stopped to rest. I'd lain it on top of me to keep warm as I slept."

His eyes were sad as he looked at it. He fell silent, his thoughts turning inward. Shea didn't push.

"We're here for you when you want to talk," Eamon told him.

Clark gave him a nod before walking away.

"He'll get over this," Eamon said.

Shea hoped so, even as she doubted it would be for a very long time.

"Looks like your Warlord has need of you," Eamon observed. He took his leave, saying, "I'm glad you're alright and were able to find Clark."

"I'll catch up with you later."

Fallon stepped close and wrapped his arms around Shea. She allowed herself a moment to be supported by his strength. Then she straightened and forced back her tears. "The men should take a brief break and then we need to move on. I want this place far in our shadow before we stop for the night," she said.

Fallon watched her for a long moment, assessing her mental state. She avoided his eyes. Sometimes she thought he saw too much with that oddly penetrating gaze of his, and right now she didn't know if she could bear having her inner self on display.

He gave her a nod and let her walk away, before he gestured for Caden and Braden to relay her orders.

*

"This isn't the path to the Wayfarer's Keep," Shea said, staring up at the mountain ridge in front of her. They had stopped halfway up the mountain, just below the tree line. If her memory was correct, this would take them west of the keep by several week's ride.

Reece took a swig of his water before capping it and putting it back in the saddle bags. Fallon had ordered a horse for him when it became clear his continued walking would only slow them down. Unlike when Shea was his captive, he had ordered a proper horse for the pathfinder, not some stunted growth mule that couldn't match a horse's longer strides.

"You're getting rusty, Shea. I expected you to figure that out several days ago."

Shea watched him with a calculating expression. It was true that she should have picked up on the divergent path earlier, but grief had made her slower than normal.

"That's the Dragon's Tail. You would never take a group like this through that ridge to reach the keep, so where are you taking us?" she asked.

Fallon folded his reins over his hand and leaned forward, his hawk-like gaze drilling into Reece. His expression was fierce. "Yes, please, enlighten the group."

Reece gave Shea a half-smile. "Come now, doesn't any of this look familiar?"

Shea's lips pursed as she considered Reece and then their surroundings. Yes, it did, but much of the Highlands was familiar. Like an old friend you had seen over and over again. Only this friend was crotchety and grumpy and would kill you should you take it for granted.

"Birdon Leaf." It made sense given their relative geographic location, the direction they were traveling and known areas of interest this path would lead to.

Reece's smile was wry, like a teacher bestowing a student with praise. "Very good."

"Why would you take us there?" Shea asked.

"Why, to visit the place where this all started." Reece prodded his horse forward, taking off before Shea could question him further.

Caden rode up on the other side of Fallon and stopped his horse as he stared after Reece. "I thought the whole point of this little trip was to go to this Wayfarer's Keep and meet with the pathfinders."

"I guess we're taking a little side trip first," Shea said, before kicking her horse into a slow-paced trot to follow Reece.

Fallon followed, though he looked no more thrilled at this turn of events than Shea.

Caden shook his head and spit to the side of his horse before he too started up the large back half of the mountain. "Oh goody."

*

One week later, Shea crested the last hill before the land flattened, giving rise to the small spit of plateau where Birdon Leaf perched. It would have taken less time had they been on foot, but the jagged ravines and steep hills were not friendly terrain to a horse. As a result, they'd been forced to take the long way around.

Shea reined her horse to a stop on the ridge and looked down on the flattened top that contained the little village. The Trateri were spread out behind her as they made their way up the last small incline.

The land between them and the village was mostly long grass, as the altitude made trees rare. From this distance, the village looked picturesque, like an innocent painting of a simpler world. One untouched by strife and pain.

Shea snorted. That couldn't be further from the truth, especially given the wasps nestled in the very heart of this little village.

There was the faint clop of hooves behind her as Witt came up on her right side. He, like she, had experienced a rather complicated relationship with this place. It should have been home, but its villagers had betrayed the two of them in one of the worst ways imaginable.

"Home, sweet home," Witt murmured.

Shea made a sound of derision.

"I wonder what they will say when they see us come riding up with an army behind us," he mused.

"Probably kick themselves for not ensuring we were dead before they handed us over."

He grunted. It was half laugh and half acknowledgement. "I would like to see Dane again, though."

"Yeah," Shea's voice was soft. She'd forgotten that he'd been close with the other man, too. The three's relationship had been short-lived, but for a short time they'd been on their way to becoming friends.

"You think he made it back?" Shea asked.

"I hope not. I hope he found a place far from here to hole up."

Shea nodded. Yeah, that sounded about right.

On both of their minds was the question of what waited down there. Would they find a thriving village, unhappy that the prodigal son and daughter had returned, or would they find a grave site? After all, the pathfinder's guild was not known for its forgiveness, and Birdon Leaf and its elders had broken the covenant in every way that counted. One way or another, there would be a reckoning.

Shea looked over at Fallon, who stared down at the village with a hard expression, one that lacked even a shadow of understanding or gentleness. Yeah, one way or another.

"Let's get this over with," Shea muttered. She flicked her reins, taking the lead down the hill. Fallon wasn't far away, though he stayed a few lengths behind her. Shea appreciated it, though a big part of her would rather not have returned here at all.

The journey down the hill and across the meadow seemed to take forever. The village and its wooden exterior wall grew as she rode closer. Jagged holes of splintered wood in the wall put paid any hope that the inhabitants had fared well over the last few months.

No villagers came out to greet them and there was no movement on the walls, something that would have been unheard of when Shea had lived here.

Shea let out a heavy sigh. Guess it was option two then.

She led Fallon and Witt and the rest around the wall. The Trateri followed, eyeing it with a deep reserve. More than one man and woman withdrew their blades and strung their bows.

Shea arrived at the entrance of the village. Normally, there would have been men standing on the wall who would give the order to open the double doors, ones so heavy it took several men working in tandem to force them to creak open.

Today, those doors lay broken and splintered, so much tinder on the ground. The village was wide open to any beast or raider who wanted to walk right up.

Shea dismounted and slid the reins over her horse's head. She left him grazing by the entrance.

"Shea," Fallon warned, looking at the village with a deep mistrust. One echoed on many of his men's faces.

She held up a hand. "I'm fine, Fallon. Whatever did this is long gone."

Fallon made a sound of frustration before dismounting and throwing his reins to Caden. He unsheathed his sword as he strode over to Shea. She didn't wait for him to reach her, crossing into the village proper as Witt, Eamon, and several of the Anateri dismounted to follow them.

Shea walked into the village, feeling cold and disconnected at the sight of the destruction awaiting her. The wooden buildings had been torn apart, the windows broken, and the doors torn off. Some were burnt, only a few timbers remaining.

Even the town hall, a building that predated the village by many hundreds of years and had withstood many attacks, looked like it had seen better days. The roof had been ripped off the top, and the heavy wooden door at its base breached.

Shea couldn't help feeling like she had failed these people. It didn't matter that they had failed her first. Maybe if she'd tried harder, been better, less argumentative, maybe things might have turned out different.

Reece stepped into the village square as Shea stared around her with a stunned numbness. She bent and picked up a child's toy, one of those mallets you were supposed to catch the ball on. The ball was missing and the handle half broken.

"Why did you bring us here?" Fallon asked Reece.

"So you could see."

"See what?" he asked.

"What you're up against. The consequences if you should fail."

"We haven't even agreed to help you," Caden said. He'd wandered close to one of the buildings and was examining it.

"Or even know what you want," Buck muttered.

"There were children here, Reece. Innocent of whatever mistakes their parents might have committed." Shea rubbed her thumb against the wood of the mallet.

His face was placid but not unsympathetic. He offered her no answer.

"You know the rules, baby girl. Sometimes you have to cut the rot from the tree, so the rest of it can survive." A man unfolded himself from where he'd been sitting in the shadows and stepped forward, meeting Shea's eyes. He was tall, taller than Fallon, and had crow's feet at the corner of each eye. Laughter had cut grooves

313

around his eyes and mouth over the years. His skin was paler than you would imagine of a man who spent the majority of his life outside.

He stared at Shea for a long moment, ignoring the weapons aimed his way. His eyes cataloged each feature, noting the grief that showed in the dark circles under her eyes and the tired slump of her shoulders. He took in all those details as if he'd come across this rare specimen, one that might disappear if he didn't memorize everything.

After an eternity of staring at each other, he gave her a half-smile. "Hello, daughter. I've missed you."

Shea took a deep breath but was unable to summon an answering smile. "Hello, father."

He lifted an eyebrow even as amusement touched his lips. "That's it? After all these months, that's all you have to say?" He turned to Fallon and the rest. "All this time her mother and I feared she was dead. We worried; we agonized. I even sent your cousin to hunt down those who might have harmed you."

Shea watched him with a careful gaze. "How long before anyone noticed I was gone?"

Some of the affableness drained out of his expression as he fixed her with a look and sighed, as if to say he was disappointed in her question. She gave him a stubborn look in return.

"Eight months."

"So, not that worried."

She'd figured as much. She was the black sheep. The golden child turned disappointment. The first couple roll calls she'd missed, they'd probably ascribed to her sulking. After that, they must have decided she was simply too busy, or maybe they had more pressing matters to attend to. A stray pathfinder wasn't that odd.

"That's hardly nice," her father rebuked.

She waved a hand at the decimated village around them. "Neither is this."

Her father nodded, taking in their surroundings with a careful eye. "No, I imagine not."

Shea spotted Witt over her father's shoulder. His face was carefully guarded as he took in the village. If she was this upset over the destruction, she couldn't imagine how he was feeling. He'd already made clear his distaste for the pathfinder method of punishing those who opposed them.

"I had friends here. People who were good to me and helped me while out there." She pointed to the world beyond the village walls. Many of which had gaping holes in them.

"I met some of them," Reece said. "A man by the name of Dane."

Both Shea and Witt looked at him with hope.

"I ran into him and a group he was leading out of the Lowlands. He's the one who told me what had happened. Otherwise, we wouldn't have even known where to begin searching for you."

And in so doing, he had signed this place's death warrant.

"You couldn't have talked to them first?" Witt asked, stepping towards them. "Gotten the children out at least."

Reece shook his head. "It was like this when we arrived. After Dane's story, I let the guild know what had happened and decided to confront the elders on my own. See the extent of the betrayal for myself. By the time we reached this place whatever had done this was long gone."

Fallon moved beside her. His fierce scowl signified the end of his patience. "I have traveled a very long way and am not in the mood to play games." He fixed Shea's father with a flat stare, the kind that intimidated most men. Her father was not most men, however. The corner of his lips twitched as if he was fighting a smile. "You sent your man to find us, and immediately after, we were attacked. A smart man would assume you and your people are a threat. Convince me not to end you and your nephew where you stand."

Her father stared at Fallon for a moment before throwing his head back and roaring with laughter. "Oh, I like this one, my dear. He's much better than that other one."

Fallon gave her father a warrior's smile, one that bared teeth as the light of battle lit in his eyes. He was enjoying this, Shea realized. Of course, he was. He thrived on combat and challenge, and her father had just proved he was capable of both.

The Trateri around them who had lowered their guard when she identified the man as her father, raised their weapons in threat. Their faces reflected similar expressions of mad triumph as Fallon's.

"Fallon," Shea warned in a low voice.

"You cannot have two loyalties in this. You must choose a side," Fallon said back. "If he is a threat to my men or you, then I will act accordingly."

Shea struggled with a strong urge to whap Fallon on the back of his head. Maybe that would knock some sense into him and force him to stop saying stupid things.

She loved her father more than words could express. He was her calm port in the storm, the person who picked her up when she fell and gave her the motivation to keep on going when she was convinced she had failed. Despite that, she recognized the ruthless and pragmatic man inside. The one who would burn the world to the ground should anything threaten the things he held dear.

That man would not have come unarmed to this fight. He would not have confronted Fallon without having some type of exit strategy.

Her father watched them with half-lidded eyes. He seemed perfectly content despite the fact there were several arrows pointed at him, in addition to the men who had raised their swords. He was calm and cool and amused by the situation.

No, he had a plan. She just didn't know how to explain that to Fallon.

"I'm not here to make war on you," her father told Fallon. "I'm here for my daughter."

Fallon's body tensed. "No."

Her father continued as if he hadn't spoken. He spread his hands to indicate the village around them. "You've seen what is happening. This village is not unique. We've lost several others over the past few months, some much bigger than this. The Lowlands are suffering as well. I've come to take her to stand trial before her people."

Shea sucked in a breath. Of all the things she thought he'd say, that had been nowhere on the list. The kernel of hurt that had taken root—after he had failed to stand up for her before her demotion—grew.

She knew he loved her, but she also knew that in many ways, she was a disappointment. Someone who had failed, broken faith, and since meeting Fallon, severely compromised her vows. Yes, he loved her, but that didn't mean he wouldn't make her pay the price of what he considered justice.

Fallon snarled, the sound angry and brutal in the desolated village. "That will not happen."

He held one arm out, pushing Shea behind him. She couldn't take her eyes off her father. She knew she needed to speak up, if only to warn Fallon to be careful that he had something up his sleeve, but she couldn't. Hurt had stolen her voice.

Family could raise you up, but they could also damage you worse than any force out there. She would rather fight a thousand beasts, lead hundreds of missions for ungrateful, obtuse villagers, than listen to her father once again tell her how she had failed, that she would stand trial.

"Fallon," she said in soft voice, raising a hand to touch his back. She tried to step around him, to come up to his side, and then had to grit her teeth as he forced her back behind him. She thumped him on the back before stepping out from behind him. She wasn't the kind of person who would hide, even if it felt like someone had just come up and sucker-punched her.

"It's not happening," he told her in a no-nonsense voice. As if by giving her an order, he could make it come true. He turned on her father, "You won't be taking her."

Her father studied him, his expression curious even as his eyes were remote as if he calculated a hundred different scenarios. He gave a sharp whistle.

Around them, in the buildings and on top of them, figures moved. They had been well camouflaged before, using the structures to hide their presence.

Fallon again shoved Shea behind him, even as half of his men pivoted to face these strangers, many of whom were clad in clothes designed to blend in with the forest and mountain terrain. The pathfinders held boomers, all trained on Fallon's men.

Fallon observed them with a sardonic arch to his eyebrow before giving them a mad grin, his teeth on full display and his eyes alight with challenge. "Your men are good. I'll give you that. My scouts saw no evidence of their presence."

Shea's dad watched him with curious eyes.

Fallon's expression turned crafty, like a wolf when its quarry had just fallen into its trap. "I've known your daughter for a while now and have gotten used to the unexpected. I haven't gotten this far without being prepared."

He let out a war cry. There was a rustle of sound as men appeared behind the pathfinders, some with knives held at their back, others with arrows nocked and drawn and pointing at Shea's father's men.

Shea's father watched with a slight smile on his face. "You'll still die," her father warned.

"We won't be the only ones. I can promise you that. We number many. Should we fall, there will be those who can replace us. Can you say the same?"

Shea's father studied him, a thoughtful expression on his face.

"Enough," Shea barked before anyone could do anything stupid and start something that would end in needless bloodshed. "I'll go with you. There's no need for any of this."

"You won't," Fallon snapped back. He didn't budge as she tried to step around him. "That's final."

This time she did slap him on the back of his head, dodging out of his arms to stand glaring at him a few feet away.

"You don't tell me what to do," she snarled. "You ask nicely, and if I feel like it, I'll listen."

Fallon glared at her, his whiskey eyes molten with anger. They spent a long moment locked in a stare down, before her father chuckled.

"Just like her mother. Never could get that woman to do anything she didn't want to." He whistled again, and the pathfinders lowered their weapons. Fallon waited a beat before giving his men the same signal. They stepped back, but kept their weapons at the ready.

"You're not taking her," Fallon told her father.

He studied Fallon with a thoughtful look. Shea waited as the two men took each other's measure. This wasn't exactly how she'd imagined introducing Fallon to one of her parents. Though to be fair, she had thought she'd never get the chance.

"Very well, then you will promise to fix this little problem we're having." He looked at Shea. "You went where you weren't supposed to go and woke something that never should have been woken. One way or another, you must take responsibility."

Shea's lips tightened. "I told you we never made it past the second marker. This is not the result of our expedition."

He shook his head. "Maybe so, but you also told me that you lost a week that you can't remember. You could very well have strayed further than you thought. Either way, it doesn't matter. The elders are looking for someone to blame and you're the only one who survived. Either you face trial, or lover boy helps end this threat with that army of his."

"His army isn't at your beck and call," Shea argued.

Her father shrugged. "Your alternative is trying to fight your way out of here. Don't think you'll get far though, and a lot of people on both sides will die."

Fallon didn't look away from him. He knew the destructive power of the boomers. Had even seen them in action a time or two. He didn't need to be told who had the advantage.

"We die or fail to make it back and my men have orders to drench the Highlands in blood. They will destroy any city or village they come across. You won't need to fear the beasts then," Fallon said in an idle voice.

Shea fought the urge to scream. Both men were being ridiculous.

"Fine, I'll sweeten the pot," her father said. "You come to the Keep with me and hear what we have to say. You do that, and we'll give you the Highlands with our blessing."

Shea's jaw dropped. She closed it with a snap. What was he saying?

"We'll even throw in enough boomers and other weapons we have in store to supply a good bit of your army."

Shea sucked in a shocked breath. This was unheard of. Even admitting how many of the boomers they had was shocking. Generations of secrecy and protecting what they hid, and her father had essentially just told Fallon where he could find a huge stockpile of weapons that would make him invincible.

A chill rushed over her. How bad were things that the pathfinders were willing to resort to this?

Fallon cocked his head. He looked interested. Shea knew he'd always planned to conquer the Highlands, and here was her father offering them to him on a silver platter.

"Shea will be free of any repercussions?"

Her father nodded. "I give you my word."

"My men will come with me."

Shea's father hesitated, his eyes going to those Trateri whose expressions had less warmth than a stone, as they watched her father and his men.

"That can be arranged," he finally said.

"Done." Fallon looked at Shea with a fierce light in his eyes. She could see the wheels already turning.

Her father kept his gaze fixed on Fallon. "As I said, you and your men will come with us. You can send some back to explain to the rest of your army, so they don't get ahead of themselves with the bloodshed and all. I'll give you the rest of the day and evening to make arrangements. We'll leave at first light."

Fallon gave him a sharp nod. Her father left, not even sparing Shea a glance, as if now that he'd gotten what he wanted he'd lost interest in her presence. The hole in her heart iced over.

Fallon summoned Caden with a look. "Pick ten men you trust to send back to our army below the fault. Darius will need to be prepared if things go bad up here."

Caden looked like he'd bitten into something sour. "This seems like a trap."

Fallon nodded. "Probably, but the potential reward will be worth it."

"I'm coming with you," Shea informed Fallon. He wasn't sending her with the ten if that was what he had in mind.

He gave her a sideways glance. "I wouldn't have it any other way. Someone has to watch my back."

Her lips tilted up. "Yes, we wouldn't want you getting stuck in another spinner web."

Caden snorted. "She can barely keep Trenton at bay during training. How is she going to protect you from an assassin's blade?"

Shea agreed with him. She gave the two men a shrug. "You'll need my help with the beasts up here. You're on your own with the humans."

Caden shook his head and strode off.

Buck stopped at her side as he stared after her father. "Your father has some serious balls. I'm beginning to see where you get some of the craziness from."

He didn't wait for her to reply before wandering off shaking his head.

Shea stood next to Fallon and watched as the Trateri prepared to make camp in the ruins of the village.

"Not exactly how I pictured meeting your father," Fallon said.

Shea snorted. "What? You didn't expect to meet him in the middle of a destroyed and abandoned village and have him threaten you with death?"

"Somehow, no. Though I should have, given he's the one to raise such an unexpected woman." He looked at her out of the corner of his eye.

She bumped his shoulder with hers.

"It would have been easier for me to just stand trial," she told him. "They're probably going to ask us to go into the Badlands and face whatever has been directing these beasts."

"I wasn't willing to chance it," he said. "Besides, I got the Highlands out of it."

She shook her head. "I don't think that's as much of a prize as you seem to think." She gestured to her surroundings. "This is what you would be ruling over."

He looked around. "This is what I would be protecting."

Shea stared up at his face. Yes. Protecting. She thought the pathfinders might have forgotten that was their role once upon a time. Perhaps Fallon and his army could take up that mantle.

"Are you ready to go home?"

She stared at him for another moment. Her father had made it clear with his talk of trial that the Keep was no longer her home. A thread of sadness fought to linger before Shea forced it away. That was before. This was now.

A smile dawned, it was slow and spoke of new beginnings. "What are you talking about? My home is standing right next to me."

DISCOVER MORE BY T.A. WHITE

The Broken Lands Series
Pathfinder's Way – Book One

The Dragon-Ridden Chronicles
Dragon-Ridden – Book One
Of Bone and Ruin – Book Two
Shifting Seas - Novella

The Aileen Travers Series
Shadow's Messenger – Book One
Midnight's Emissary – Book Two

CONNECT WITH ME
Twitter: @tawhiteauthor
Facebook: https://www.facebook.com/tawhiteauthor/
Website: http://www.tawhiteauthor.com/
Blog: http://dragon-ridden.blogspot.com/

ABOUT THE AUTHOR

Writing is my first love. Even before I could read or put coherent sentences down on paper, I would beg the older kids to team up with me for the purpose of crafting ghost stories to share with our friends. This first writing partnership came to a tragic end when my coauthor decided to quit a day later and I threw my cookies at her head. This led to my conclusion that I worked better alone. Today, I stick with solo writing, telling the stories that would otherwise keep me up at night.